AF413439

Also by Jessica Lewis
Nav's Foolproof Guide to Falling in Love
Bad Witch Burning
Monstrous

HALLIE'S RULES
FOR A
RECOVERING

Romantic

JESSICA LEWIS

HARPER
An Imprint of HarperCollinsPublishers

HarperCollins Children's Books, a division of HarperCollins Publishers,
195 Broadway, New York, NY 10007

HarperCollins Publishers, Macken House, 39/40 Mayor Street Upper,
Dublin 1, D01 C9W8, Ireland

ISBN 978-1-335-00847-3

Typography by Julia Feingold
26 27 28 29 30 LBC 5 4 3 2 1

First Edition

To Grandma, always <3
And to girls who feel like they're too much, not
enough, too loud, too quiet, too *everything*—you're
perfect just the way you are.

CHAPTER 1

As my best friend helps load my bags into the car, heroically trying not to cry, I know this is going to be painful.

Nav lugs my duffel bag containing three weeks' worth of camp supplies into the trunk. I move to help, but she waves me off. She won't look at me, but I know she's blinking back tears. I fidget with my heavy backpack, struggling not to cry too.

"Got all your underwear and shit?"

"I hope so." I try to smile, but I'm mentally cycling through my triple-checked heavy suitcase and duffel bag. I don't have enough clothes for six weeks, but the brochure for Carnegie Camp for Young Scholars said there'd be a laundry room, so I should be good there . . . but how do you pay to use the machine? Will they accept a card, or is it one of those old ones that only accepts quarters? What if I have to wear dirty clothes all summer?

"What about bug spray?" Gia, Nav's girlfriend, asks. She's frowning seriously, like she's thinking about the laundry situation too. "Sunscreen?"

"Got it, I swear."

"Okay. I guess this is the last of it." Nav picks up my suitcase and hauls it into the trunk of the car, then pulls it back out. Gia gently lifts it back into the trunk again. Nav sighs but allows it to stay put this time. "Don't go off doing random sports and get hurt. I can't drive two hours to a hospital."

"I don't do sports anymore."

I decided to quit the basketball team ahead of camp, something Coach Underwood took like a blow to the face. She begged me to reconsider, and I weakly told her I'd think about it, but I'm determined. This is the trip, the summer, to change my life. And basketball no longer has any part in that (even if I'll miss it).

Nav waves her hand in the air, dismissing my words. She, like Coach Underwood, thinks I'm bluffing. "Whatever, just be careful. And no fuck boys—like, seriously, Hallie. If a greasy-haired guy named Aiden approaches you, pepper spray him."

That gets me to laugh. "I'll look out for any Aidens, I promise."

Nav finally looks up, her eyes wet with unshed tears, a wobbly smile on her lips. "Sorry. I'm just gonna miss you."

I grab her and squeeze her as tight as I can. My throat constricts, and even though I swore I wasn't going to cry, tears prick at my eyes. "I'm gonna miss you too."

"Come on, Hallie," Mom calls from the car. "It's not a funeral. You'll see each other again in six weeks."

"Just a minute, Aunt Cathy!" Nav yells. Nav frowns at me as we break our hug. "Call me any time, okay?"

"Okay. And you too! If your new employees get pissy, I'll come back and we can kill them."

Nav cracks a wider smile. "Wouldn't go to prison with anyone else."

We hug one more time. I can feel Mom's eyes boring into my back, so I grab my camp backpack and shoulder it. I wave to Nav and Gia. "I guess I'll see you both in August?"

"You better!"

Gia shakes her head slightly, an amused smile on her face. "Bye, Hallie. I hope you have a good time. Oh, and you can always ask my mom for help if you need anything."

I nod, though I have no intention of asking the millionaire sponsor of the camp anything, tangentially related or not. This is my chance to start over, and I can't do that if I'm calling in favors from my best friend's girlfriend's mom.

"*Hallie*." Mom's voice is thick and short, so it's time to go.

I scramble into the back seat, squished against the window by my stuff, and wave at Nav and Gia as Mom cranks up. They wave back, and we keep waving until the car is almost out of sight. Then, just before I can't see them anymore, Nav breaks down and hugs Gia. Gia rests her cheek on the top of her head, patting her back gently.

I turn around to face the road ahead, an ugly bit of jealousy curling under my ribs.

I don't even want to acknowledge this horrible feeling, but it's been in the back of my mind for a few days, and it looks like it's not going away. I don't like Nav's girlfriend, Gia Flores, romantically, though we did go on one disastrous date a month ago. The more I'm around Gia, the more I'm certain it wouldn't have worked between us. But the part that keeps me up at night is that Nav has found her person and I'm still looking. Nav Hampton, heartbreaker of Mapleton High, famous for shooting down any and every girl who even tried to suggest a relationship, is now dating Gia. And when I say dating, I mean *dating*—Nav would get starry eyed whenever she brought Gia up, even before they got together. I'm talking sobbing on my shoulder when she thought she messed things up with Gia type of love. I'm talking big declarations of love outside a mediocre ice cream shop. And I'm happy for her, I really am, but it's just like . . . what the hell am I doing wrong? I was always the one who wanted a partner, and somehow Nav not only lapped me but also had everything I've ever wanted dropped into her lap when she wasn't even looking for it. All I have to show for two years of sincere effort is six failed relationships and probably a few new insecurities.

I sink lower into my seat, part embarrassed, part annoyed, part in despair. I can't keep thinking like this. It's frankly pathetic. I have to change. And Carnegie Camp for Young Scholars is the perfect place to do it.

"You okay, Bean?" Dad asks from the passenger seat. "You look deep in thought."

"Probably just excited for the camp," Mom answers before I can. She meets my eyes in the rearview mirror. "But you know you'll have to work hard and not just laze around. You're there to learn and study."

"I know." I struggle to keep the residual annoyance out of my voice. Carnegie Camp is famous for its parties—not that Mom knows that—but I'm not stupid enough to squander an opportunity I worked hard for.

Mom doesn't look away, which is unnerving because she should be watching the road. "You know what happened last time you lost your focus."

Acid creeps up my throat, and I want to be sick right here in the car. "Yeah."

She's talking about in March, when I took the SAT the first time. I studied so hard, really pushed myself, and did every practice problem three times. I felt ready to ace that test. I *was* ready. And then the night before, my now-ex-boyfriend Peter and I fought about me missing one of his band practices because I was studying. Just practice, not even a show! It threw me off so bad that I bombed the test. Mom was so disappointed when we got the feeble 1370 score. Which is still good, but it crushed me because I know I can do better.

But that's where Carnegie Camp for Young Scholars comes in. Carnegie Camp is a six-week academic camp located on a beautiful lakefront in middle of nowhere, North Alabama. There will be some traditional camp stuff, like s'mores probably, but it's mostly for prepping for the SAT we take at the end of the camp. I *will* do better this time. I'll study those practice materials like my life depends on it and get a way better score.

I watch a few black cows munching on grass in the summer heat, my mind drifting. I think my vow to get a great grade on the SAT is a good goal, but is it enough? I can't stop thinking that this is my chance to really audit my life. The academic problems are just the tip of the iceberg. I've been struggling with my relationships; I've had six partners, and now I have six exes. Clearly something is wrong with me, and now is the perfect time to figure out what it is and change.

But I don't really know where to start. I don't even know who the real Hallie is. Sometimes it feels like my whole personality comes from my exes. Ashley got me into horror movies, Gabriel was a fan of K-pop. I even joined the basketball team for Ginger Banks, and then she turned out to be straight! I've wasted my life on other people's dreams. I get depressed if I think about it too much.

But camp—I did that on my own. I had to test into Carnegie, and though lots of people applied, I'm the only one from Mapleton High who got in. And even before I suddenly noticed that everyone around me was hot, I did well in school. I've always liked math and science, and school comes easy to me.

So maybe that's the real me. I'm Smart Girl Hallie, not Basketball Hallie or Horror Movie Hallie, and certainly not Bombed My SAT Test Because I Was Crying Too Hard to See the Page Hallie. I can do well at Carnegie Camp and leave behind all my exes and my jealousy over my best friend and the old, stupid Hallie who cried for two weeks over Peter cheating on me. I'm throwing that Hallie away and embracing a new, better me. Hallie, but refined. Hallie 2.0.

"As long as you know," Mom says, bringing me back to the present. She gives me a faint smile. "You'll do great."

"We're incredibly proud," Dad adds. "One of forty-eight! In the whole state!"

"And the guaranteed scholarship," Mom says. She's practically beaming now. "Five thousand dollars will pay for all your books for all four years!"

I don't say anything, but I'm secretly basking in their praise. Mom and Dad are strict, and they expect a lot out of me, but man does it feel good when I do something right.

But I need to keep it that way. Change won't be easy, but

I'm mostly worried about what happens when—if!—I see a cute person at camp. Nav's made-up Aiden floats into my brain, and I shudder. I can't even laugh about it because I wouldn't put it past me to fall in love with him if he was remotely interesting.

But no! That's the old Hallie. New Hallie doesn't fall in love with greasy-haired Aidens, whether they ride Jet Skis or not. Before I get lost in dreaming about the mythical Aiden, who also has well-defined biceps in my imagination, I make a new rule for myself: no romance. The new, smart Hallie doesn't need romance. She gets a 1600 on her SATs and doesn't worry about what the cute fellow campers are doing. I nod to myself, eyebrows scrunched in determination. This isn't so hard. I can do this. I can resist any charm that comes my way. I mentally push the handsome Aiden off his Jet Ski and grin to myself. Hallie 2.0, here we come.

Mom and Dad keep talking about the camp, and I turn my daydreaming to winning a Nobel Prize and dedicating my speech to Carnegie Camp for changing my life. And, after an hour and a half of bad road trip sing-alongs with my parents, the Carnegie Camp for Young Scholars sign comes into view.

Dad looks back at me, grinning. "You ready, Bean?"

I grin back, heart hammering with anticipation. "I'm ready."

CHAPTER 2

The camp that's going to change my life is full of dust. Specifically gravel dust, kicked up by the forty-eight cars all trying to squeeze in the minuscule parking lot at once. And it's *hot*. It's July in Alabama, so I should be used to it, but the humidity is out of control thanks to the nearby lake (allegedly—I can't see it over the cluster of buildings and trees and parked cars). I'm swimming in soup-air, then getting coated with a fine layer of dust. Dad hacks up a horrible cough, causing a white girl and her mom to stare at us. Mom wipes her brow, and it comes away gray.

Not a great start.

But it's fine! Plenty of things have terrible starts. Basketball was pure misery until my body got used to workouts. Some of the best horror movies have slow or clumsy openings. Everything will be fine. Encouraged from my mental pep talk, I grab my suitcase and follow bright yellow signs pointing up the long gravel road to a massive log cabin–type building.

"This is nice," Dad ventures.

But as we get closer, it's clear he's exaggerating. The building looks partially run-down, with kudzu climbing the sides and the wood washed out by the harsh sun. Mom regards the building with disgust.

"It's rustic," I offer.

"Hmm."

Dad and I share an uneasy glance. Mom isn't just intense with me; her personality is quintessential type A, no-nonsense, borderline drill sergeant. It's helpful when a restaurant gets my order wrong, or when I'm arguing with a teacher about a grade, but it can be lethal in situations like this, when I really don't need her to embarrass me.

We finally reach the lobby, panting and sweating. I open the door, praying for a blast of cool air, but it's stuffy and stagnant and hot. Uh oh. A young Indian woman sits behind a folding card table near the front door. She has gorgeous dark hair (How is it so beautiful in this humidity?!) and a name tag on a dark blue lanyard that reads "Amira Patel: Registration." Amira brightens when she sees us.

"Welcome to Carnegie Camp for Young Scholars! So happy to see you. Unfortunately, the air-conditioning is broken in here and the meeting hall, but please take a fan!"

"Oh, hell no," Mom mutters under her breath.

I spring into action to avoid a Mom-tantrum and grab three paper fans from the table. "Thank you! I'm Hallie Griffin; these are my parents!"

Mom gets distracted by introductions and the fan I shove into her hands. She compliments Amira on her earrings, and I sigh in relief. Crisis averted for now.

"Hallie," Amira says after laughing with Mom for a few minutes, "campers will go back there, but it'll be half an hour until we start. You can use that time to say your goodbyes."

"Already?" Dad's shocked, his eyes wide.

Amira smiles sympathetically. "Already. We'll take good care of her, I promise."

"Don't make a scene," I joke to Dad, but when I hug him, his embrace is strong and tight. I'm almost as tall as him now, but for a second, I feel like a little kid again.

"Love you, Bean," he says, and presses a kiss to my hair. "You're gonna do great."

"Of course she is," Mom says after Dad lets me go. She hugs me next, and her hug is just as tight as Dad's. She lets go quicker and adjusts my shirt. She smiles, her sharp brown eyes softer than I'm used to. "Call us at least once a week."

"Yes, ma'am."

"And if you need anything, we can overnight it." Mom waves a postcard she picked up from the card table. "Got your address here."

"Thanks, Mom." I take a deep breath. "I love you both."

They hug me one more time, and then they're backing out of the hall. We're not a sappy family, but they keep looking back at me anxiously, and I want to tear up again. I wave until they're gone, and I can't watch them through the age-fogged windows anymore.

Amira smiles at me. "Go ahead, Hallie. And welcome again!"

I smile back. I'm sad, but I'm excited now too. Day one of my new, better self.

"Thanks!" I haul all my luggage to the door behind her and enter the meeting hall for the first time.

It's no cooler in here. That's my first thought. The second

is a blank panic as at least twenty pairs of eyes look directly at me. I lift my hand in a lame wave, then change my mind halfway through and focus on wrestling my heavy luggage into the room. I like meeting new people, but there's a hushed air of seriousness in the meeting hall. It's a cavernous space with a full-sized stage at the top of the room, so everyone's whispering to each other so their voices don't carry. I slowly wheel farther in, wanting to die from all the noise I'm making. I'm regretting my giant suitcase and duffel bag and my very existence when the person nearest to the door looks up and smiles at me. I make a beeline to them immediately.

"Hi," I say, sweating with nerves and the thousand-degree heat. "I'm Hallie."

"I'm Cam." Cam smiles, and I clock a cute little dimple on one side. And freckles! So many across their nose and under their eyes, like a constellation. They're white and have a cool, androgynous style: loose-fitting white polo, new jean shorts, pristine purple Jordans. An expensive style, I note. They have a mop of short brown hair, light brown eyes, friendly smile.

My cheeks warm as I return it. They're cute.

No! I want to strangle myself. I'm already trying to break the one rule I made for myself in the car: *no romance*. I have to take a break from dating until I can fix my life. Smart Girl Hallie isn't interested in kissing friendly strangers. She's interested in SAT tests. Books. Freckles? No! Math and science and essays!

"Guess things haven't started yet?" I say, desperate to get out of my own horrible brain.

"Not yet," Cam says, hopefully unaware of the war going on

in my head. My gaze drops to the lanyard around their neck. It reads "Cabin 8" in blocky letters, but it also has a white, yellow, and purple flag pin.

I point to it, excitement blasting away my earlier mortification. "Where did you get this?"

"The lanyard?" Cam points behind them, to another card table with a man seated behind it. "That guy will get you checked in."

"No, I mean—" Because I'm too excited to speak coherently, I turn so they can see my backpack. It's a simple green, but I've covered it in enamel pins. Some are from school and my favorite—ex-favorite, we don't like horror anymore, Hallie—slasher, *Halloween*, but most are fun flowers with colors from the bisexual flag.

Cam's whole aura changes. Their face lights up, and their posture, once guarded but friendly, eases. They lean closer to me, like we're already friends. "One of us!"

"One of us!" I repeat, caught up in the hype. I shouldn't be this excited to see another queer person, but in Alabama, they're rarer than you'd think. Nav and I were the only out middle schoolers in Mapleton for a long time, and even now there aren't that many.

Cam grins as I turn around to face them again. "I was so worried I'd be alone out here. I almost didn't come. They/them, by the way."

"She/her," I add. "And me too! I mean, I was always coming. I can't turn down excellent parties." Shit, why did I say that? Smart Girl Hallie doesn't party!

Cam at least finds my slipup funny. They laugh, a cool, lower chuckle. "A party girl! I love it."

No! I'm already fucking this up. I open my mouth to clarify, but Cam playfully nudges me toward the card table with the older white guy sitting behind it.

"Go get your lanyard and then we'll talk. I hope we're in the same cabin."

"Okay, be right back." I leave my stuff with Cam and head to the table. More people are filing in now, so there are three people ahead of me. I listen closely—"Maverick, Cabin Four, welcome to Carnegie Camp. . . . Oscar, Cabin Two, welcome to Carnegie Camp. . . . Julia, Cabin Eleven, welcome to Carnegie Camp."

And then it's my turn. I step up, smiling. "Hallie Griffin. And I know, welcome to Carnegie Camp."

The man chuckles and cross-references my name on a handwritten piece of paper. His lanyard reads "Mr. Green: Communication." What does that mean? Amira's said something about registration, so it's interesting that his is different. He digs a magenta lanyard out of a box and gives it to me. "Here you go, Hallie. Cabin Eleven. Have a good time at Carnegie Camp."

I take it, a little disappointed I won't get to see Cam's cute freckles every morning. God, there's something wrong with me. But wait! The girl ahead of me was also Cabin 11, right? I jog to her side, where she's paused by her small suitcase and some sort of instrument case.

"Hi!" I say, smiling.

The girl, Julia, turns to face me. I'm momentarily stunned.

She has the prettiest, clearest dark skin, a diamond stud nose ring, and a single strip of purple in her intricate braids. She's wearing a simple gray T-shirt and army green shorts that look well-worn, but I like that; it's too risky to bring new clothes to a camp where anything could happen. She's not smiling, but her dark brown eyes are piercing and intense.

Gorgeous, my traitorous brain sings.

"What do you want?" Julia's voice is soft, but not in a good way. Kind of a *Leave me the fuck alone* way.

The stars fade from my eyes as I sense a hint of danger. But maybe she's just tired. She could have had a long drive. That hour and a half just about killed me.

"I'm Hallie! I heard we were in the same cabin." I lift up my lanyard as a helpful visual aid.

Julia's icy eyes look at my lanyard, then up to my eyes. "Okay."

I stare at her for a second, smile frozen on my face. Uh oh. That danger signal from before is getting stronger. "Umm, I just thought it would be good to get to know each other. As cabinmates."

Julia doesn't say anything. And not because she's thinking of a reply; she's just staring at me, eyes half hidden with clear annoyance, posture stiff and hostile, perfect brows slightly furrowed. I take an involuntary step back. I'm feeling distinctly like a rabbit staring down the maw of a wolf.

"Campers," a woman calls from the stage. "We're about to start. Everyone get checked in."

"Umm, I guess we'll talk later?" I don't wait for her to respond. I get my ass back to Cam and my luggage as fast as possible. I glance at Julia once I'm a safe distance away, and she's not looking at me anymore. She's packing something carefully into her backpack, moving incredibly slowly. Maybe I interrupted her at a bad time?

"What happened?" Cam asks as the woman fiddles with the mic onstage.

"I think I almost died just now."

Cam looks confused, but there's no time to explain. The woman finishes fixing the microphone and steps up. I start as I recognize her—Gia's mom, Ms. Flores, sponsor for this year's Carnegie Camp for Young Scholars. She's a short Latina woman dressed in a stunning white pantsuit. She's wearing a lanyard too, hers jet black with a simple "Ms. Flores" on her tag.

"Hello, campers! Welcome, welcome! I'm Adela Flores, this year's sponsor for Carnegie Camp for Young Scholars." Ms. Flores waits while a few applaud, me included. "So sorry about the heat; we should have everything up and running again soon, and your cabins have fans, don't worry!"

Another shock. Gia's mom is the opposite of the Gia I know: talkative, animated, intense in a fun way. She grins at us, brilliantly white teeth beaming in the gloom of the massive room.

"I won't keep you long because I know it's hot in here, but I wanted to welcome you—and also say there will be changes to camp this year."

Murmurs break out among the campers. Cam frowns at me, and I frown back. What does Ms. Flores mean? I have a bad feeling this perfect summer isn't going to go how I thought.

CHAPTER 3

Ms. Flores gazes out at us serenely, like she isn't shaking up our existence. "I'm sure you've all heard that in previous years, this camp was known less for academics and more for lackadaisical days lounging in the sun." Ms. Flores beams at us. "Those days are over."

Uh, that doesn't sound good. I bet she's talking about the famous wild parties counselors would throw. I was ready to learn, of course, but I thought a party once a week wouldn't hurt. . . . The people around me seem to feel the same; murmurs and shuffling fill the cavernous room.

Ms. Flores continues, apparently unbothered. "There's no reason to only have a single hour of studying and then twenty-three of relaxation. You had summer in June! You came here to work hard, yes?"

There are a few half-hearted cheers. Cam looks like they might be ill any second. I glance at Julia, by the wall. She's staring at Ms. Flores with a blank, unfocused expression. At least I'm not alone in my dread.

"You'll have an hour of SAT prep each morning, but also three hours of other classes. You'll have a break on most Wednesdays, and weekends free, no worries!"

That's not so bad. Four days on, three days off. And it's just three extra hours. I can handle three hours of math or science—

16

"There's a catch." Ms. Flores is practically vibrating with glee. "Your classes won't be the normal academic classes. The fact that you're here means you can study. You all know how to do complex math and know US history. But do you know how to cook a simple meal? Do you know what taxes are and how to pay them? Can you derive joy from the things in life we can't quantify?" Ms. Flores scans the audience, smiling. "There is more than one way to be a scholar, campers, and you'll learn those ways here! The goal is to be a well-rounded individual as you leave high school and enter adulthood. A perfect SAT score is great, but it won't do you a bit of good when you're stranded on the side of the road with a popped tire."

The room is completely silent. I glance at Cam and the others beside us as I fight rising panic. I know I would do well in STEM stuff, but what does it mean to "derive joy" from unquantifiable things? I mean, I can cook okay (I practiced a lot the summer Mom took a sabbatical because Dad burns water), but I'm not confident in doing taxes. Smart Girl Hallie can contend with math and science no problem, but I didn't know I'd have to learn how to do all these other things too.

This is going to be a lot harder than I thought.

"Don't fret." Ms. Flores is trying to sound soothing, but she's grinning like she's a sponsor for the Hunger Games. "I know it's a big adjustment, so I've made a system to encourage you to do well." Ms. Flores holds up one finger. "First, every time you excel in classes, you will get points. Points can be redeemed for extra amenities, including but not limited to sweets, comforts, and even electronics."

Now everyone's paying attention. Cam stands straighter beside me.

"But you may want to save your points, because at the end of camp, we'll total them up and the top scorers will be eligible for some grand prizes." Ms. Flores beams at us. "Top prize being a twenty-thousand-dollar scholarship to a college of your choice, a brand-new laptop, and a medal of achievement for excellence."

Ms. Flores keeps talking, but I don't hear her. That's it. That's what I have to do. I can see it in my head—I win the most points, I get onstage, I get the medal that says, *Yes, I am Smart Girl Hallie.* Smartest girl at Carnegie Camp. Ashley won't ever accuse me of not getting the point, and Peter won't ever call me a dumb jock again. It's the pinnacle of academic achievement. It'll be a tangible, visible reminder that I've officially changed.

I have to win that medal.

"Anyway!" Ms. Flores claps her hands, returning me to the present. "I'm proud of everyone here already, and though I hope you'll learn many new things in the next six weeks, I hope you'll have fun too. Good luck, campers, and have the best time!"

Now the room cheers, and it's sincere. Ms. Flores waves at us before leaving the stage, and we're done.

Cam hops on one foot, ecstatic. "That turned around! Twenty K?"

"And a medal." I'm practically burning with excitement. "I need it."

Cam laughs. "You can get a medal anywhere."

I smile but don't explain. Normal Hallie would word-vomit

all over Cam, but not Refined Hallie. She holds her cards close to her chest and wins medals. And is probably way hotter and more confident than me, but we'll work on that after I have the medal around my neck.

"What now?" I ask instead.

"Cabin time, I guess." Cam's grin fades. "I hate we're not in the same cabin! You're cool."

I can't help beaming. I'm not Cool Girl Hallie, but I mean, I can make an exception right here at the beginning. "Me too. I met one of my cabinmates, but . . ." I trail off as I look around for Julia, but she's already gone. "Never mind. Let's go!"

Cam and I leave the meeting hall, chatting the whole time as we follow the line of kids walking toward the cabins. The buildings are all in a neat row, a sizable gap between the first six and the last six. They're much newer than the meeting hall; the wood gleams in the sun, as if someone polished it just before we got here, and the cabins all have massive numbers at the top. They're also much bigger than I was anticipating. I thought there were only four people per cabin. . . .

Cam stops at Cabin 8. I hesitate, but as a girl emerges from the door, waving Cam in, I nod to them.

"See you later?"

"Yeah! I'll find you at dinner. Whenever that is." Cam waves at me, and I wave back, then keep trucking to Cabin 11.

There are no friendly greeters outside my cabin. In fact, the screen door is closed, and raised voices float to my ears. I look to my right; four girls are happily taking pictures outside Cabin 12. I look to my left; silence and no movement in Cabin 10.

And then in mine, muffled yelling as something heavy slams into the floor.

"Oh God," I mutter. But no, I have to be positive! I'm sure we can work this out, whatever the problem is. I take a deep breath and open the screen door.

Julia is standing next to a bunk bed, arms folded, posture rigid and ready to attack. Opposite her, a white girl wearing a really nice red shirt with frills at the bottom glares at Julia. Her face is turning as red as her shirt. I take in the spacious cabin and apparently private bathroom—wow!—but push those details away. Deal with the crisis in front of me first.

"Hi," I say, dragging my suitcase into the cabin. "I'm Hallie! What, uh . . . what's going on?"

The white girl turns to me. She sizes me up and appears . . . relieved? Her lanyard reads "Michelle" in bold letters. "Oh thank God, someone normal."

I glance at Julia, confused. She's a silent dragon, sharp eyes trained on Michelle. I'm getting a bad feeling about this. Julia is deeply unfriendly, but I don't like how Michelle looked at me once and called me "normal" in comparison. I edge closer to Julia's side of the room, still smiling.

"What's the problem?" I study the room closer, and there are gift baskets on three beds. One is on the floor, knocked off the bottom bunk to the right. "Beds?"

Michelle snorts. "That started it, but they can't expect me to stay in a cabin with a lesbian. Like, you agree, right?"

I stare at Michelle, shock robbing every thought in my head for a second. Talk about bad feeling confirmed. I know we're in

Alabama, but good God. I was sort of expecting some racism, but the homophobia is disappointing.

I stand next to Julia and cross my arms too. "If you have a problem with us, you can get out."

All the color leaves Michelle's face. "You too?!"

"Bi, if you have to know. But that doesn't matter, because I don't want to share a cabin with a homophobe either."

Michelle makes a choking sound in her throat. While she's trying to breathe, Julia finally speaks.

"Feel free to change cabins," she says. Her voice is low and lethal. "You don't have to, though. Neither of us want to fuck you."

I almost laugh, but I hold it in to seem severe and intimidating. Michelle doesn't speak, just snatches her duffel bag and storms to the door. She leaves, letting the screen slam behind her.

Julia picks up the fallen gift basket and tosses it outside. She yells, "Take your basket with you, asshole."

When Julia comes back, her eyes meet mine. She almost seems surprised, like she forgot we met before. Or maybe she wants to be friends now . . . ? I smile at her and open my mouth to speak, but she turns away. She points at the bottom bunk on the left.

"This one's mine."

I wanted the bottom bunk . . . my legs will hang off the top . . . but that's fine, I can sleep on the bottom on the right—

"Fan's broken on that side." Julia puts her small bag and instrument case on the bottom mattress. And then she leaves the cabin without another word.

I stand in the middle of the room, at a loss. Okay. Okay, I

guess I have to take the top bunk. Not at all what I wanted, but it's better than roasting to death at night. I also wanted nice roommates, but I got stuck with a homophobe and Julia, who is mysterious and beautiful and also deeply uninterested in being friends.

I kind of want to cry.

But I don't. Smart Girl Hallie doesn't cry when things are bad. The days of me sobbing for weeks after my ex cheated on me are over. I take a deep breath and inspect the private bathroom (it's small but really nice!) and the mini fridge next to the forbidden bunk bed. Empty, but a decent size. There's also a desk between the two bunks. The gift basket atop my bunk is untouched; it has a schedule, a map of the camp, some basic toiletries, a water bottle, and a bright red T-shirt with Carnegie Camp's logo on the front. And a massive chocolate bar.

I almost shove the chocolate bar into my face on sight, but I pause. This is a good opportunity, right? The old Hallie is impulsive and falls in love at the drop of a hat. New Hallie has restraint. She doesn't fall in love with Cam and their dimples, or Julia and her intense eyes, or the fictional Aiden and his Jet Ski. She doesn't cry when her roommate hates her for simply existing. She doesn't eat an entire chocolate bar before dinner and get sick. New Hallie is better than that.

I place the chocolate bar carefully in the mini fridge so it doesn't melt. I'll only eat a piece at a time, to celebrate when I ace my classes and when I've successfully changed for the better. And the rest when I win the medal.

I nod to myself, encouraged. I put Julia's bar in the fridge too (it's absolutely boiling in here, even with the fan), then grab my map and schedule.

The map is straightforward: there's the meeting hall close to the parking lot, and a mess hall located straight ahead from my cabin. The mysterious lake is to the far left of my cabin, but it's apparently surrounded by a forest, so I will not be going there. I'm a city girl at heart, and getting lost in the wilderness is the last thing I need. There are a few more buildings labeled *auditorium*, *canteen*, *nurse's station*, *library*, and *laundry room*, but I need to see them in person. These cute little dots mean nothing to me.

The schedule, however, is interesting. It's organized like a weekly calendar, with *CABIN 11* printed at the top. This week, apparently, is different from the rest; today is Monday, and it simply says *orientation*. But every other week, we have Wednesday off as a free day. I take a peek at tomorrow's schedule, Tuesday.

BREAKFAST: 7:00–8:50 A.M.
SAT PREP: 9:00–9:50 A.M.
FINANCE: 10:00–11:20 A.M.
LUNCH: 11:30 A.M.–12:50 P.M.
COMMUNICATION: 1:00–2:20 P.M.

I frown at the schedule. I don't know much about finance . . . but maybe it's just balancing budgets? And what does communication mean? I flashback to Mr. Green's name tag, and it clicks. I bet he's our instructor. Wednesday's schedule is the same, but *Finance* has been replaced with *Life Skills* and *Communication* with *Fine Arts*. My stomach aches at that last one. I can barely draw stick figures. My chances at a medal seem further away than ever.

But I can't get down about it! I haven't even attended a class yet. Maybe it's totally fine and easy, and it'll be a breeze. I nod, determined to gaslight myself into being positive, and put my suitcase and duffel bag away. And then I take my map and leave Cabin 11 to explore my home for the next six weeks.

CHAPTER 4

I stare up at the dark ceiling, wide awake, my feet hanging off the top bunk like I knew they would. The ancient fan whirs at my head, circulating cool air with an obnoxious, cyclical squeak. I listen for Julia beneath me, but I can't hear anything, not even her breathing. Which makes me think of an ambush predator in the wild, watching and waiting for me to close my eyes so they can eat me.

Sometimes, I regret every decision I've ever made.

This happens whenever I'm still for too long, or have too much free time. Especially at night, especially from one to four a.m. I'm minding my own business, and suddenly I'm thinking about the time Ashley clowned me for not knowing who Alfred Hitchcock was. Or when I tried out for the basketball team and the middle school coach said she only picked me because I was tall, not because I was good at it. Peter jokingly (allegedly) saying I was "just a dumb jock" so I should stop studying for my SAT to hang out with him, and the catastrophic fight that followed. And now, currently, thinking about how Michelle never came back and our mysterious fourth roommate never arrived and Julia hasn't said a word to me all day except to claim her bunk.

I roll over to my side and check my phone. 1:12 a.m. Yep, peak Sad Girl Hours.

If I were at home, I'd do something to tire myself out. A

workout, watching a video on physics (it really puts you to sleep), *something*. But it would be rude to wake Julia, right? Not that she's been nice so far. . . . Nav would probably play music from her phone on full blast to get revenge.

I could text her. She keeps goblin hours in the summertime. I pull up our chat, which ended only a few hours ago.

I can't sleep.

It's hot. This fan is too loud.

I'm hungry and I don't have any food in my cabin.

My heart leaps when Nav's text bubble pops up.

im on my way with snacks

I touch my phone to my forehead, close to tears. On the way here, I thought I was sure about coming to camp. But now, at 1:12 a.m., half thinking about my disastrous attempts at friendship with Julia, I wish I were back in my hometown with my best friend.

My phone vibrates gently in my hand.

do you have melatonin to help you sleep?

No

tequila??

I chuckle at the memory.

I told you never again and I
meant it!!

you probably can't sleep because
you didn't do your workout shit

I quit the team remember?
I don't have to do workouts

yeah ok lol

either way you can't quit cold
turkey. do some tomorrow

I scratch my thumbnail against my phone case. I didn't think
about that. My body is used to a routine, whether I like it or not.
And suddenly not doing any exercise at all and being in a new
place and going to bed at nine o'clock because I can't bear hours
of awkward silence is brutal. Maybe I can borrow a little from
the old Hallie.

falling asleep. it'll be better
tomorrow, okay?

"It'll be better tomorrow," I whisper into the dark, then

hate myself a second later because if Julia's awake, she probably thinks I'm a psycho. I quickly type out a message to Nav before darkening my phone.

Okay. Love you Nav

love ya babe.

* * *

It's tomorrow, and it's not better.

I drag my toothbrush across my teeth, nodding off into the sink. I slept maybe three hours, and woke up right at six a.m., when the sun ran into the window and stabbed my eyes.

I'm in a bad mood.

"New Hallie doesn't have bad moods," I mumble through the froth of toothpaste. "She is positive. She is optimistic and smart and hot."

I don't feel optimistic. Or hot. My eyes are exhausted, and my hair is a curly mess from the humidity. Julia is fast asleep, so I'm being extra quiet. And I have a sudden paranoia about her hearing me pee? This is the first time being an only child has come to haunt me.

I pat both cheeks to get it together. I said it'll be better tomorrow, but it won't if I don't *make* it better. I gather my toiletries and take the quietest shower of my life, get dressed, and straighten my hair as much as possible in this god-awful humidity. By seven thirty, I'm a new person! And hungry now, but at least presentable.

I peek out of the bathroom. Julia is still fast asleep, motionless under her plain gray comforter. Does she want to get breakfast? Should I ask? I run the scenario through my head: I wake her, she sits up in bed, she immediately murders me with her bare hands.

That's a no, then.

I grab my backpack and slip out of the cabin, easing the screen door closed behind me. It's oppressively hot already; my skin is immediately sticky and wet, rendering my nice shower worthless in minutes. The gloomy mood is crawling back, but I ignore it as I follow the gift basket map to the mess hall.

It's another massive building, but this one thankfully has air-conditioning. There are long, wooden tables in six identical rows, complete with wooden benches. There's a cafeteria-style breakfast bar, but no lunch ladies behind it. The food is under heat lamps, but it looks pretty decent. It's almost untouched, because there are only a few campers in the mess hall so far. I get eggs, toast, and bacon, and put it on a steel tray (reminding me of elementary school or, much less pleasantly, prison).

When I turn, stomach growling happily in anticipation, I meet Michelle's eyes immediately. She's sitting with three other girls near the middle of the room. She grimaces and leans closer to the others, and then she *points* at me.

I run a scenario through my head. I stomp over there, dump my eggs on Michelle's head, she screeches like the idiot and homophobe she is. It's tempting, honestly, but then I'd still be hungry and they might not let me have a second breakfast. No, I'll get revenge by being the number one camper, and I can give her the middle finger while holding my medal.

I turn away, dignity intact, and scan the rest of the tables. I hate eating alone, but Michelle has made me paranoid. What if I sit with a bigot and they dump their eggs on *me*? I just took a shower!

My eyes lock on to a boy sitting by himself, picking at a bowl of oatmeal. I have to take the risk. I can't stand here looking like an idiot or Michelle will have more ammunition against me. I take a breath and make a beeline to the boy's table.

"Is anyone sitting here?" I ask.

He looks up from his oatmeal, startled. He has curly black hair that swoops low over his forehead, dreamy dark eyes, and sun-kissed tan skin. *CUTE*, my traitorous brain screams before I beat it into submission again.

"Uh, no, go ahead." He gestures to the seat across from him.

Instead of blurting out my embarrassing thoughts, I sit down on the hard bench and smile. "Thanks! I'm Hallie, and I hate eating alone."

The boy cracks a smile, and I'm momentarily enraptured by the little gap in his front teeth. "I'm Teddy. I don't hate eating alone, but happy you're here."

I know my smile is widening, because my ears are burning with glee. See, Old Hallie would take this as flirting and maybe even imagine our life together as a scientist-archaeologist duo (I don't mind either, his choice). But New Hallie has a handle on her life and hormones, and will not be weird right off the bat. Or ever! No romance this summer!

"Nice to meet you, Teddy," is what emerges from the hurricane that is my thoughts. "How do you like camp so far?"

Teddy grimaces at his bowl of oatmeal. "Well, the food's shit."

Uh oh. I take an experimental bite of my scrambled eggs and nearly gag. It's certainly . . . food? If I squint. But it's painfully bland, and the eggs are somehow *wet*. "Shit. We're doomed for the next six weeks."

Teddy chuckles. His voice is much deeper than I thought it would be, and he has a fascinating birthmark on his neck, near his collarbone. Not that I'm staring, just observing my new friend, that's all.

"Can't be worse than my mom's cooking, so I'll live."

My mom's cooking is pretty good, but now isn't the time to brag about that. "At least we can buy snacks at the, uh, canteen? But I don't want to use my points if I can help it."

Teddy shrugs. "I'll probably cave soon. I doubt I'll get to the top."

I can't hold in a gasp. "Why do you think that? We're all here for a reason."

"Sure, but I know I'm not the smartest here." Teddy lets out a small laugh. "My bunkmate is preselected for Harvard, and his whole family has gone for like a hundred years or something. I'm cooked."

Damn. That is a problem, but I'm pretty smart too. No reason I couldn't go to Harvard if I wanted (which I don't, because it's too far from home). Teddy could too! This is literally a camp for smart people. He should have more confidence.

"You can do it! Nepo babies aren't the only ones Harvard-bound."

"Amen," a voice says behind me, and then Cam is sitting next to me. Before I can squeal with glee, Cam waves at Teddy. "Hello, I'm Cam, they/them and all that!"

"Oh, uh, hi. Teddy. He/him." Teddy points at himself, then puts his hands in his lap. Probably self-conscious, poor guy.

"Nice to meet ya." Cam looks at me, and my heart skips a beat as I remember they have those cute freckles and the one dimple.

I swear, being alive is a fucking curse. Why is everyone so hot?! The only ugly person I've met here is Michelle, and that's because she's a bigot. She's basically an overgrown slug to me.

"How'd last night go? I was going to text you, but I forgot to get your number!"

I try not to have a stroke over a hot enby asking me for my number. But my dazzlement is over quickly because the thought of last night and the Michelle incident sours my already grumpy stomach. "Horrible. My roommate is homophobic. She left— and changed rooms, I guess—because she didn't want to room with someone queer." I phrase it carefully so I don't out Julia, just in case she doesn't want anyone to know.

Cam is immediately outraged. "What a monster! Is the bitch in the room with us right now?"

I laugh and start to point her out, but I catch Teddy's eye. He's watching us with a complicated, hard-to-read expression. Anxiety leaps into my chest. Don't tell me he's homophobic too! I might have the worst luck imaginable.

"You okay, Teddy?"

"You're both queer?" he blurts out.

Cam and I nod.

"Bisexual," I add.

Teddy seems relieved. "Wow, uh, me too! I mean sort of."

I grin as Cam gasps. "One of us!" I cry.

"What does 'sort of' mean?" Cam asks.

Teddy fidgets, stirring his too-liquidy oatmeal with his spoon. "I'm ace. I think so, anyway. And aromantic. But that doesn't feel queer enough sometimes."

"Shut up, it definitely is." I want to grab his hands, but they're still in his lap.

"Ditto," Cam says. "The A isn't for ally!"

Teddy gives us a tentative smile. "I guess that's true."

I smile back. I bet someone's given him a hard time about this before. The curse of living in Alabama. "Welcome to the club! Membership is low, but we're building the program." I gasp as an idea pops into my head. "Queer cabin!"

A few people look at us, eyebrows raised. Whoops. Cam and Teddy look equally confused. I lean closer and lower my voice.

"I just had a great idea. We should be the queer cabin! We can eat and study together. That way we don't have to deal with homophobes."

Teddy nods, but Cam frowns. "Yes to the eating together! But we shouldn't study together."

"Wait, why not?" My joy was short-lived. I work so much better in groups. . . . I thought I'd find a study group here.

Cam looks at me like I'm an idiot. "Because it's a competition? We can't help each other win."

That doesn't seem fair. Or fun. We can't all be good at

everything, right? But Cam seems sure, so I hide my disappointment and nod along.

"To be fair, I hate studying," Teddy says. "I got in because I go to an artsy high school, but SAT prep is going to kill me. I'm a terrible test taker."

I perk up at that. I've already taken SAT prep at school, so I'm hoping it's more of a refresher. "I can help—"

"Hallie," Cam interrupts, a laugh in their voice. "Competition, remember?"

Cam's competitive spirit cows me into shutting up. Teddy laughs and I join in, but I'm feeling kind of rotten. I've always helped Nav with her schoolwork, and I never minded sharing notes with classmates. Maybe that's a bad thing? Maybe I've been too soft this whole time.

"Besides SAT prep, I'm worried about Finance," Teddy says, unaware of my depressing spiral.

"I'm not," Cam says. They seem a little embarrassed now. "My dad's an investment banker."

"You're a nepo baby too!" I blurt out. I want to die right after I say it, but Cam ends up laughing so hard, they spill their chocolate milk all over the table, and then we're too busy cackling and cleaning up to discuss queer cabin anymore. Underneath the joy of hanging out with my new friends, there's an undercurrent of unease. I wish I'd said how I really feel, but I don't want to rock the boat so early. I just made friends; I don't want to lose them over something as stupid as not wanting to study alone. I'll simply have to study harder on my own. New Hallie can surely do that.

"Campers," Amira—wearing a lovely pink halter top, excellent style—calls from the door as we dump the soiled paper towels into the nearby trash can. "It's eight forty-five! Please head to the auditorium for SAT prep soon."

"Speak of the devil," Teddy mutters. He chokes down another mouthful of oatmeal as Cam and I scarf down the rest of our breakfast. When we're done and the rancid "food" is in the garbage, Cam claps their hands on both our backs.

"Queer cabin, assemble! Let's crush it."

I cheer, and Teddy gives a meek "Hooray." I'm a little bummed, but it'll be fine. I can be cool and smart and not spontaneous. I can resist falling in love with my very attractive friends. I'm doing all right so far, even if I can't study in a group with them. Things are looking up.

CHAPTER 5

Right after breakfast is SAT prep. Which seems like it's the only easy thing about Carnegie so far, but I can't even enjoy it because I'm worried about Julia.

We're gathered in an auditorium, big enough to fit forty-eight students and then some. Our instructor, Mr. Lin, is explaining the intricacies of the test at the front of the room, but so far, it's all info I've heard before. I dutifully take notes from my position in Tall Jail aka the back row (thank goodness I have good vision), but I keep glancing at the time on my phone. Class started at nine o'clock sharp, and everyone's here . . . except Julia. It's 9:14 already! I bet she overslept. I feel so bad. I should have woken her up, and we should have gone to breakfast together. She could have joined queer cabin, if she wanted. I know Cam said I shouldn't be worried about the competition, but I can't help myself. I'd want someone to wake me up if I overslept, points on the line or not. Being New Hallie is so hard.

Mr. Lin goes over each section, plus a little history about the test, but I'm barely paying attention. I watch the minutes tick by, and I feel worse and worse.

Finally, at 9:19, the door creaks open. Julia strolls in, seemingly unconcerned about being twenty minutes late. Mr. Lin doesn't call attention to her, and I'm relieved for her. I would die of embarrassment. But Julia just sits at the closest available chair, ignoring every eye on her, and opens her notebook. I'm in awe, so much that I'm staring long after everyone else looks away. Julia's head is held high, chin up, unbothered. I wish I was that cool. I'd have been a puddle of tears by now. Julia starts writing, but thanks to said perfect vision (and the fact that I'm still staring at her), I notice how tightly she grips her pencil. I see how tense her shoulders are, how she keeps her head dipped low for the rest of the class.

She is embarrassed. She does care.

It's the first instance of anything fazing Julia, and I have a knee-jerk instinct to do something to help. But I don't know what. Even as class ends at 9:50, and we troop off to the first Finance course, I can't bring myself to ask her about it. Old Hallie would swoop in and ask her if she's okay, grisly rejection be damned. But Cam's warning hangs heavy in my mind, and Julia's dangerous expression does the rest. So I don't say anything, through both Finance and Communication courses, and even when it's evening and we're getting ready for dinner.

I watch Julia, unsure. She's been exuding a menacing aura since this morning, and that's continuing now, as she scratches notes at the sole desk in the cabin. I fidget with my backpack, debating if I should just leave her alone and go to dinner solo. But Julia was so upset this morning. She's probably having an equally bad time here. I know how that feels, so I clear my throat. Here goes nothing.

"Julia?"

Julia turns her head, painfully slowly, to glare at me with one eye. I'm a mouse again, about to be eaten by a tiger. A stupid mouse at that, because I'm momentarily dazzled by how pretty her glare is. I wait for her to answer, but a second later I realize the glare is her answer. She's not ignoring me; this is my invitation to speak.

"Do you want to eat dinner with me? Maybe the food'll be better this time!"

"No." Julia turns back to her notebook and keeps writing.

I guess that's the end of that. I tried. I squeak out an "Okay, bye!" and hightail it outside.

I look up at the sky full of stars. It's beautiful here, despite the heat, and yet I'm already so sad. I hate that my roommate doesn't like me. I know it shouldn't bother me, but it does. I thought I would come here, make a great score on the SAT, make some lifelong friends, and change. But so far, even though I've stuck to my rules, everything feels off. There are too many variables. How could I plan for confronting homophobic Michelle, bending to competitive Cam, and avoiding the dangerous (yet mysterious and beautiful) Julia? And I was so distracted by Julia all day, and my guilt for not waking her up, that I took half-assed notes in Communication and Finance. That's definitely going to bite me later if I can't get myself under control. I breathe in the heavy, warm air and scratch at two mosquito bites forming on my ankle. I thought becoming New Hallie would be a piece of cake. I see now that I'm dead wrong.

I sit up straighter and slap a mosquito off my arm. I can't keep whining and feeling sorry for myself. Coach Underwood says nothing worth doing is easy. I'm pretty sure that was an excuse to get us to run more laps, but I cling to the mantra now. It won't be easy, but it's worth it. I have to keep going. I have to get that medal, and nothing will stop me.

Determined, I head to the mess hall to eat some crappy food and hopefully have a better tomorrow.

* * *

"Okay, campers!" A small white woman claps her hands. "Welcome to Life Skills! I'm so happy to be your instructor. I'm Sharon, and we'll be learning about how to make basic meals today."

"Hi, Sharon," I say automatically, and then I'm embarrassed because no one is on the same joke wavelength.

The girl beside me giggles a little, so that's encouraging. Julia is on my other side, but she's in an even worse mood today (she was late for SAT prep *again*), so I'm trying not to look her in the eye.

Sharon winks at me. "Glad to hear some enthusiasm this morning. Today, I'll be demonstrating how to make simple scrambled eggs."

It's Cabins 3, 5, 8, and 11's turn at Life Skills. I'm feeling pretty confident—well, I was. Because if Sharon is making our daily breakfast, we are dead. I know how to make scrambled eggs already, but not the bland rubber bullets they serve at the mess hall. Still, I pay polite attention as Sharon goes over how to safely operate a stove. We have individual burners, but

Sharon talks about a full stove. Julia takes extensive notes, her pencil flying across the page. The girl next to me is also taking notes, but hers are slower and sloppier—wait, I think she's writing something different. I sneak a peek and read a sentence about a man-eating bear. She's writing a book in the middle of class? I already love her.

"Okay, let's try it! Everyone grab their frying pans."

I do, and I'm on autopilot as I add a little bit of vegetable oil. I glance at Julia's pan and start when I see it—the entire bottom is covered in oil.

I know Cam said we shouldn't help each other, but I can't help myself. Before I overthink it, I lean closer to Julia.

"I think that's too much."

Julia jumps, like she didn't expect anyone to speak to her. Her gaze flickers to my pan, then hers. She has a deep frown on her face. But then she carefully pours half the oil back into the bottle. I beam at her and give her a thumbs-up. Still too much, but less chance of a grease fire! When I look up, Cam catches my eye from across the room and shakes their head in disappointment. That brings down my positive mood.

As Sharon talks us through the process, I watch Julia from the corner of my eye with increasing alarm. She smashes three eggs with too much force before she's able to coax an intact one out of its shell. And then half the shell ends up in her pan, which is way too hot. The oil is sizzling fiercely because she takes too long to add the eggs to it, and the edges burn almost immediately.

Holy shit. My roommate cannot cook at all.

"Good job so far," Sharon says, unaware of the massacre going on to my right. "Now we gently agitate the eggs until they're firm and no trace of liquid is left."

What about seasoning? Milk? Cheese? Anything? No one else seems to care, so I sadly stir my eggs until they're bland lumps like we choke down at breakfast. "Fucking prison food," I mutter under my breath.

Julia hears me. She tilts her head slightly away from me. And, though it's quick, a ghost of a smile graces her lips.

And then it's gone a second later, because somehow, she catches her entire pan on fire.

There's a brief panic while Sharon screams and gets the fire extinguisher, but it's a short crisis. Julia looks absolutely horrified, so I search for some encouraging words. I would want someone to console me, and I can practically see Julia beating herself up. I finally come up with something to say as Sharon calms down and checks our eggs.

"It's okay," I tell Julia. "It'll be better tomorrow."

Julia gives me a weird look, but she doesn't snap at me. Progress! I'll take anything at this point. It's stupid, because she's made it clear that she doesn't want anything to do with me, but I want to know more about her so bad. I've never met anyone like her. I can usually read people well, but Julia's like an attractive, mysterious brick wall. I can match Cam's no-competition energy, or Teddy's gentle friendliness, but Julia's giving me nothing. Old Hallie would be deeply intrigued by someone who's so closed off and would find that attractive and alluring, but New Hallie doesn't think like that. I just want us to be friends, that's all (I swear). The queer cabin won't study with me, but she might.

Sharon reaches our table and is aghast at the runny eggs from the girl next to me and Julia's burnt disaster.

"Well, good try, girls," Sharon says. She gives me a smile. "Excellent work, Hallie! You get five points for today."

Yes! Fuck yeah! I know I'm beaming, but I can't help it. I only got three points in Finance and Communication each yesterday, so this is amazing! I'm crushing it. I'll have that medal, easy.

Sharon walks away, and as we clean up, I'm on top of the world. Bring it on, Carnegie Camp. You won't break New Hallie, no matter how hard you try.

CHAPTER 6

My Life Skills victory is short-lived.

I don't know why I thought I could do well in Fine Arts. We're starting on music, and I'm in trouble. I've never been able to carry a tune, and no one in my family can either. Nav and I got into a bad fight once because she begged me not to sing along to a song on the radio when I was in her car. Which is why I'm staring at a piece of sheet music that might as well be written in Klingon.

"Can anyone tell me what this note is?" Our instructor, Mrs. Jenny, asks. She's a beautiful tall Black woman wearing an intricately designed headscarf. She makes me miss Mom, which is pathetic and childish, I know. But Mrs. Jenny is a lot better at music than anyone in my family, so that's where the similarities end.

Mrs. Jenny points at a squiggle with a flag at the top on the board. I stare at it blankly. I've never seen this in my life. Mrs. Jenny makes eye contact with me, and I duck my head, but it's too late.

"Hallie, right? Can you tell me?"

Oh God, oh fuck—I can't even guess! Why does it have a little hat on? Why is it on some lines? What am I even looking at?! I glance at my notes for some help, but all I've written is *????*.

Something nudges my knee. I glance at Julia, and she nods her head subtly downward. I blink at her notes, and she's written the number 8 in pencil in the margins.

"Hallie?" Mrs. Jenny prompts, her voice gentle.

"Umm . . . eight?"

"An eighth note, that's right!" Mrs. Jenny seems pleasantly surprised, and I am too. Why did Julia help me? I try to catch her eye again, but she's staring serenely at the board, lightly tapping a rhythm on her leg with her pencil. As Mrs. Jenny continues the class, I can only really look at Julia's profile, at her nose ring that shines in the light, at the way her eyes are softer when she's listening to the invisible song in her head.

No. *No!* I'm doing it again. My brain is halfway to a crush, so I fight to claw it back to real life. Julia is just returning the favor from this morning's cooking class. I can't read into it, or imagine that we'll be friends and study together by the lamplight in our room and it's just us, so . . .

I rub my temples to scrub these evil thoughts out of my brain. I need a lobotomy.

The rest of Fine Arts class is pure misery. Sixteenth notes and eighth notes and "trouble" something that tells you what key something is in? What the hell is a key, and why is it a unit of measurement in songs in the first place? I'm doomed.

But Julia's killing it. She answers every answer correctly, and when Mrs. Jenny asks her to come to the front to demonstrate the types of notes, she sits at the piano and plays it! I watch her with a mix of intense awe and jealousy. She may not be able to cook, but she certainly knows music.

When Julia sits back down beside me, I don't know what to say. My instinct is to immediately beg for her help, but I stop myself. No, I can figure this out on my own. I'm smart! I'm capable! This was a onetime thing. Still, it hurts, just a little, when Julia gets five points and I get zero.

If I want to win that medal, I have a lot of studying to do.

* * *

I decide to go for a walk.

I've spent the past few hours trying to figure out music class, but I don't even know where to start. I don't know what I don't know. I'm so overwhelmed I'm about to cry, and I don't want Julia to see me, so I'm outside in the horrific heat.

The sun is setting, casting a pretty orange glow over the sky. I walk past a few people studying together under a gazebo, but as soon as I meet their eyes, they look away. I don't know if Michelle is spreading rumors about me and Julia or if everyone really is that competitive, but this is torture.

"Hold it together," I tell myself. Everything is threatening to crash down on me. I could use some chocolate right now, but I haven't done well enough in anything to deserve it. I'm at an all-time low.

I find an abandoned track that seems to circle an empty area of land. A faded sign declares something is coming soon, but obviously, whoever owns this camp has long abandoned that idea. I walk around it, dejected. My body aches to do some workouts, or sprints, or the hundred free throw game I was actually good at, but all I have is this empty, uneven track. I miss basketball. I miss home. I miss Nav.

I pull out my phone and touch Nav's name on FaceTime. She answers right away, one cheek puffed out.

"Hallie! How's camp? You go to a party yet? Tell me everything."

Her voice is muffled by food, and I catch a glimpse of half-mutilated egg rolls. I laugh at the gross, comforting image, and my day is a little better.

"No parties. Actually, they've been outlawed."

"No!" Nav groans, then coughs as she inhales some stray food. "Is nothing—shit, I'm dying—sacred anymore?"

"Are you all right?" a muffled voice asks from beyond Nav's screen.

My laughter dies in my chest. I should have noticed—Nav's not in her bedroom. Unfamiliar gaming posters and a messy, massive bed are in the background. She must be with Gia.

"I can let you go if you're busy."

"No, no." Nav waves to me, then to Gia's voice. "Gia, I'm fine. Hallie, you hang up and I'll drive two hours to kill you."

A small smile returns. At least Nav still has time for me. I shouldn't be worried, but I don't know. I don't even like to let my brain go down that dark jealousy road.

"Tell me about camp," Nav says after she drinks some water.

"It's hot."

"Obviously. Is it fun? I mean, as much fun as studying can be?"

I wish I could lie to Nav, but I can't. She knows me too well. "No. It hasn't been much fun at all."

Nav frowns and leans closer. "What happened?"

I walk around the track and unload everything on her. How parties are canceled and we have to study way more than previous classes. The competitive campers. How bad I am at music. I don't even get to how painful my bunkmate interactions have been before I have to stop so I don't burst into tears.

"Shit." Nav looks stricken too. "I'm sorry. I thought it would be a lot better."

"Me too." I wipe the sweat pooling under my eyes. I feel a little better after venting, at least. "And I feel so stupid because I just want someone to study with. Is that crazy?"

Nav opens her mouth, but Gia's voice answers from beyond the screen.

"Not crazy! You need body doubling."

Huh. I guess that's true. Even if Nav's clowning around, having her there helps keep me on task. And not give up, like I'm doing now.

"No clue what that is, but listen to Gia." Nav nods sagely. "I'm assuming your roommates are also competitive assholes?"

"God, worse than that. One's a bigot." I tell Nav and Gia, who is leaning into frame now, about the Michelle incident. They're both outraged at my story.

"What a bitch!" Nav practically roars. "I'm coming down to kill her."

"No need," Gia adds. She's normally mild-mannered, but her face is red with outrage. I've never seen her so angry. "I'll tell Mami, and she'll kick her out."

"No, don't." I walk for a while before I can gather my thoughts.

"I think if I can win the medal, I'll show her I'm better than her, you know?"

"Hell yeah." Nav nods fiercely. "We gotta get you a music tutor so you can smoke her."

My mind slips unhelpfully to Julia. She really is great, but I'm sure she won't want to help me. And New Hallie should be able to do things on her own, right? She should have a handle on her emotions and not let a setback reduce her to tears. I shouldn't even be calling Nav every time I'm slightly sad.

"Your other roommate sounds cool, though," Gia says while I'm thinking. "Maybe you could study with her?"

"She isn't the type," I admit.

Nav narrows her eyes suspiciously, so I hurry to continue.

"How's the new job going?"

Nav was recently promoted to manager at the local ice cream/bakery combo store. She was terrified of the responsibility at first, but I know she's doing fine. She's an excellent baker, and also good at demanding things from people with no fear. Perfect manager skills.

"It's hard. Ethan was so shit, I swear to God, so I'm having to do twice the work I did before. And hiring is a disaster. The first two applicants were rude right to my face, and one said he didn't want to listen to a kid." Nav rolls her eyes, but then she gets a rare, tentative smile. "But other than that, it's good. Honestly."

I smile back, but the ugly jealousy is back and biting. Nav, notorious for hating change, is doing something hard and scary, and somehow doing it well. And I'm having a meltdown because I don't understand the difference between a treble and a bass clef. I can't help it—I'm jealous as hell. God, I'm awful! I know, but I can't help thinking that if Nav is handling her hard, scary thing well, why can't I?

Why can't I do anything right?

"You're going to be the best manager that store has ever seen," I tell her before I can break down. "But I have to go figure out what the hell is going on in music. Talk later?"

"Absolutely. And, Hal, you've got this, okay? I believe."

"Me too," Gia says. She smiles at me, a sympathetic look on her face. "And I really will tell Mami about Michelle if you want."

"No, it's fine, but thank you. Bye, Nav, bye, Gia!"

"See ya!"

Nav ends the call. I stare at my sweaty, crestfallen expression in the blackness of my phone screen for a long time, then turn to head back to the half-empty Cabin 11.

Julia's sitting at the desk when I get back, heavy headphones hanging around her neck. She looks up when I walk in but quickly goes back to studying. I take a self-pitying second to wish I had the courage to ask her for help with music, but I shake my head and go to the bathroom instead. I take a long shower and wrap my hair in a silk cap, and just stand around to avoid studying. I want to clean up, something to take my mind off things, but my clothes are neatly put away already while Julia's are scattered across the room and hanging out of her bag. And I'm too scared to ask if I can help her clean so my brain doesn't explode from stress. God, this sucks. I'm having Sad Girl Hours way before one a.m.

But I can't let the depression drag me down. I sit on the

floor by the beds, sandwiched snugly between the frame and my suitcase, and study like my life depends on it. All SAT stuff, but the familiarity soothes me. I can worry about music later; if I'm okay at everything else, I'm golden. Surely I can fail one class (the thought makes me itch) and still be number one? I chew on my thumbnail as I make vocab-word flash cards. Cam is good at everything so far. They're going to be hard to beat if I'm failing music.

Eventually, eleven o'clock comes. I get dressed in pajamas and climb into the top bunk, though Julia is still studying. She has her headphones over her ears now, and she looks like she's writing out math problems. From SAT prep, probably, but Finance too maybe. I roll over to face the wall, fighting tears.

"It'll be better tomorrow," I whisper to myself. I've said that three days in a row, but so far, tomorrow isn't coming. I close my eyes and wish for sleep.

"Hey."

My eyes fly open. My instinct is to stay very still, in case a murderer is trying to lure me outside. But the voice isn't coming from outside—it's right below me. I roll over, and Julia's looking up at me from the desk.

"Are you talking to me?" I hate myself immediately after asking. Of course she is! Who else is in here? I'm the only freak who talks to herself.

Julia doesn't smile or laugh, but her severe expression softens just a little. Or I'm imagining it. "Yeah. Is the light bothering you?"

I stare at her stupidly for a second. The light. The lamp? It's casting a soft yellow glow over the room, but I'm so defeated that it doesn't matter. I've always been a hard sleeper, so I'll be asleep in minutes. "No—no, it's okay! I'm fine, thank you."

Julia nods and goes back to studying. I watch her for a second, stunned. She talked to me. She talked to me! And she asked me about my comfort! I roll over before she can look up and see the stupid grin on my face.

Maybe Carnegie Camp for Young Scholars isn't so bad after all.

CHAPTER 7

I wake up at five a.m. sharp, the blue light of morning already stealing into the window, but I'm not tired. Or sad.

I'm determined.

If I'm going to wake up at five anyway, I might as well use this time. I get to my hands and knees, moving carefully so I don't wake Julia, and scurry down the ladder of the bunk bed. I wait at the bottom, fearful I woke her up, but her breathing is soft and even. Success!

I tiptoe into the bathroom and brush my teeth, then pull my hair into a loose ponytail. I also pull on shorts and an old T-shirt, and tie my tennis shoes. I sneak out of Cabin 11 as quiet as I can into the early morning.

No one is out, not even the counselors and instructors. I head to the track I discovered yesterday, in a better mood with each step. I've never been a runner, but I miss basketball so much that I have to make a concession. I need to do *something* or I'll go mad. And maybe it'll help me be more tired when I go to bed tonight and I'll miss Sad Girl Hours. I reach the track and stretch, then launch into a light jog.

I immediately feel better. Endorphins have a party in my brain with each footfall, and the sting of failures and chocolate-free days turns muted. I don't even care that it's hot and muggy before the sun is even up, because I'm taking a shower when I get back. This was an excellent idea.

I run two laps before movement catches my eye. I slow, panting, and a large, bulky shape slinks onto my path. It stalks closer, and I gasp—a dog!

"Here, puppy," I call.

The dog steps closer, sizing me up. It's a handsome black and tan, with a nubby tail, short floppy ears, and the cutest little tan eyebrows! It's wearing a vest and a collar, both of which have "Security" in reflective metallic print.

"Aww, are you lost?" I pat the dog's head; it just looks at me, brown eyes intense. "I have to keep running, but you're a good boy! What a cutie."

I don't know anything about dogs, but I like that this one is big and friendly. Well, not friendly. More like tolerating my presence. My mind inadvertently slides to Julia. Progress is progress, I suppose.

I keep running, and the dog follows behind me. Halfway through my lap, I slow again as a human-shaped shadow emerges from a cozy little cabin close to the track. As I get closer, I see an older white woman in a vest, scanning a flashlight across the ground.

"Walter? Here, boy!"

Oh, the dog! I stop and turn, and apparently-Walter stalks by me and returns to the woman's side. I jog up to her, and she smiles.

"Hi, a camper, right?"

"Oh, yes, ma'am." I point to the dog. "Sorry if he got lost. He was following me on my run."

The woman rumples Walter's ears affectionately. He doesn't move, sitting stoic and regal like a statue. "It's okay. Walter here takes his job very seriously. He must have heard you running and didn't like that a camper was out of bed."

I laugh. "Sorry, sorry! I couldn't sleep." I pause, uncertain. Now that I'm closer and the sun is peeking over the horizon, I see the woman's vest also has the *security* labels. I don't see any weapon at her hip, but I'm automatically nervous. "Is it okay if I run here? In the mornings, I mean?"

To my relief, the woman nods. "Totally fine. Just don't be surprised if Walter tries to herd you back to your cabin."

We both laugh while Walter looks at us like we're idiots.

"Okay, thank you. What's your name? I'm Hallie."

"Maxine." Maxine shakes my hand, smiling warmly. "Enjoy the rest of your run, Hallie."

"Thanks. And bye, Walter!" I pat his head again, and he snorts. Good enough for me.

I wave at the security duo and run two more laps before I'm too hot and exhausted to continue. I head back to Cabin 11, in a great mood. This was an excellent decision. I know I said I was going to focus on academics, but physical fitness is important too, right? I'm having doubts, but I quickly drown them out by diving into the shower for a long scrub.

It's seven thirty by the time I'm done showering, straightening my hair, and putting on presentable clothes. And Julia is still asleep. I hover by the bed, uncertain. I'm starving, but I've been up for two hours. And I don't know when she went to sleep; I conked out minutes after she asked me about the lamp. I'll let her rest.

I ease out of the cabin for the second time, headed to the mess hall to eat an undoubtedly terrible breakfast.

The queer cabin is already seated, plus a new girl sitting by Teddy. I hurriedly grab my burnt toast and rubber eggs and join them.

"A new member?" I blurt as soon as I sit down by Cam.

Cam beams at me. "Hallie, meet Caroline! I've been recruiting."

"Hi," Caroline says, and I recognize her.

"You're the author!"

When Caroline looks confused, I clarify.

"In Life Skills, when we were making eggs, I saw your notebook. I'm sorry I peeked, but I wanted to see what kind of notes you were taking to make these horrible eggs."

Recognition flashes in Caroline's eyes. Which are a pretty blue, I'm realizing. And her hair is a gorgeous shade of reddish blond. *She's cute*, my brain whispers, and I barely hold in a groan. Not again! This can't keep happening. I'm never going to eat a piece of chocolate.

"You're the one who got the perfect score! And your roommate almost burned the place down."

"That I did, and that she did. But she's getting the hang of it now." I'm sure I'm lying, but I feel a protective instinct to defend Julia's honor. It's pretty pathetic; Julia talks to me one time and now I won't even let my friends say a single word against her. But I remember how frustrated she was in SAT prep, and how she really did try with the eggs. They're not making fun of her on my watch.

"Sounds like my first attempt at cooking," Teddy says. "We had to make pancakes. Fucking brutal."

"I can't do pancakes on a good day," Caroline groans.

I can, but now doesn't seem like the time to mention it. "We can do it! Maybe they'll let us practice after-hours?"

Cam shrugs. "I'm not too worried about it. Cooking can't be that important. I'll just coast until we switch to something else."

That strategy worries me. Cooking is an important life skill, maybe *the* most important. We have to eat every day! I want to say something, but I don't want to disagree with Cam and start a fight for no reason.

"Important or not, I'm sure we could do better than this," Caroline mutters, stabbing a tough sausage link.

We eat for a minute in disgusted silence. When I swallow a bite of my burnt toast, I turn to Caroline. "What cabin are you in?"

Caroline sighs. "It's complicated."

"What do you mean?"

Caroline fidgets with the hem of her shirt. "I'm trans, so there was a whole thing about where I'd stay. Ms. Flores wanted me to stay in one of the cabins like normal, but some parents complained."

I'd bet my life that it was Michelle and her probably-just-as-evil parents. That bitch. I narrow my eyes, searching for her in the cluster of campers in the mess hall. I don't see her, and it's a good thing too because I'm feeling pretty stabby. No wonder Cabin 11 is missing a person; I bet that was Caroline's spot. "We had trouble with bigots too, but the trash took herself out. You can come stay at my cabin!"

But Caroline shakes her head. "Ms. Flores was really

nice about it and gave me my own private cabin. It has air-conditioning, and I don't have to share my bathroom, so I'm never leaving."

I laugh and Cam grins, but the mood is still a little sour. It just fucking sucks that we can't exist without people like Michelle getting in the way. I'm happy Caroline has a nice cabin all to herself, but she shouldn't have had to move. I wish Ms. Flores could have won that argument, but we are in hellish Alabama, so I don't know. I want to love my state, but more often than not, it doesn't love me back.

Teddy eventually starts talking about Finance, and he and Cam get into a heated debate over the best way to balance a budget. I glance at my phone, anxiety welling in my gut. It's 8:20, but Julia's still not here. I join in the discussion, adding that I think we should leave room for emergency-fund savings, but my heart's not in the debate. I keep glancing at the door, waiting for Julia's familiar scowl to stroll in. But she never comes.

At eight thirty, I get up from the table. Caroline and Cam start in surprise.

"You okay?" Cam asks.

"I'm fine! I just—I gotta go do something. I'll see you in SAT prep!"

I hurry away before I can talk myself out of my dangerous mission. I make a beeline to my cabin, and sure enough, despite it being 8:34, Julia is fast asleep in the bottom bunk.

I shouldn't wake her. Cam's warning about helping opponents hangs heavy in my head. If I was truly cutthroat, I would let her sleep, because Julia getting a bad score in SAT prep means I'm one step closer to my medal. But the mere thought of being cruel makes my stomach hurt. Even if Chelsea, the incredible and foul-happy point guard from our rival basketball team, tripped and fell right in front of me, I'd help her up. And I like Julia way more. In a potential-friend way, of course. I can't leave her to drown when I have a life ring right here, risking valuable points or not.

"Julia?" I call. My voice is nervous to my own ears. The morals of helping my opp aside, she might not want me to wake her up. She might yell at me, and then I think I'd die.

Julia continues to snooze. I clear my throat and try again.

"Julia? It's me, Hallie."

Nothing. She's a hard sleeper. I could shake her shoulder, but I might scare her. I look at the rickety bunk bed and get a better idea. I tap the side with my foot, and it wobbles. I rear back and give it a good kick. The bed screeches in protest and shudders like a tree in a storm.

Julia shoots upright like a bear is attacking her. She looks at me, eyes wide with blank shock.

"Hi," I say, suddenly awkward. "It's eight thirty."

Julia just blinks at me. "What?" Her voice is muffled with confusion and sleep, and I inwardly squeal a little. She's so cute!

"It's eight thirty," I try again. "SAT prep is at nine."

The sharpness leaps into Julia's eyes like lightning. She's wide awake now. Her shoulders tense up, and she watches me warily, like she isn't sure what to say. "Okay."

A better response than I was expecting! I hate that she seems so wary of me, but I'll take it. "Do you want me to wait for you . . . ?"

"No." Julia swings her legs out of bed. I see her pajamas for the first time—a plain black tank top and surprisingly festive white-and-red shorts with tiny Christmas trees on them. She ignores my staring and waves her hand at me. "Go on."

"Okay," I say. "See you soon!" I leave the cabin, thinking about off-season pajamas all the way to SAT prep.

I sit next to Caroline in the back row (she is also in Tall Jail), and she chatters to me about how difficult the math section is, but I'm not paying attention. I watch the door, counting seven students; Mr. Lin; Ms. Flores, who's come to observe . . . and Julia, dead last, at 8:55.

I smile and open my notebook as she sits near the front. All the anxiety and nerves melt away, and I can finally focus on SAT prep.

CHAPTER 8

I'm in a groove.

Coach Underwood used to say that about when we're shooting, and every ball goes in the basket. That's how I feel now. Things are finally working out.

Every morning, I run on the track from five thirty to six thirty a.m. Walter runs with me as well, trying his best to bully me into going home. At six thirty, I head back to my cabin, and he sighs heavily like he's saying *finally*. Then, I take a shower, eat breakfast with the queer cabin (still a party of four, alas), kick Julia's bunk bed so she wakes up, and we're both on time to SAT prep. I go to the two courses per day, and in my free time, I study for hours. I feel good! Smart, even! Some maniac thought it would be a good idea to start a leaderboard written in chalk on the side of the main building, so I can see my ranking. The good news is that I'm above Michelle.

The bad news is that I'm not even in the top twenty.

When I think about it, I want to scream. It's music. It's the damn music class. I'm so lost that I'm in tears after I get done. I don't know what an eighth note is or why the little beans are all in a line sometimes and other times not. I don't know how to name notes on the piano. Julia raised her hand and said the piano was out of tune. I didn't even know pianos could do that!

I'm so fucked. I'm cursing my parents for saying that I could skip all art and music electives in favor of sports. Is anyone giving me points for running stress miles every morning with a security dog nipping at my heels? I think not.

I'm getting negative again. I take a deep breath to calm myself. I'm in the cabin, trying to make sense of the sight-reading book I borrowed from the tiny library in the music room. But it's currently sitting open and neglected on my pillow as I pout. I can't focus because of the heat and also because I can see Julia's notes as well. She's watching a video on how to make an apple pie. She's also chewing her thumbnail to bits. Julia is ranked twenty-two and I'm at twenty-three, so we're the same. One class is sinking each member of Cabin 11, and we do not have a life boat.

A polite knock shocks me out of my pity party. I sit up, but Julia just shoots an annoyed glare at the screen door. I climb down and open it, and I'm shocked again.

Ms. Flores stands on our porch, smiling. "Hello! Can I come in?"

"Oh, uh, sure." I step back to let her in, then tap Julia's shoulder. She turns her annoyed beam at me but stiffens when she sees Ms. Flores. She doesn't get up, but she does pause her video and takes her headphones off.

Ms. Flores seems deeply interested in our cabin. Her gaze roves gleefully over my emotional-support suitcase and Julia's messy spilled duffel bag on the hot side of the room. She points at our bunk. "On the same side? I thought you'd spread out!"

"Fan's broken on that side," Julia grunts.

Ms. Flores seems dismayed. "I'm so sorry! I should have gotten that fixed before you got here."

"It's okay. There's only two of us anyway!" My voice is terribly high-pitched. I'm a nervous ball of energy. Why is Ms. Flores here? Are we in trouble? Did I do something wrong? Am I getting kicked out for being so bad at music?

Ms. Flores smiles. "Glad to hear it. And you can relax, girls, this is a social call." Ms. Flores lifts up a sparkly gift bag, one I'm just noticing. "My daughter and her girlfriend insisted I bring this to you, Hallie. I told them you'd get it in the mail, but they wanted you to have it ASAP."

Oh. A gift for me? From Nav and Gia? I take a hesitant step forward, but when Ms. Flores nods, I close the distance and take the bag. I open it and gasp—

"A Snuggable?!" And it's the seahorse! The orange, limited edition, so-ugly-it's-cute stuffed animal that Ms. Flores's company makes. And there's a card. I pick it up, and inside, Nav's messy handwriting says, *Since everyone at that stupid camp is a dickhead, here's a study buddy for you!*

My eyes get misty. I pick up the stuffed animal and hug it. It smells like honeysuckle and lavender. I'll never get a better gift.

"Thank you so much, Ms. Flores."

"Thank your friends. I had to have it overnighted, so I took it out of Gia's allowance."

"Oh, uh . . ." Yikes. How much did this cost? Do I have to pay her back?

Ms. Flores smiles. "Just kidding! She doesn't get an allowance."

I don't know what to say to that, so Ms. Flores keeps talking.

"Putting my camp-sponsor cap on now—how are you both doing? Anything you need? I'm so sorry about the cabin arrangements, I'm making some steps to prevent this from happening in the future. Are you enjoying yourselves?"

Goodness, she talks so fast. I hug my seahorse for strength. "Umm, we're good! Feeling adequately challenged from our classes."

Ms. Flores laughs. "You have a future in politics, Hallie. Tell me how you really feel."

Honestly, like shit, but I can't tell her that. She's done her best! And it's cool that we get to come here for free. I would be a brat if I complained about the food, or that it's not fair that no tutors are available because I *want* to learn, but I'm lost. . . .

I clear my throat. "I'm having a great time, really. I wish the cabins had air conditioners, but the fans work fine."

Ms. Flores shakes her head but accepts my answer. "Fair enough. Julia? What about you?"

Julia seems surprised that Ms. Flores called her name. But it quickly melts back into her usual disinterested look. "I think there should be more opportunities for us to earn more points."

Ms. Flores raises her eyebrows. "Elaborate."

"We're working hard in our courses, but some aren't compatible with us. We should have opportunities outside the courses, such as volunteer work, to make up the deficit." Julia speaks with conviction and without fear. And she's still sitting at her desk! I expect to feel the ugly twinge of jealousy at her composure, but I'm just in awe of her courage.

Also she said *we*. Is she including me?

"Hmm." Ms. Flores nods slowly. "Fair assessment. I'll think on it."

Ms. Flores breezes to the door. "See you later, have to go! Enjoy your Snuggable, Hallie! And let me know if you want one as well, Julia, as a thank-you for answering my questions. Okay, bye!"

And then she's gone, our screen door slamming behind her. Like a gift-giving tornado.

I glance at Julia, and she meets my eyes. But only for a second—she turns back to her phone and restarts the video of the apple pie.

The seahorse's soothing scent fills my nose as I hug it again. I'm trying to sort out what just happened. Julia being hella cool is one thing, but she said *we* and *us*. Does that mean she thinks I'm trying hard too? I shake my head to dispel the bubblegum thoughts that brings. More important, by her own admission, Julia recognizes Life Skills isn't going well for her. And it's not just cooking; she was nearly in tears when she had to learn how to fix a leaky sink. But Julia is a musical prodigy. She even has that instrument case, though I haven't seen her touch it since camp started. And music is horrible for me, but I'm good at the rest of Life Skills. Whatever my parents didn't teach me, I learned from experience. I'll never forget having to learn how to change Gabriel's tire when he was freaked out and I had 2 percent battery on my phone.

We can help each other.

I put the seahorse on my bunk. Julia is giving off major *Don't bother me* vibes, but I have to be brave. Volunteer work is a fantastic idea, but Ms. Flores just said she would consider it. There's no guarantee it'll help us now. Emphasis on *us*.

"Julia?"

Julia pauses her video. She looks at me like she wants to claw my eyes out. My lizard brain is crying, begging me to leave the scary girl alone, but I forge ahead.

"I have an idea."

Julia doesn't say anything, but she doesn't restart the video either. I take the opportunity to speak.

"I know you've seen that I'm pretty bad in music class."

"Yes," Julia agrees immediately.

Which is like, wow, okay. She could have hedged her words a little. . . .

"And I know Life Skills isn't your favorite class either."

Julia doesn't agree this time, but her expression is immediately stormy and closed off. Bingo.

"What if we helped each other?"

Julia eyes me warily. "What do you mean?"

"Like I'll tutor you in Life Skills, and you tutor me in music."

"I'll get better at Life Skills." Julia doesn't sound nearly as certain as when she was talking with Ms. Flores. "And it won't be music forever. I'm sure we'll swap to art soon."

"I can't do that either!" I take a deep breath to stay calm. "We're in the middle of the leaderboard. If we don't do something, we're gonna stay there. One class is sinking us both."

Julia is quiet for so long that I think I've lost her. But finally, she says, "I would at least like to do better than Michelle."

"Yes! Fuck her!"

Julia breathes out, and it could be a laugh if I squint. "Okay. Let's do it. But," she adds before I can cheer, "let's lay some ground rules. We focus only on Fine Arts and Life Skills, nothing else. No socializing. We're not friends. You will not interrupt my focus. I'm winning that laptop if it kills me."

"Okay," I agree, ignoring the disappointment at the *We're not friends* statement, "but I'm winning first place to get the medal. Sorry."

Julia looks into my eyes, and she smiles. A real, natural smile, one that curves the right side of her face. One I've never seen. One just for me.

She stands up from the desk and puts her hand out. I shake it, trying not to focus on how soft her skin is, and I smile back. The Hallie-Julia alliance has begun, and I have a feeling it's only getting better from here.

CHAPTER 9

Julia points to her notebook. She's drawn some little black beans on the page.

"What note is this?"

I smile, hoping my winning personality convinces her to not kill me on the spot. "I have no idea."

Julia closes her eyes for several seconds, probably contemplating my continued existence. She's been trying to teach me music stuff for the past ten minutes, but I'm not getting it at all. I like K-pop! My ex was a drummer in a real band! I've never had to look at it on paper a day in my life!

Julia opens her eyes again. They're looking at me with pure exhaustion, which makes me feel bad. I'm trying, I promise. "Okay, let me ask you something. Have you ever taken a music class?"

"No."

"No band, no choir?"

"No."

"Do the words 'octave' and 'key change' mean anything to you?"

"No."

Julia pinches the bridge of her nose. It's really cute, but it's overshadowed by how tired she looks. I want to shrink down and disappear. Tutoring was my idea, but maybe it was a bad one.

"I'm sorry, I know it's frustrating. Maybe I can get it on my own."

"You most certainly cannot." Julia scribbles some notes in her notebook, sniffling occasionally. I pay attention to that; maybe she's late for SAT prep because she's not feeling well. Should I offer allergy meds? Mom packed them for me, but so far, I've been fine.

Julia finishes her notes and shoves the book into my hands. "Study that. And I'll quiz you tomorrow."

I take the notebook, dejected. "Okay. Sorry I'm so bad at this."

"Don't apologize." Julia says it with such authority, I have no choice but to listen. "I'm shocked, but you can learn. Just like I can learn how to cook."

I perk up at that. "Exactly! Should we practice that now?"

Julia seems uncertain. "Don't we have to go to the kitchen?"

"No, we can do theory in here." I sit up straighter, relieved the heat is finally off me and how musically stupid I am. And maybe Julia will give me more info about herself! "What's your relationship with cooking?"

Julia sits on the floor and draws her knees to her chest. She has a tiny scar on her right knee, shiny from age. This is the first time we've been so close, and my brain helpfully catalogs little details I missed before: a tiny flat mole under her left eye, narrow shoulders that slump inward like she's tired, irises such a dark brown that they're close to black.

"I don't have one."

It takes a second for me to stop staring and remember what we're talking about. "At all?"

Julia's shoulders hike up to her ears and her expression turns stormy. I'm reminded of a hissing cat.

"I said I had none. I don't cook."

"No big deal." I try to sound soothing. If she's feeling half as ashamed as I am about music, I get the defensive stance. "I don't know that much, but there was a summer my mom traveled for research, so my best friend and I teamed up so Dad wouldn't starve. That's the only reason I know anything."

Julia looks away, to the wooden floor. She's quiet for a few moments before she says, "I don't have a foundation. I've never even boiled water."

Okay, not a great situation, but not impossible. "I can send you some links to recipes I used when I was first starting." I pause, thinking that over. Julia's already in a bad mood, and I'm in a sad one, so we won't study well together right away. We have too much to build on. "Let's get the basics down and regroup tomorrow. Sound good?"

Julia sighs, but meets my eyes and nods. "Deal. Study that notebook like your life depends on it."

"Does it?" I'm making a joke, but I'm a little worried she might murder me if I keep dragging her down.

Julia gives me a small half smile. "You bet it does. Send me the baby recipes."

I pull out my phone, but . . . I don't have her number. I'm flooded with panic. Should I ask? This feels horribly like an excuse to get her number, like we're at a party or something. This is so embarrassing—

Julia puts her palm out and raises one eyebrow. I give my

phone sheepishly to her, who types her number in without a word. When she gives it back, she's saved herself as simply "Julia."

"Text me yours." Julia gets up and heads to the door.

"Where are you going?"

Julia doesn't turn around. "Out. You better study, I mean it. I'll have a stroke if you don't know what an eighth note is when I get back."

And with that, she's gone.

I hug my own knees, recovering from the interaction. That was the first time Julia's spoken to me for so long! And she wasn't mean; just tired, maybe. That reminds me of her stuffy nose, and I pull the allergy meds from my bag. I cart them to her desk, but pause when I see the surface.

Julia's notes are wide open, familiar ones from Finance today. But one notebook is unopened, and the front is covered in doodles. They're mostly squiggles and intricate lines (I know about as much about art as I do music), but they're obviously hand drawn. She's good at music *and* art? I love this.

I try to ignore my increasing interest in Julia. If I was just starting out in a new crush—which I am *not*—this would be the final blow. I always seem to be attracted to artists and musicians, and Julia is both. I shake that cursed thought out of my head as I observe the rest of Julia's study materials.

Mechanical pencils are haphazardly strewn across the desk, and her (empty) blue-and-white pencil case reads "Novia Eagles." I know where that is! We played Novia in a tournament last year. It's about two and a half hours from Mapleton, but can't be more than twenty minutes away from here. I wonder how she feels about being so close to home. My brain also wonders about long-distance relationships and if I'd be open to trying one out.

Stop. Stop! I place the allergy meds on Julia's desk before my daydreaming gets out of control and write a quick note. Then I pick up her notebook to learn what the heck an eighth note is.

* * *

I'm doomed. I'm so freaking doomed.

I'm just getting back from Finance, which is going well, but music is not. I think I know the basics now, after Julia's extensive notes and links to beginner websites, but I'm still not entirely sure what a time signature is. And why are the speed-up/slow-down words in Italian? I don't get it.

I turn to my seahorse, dejected. "Help me. What am I going to do?"

The seahorse, who I've named Reginald, has no answers for me. No one else does either, because Julia left Finance and walked off somewhere else. I'm sad. I'm lonely. I'm deeply pathetic. I hug my gift, feeling Sad Girl Hours coming on way sooner than they should.

I take an emergency study break and call Nav. I wait, and wait, and wait . . . but she doesn't pick up. I check the time—four o'clock. She should be out of work by now. But maybe she changed her hours as a new manager.

Or maybe she's busy hanging out with Gia.

I'm wallowing in a well of jealousy when Nav sends me a text.

71

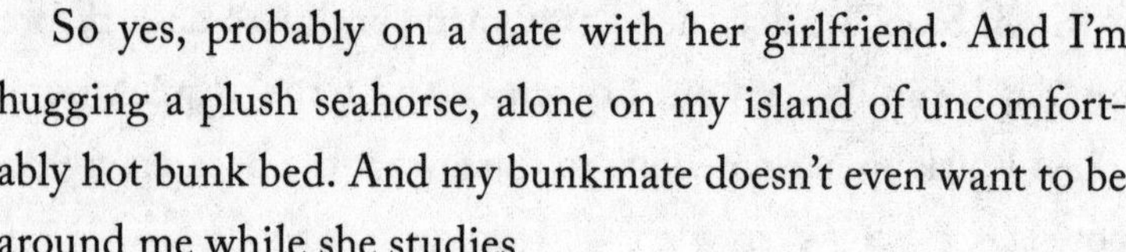

So yes, probably on a date with her girlfriend. And I'm hugging a plush seahorse, alone on my island of uncomfortably hot bunk bed. And my bunkmate doesn't even want to be around me while she studies.

I scroll through Instagram to blunt my sorrows. Chris is having fun on his trip to Cancún. I heart his post of clear water and a seagull grabbing his food. I heart everyone's photos on autopilot, but pause when Nav's picture pops up. She's taken a selfie with an embarrassed-but-also-pleased Gia at the local aquarium. The caption says: *third time we've been in two weeks!! never gets old* ♥

The picture was posted just a few minutes ago, so suspicions confirmed. I can't believe Gia convinced Nav to do something educational not once but *three* times. And look how she's smiling! She's so happy!

I heart the picture through gritted teeth.

A text alert saves me from drowning in the jealousy swamp. Sarah Knight, point guard on the team, texts me a picture. I touch it, and the entire team smiles back at me.

I stare at the picture, Sad Girl Hours practically strangling me. A horrible part of me wishes I hadn't skipped basketball camp for this one. I wish I was at home.

I frown at my phone. I didn't know anyone else from Mapleton was here.

I sit straight up in bed, shocked. No fucking way! Julia picks that time to come back, and I can't help myself.

"Julia! You didn't tell me you were Sarah's cousin!"

Julia freezes halfway to her bunk. She looks up at me like I've shot her. "How do you know that?"

"Sarah's on the basketball team with me! Well, she was, long story—anyway, I had no idea! Did you go to her birthday party this year? I must have missed you!"

Julia doesn't seem to know what to do with this information. She drops her bag by the desk (which is clear of allergy meds). "I was there. Mostly cleaning up after drunks who puked on the pool table."

I wince. That had to suck. "Yeah, it was a wild one. I've had vodka before, but I swear she picked the strongest one possible. I don't think the Sprite helped at all."

Julia's once again looking up at me like I'm an alien. Did I say something wrong?

Julia finally shakes her head and sits at the desk. "Enough. Have you been studying?"

"Yes," I say, but it's more of a whine.

Julia shoots me an annoyed glare. "Quit yapping to me and start reading."

Well, conversation over. I retreat to the safety of my phone, where another message from Sarah waits.

She can be kind of standoffish? But she's a great person once you get to know her!

I peek down at Julia from my lofted bed. She's already hard at work, headphones covering her ears. But I can see what she's working on: music notes for me. I smile to myself and type out a reply to Sarah.

I think you're right:)

CHAPTER 10

I'm packing my things at the end of SAT prep when Mr. Lin clears his throat.

"Hold on, everyone. Ms. Flores says normal classes are canceled for today."

Murmurs of surprise instantly start up around me. I glance at Caroline in disbelief, and then my eyes find Julia. I jump a little when she glances at me too, but she quickly looks to Mr. Lin again.

"Instead, we're all to report to the main hall." Mr. Lin seems a little bemused, but his body language doesn't say we're in trouble or anything. He walks out first, and after a few seconds of stunned silence, campers start to file after him.

"Wonder what this is about," Caroline says as we shuffle out of the room. We're last because we're in the back, and I can already see some of the front row-ers enter the main hall from the window.

"I don't know. Maybe we're having a drill or something?"

"I came here to get away from that," Cam groans as they join us from the middle row.

Yeah . . . I don't like the idea of an active-shooter drill even here. "Don't worry, Walter and Maxine will protect us."

"Who?" Cam asks.

I start to explain, but trail off just before Walter's appearance as we get closer to the main building. Outside the main hall, on a big banner, someone's written *Pop-Up #1* in bright green letters.

"Uh." I blink at the banner. I don't know what to think. I look at Caroline and Cam, but they seem as lost as I am. All right . . . guess I'll go see what surprise this camp has in store.

Amira (wearing a pastel pink jumper today! Love!) herds everyone through the lobby, smiling warmly. "Everyone, please stand with your cabins once you get inside. And we fixed the AC, so no fans required!"

Thank goodness for that. We shuffle inside, and I'm stunned again. The main hall is full of card tables . . . and games? Board games, hopscotch, cornhole near the stage. It looks like the cheap carnivals we used to have in elementary school. What on earth?

Near the door, someone has sectioned off twelve squares with a number in them. Our cabins, I'm assuming. Lots of kids are already in place. I start to say goodbye to Cam and Caroline, but they're gone before I can say anything. I sigh and look for Cabin 11. It's in the back corner, where Julia already waits.

Julia doesn't say anything as I stand beside her, but she doesn't seem annoyed I'm so close. In fact, she seems intrigued as she observes everyone get into their groups. Some of her perpetual tiredness is gone.

Ms. Flores takes the stage, and we all immediately shut up. She's wearing a fantastic blue-and-white gingham dress and beautiful white heels. And her earrings are little white cats! I love Ms. Flores. She leans close to the mic, grinning like the felines dangling from her ears.

"Welcome, campers! I hope you're all settling in. And having fun!"

I clap, but then I stop because hardly anyone claps with me. My ears burn in embarrassment, but Ms. Flores grins right at me before continuing.

"I've heard your pleas and lamentations. Some of you say, 'Hey, I'm not good at finance!' Or maybe some struggle with communicating with friends, or making a meal, or with finding the key a song is in. I hear you. But"—Ms. Flores pauses for what I assume to be dramatic effect—"is that so bad? Is it the end of the world to not be good at something?"

"It is if you want to win twenty thousand dollars," Julia mutters to my right.

Sorry, Ms. Flores, I agree. Failure isn't an option here.

Ms. Flores shakes her head good-naturedly at our thick silence. "I would love for you kids to sit with this feeling, why you feel like you have to be perfect, but I'll give it time. You'll see." Ms. Flores spreads her arms wide. "So! I've come up with a way for those of you who feel slighted by my class choices to get some bonus points."

Oh! She listened to Julia's suggestion! I look at Julia, and she meets my eyes, hers round with shock.

The rest of the room is surprised too. They murmur to each other and eye the card tables. One of the boys in Cabin 1 steps close to a table full of checkers. Ms. Flores wags her finger at him.

"Not yet! Let me explain the rules. These special events are called pop-ups, and they're random. Think of them as pop quizzes. They won't focus on any skills that could be assessed in your normal courses. These are to judge you on less easily quantifiable abilities, like your ability to adapt or think fast and critically. In this round, as you can see, we'll evaluate that by playing games.

"Also important to note: pop-ups are optional. If you don't feel like playing games, you don't have to. If you feel secure in your points, no problem! You can take this afternoon off and relax. Oh, that reminds me . . ." Ms. Flores gestures to somewhere offstage. "It seems I've made you all work a bit *too* hard, so I've set up some activities for you to do outside of class hours to help you relax. There will be hiking and bird-watching in the afternoons, swimming in the mornings, and s'mores every night."

Oh hell yeah, I love s'mores! It'll actually feel like camp for once, and that could be nice. I've never been to a sleepaway camp before this one, so it's cool that it's not entirely math and essays and realizing how stupid I am about music. I glance around the room, but no one seems nearly as excited as I am. They're all staring down the games or whispering in their groups. Even Julia is laser focused on the table in front of us.

"Okay, that's all! Talk among yourselves and figure out who's staying and who's going. When you're ready, pick a table and have fun!"

I look at Julia. "Do you want to . . ."

"You don't even have to ask." A ghost of a smile plays on Julia's lips. "We're winning this whole thing."

I nod, determined. No one is leaving, despite Ms. Flores waiting patiently. Cam's competitiveness comes to mind. I don't think anyone is thinking of this first pop-up as simple fun. But now that I'm in it . . . am I even going to be good at this? I haven't played a board game in years. Only child problems strike again.

"Are you good at any of these?" Julia asks, like she can read my mind.

I cringe, but I have to be honest. "I don't think so . . . maybe cornhole?" I was on the basketball team, so surely that counts for something.

Julia nods. "Jenga first, then cornhole. We'll go from there."

Okay . . . ! I was panicking, but Julia's quiet confidence gives me a boost. I follow her to the table with several wooden blocks on it, stacked in a tower. No one challenges us, but a lot of cabins still haven't chosen their game. Cam looks like they're arguing with their cabinmates, and Caroline is chatting with another cabin that seems to be down a member. I search for Teddy and find him at the checkers table with his cabin. I try to pick out which one is Harvard-bound, but they're all blond white boys in board shorts, so who knows.

"I can't believe she took your suggestion," I say to Julia as a few more cabins choose their tables.

"Me neither." Julia watches Ms. Flores warily, like a cat sizing up an opponent. "I feel like she's up to something. She's like a prettier Ego from Blue Lock."

I've heard those names before . . . . I cycle through my memories until I get to Natalie, my ex who adored all things Japanese. "The soccer anime?"

Julia physically jumps. "How do you know that?"

I smile. "My ex was super into anime. She showed me that one because she knew I liked sports. I like it! I was so sad about how the leader guy made everyone so weird and paranoid, though. Ms. Flores isn't like that."

Julia is staring at me with blank disbelief. What? Is it so weird that I've seen anime? It's not my thing, but for Natalie I was willing to try. It was a lot better than Peter's bonsai stuff, I'll tell you that much.

Julia opens her mouth to speak, but a group of girls approaches us. I'm momentarily anxious it'll be Michelle, but it's the quiet group from Cabin 10. One even smiles at us. The other three seem deadly serious though.

"We'd like to challenge Cabin Eleven," the lead girl says. Her name tag reads "Samantha." "Umm, if that's cool?"

"Fine with us," Julia answers.

I nod, though I'm internally panicking. How do you play this one again? And how is this going to assess critical thinking or whatever? Ms. Flores is such a mystery.

Mr. Lin approaches our table, smiling. "If we're all ready, I'll be the judge. Everyone know the rules?"

We all nod, but Julia leans in to whisper in my ear. "I got this one." Louder, she says, "I'll be representing Cabin Eleven alone."

Samantha blinks, and the other girls exchange uneasy looks. "Can she do that?" she asks Mr. Lin.

Mr. Lin shrugs. "Sure, why not? Do you want to choose a representative? I'm not sure how the points will shake out, though."

I see Julia's strategy immediately. Cabin 10 is agitated, arguing with each other about who will get the points if they win. Julia seems calm and confident, so she must be good at this one. She'll probably get all the points if she wins, which isn't fair, but . . . Julia catches my eye and glances at the cornhole station, where Cam's cabin is cleaning up. I understand; I'll be the one to carry us to victory there and thus get the maximum amount of points. If we take turns here and I lose it for us, we go home with nothing. Risky, but based on how Cabin 10 is acting, I think it'll work. I take it back—this is clever critical thinking indeed.

I step back and watch it unfold. Samantha's group can't agree, so all four end up playing against Julia. But Julia is somehow a Jenga master. Her hands are still and steady as she pokes each wooden block from its station. She whittles away at the tower as Cabin 10 clumsily lasts a few rounds, but one of the girls' shaky hands topples the tower.

Mr. Lin taps the table as Cabin 10 groans. "Sorry, Cabin Ten, you're out. Five points to Julia of Cabin Eleven."

"YES!" I run to Julia's side. I almost give her a hug but then remember she would probably kill me. She gives me a half smile instead, and I'm warm all over. Julia trots away from the card table without another word, but I stop to chat with Samantha. She's clearly bummed but nice enough.

"Good luck with the rest of the games," she says. "You beat us, so you better win the whole thing."

With Julia's strategy, we just might. I wave at Cabin 10 and join Julia at the cornhole station. She has her hands in her pockets, carefully observing the cabins ahead of us. "Are you sure you can do this?"

"Yeah, it's pretty simple! I'm on the basketball team, err, was, so I think I can do this. It's just a smaller hoop, right?"

Julia raises her eyebrows, but doesn't say anything else. We wait in silence for a few minutes until I can't keep my curiosity at bay.

"How are you so good at Jenga? You didn't make a single mistake."

"I have a brother" is all Julia says, and then she's quiet as we wait.

Huh. Is that . . . the first non-camp-related thing she's ever told me about herself? I'm grinning as it's my turn to win it for Cabin 11.

We're challenged by Teddy's cabin, and they're super arrogant when they see it's just me and Julia. But Julia's strategy works again; I claim to be the representative, and it throws the boys off. It only takes me three perfect rounds before one of the blond boys sends his bean bag sailing high over the wooden board and nowhere near the goal. Teddy's cabin groans, and Amira congratulates Cabin 11 again.

And that's how it goes all day. Julia picks games that require concentration and focus, and I pick anything athletic. Soon, we've racked up twenty-five points each, and we're one of the last two teams left.

Unfortunately, Cabin 8, Cam's cabin, is our opponent.

Also unfortunately, the last game is Monopoly.

"I'm, like, really bad at this one," I whisper to Julia before we face Cam. I have played this, and it ended in many tantrums and board flipping while Mom cackled with her pile of fake money.

"Me too," Julia says, and my stomach drops. She's frowning fiercely at the old bald man in the middle of the board. "I've never won once."

"Also I don't want to alarm you, but Cam's dad is an invest-ment banker."

"Well, fuck." Julia shakes her head, and for some reason she smiles. She looks at me, and her brown eyes are alight with a fire I haven't seen before. "Everyone likes an underdog story, right?"

Unfortunately for us, we're not in a kid's baseball movie. Cam's cabin completely demolishes us in late-stage capitalism. My shoulder slump as Sharon calls the game when I'm penniless and Julia's stuck in jail. Cam cheers, and their cabin hugs each other.

"Sorry," I say to Julia. I thought maybe if we came back and won it all . . . if we could sweep the entire day . . .

Julia puts a hand on my arm, and the sheer contact short circuits my brain. She gives me a half smile again. "Can't win 'em all. Twenty-five points isn't bad."

I want to say so much. *Thanks for being so cool, that strategy was amazing, how are you so good with your hands?* (Maybe the art has something to do with it?) *Can we be better friends now?* Because surely this has bonded us and we're on the right track to rising in the ranks. . . .

But "yeah" is all I'm intelligent enough to say. Julia nods and takes her hand off my arm. She's in business mode again, arms folded over her chest as Ms. Flores crowns Cam's cabin as the winners. She narrows her eyes as Ms. Flores gives boxes of candy to the delighted campers.

"If pop-ups are gonna be a regular thing, we might not need to help each other study."

Panic lances through my heart. We can't quit now! I was just getting the hang of music. Sort of. I know Julia doesn't want to be friends, and I know it's pathetic, but I don't want to lose study time together. "We don't know if it'll be regular enough. Or if we'll win enough to make up for it."

My heart dances with hope as Julia considers my words. She starts to speak, but Cam bounds to my side, grinning. They're wearing a cute paper crown, like the ones you get at Burger King.

"That was awesome! I love pop-ups!"

I smile back. I'm jealous, but just a little. I'm a lot more worried about what Julia has to say about studying together. "Good job, Cam. You crushed it!"

A red blush crosses Cam's face, right over their nose. They look more pleased than I've ever seen them. "That felt so good. But Brittany almost folded at Jenga. I about lost my mind."

"Julia was great at that one," I say, but Cam's not listening. They're shooting their cabin a sour look over their shoulder.

"I'm glad we won today, but it was too close. I hope the next pop-up is for singles. Group work sucks."

Well . . . it can, if not everyone's heart is in it. But Cam's cabin seemed to be doing their best. "We can't be good at everything! Next time—"

"There won't be a next time," Cam snorts. "That's why I told you not to study with anyone else. They'll just bring you down."

I flinch before I can help it. I know Cam doesn't mean it, but they've pressed on a sore spot. I don't want to bring Julia down. Maybe she would be better off without my tutoring help.

Julia, who hasn't said a word yet, gives Cam an odd look. It's almost a glare. She turns her glare to me, and I'm terrified for a second.

"You know what, Hallie?" Julia says. "I changed my mind. Keep studying music. I'll see you back at the cabin."

I'm too stunned to answer as Julia stalks away from us and out the door. Cam blinks in bewilderment.

"Your roommate is kinda intense," they say.

I blink at the space where Julia disappeared. But the shock has worn off, and now all I'm feeling is gratitude. I smile at Cam. "Yeah, she is."

CHAPTER 11

As soon as I get back to the cabin (Julia mysteriously absent), I FaceTime Mom. She answers after three rings, her face too close to the camera.

"Hallie? Are you all right?"

"I'm okay," I reassure her.

We're not a sentimental family, so I've been texting her and Dad minor updates about camp. But after today's point win but emotional confusion, I don't know. I wanted to see her.

"Where's Dad?"

"He went to pick up food." Mom smiles into the camera. "We miss your cooking!"

"Me too." I sigh and explain the terrible food situation.

Mom snorts when I'm finished. "I can't believe they're feeding you slop. I should complain."

"You really shouldn't." I smile at my phone, already feeling a bit better. At least this is familiar. "But anyway, food aside, I did well in a tournament today!"

"Oh? Math, science?"

"No, we uh . . ." I'm just now realizing Ms. Flores's wild challenges are going to sound nuts to my mother. I scramble for a way to doctor up that I dominated in competitive cornhole. "We played games that assessed our critical thinking and reaction time."

Mom seems impressed. "Did you win?"

"No, but we got second place. My cabin, I mean."

Mom frowns. "You have to try harder, Hallie. You're not slacking, are you?"

Oh no. My former happiness evaporates in an instant. Second place is pretty good, but Mom is always like this; if I get an A, why isn't it an A+?

"No, I just—"

"You're not dating someone, are you?"

I sink lower into my bunk. Mom was furious when we got my SAT score back and it wasn't a 1500+ like she expected. I tried to explain that the fight with Peter really threw me off, and honestly it was hard to see the questions through my puffy eyes, but she wouldn't hear of it. Since then, she's been breathing down my neck about prioritizing school and not letting my relationships get in the way. But she's never satisfied! I got all A's in my regular classes and all 5's on my AP exams, and she didn't even celebrate with me. She said, "That's what you're supposed to do."

"No. I'm not dating anyone. And I'm doing okay, but—"

"Okay isn't good enough for med school," Mom says, and I know I've lost. When Mom gets started on me being the first Black doctor in the family, there's no stopping her. Never mind that I don't think I want to be a doctor. It feels like a lot of pressure! I don't want to be in charge of people living or dying. I can't even get my own life together, much less handle someone else's.

I listen to the rant I've heard a million times before, my mood sinking lower and lower the more she speaks. When she's done, she finally takes a deep breath.

"I just want you to do your best."

"Yeah."

"And I know you will, but you have to stay focused. Okay?"

I swallow hard against the burn in my throat. I'm about to cry if we don't end this conversation right now. "Okay. I have to go."

Concern flashes across Mom's face, but it's gone so quick I might have imagined it. "All right. Study hard! We'll talk later."

Mom mercifully ends the call. I lie face down on my bunk, more depressed than I've been in days. I wanted familiarity, but boy did I pay for that.

I listen to the rhythmic squeak of the fan above my head and hug Reginald. Mom just told me to study hard, but I'm so down I don't feel like doing anything except wallowing in despair. I hug the seahorse tighter, and the soothing lavender reminds me of Ms. Flores . . . and her s'mores. I sit up, a sudden burst of energy flooding my system. I need away from this cursed cabin and my mother's haunting words. Some roasted marshmallows sound like the perfect distraction. Oh, and maybe the queer cabin will be there! Or Julia! I should be looking up music notes, but I feel like I need this. I hurry from my bunk before I can change my mind, slip on my tennis shoes, and head outside to hopefully drown my sorrows in free sweets.

But when I show up to the s'mores station, no one is here.

I stand around the hot fire, a little shocked. There are plenty of marshmallows and chocolate and the good graham crackers on a table, complete with long metal pokers for roasting. And *no one* came? Not a single camper? It's not late, and other campers are studying on their cabin porches or at gazebos, but they're all pointedly ignoring the s'mores. Maybe I'm the only one who is stupid enough to want a break. Maybe Mom's right and I do need to focus. I turn around to sulk back to my cabin, disheartened, and almost run smack into Ms. Flores.

"Oh—sorry!"

"No worries," Ms. Flores says. She's changed out of her pretty dress and is in more casual light sweatpants. They have a dalmatian on the cuffs—cute! She gestures to the table. "S'more?"

"Oh, uh . . ." I can practically hear Mom's voice warning me to stop slacking off. And if no one else is here, then I must be the one who's wrong. "I'm the only one, so—"

"Even better," Ms. Flores interrupts. "More for me and you!"

Ms. Flores sidesteps me and heads to the table, where she enthusiastically spears an unsuspecting marshmallow.

I hesitate. It would be rude of me to leave now . . . right? Mom wouldn't like it if I was rude to the leader of Carnegie Camp either. I can stay for like ten minutes, surely. Then I'll study. Before I can overthink it, I grab a metal stick and marshmallow and sit next to Ms. Flores on the log she provided for us.

We don't talk for a long time, but it's kind of nice. It's not so blisteringly hot now that the sun's gone down, and the fire makes soothing popping noises. I could live without the constant buzzing of flies and mosquitoes, though. I want to plunge the marshmallow into the fire, but I rotate it patiently above the flames. New Hallie is patient and cool-headed. She can wait for her sweet treat. Especially when she hasn't earned it and got second place in a tournament she should have won.

That brings out an audible sigh, and I'm embarrassed when Ms. Flores turns to me.

"That bad, huh?" Her eyes sparkle with what can only be mischief in the firelight. I remember Julia's comparison to the anime guy and smile.

"It's nothing. Not really."

Ms. Flores rotates her marshmallow. "If it was nothing, you wouldn't be worried about it."

I stare into the fire for a minute, blinking against the stinging smoke. She's right, of course. I don't want to whine to the sponsor of Carnegie Camp; it's already incredibly pathetic that I'm the only one who showed up to a kiddie activity. But then again, something tells me Ms. Flores wouldn't make me feel bad about getting second place. I bet she's not pressuring Gia into becoming a doctor.

"Do you ever feel like you've made so many mistakes that it's impossible to come back from them?"

Ms. Flores considers my question for a few seconds. I like that—she doesn't just blurt out the easiest platitude.

Finally, she says, "I've definitely felt the weight of mistakes. Marrying a douchebag is at the top of that list."

I don't know whether I'm more shocked that Ms. Flores said the word "douchebag" or that she was married before. I guess I assumed she was always this bad-ass millionaire entrepreneur?

Apparently not. Apparently, I'm not the only one who's not great at picking partners.

"But," Ms. Flores continues, "mistakes are part of being human. I didn't make the best choice then, but he gave me the light of my life. If I didn't choose him, I wouldn't have Gia." Ms. Flores smiles at me. "You have to take the good with the bad. That's life."

I sit with her words, turning them over carefully like they're a puzzle to be solved. I get where she's coming from: she married a loser, he sucked, but she got Gia out of it. I mean, I understand. It wasn't a net loss. But I feel like I haven't gotten anything out of my mistakes. I cried for literal weeks after my breakup with Diya when she said long distance wouldn't work. And it's not just my exes. Mom isn't satisfied with my work, even if I do my best. Nav is off having the time of her life with her girlfriend while I roast marshmallows with the first adult who's been kind to me in weeks. Time after time, I throw everything into my relationships, and I'm always burned. Even the non-romantic ones.

If I don't change, I'm going to be miserable for the rest of my life. And I don't think I can take it.

"Okay" is what I say to Ms. Flores. "I get it."

"You don't, but that's fine." Ms. Flores chuckles. "You will."

Now I'm a little annoyed. She acts like I'm missing something! I can't see any other way around it. "How do you know?"

"Because you're here. Even when everyone else is stuck, you're the first to kind of understand what I want you kids to get out of this camp. So I know you'll get it. You're already on the right track."

I pout into the fire. I don't feel like I'm on the right track. I feel like I'm lost in a sea of my emotions: fear, shame, determination tinged with guilt, jealousy. It's no wonder Julia doesn't want to be friends with me. I'm a certified mess.

Ms. Flores can apparently sense my broodiness because she smiles. "I'll give you something to think about. You have to look at the whole picture."

I frown at her. "What does that mean?"

"I can't tell you!" Ms. Flores looks absolutely gleeful, and her enthusiasm cheers me up a little. "I want you to think it over, and then— No!" Ms. Flores gasps when her marshmallow falls off her stick and into the fire.

I look over at mine, startled, and it tumbles to its fiery grave as well. We both groan, and then Ms. Flores laughs. She retrieves two marshmallows from the table and comes back. I take one and reload my stick. Round two, marshmallow. I can do this.

Ms. Flores stays standing. "Anyway, Hallie, you can talk to me anytime. Try to have some fun between all your studies, okay? Promise me."

"Okay," I say, because I'm supposed to. But I genuinely don't get what Ms. Flores is saying.

Ms. Flores grins and gives me the second marshmallow. I take it, and at my questioning look, she winks.

"I hate marshmallows. Enjoy mine for me!" And then she's gone, motoring off to save the world, one Snuggable at a time.

Or maybe she's headed home to spend time with Gia, who she clearly adores.

I add the second marshmallow to my stick, deep in thought. *See the whole picture.* What does that mean? I watch the marshmallow brown, but my mind is on a million little things at once—Julia's confusing response to our pop-up, Cam's competitiveness, Mom's harsh warnings. They're all jumbled in my mind, equally loud and fighting for my attention. It's hard to focus on which problem to tackle.

Wait a minute . . . Ms. Flores said I should look at the whole picture, but I'm looking at the pieces right now. The top marshmallow deepens from lightly toasted to a deep brown, but I jump up, excited. Maybe that's it! I need to look at the whole problem, not just the pieces. I need a unifying structure—not just fragments of who I want New Hallie to be. I need some defining rules.

The marshmallows, forgotten amid my brainstorming session, tumble into the fire, but that's fine. I carefully return the metal stick to the table (after wiping it off best I can with water and paper towels) and hurry back to Cabin 11. New Hallie, here we come.

I arrive at my cabin, hopeful to see Julia, but it's still empty. It's getting late, and the mosquitoes were murder by the fire . . . I hope she's okay. I shake my head. I need to focus. New Hallie first. I stare up at my messy bunk. I know what I need to do, but I need some clarity. The big picture of what's wrong with me and not a bunch of tiny things needling at me all the time. I just need a reminder . . . a visual one. That's it! A vision board!

I rummage in my bag for tape, scissors, pens, and a lot of notebook paper. And I get to work.

It takes me an hour, but soon I have a big sign in blocky letters:

HALLiE'S RULES FOR
REiNVENTiON AND REFiNEMENT

ABSOLuTELY <u>NO</u> <u>ROMANCE!</u>

GET A 1550+ ON THE SAT

LET Go OF OLD HALLiE

GET FIRST PLACE AT CARNEGiE
CAMP AND WiN THE MEDAL

I tape the rules on the wall above my bed, nodding to myself. There! They're more like goals, but it still counts. If I see the list every day, the whole picture and not the tiny details, I'll be forced to do better, right? But I probably need more reminders. I write the word "basketball" on a piece of paper, cut it out, and draw a red X over it. I do the same for "horror movies" and "Jung Kook" (RIP me). I'm in the middle of taping up "slacking off" when the screen creaks behind me. I glance over my shoulder, and Julia is staring up at my bunk.

"Hi," I say. I want to wave, but my hands are covered in tape.

Julia doesn't say anything. She looks at the desk and takes

a step toward it, but then looks back at my vision board. She takes another few steps, but then doubles back and stands directly under the bunks.

"All right," she says, folding her arms. "You got me. What the hell is this?"

"My vision board." I move out of the way so she can see it better.

Julia doesn't seem to understand. She just stares at me.

"So before I came here and we learned about the points thing, I kind of wanted to restart my life, you know? Like change some things up. But I haven't been doing a good job, so I thought I could post some rules where I could see them every morning."

Julia nods slowly, but her expression is still incredulous. "What does Jung Kook have to do with that?"

Oh no. Now I have to explain the whole thing! She's gonna think I'm nuts. I give her a highly edited version. "Okay, so I'm trying to reinvent myself this summer. No more screwing up the SAT or pop-ups or anything. I have to lock in."

"And that means no Jung Kook?"

I nod seriously. "No Jung Kook. He will only distract me."

"Hmm." Julia points upward. "What's the 'no romance' about?"

"I can't date anyone else until I figure out what the hell is going on."

Julia cracks a smile at that. I'm momentarily dazzled by how pretty she is when she's smiling, the rare tiny moments when she's happy and not laser focused on studying.

"Heard." Julia goes to the desk and sits down, already pulling out her study materials. "Figure out music first, though."

"Maybe we can study together?"

"No." Julia doesn't even look up from her notebook. "That's what you have the ugly seahorse for."

"Ugly?! Apologize to Reginald right now."

"You named it what?" Julia is smiling at her notes and shaking her head in disbelief. "Never mind. I'm studying. Don't bother me."

I quiet down, one arm around Reginald. I think that's the most Julia's ever spoken to me. And she's smiling. At what I said! I look up at my vision board, at all my goals and aspirations for this summer. My gaze lingers on *no romance*, but I force myself to look away. I don't *like* Julia. I'm just hoping we can be better friends, that's all. I'm glad she's smiling more. I'm extra glad it's because of me.

I pull out my music notes, and somehow, even though we're not talking and Julia's carefully transcribing my notes on how to reduce stress, I feel like I grasp the music concepts a little better.

CHAPTER 12

Julia looks over the worksheet she made me, eyebrows raised. "Okay, not bad."

I'm beaming. I studied all day and night, and I think I'm getting the hang of it now. I know the difference between a treble and bass clef, and I recognize all the beans as different notes and that they tell you what sound they make. I still don't really . . . get the sounds? Like I don't hear the difference, even when kind YouTubers meant to teach babies explain it, but I know enough to pass a written test. On the basics, at least, which we've already covered and so I'm still behind.

Ugh. Sad Girl Hours are creeping back.

But Julia's slight nod gives me strength. If she's impressed, then it's not hopeless.

"We can get into more complicated stuff later, but this is a good start. We should pick an instrument for you to play for practical practice, because I'm sure that's coming. Piano is the obvious choice, but . . ."

Julia trails off, staring out the window with glazed eyes. I patiently wait for her to finish her brain blast, but my eyes wander to her instrument case.

"I could play whichever one you do?"

Julia's attention snaps back to me. "Who says I play anything?"

"Umm . . ." I point to the case, where the neck is barely peeking from under her bed. "You have it right there? Must be a small guitar. Ukulele?"

Julia's expression turns to pure horror before she quickly regains composure. "I'm gonna pretend you never said that. Do I look like somebody who plays ukulele?"

I don't know how to answer that. "I mean, I don't know! I don't know you that well."

Julia seems taken aback for a second, but her expression quickly morphs back to neutral. "It's a violin."

Oh! That's so freaking cool! My brain immediately fills with fantasies of Julia playing in front of a packed auditorium, her eyes closed and chin resting on the smooth wooden instrument. "Can you play a song—"

"No." Julia cuts me off. She pushes the case further under the bed with her foot until it's out of sight. "I'll send you some links to more advanced music theory. And we'll try the piano tomorrow."

That doesn't sound fun, but fine. Julia is so interesting. She seems wrapped up in her own world a lot of the time, and she's so tight-lipped about herself. I guess I don't need to know anything about her for her to be a good tutor, but I'm a little sad. I know she said we weren't friends, but I was hoping that in time, we could be.

"Okay. My turn!" I get to my feet and shake off the tingly feeling in my legs, and also the disappointment. "How's cooking going?"

Julia shrugs. "Okay. I watched a lot of *Hell's Kitchen*."

I try to hold back my horror. Reality TV is the worst on a good day, and now she's getting advice from a screaming maniac? And even if he can cook, we're not trying to make beef Wellington! Julia set scrambled eggs on fire! "Please tell me you watched other things."

Julia looks away, toward the opposite bunk. "Sure. But I doubt we'll be on cooking much longer."

I want to freak out, but this is fine. I can make some beginner worksheets for her, like she did for me. And she's right; we've been cooking less and less lately. Unlike music, Life Skills changes almost every day. We started with making basic meals, but we've bounced between changing tires to water safety. I thought Julia would be okay with some other things, but she seems uncomfortable with all three.

"How about car stuff?"

And she's uncomfortable now. She fidgets, looking out the window again. "Fine. In theory?"

Hmm. I don't like that answer. "Do you know how to drive?"

Julia's silence is deafening. But that's fine; I was scared at first, and lots of people on the team don't drive because it stresses them out.

I cross the room and slide into the bottom bunk of the bed we don't use. I smile and pat the space beside me.

"Let's learn how to drive."

Julia looks like I asked her to crawl into a vat of radioactive snakes. "I don't need to know how."

"You don't if you live in New York or Seattle. But you do if you want to get points in Life Skills. Sorry."

Julia heaves a sigh but eventually trots over. She sits beside me, her movements tentative and unsure. And her muscles are tensed like a rabbit ready to bolt.

"We'll just practice for now," I say, trying to be encouraging. "First, do you have driving anxiety?"

Julia's shoulders are up to her ears again. She won't look at me. "I don't know. I've never done it before."

Oh, makes sense. She's never been behind the wheel, and she's clearly embarrassed about it. Why didn't her parents teach her? I scold myself for that thought as soon as it appears. Not everyone's parents are around, or up to it. My mom taught Nav and me at the same time, after all. But I'd be lying if I said I wasn't curious.

I mentally rewrite what lessons I was going to do and instead pretend I'm Mom, watching me anxiously climb into the driver's seat of our family car for the first time.

"First things first, you have to put your seat belt on."

I mime the action, then stare pointedly at Julia. She gives me an impressive eye roll but mimics the motion. I grin and face forward.

"Let's go over the parts of the car first." I trace an invisible steering wheel in front of me. "Here's the wheel. It tells the car where you want to go." I move my hand to the right, mentally in the driver's seat of my beloved SUV, Daisy. "Behind the wheel is a little stick. That's your turn signal, but it can also control your windshield wipers."

I worry this might be insulting, but Julia's listening closely. She has a notebook in her lap, and she's furiously writing notes. I glance at the page quickly; it's a mess of music notes, Communication exercises, and now driving notes. The lack of organization makes my head spin. How does she keep it all straight in her head? If I don't have color-coded notebooks for each subject, I want to cry.

I return my attention to the invisible car. "Here's the ignition, where you crank the car up. I have a manual key on my car, but Mom's is a push-button start. Same idea, though, and it's in the same place."

Julia nods gravely. She looks like she's about to go to war. "Is the gas on the right or left?"

I think for a second. It's alarming how much driving becomes autopilot after you do it for a while. "Right. Brake is on the left. You have to put your foot on the brake before you can put the car into drive."

Julia seems vaguely anxious. "I should have paid a lot more attention when my parents were driving me around. Instead of looking out the window and imagining myself in a music video."

I laugh. "We've all been there. Here, let me see that." I reach for Julia's notebook, and she hands it over. I draw her a picture of the gear shift, in the order they appear on Daisy. "P is for park, R is for reverse, N is for neutral, and D is for drive. Pretty easy, yeah?"

Julia nods uncertainly. "What's neutral?"

"Honestly, I have no idea. My dad just told me to stay away from it."

Julia cracks her first smile all day.

I explain the mirrors and how to adjust them, and the controls to the windows. She takes notes while I talk about what to do in heavy rain and fog. When I'm finished, we swap places and I coach her how to pretend drive the empty bunk around the cabin. Soon, we're done, but we don't get up right away. I'm aware of her beside me, her breathing that started nervous but is calm now.

"Do you think we'll have to drive a real car?" Julia asks.

"No shot. Huge liability. They'd be sued into oblivion if we ran someone over."

Julia frowns at me. "Then why be so thorough?"

I guess I didn't have to. I could have just been satisfied with the basics. But . . . she seemed like she wanted to know. It wasn't like she was anxious, like Madison or Penny from the team. She seemed interested in what to do and embarrassed at first that she didn't. I smile at Julia. "You could have stopped me at any time."

Julia smiles back, her characteristic half one.

I'm taken in again by her dark eyes, the cutest mole, the way she seems so serious all the time but relaxes just a fraction in moments like this. It's almost a compulsion when I say, "Do you want to eat dinner with me?"

Julia snorts. "No." But she's still smiling when she says, "But thanks for asking."

CHAPTER 13

I chew on my thumbnail as Ms. Flores proudly presents her Mercedes to us. "Let's practice driving!" she says, beaming at the assembled cabins.

Julia is glaring daggers into the side of my face. Okay, turns out I was wrong and millionaires don't give a shit about liability. I can't believe she's using her personal car! Adela Flores is a maniac.

We're in Life Skills, and I should have known it was gonna go badly when Ms. Flores appeared instead of Sharon. Still, I was in denial right up until we followed her to the nearly empty parking lot, with a single brand-new sixty-thousand-dollar car in the center. Ms. Flores gazes at us serenely, ignoring our rising panic.

"First, how many of you have a driver's license?"

I raise my hand, and I'm surprised I'm one of only six who do. The other ten, Julia included, keep their hands down. Ms. Flores shakes her head.

"Unfortunately, driving is a skill you need as an adult! At the very least, what to do in an emergency. Licensed drivers, stand over there. Unlicensed, stay here."

"You've got this," I whisper to Julia as the others move to the side. "Remember, foot on the brake at all times until you want to move. Check your mirrors. Stay away from neutral."

Julia nods, face grim and determined.

I want to say more, but Ms. Flores is staring at me, so I hurry away. I can barely hear what she says as she opens her car door and beckons Julia closer. Oh God. I'm so anxious I'm vibrating.

"You look like you're about to have kittens," Caroline says beside me.

"I feel like it too." I don't take my eyes off Julia as Ms. Flores gets into the passenger side. "This cannot be legal."

"Definitely not," Caroline says, laughing. "Though we should have expected it, because she's so chaotic. Did you know Ms. Flores asked me about my book? She caught me writing it in Finance. She didn't even get mad that I was writing and not taking notes. She said I should finish it, no matter what."

That does sound like Ms. Flores. She's intense and kind in a way I've never seen before. Gia is so lucky to have her as a mom. I respond to Caroline, but I'm still watching Julia. "She's so nice! And she's right. You should finish your book."

Caroline pauses for a heartbeat, then says, "Are you helping your roommate out with Life Skills?"

That gets my full attention. I know Cam would scold me for helping the competition, but Caroline just looks intrigued.

"Yeah . . . and she's helping me with music. I'm terrible at it."

Caroline nods. "Hey, good for you! I'm not great at music either, but I've decided to give up on getting the top prize."

I'm momentarily stunned. I thought everyone would be cutthroat until the end. I glance at Julia, but she's still talking to

Ms. Flores inside the car. I turn my full attention to Caroline. "What? Why?"

"I'll never beat Cam. Did you know they have a photographic memory?"

Well, I do now. I feel the depression creeping in, but I beat it back. Cam's superpowers don't have anything to do with me. I can't get that medal if I give up, so I have to keep trying. And Caroline should too. "I bet you could still do it. I mean, I'm aiming for number one too, but you know what I mean."

Caroline smiles. "I do. I think it's cool that you're helping each other out. It doesn't feel good to be so competitive all the time. Honestly, I came here to party, so this is a lot."

I laugh and start to agree, but my words are cut off by disbelief. The car is moving . . . ! With Julia in the front seat! Julia looks slightly nauseous, but Ms. Flores doesn't seem afraid at all. She says something, and Julia makes the slowest circle around the parking lot before pulling slowly, painstakingly, *perfectly* into a parking spot. She cuts the car off, and Ms. Flores nods enthusiastically. They both get out, and Ms. Flores pats Julia on the back. "Excellent job for a first try! Four points. Next, Andrew! Come on down!"

Julia walks to me, looking like she just survived a war. But when she meets my eyes, a tentative smile blooms on her face. I'm so happy, I feel tears prick my eyes.

"I'm gonna hug you."

"No, you're not." But Julia's smiling for real now, her characteristic one that only affects half her face. She joins me on my other side.

"You did so good! Was it scary?"

"A little," Julia admits. "But it was okay? Her car matched your diagram almost perfectly."

I puff out my chest a little. I'm a good tutor after all. "Do you think you'll continue driving? After camp, I mean."

Julia nods thoughtfully. "It wasn't so bad. I think I'd get better with practice."

"You absolutely would! Ms. Flores would probably let you use her car, the madwoman."

We laugh, and Caroline leans closer. "Good job, Julia!"

Julia freezes, then gives Caroline a curt nod. All trace of her smile is gone. "Thank you." Then she looks straight ahead and doesn't say anything else as Andrew very narrowly misses the gate post to the parking lot.

Caroline looks at me, bewildered, and I can't help smiling back. For a second, Julia forgot her strictly-business rule. Don't I know about slipping up. But Caroline's nice! Julia should get to know her.

Ms. Flores finishes with the unlicensed drivers (never awarding a perfect five points—is she a tough grader?) and then it's our turn. She goes down the line and asks car-related trivia questions we went over in an earlier class. How to pump gas, what to do when your tire pressure is low, that stuff. But she also throws curveballs, like what you should do if you suspect a car is following you, or if you hit a deer. I listen, intrigued. I feel like I'm actually learning something. Caroline stumbles when she's asked how to drive on ice (honestly not fair because, hello, we live in Alabama?), and then it's my turn.

"If you want to turn right, what should you do first?"

"If I'm at a stop sign, stop obviously. And then turn my blinker on and wait until the road is clear."

Ms. Flores nods. "Let's say you're hydroplaning. What do you not do?"

I remember this from a particularly painful night with Gabriel. That's how he popped his tire. "Avoid hitting the brakes too hard and jerking the wheel."

"Correct! One more. How do you know when it's time to get your oil changed?"

. . . Huh. I've never actually had to take my car to the shop. Dad just grabs my keys, disappears for two hours, and Daisy comes back sparkling and with a little tree hanging from the mirror. "I wait until my dad tells me to?"

Ms. Flores laughs, and I'm surprised when Julia does too, though she quickly smothers hers. Ms. Flores shakes her head, clearly amused. "Depending on your car, it will alert you when it's time. But if that fails and you're way overdue, you'll start to smell burnt oil or hear unusual sounds from the engine. Proper, regular maintenance should keep everything working smoothly. But I'll give you half credit, because dads can be pretty reliable. Four points!"

Hey, not bad! I'm beaming when Ms. Flores steps back and claps her hands.

"Great job today, everyone. I'm proud of you for facing your fears, steeling your resolve, and doing the hard things. Driving can be intimidating, but it's good to at least know the basics in an emergency. Anyway, don't forget to take advantage of the camping activities every day and s'mores at night. They are free, after all! Class dismissed!"

Wow, she even let us go early! Ms. Flores is the best. Julia starts to walk away, but I keep pace with her. I wave to Caroline, who heads to the mess hall for a snack. I'm still full from my mediocre lunch, and I want to get back to my music notes.

Julia is quiet, but I don't mind. She's not tense like she was with Caroline. She looks distant, as if she's deep in thought. I don't interrupt. I don't feel the usual urge to fill silence with conversation. I listen to the crunch of gravel under my shoes, the cicadas humming, the distant talking and laughter of the other campers. The swish of Julia's backpack against her clothes. The sun is trying its best to murder me, and I'm terribly sweaty, but right now, Carnegie Camp isn't so bad.

I jump when Julia finally speaks. "Did your dad teach you how to drive?"

"My mom. You wouldn't believe it, but my dad is such a softie. He said I made him nervous. He still won't ride with me!"

Julia doesn't smile, but her eyes are amused. "I take it you weren't the best when you first started?"

"Nah. But no one is."

Julia's quiet again as we pass Cabin 1. I wave at Teddy, who's reading a book outside Cabin 3.

"I'd like to practice more." Julia's voice is so quiet I almost don't hear her.

"If I had my car, I'd let you use it! But Ms. Flores would seriously let you use hers. She's amazing."

Julia glances at me. "How do you know her?"

"My best friend is dating her daughter. So I don't really know her, but we're from the same town. And sometimes we'll talk." I gasp at the realization. "Oh my God, am I also a nepo baby?"

Julia snorts out a laugh, and her half smile is back. "I think you're in the clear. I haven't seen your silver spoon lying around anywhere."

"If I had one, I would have pawned it by now. Basketball uniforms are not cheap."

Julia laughs again. She stops right after, like she's annoyed that she made any sound. But she's still smiling. "It's disturbing how many rich kids are here."

Yeah . . . you'd think they'd prioritize people who can't afford it, but most of the campers are visibly well off. Designer bags and spotless tennis shoes galore. Even Cam and Caroline have clothes that cost more than my entire wardrobe put together. I'm sure I'd have a complex about it if I wasn't so worried about not letting Fine Arts sink me.

"But it's cool that we're here, if you think about it. We tested in and we didn't have any access to fancy tutors or whatever." I hesitate. I just assumed Julia was in my tax bracket, but maybe not? I desperately want to know more about her, even if it's just a little. But I don't want to cross the boundary of our agreement. . . .

Julia considers my words for a second. Then, miraculously, she says, "Yeah, you're right. My parents run a car wash. Not exactly made of money."

I'm beaming as we reach Cabin 11. She told me something personal! I feel like I've won the lottery. Slow, but maybe surely,

Julia is opening up. I start to say something, but before I can, she points to the desk.

"I'm studying now. And you should too. We need a music win like we had today."

"I'm on it." Though I'd like to talk more, I know when to quit. Still, it's nice to win for a change at this camp. In both points and tentative speaking terms with my cabinmate. Though I have to worry about Cam and their photographic memory as my future competition now. . . .

No, no negativity. I've had a good day and I can hang on to that. I pull out my notes and settle into my cubby hole between the bed frame and my suitcase. Hearing Julia's faint music from her headphones keeps me focused, and soon I'm lost in music notes and treble clefs and time signatures. And imagining the way Julia's eyes lit up when she left the driver's seat, triumphant.

CHAPTER 14

I roll around my top bunk, music notes across my face. Julia's at the desk, furiously scribbling some practice problems into her catch-all notebook, headphones tight around her ears. She's been at it for hours. Julia's locked in, but I'm not. I can't focus; I hear the aggressive bass from Julia's headphones, the annoying squeak of the fan, someone talking on the phone at full volume outside. I don't understand the music notes I took or Julia's kind worksheet. I'm restless.

I sit up in my bunk, sighing. The cabin is part of the issue. Despite Julia being mysterious and aloof, I'm slowly learning things about her. And I've discovered something less than pleasant—Julia is messy. Not just her notes, but also the cabin. She has her clothes scattered all over the place now: the unused bunk, the floor, the bathroom. My bunk is the only place safe from a random shirt or pair of pajama shorts. But I hate studying up here! I keep getting distracted, and the fan is too loud. I should ask Julia to pick up her clothes, but I'm scared. As pathetic as it is, I don't want her to be mad at me. We're only now finally able to speak about things other than music or Life Skills. I don't want to ruin what we have. I look hopelessly up at my vision board.

Sad Girl Hours threaten me like an impending storm, so I

scramble down from my bunk. I should be focused like Julia, but that's clearly not happening, and being trapped inside this cabin is going to give me a mental breakdown. I need a break. It's one of our off days with no classes, so I can wander around camp until I'm ready to concentrate on studying. I already ran this morning but looks like I need to do something else. I shoulder my backpack and tiptoe out of Cabin 11 so I won't disturb Julia.

I squint into the bright sunlight; there's not a cloud in the sky. The sun breathes down my neck as I walk around camp. I'm not really going anywhere in particular, but I wave at Maxine and Walter as I pass their cabin. I linger near Cam as they read beneath a wide tree, but after a quick wave, they go back to studying. I sigh and keep moving. Michelle glares at me from the mess hall's porch, and I resist the urge to flip her off.

I end up near the lake. Two kids are laughing and splashing near the dock while Sharon yells at them. She launches into a lecture about water safety and not swimming without supervision. I listen, fascinated. Who knew you weren't supposed to go into lakes with an open wound? I'll have to tell Julia.

I wander around for two hours, exploring parts of the camp I've never seen. There are hydration stations dotted around the camp that I swear weren't here before. I fill up my water bottle as a test, and the water is cool and doesn't have a metallic taste like it does in our bathroom. I pass Ms. Flores talking to Samantha, the girl we beat at Jenga. She's nodding gravely while Ms. Flores chatters about the pros and cons of majoring in business. I listen but not too closely. I'm not sure I'd do well in business. I like team stuff but not being in charge. Coach Underwood asked me if I would consider becoming captain for my senior year, and I almost had a heart attack. I can barely be responsible for myself, much less a whole team!

I make a lap of the entire camp, meeting Barbara the nurse for the first time and a shy cafeteria worker named Josh and end up back at Cabin 11. A perfect loop. I'm hot and sweaty, and I'm sure I have three more bug bites than I did before, but I'm calmer. Maybe now I can focus on those music notes. I take a deep breath and open the screen.

All the peace I gained on my walk disappears when I see the state of our cabin. I can't study with all this mess! Even Julia seems to have given up. She's face down on her desk, fingers and cheek smudged with ink. Her headphones around her neck are silent.

I have to say something. The mere idea makes me break out into a sweat worse than ninety-degree heat and 100 percent humidity. My body is screaming at me to just suck it up, and honestly my brain is starting to agree.

"Have you been studying music?" Julia surprises me by speaking. She doesn't look up.

"Kind of." I hesitate, then cave. "I went for a walk. I can't focus."

"Same." Julia still doesn't sit up. She sounds exhausted. The annoyance at the state of our room fades into concern. Is she sleeping enough? Maybe we're overdoing it. I don't remember studying this much in my entire life, including in the spring when I had five AP classes.

But Julia isn't going to want to stop. I get it; the pressure of the ranking is intense. But we have *got* to do something about this room. I stare at her back, at the tension in her shoulders, and I'm reminded of how uneasy she was about driving lessons. Slowly, an idea forms.

"I'm going to do some laundry," I say.

"Okay," Julia grunts. I hold in a sigh. She didn't pick up on my hint, so now I have to be more direct.

"I think you should do some too. We can go together!"

Now Julia moves. She tilts her head to the side, revealing one intense, annoyed brown eye. I want to wither under her gaze, but I stay strong.

"I'm not goofing off—it's practice for Life Skills. Laundry is a life skill."

Julia frowns. She hesitates but finally sighs and sits up. She turns and I smile. She has a big round indentation on her forehead from the desk. She must have been having her own Sad Girl Hours.

"All right," Julia says. "Give me a second."

"Okay!" I happily gather my dirty clothes into the drawstring laundry bag that was in our welcome kits. I grab the red shirt Ms. Flores gave us too. I haven't worn it yet because I like to wash my clothes before I wear them. I wait for Julia to track down all her scattered clothes. When she has everything packed into her bulging bag, the cabin looks sparking clean. I can already feel my blood pressure lowering.

"To the laundry room!" I lug my clothes bag outside and hold the door open for Julia, who looks like she's passing a kidney stone. But she doesn't say anything as I lead the way to the laundry room, which is located in the basement of the library building. I've been here just once, and honestly it's impressive. It's almost like an old-timey laundromat, with rows of washing machines on one wall and dryers on the other. The washers even take quarters! But Ms. Flores has a basket full of them atop every machine, so we don't have to pay. I love her.

Julia looks around, her shoulders inching up to her ears as she takes it all in. No one is here, so we have the room to ourselves. Still, I pick a few machines far away from the door. "Okay, let's do it! There are a bunch of types of detergent over there, but I just use the squishy detergent balls. Way easier."

Julia nods. We go to the supply cabinet together and pick up the multicolored detergent. I drop two detergent packets into the bottom of the nearest machine and then dump my clothes in.

"Aren't you supposed to separate white clothes from the darker clothes?" Julia asks.

I pause. I guess . . . I should do that? But I never have before. Admittedly, Mom doesn't let me do the family laundry, but I have to do my workout clothes and basketball stuff separate. It's always been fine. I shrug. "Nothing bad's happened to me yet."

Julia cracks a half smile and dumps her clothes into the machine next to mine. I don't say anything, but I notice Julia watching me closely as I adjust the controls and start the machine. She picks the same settings that I do. Looks like my hunch was right. Julia is messy, but only because laundry is another Life Skills weakness. She didn't want to ask for help, so our cabin just accumulated her clothes. I'm feeling a bit emotional as I close the lid and start the load of laundry. I feel like

I'm not just noticing things about Julia but understanding her. I think so, anyway. There's still a lot to learn.

When Julia's done (she ends up using two machines), she looks around. "Now what?"

"We wait." I sit on a bench and shed my backpack. My T-shirt has a perfect oval of sweat where it rested against my back. Ugh. Thank goodness this place is air-conditioned. "We can study."

Julia nods and sits next to me. "Yeah. I bet you can study better now that our cabin's clean."

I freeze, my breath caught in my chest. "I didn't mean—"

Julia waves me off and sits next to me on the bench. "I wasn't born yesterday. But it's cool, it was starting to get to me too."

She pulls her notebook out and begins studying without another word. I'm speechless. I thought for sure she'd be upset with me if I asked her directly, but turns out I cooked up this elaborate scheme for nothing. She saw through my ruse right away . . . and still went along with it. I smile into my lap and open my notebook too. I'm trying so hard to rein in my crush on Julia, but moments like these make it really difficult.

We study in silence for twenty minutes. I bite the end of my pencil, frowning at my Communication notes. It's subtle, but Julia and I are truly opposites. She breezes through Communication and Fine Arts, always getting maximum points, but she struggles a bit with Finance. Where I'm great at Finance, but some of this Communication stuff . . . I don't get. Communication is more abstract than I thought it would be. I'm perfectly fine at public speaking, but sometimes Mr. Green will talk about the "concept of self" and boundaries, and I'm lost. I'm frowning at a note that says *sometimes you have to be firm with friends and family to get your point across* (my mom would kill me if I was "firm" about anything) when my phone buzzes in my pocket. I pull it out, and it's a text from Sarah.

What're you up to at smart people camp

We're doing laundry!

We??

A second later, Julia's phone hums. She pulls it out of her backpack, reads the screen, and does an impressive eye roll.

"Sarah?" I guess.

"Yes. She's so fucking annoying." Despite Julia's harsh words, her tone is soft with exasperated affection. She smiles at her phone as she types out a rapid reply. Sarah responds immediately, and Julia's grin widens.

I observe, fascinated. This is the first time I've seen Julia remotely happy about something not study-victory related. "Are you and Sarah close?"

Julia nods, still typing. "As close as cousins can be, I guess." She pauses, then glances at me. "We're actually second cousins. It's complicated, but we spend a good amount of time together, even though her dad is technically my first cousin once removed and our parents aren't the closest."

"Whoa! That's so cool." I try to pull apart the tangled family web, but I can't picture it.

Julia shrugs. "It's a thing. Sarah used to pout all the time that I'm like her aunt." Julia's smile turns mischievous, just for a second. "To be fair, I won't let her forget it."

I laugh. I picture Sarah: cheerful and helpful to everyone, but also with a bossy streak. She had to die every time Julia brought it up. "So do you stay at Sarah's every summer? Or were you just there for the party?"

Julia's smile slips, and she stares at her phone. "I don't usually make it to the parties. I was just there this year by chance." Julia rubs her shoulders. "I was shocked, honestly. She's so quiet and shy, and then she throws ragers."

I wouldn't describe Sarah as quiet or shy. She's the heart of the team, always pumping us up and cheering everyone on even when she's on the bench. She's the perfect candidate for captain, and I told Coach Underwood so. But I guess Julia doesn't see Basketball Sarah. Maybe we all have versions of ourselves that we don't let anyone else see. I frown at my own phone. Ominous thoughts for New Hallie. I might have to add subcategories or something. Does that still count as changing?

"It was a good party," I say instead of vocalizing my worries. "I got so drunk that I got into a horrible fight with my best friend and then passed out for ten hours."

Julia looks amused. "It was insane. People were puking everywhere. We were cleaning for hours before Red and Cricket got back. And they still caught us! Miserable experience."

I smile at the nicknames for Sarah's parents. I bet they're closer than Julia's letting on. "I'll help you clean up next time. Provided I'm not wasted."

Julia shakes her head, a small smile on her face. "I wouldn't expect you to be a party girl."

"I was, but that was the Old Hallie. New Hallie doesn't party." I haven't thought about it in a while because I've been laser focused on the SAT and the ranking, but I'll miss parties. Sometimes I'm so stressed that I feel like the spring in a windup toy, just ready to explode or have a meltdown. Some alcohol and dancing every once in a while really helped that. But if New Hallie doesn't party, then what's going to happen when I'm wound up?

"Right," Julia says, oblivious to my fretting. "I wish we still had them here. I don't drink much, but beer loosens me up." Julia rubs her shoulders again.

"Maybe we need to find better stress relief," I say, half to Julia, half to myself. "That's a Life Skill, surely."

"Don't say that where Ms. Flores can hear you. She'd probably make us do goat yoga or something."

"I like regular yoga," I offer. "I took some classes before I came here, and they were fun."

Julia finally meets my eyes, turning that cute half smile to me. "Of course you did."

My pitiful heart speeds up, but Julia seems to catch herself. She blinks and straightens. Her smile disappears. "Back to studying. We've wasted a lot of time."

Learning more about Julia, piece by piece, is never a waste of time. But I shove that bubblegum, borderline crush thought back into my brain and nod weakly.

"Okay. We'll take a break when we switch the clothes to the dryer."

We study for twenty more minutes until the washer beeps merrily that it's through. I open the lid, thinking about the different Sarahs, the party where Julia and I missed each other, and Julia slowly unveiling herself to me one precious piece at a time. Then I grab the wet clothes, and my thoughts crash to a halt.

All my white clothes are baby pink.

"Uh," Julia says, peering into her machine. "I think we messed up."

I pull out a pair of formerly white socks, in shock. How . . . ? How! This has never happened to me in my whole life! But then I spy the bright red shirt with Carnegie Camp's logo on the front—brand-new, never been washed. A half-remembered warning from Mom pops unhelpfully into my brain, about an hour too late. Always wash new clothes on cold and with dark ones. I look at Julia, a frantic apology on my lips, but she takes one look at my socks and bursts out laughing.

I'm still shocked when she pulls out her formerly white Christmas shorts, still cracking up. "Oh my god, they're even uglier now! This is amazing."

"I'm so sorry, Julia. I didn't think—"

Julia waves me away, still chuckling. "Stop, stop. You were right—this is perfect Life Skills practice. Now we know we *do* have to separate the white clothes."

I watch Julia cart her clothes to the nearest dryer, still laughing. That . . . that's it? She's not angry with me for staining her clothes? She not upset my mistake caused such a mess? I blink down at the damp pink socks in my hand. My heart is still racing in anticipation of . . . something. These should be a visual representation of me fucking up, again. Of how far away

Hallie 2.0 really is. But now that I look at them, Julia's laughter echoing through the laundry room, baby-pink socks with tiny cacti aren't so bad either.

"Come on, Hallie," Julia calls, finally over her laughing fit. She's shooting an annoyed glare at the dryer, but for the first time in over a week, her shoulders are relaxed. "Show me how to use this dryer thing. I think it ate my quarter."

I smile back and carry my pink clothes to Julia's side.

CHAPTER 15

"I just think I should be making more progress by now, you know?" I pant to Walter on my third lap around the dusty track.

He keeps pace with me, jogging silently in his shiny vest. He doesn't even look tired! What an athlete.

"I haven't gotten a single piece of chocolate. But maybe I'm being too hard on myself?"

We pass Maxine, who's drinking a cup of coffee on her porch. I lift my hand in a wave, and she waves back. "I mean, I have kind of been crushing SAT prep. But that's hardly an accomplishment. I already took that class at school."

Walter says nothing, but I'm just relieved he's here. Reginald is great, but there's something nice about talking to a living creature for a change.

"And I haven't given in to any of my crushes yet." That admission shocks me. I guess it's true—I haven't! It was dicey at first being around all the very hot members of the queer cabin, but I haven't thought about them like that in over a week. I've somehow settled them firmly into friend territory. "I *should* get some chocolate. I'm doing it. I'm changing."

But I don't feel like I'm changing, not really. The crush part is under control, allegedly, but I still miss basketball. I look through Sarah's Instagram every night, nearly in tears. I miss listening to K-pop. I really miss horror movies. I would kill to watch *Halloween* right now, summer be damned.

"Maybe it's impossible to change, Walter. Maybe we are who we are."

And that means I'll always be the jealous, heartbroken, dumb jock I've always been. I stop running abruptly, my stomach so queasy I lean over in case I throw up.

Walter tentatively noses my hand. I look at him, and he's staring at me, head cocked to the side. I pet his back, trying to breathe. No. No, that's not a future I'll accept. I *am* changing, and winning that medal is the start. I just have to keep working hard.

"I'm okay. Don't worry." I straighten, and Walter licks my knee. I laugh, and his tail wags. Just once, but hey, I'll take it. "Okay, buddy, that's enough for today. See you tomorrow."

I head back to Cabin 11, but this time Walter escorts me the whole way. When I get to the door, he turns and trots back toward the track. I smile at his receding form. I may not have many human friends, but Walter's pretty great. I see why Nav's so obsessed with dogs now.

I ease the screen open and slip inside. It's quiet as usual, so I go to the bathroom to scrub the sweat and fear and nausea off my body. When I'm out of the shower, I glare at my suntanned face in the foggy mirror. Today's a new day. I *will* get maximum points in Communication today. I *will* earn chocolate today. I *will* change. I believe. I'm manifesting it. I might have been incredulous when Sarah said she was manifesting a tournament win last year (we lost), but I'll take anything I can get right now. If I keep at it, things will eventually change, right?

When I step out of the bathroom, I freeze. Julia's sitting upright in her bunk, blinking sleepily at me. At seven fifteen? No way!

"You're awake!"

Julia grunts something unintelligible. She is upright, but just barely. Her eyes are closed, and her shoulders are slumped with exhaustion. She's more like a zombie than a person ready to start her day.

"You go back to sleep," I say, almost laughing. "I'll wake you up at—"

"Where do you go?" Julia asks suddenly.

I blink at her. "What?"

Julia struggles to keep her eyes open, but she lifts them to meet mine. "In the mornings. Like just now. Where do you go?"

"Oh! I run every morning. There's a track behind the main building."

Julia nods, then promptly collapses back into bed and right to sleep.

I watch her for a second, a grin on my face. She's noticed I'm gone? I thought I was careful about not waking her up. But more than that, it kind of makes me feel warm and fuzzy that she's curious about me as well. Julia is such an *I'm going to mind my own business* person. I never expected her to take an interest in me.

The warm feeling persists through breakfast, where Cam teases me about the blush on my ears. And through SAT prep, where Julia and I both ace our pop quiz and grin at each other like idiots. And it lasts through Finance, where I successfully balance a budget and receive maximum points. And when Julia says I'm doing a good job with music and she's proud of my progress before she disappears to study at her unknown location. When I get back to the cabin, I'm practically burning up with secret pleasure. What a great day! Julia asked about me, and she smiled at me, and she complimented me about music, and she looked so nice today, wearing the cutest blue shirt with an interesting decal on it . . .

I stop cold in the middle of the room. Wait a fucking minute. I'm not in a good mood because I did well at camp. It's because of *Julia*. I'm literally walking on air because she smiled at me. And I haven't thought of anyone else lately because I'm thinking of Julia and her quiet strength and mystery and sharp eyes that sometimes turn soft when they're looking at me. I know this spiral because it's been happening since puberty hit me like a truck.

I have a full-blown crush on Julia, which violates my number one rule.

Oh, goddammit.

"This can't be happening!" I know I'm wailing like a maniac, but this is a crisis. I tried so hard! And I thought I'd be safe because Julia is so intense and standoffish. But . . . she's not? Not really! Every day she relaxes a little more, talks to me a little more. And I fell hook, line, and sinker. I want to die. I want to scream. Instead, I race back to the track to call Nav.

It's after three, so I'm praying she's off from work. If she ignores this call, I really might drop dead. I touch the Face-Time button and, thank goodness, Nav's face appears. She's at a weird angle, like she's lying down, and she has a bit of pink frosting in her hair. She grins, and some of the panic gripping my heart eases.

"Oh, *now* the scholar decides to grace us with her presence."

I roll my eyes, but I'm already feeling better. This is so Nav, and I'm already at ease. "Shut up, I'm on a break." I pause when I catch a glimpse of Gia in the corner of Nav's screen. She must be at Gia's house again. "Hi, Gia!"

"Hi, Hallie." Gia waves, but doesn't take her eye off the TV in front of her. She must be focused.

"Why're you sweaty?" Nav asks.

"It's July in Alabama?" I pretend to be offended, but I'm secretly pleased. The familiarity is distracting me, thank goodness.

"You should be careful of heatstroke," Gia says, still hyper-focused on the TV. "Drink plenty of water."

"Yeah, listen to Gia! Why aren't you in your cabin?"

I rub the back of my neck, looking down at my shoes for strength. "Don't laugh."

"I'm not."

I know she's about to, the asshole. I sigh and spill my news anyway. "Well . . . there's this girl . . ."

"Oh, here we go." Nav rolls her eyes and smiles. "Tell me everything."

I hate that reaction. That *"Oh yeah, of course Hallie is in too deep with her crush because that's all Hallie is and all she does"* reaction. I know Nav doesn't mean it like that, but it hurts.

"Nothing. Never mind."

"No, tell me!" Nav moves the phone as she sits up, then refocuses it. "I'm here, seriously."

I walk around the track for a bit, distressed. I don't see Maxine, but Walter lifts his head when I pass the guard cabin. He trots after me, slower paced than in the morning. "I don't know. I think I have a crush on my cabinmate."

"Straight or queer?" Nav asks, all business now. As much as I hate to admit it, this isn't her first rodeo. This is how it always starts. Nav helps me through all the early butterflies, helps me come up with schemes to get close to them, listens to all my angst. She must be so tired of me.

Almost as tired of me as I am.

"Queer," I whisper, close to tears. "I think. She hasn't told me for sure."

"Okay, you have a shot!" Nav seems excited, at least, and not scolding. Or ashamed of me. "What's she like?"

"Cool. Kind of mysterious. And she's so smart and serious, but I like that. We agreed that we wouldn't be friends, but sometimes she'll laugh at a joke and yesterday she told me a little about herself and I was so happy—oh God, I hear it. I definitely like her."

"Cute?" Nav asks. She tries to play it like an innocent question, but her eyes sparkle with mischief.

"Please don't tease me. I'm having a crisis." I pause, feeling my ears burn that have nothing to do with the afternoon sun. "But yes."

"If you like her this much, you should tell her," Gia's voice calls from off-screen. "I remember feeling something similar and suffering while Nav tried to get me to date someone else."

"Oh, shut up," Nav says, all the affection and love in the world in her eyes for Gia. I want to puke. She looks back at the camera, still smiling. "I have to agree, though. Don't suffer like we did."

"You don't get it. I said I wouldn't do this!" The words burst out of me. I said I would change, and here I am, back to square one. Negative squares, if that were a thing. And it's clear Julia doesn't like me back; she said no friendship and I've never seen her take anything camp-related not seriously. I'm just setting myself up for failure. And I've had so much of that for so long, I don't know if I can do it again. I rub my eyes and point my phone away from my face so Nav can't see me cry.

"For what it's worth, I think a crush is fine." Nav's voice is gentle. "And honestly, you work best when you— Oh fuck, Hallie!"

I bring the phone up again. "What?"

Nav's eyes are wide and now Gia is in the frame too, looking alarmed. "Don't panic," Gia says, "but there's a rottweiler right behind you."

I smile, my mood lifted. I turn, and Walter tilts his head quizzically. "That's Walter. He's my friend, aren't you, boy?"

I crouch and Walter stalks toward me. I give him a one-armed hug, and he sighs, like he's tired of my shenanigans and just wants me to stay in my cabin for once. Sorry, boy, I'm in the middle of a romance emergency.

"How the hell did you manage that?" Nav's voice crackles from my phone.

I pull back so she can see him better, and I sit on the dirt track. My clothes will be filthy, but I'm too exhausted to care. Walter takes a seat next to me.

"I run every morning. He doesn't like that I'm out of my cabin, so he follows me."

"Fucking athletes," Nav mutters.

Gia beams into the phone. "He's a gorgeous dog. Did you know that though they're excellent guard dogs, rottweilers are really needy?"

Just like me, apparently. I pet Walter's head, feeling pathetic. "I didn't know that."

"Cute dog aside," Nav says. "I don't think you should worry about it. A crush isn't a bad thing, Hal."

It is for me. Romance is a distraction. It makes me fail SAT tests. It makes me ignore every red flag imaginable. It always ends with my heart torn to shreds while my crush moves on without a care in the world. I can't do this again. Not when I'm so close to changing my life for the better.

"I'm just going to ignore it."

"Yeah, okay." Nav sounds doubtful.

"Maybe you can just be friends?" Gia suggests.

That's not a bad idea. I can't stay away from Julia for practical and academic reasons, but we can be friendly. I can be normal. Yeah! I stand up, encouraged. "Thanks, Gia! That's what I'll do. We can be friends. I can be friends with her, easy."

Nav still looks like she doesn't believe me, but she nods. "I still don't think it's a bad thing, but all right. We're here if you need a pep talk, okay?"

I give her a mock salute. "You got it, captain. What're you guys doing?"

I walk around the track for an hour, listening to Gia explain the insanely complicated game she's playing and Nav fret over her new cupcake recipe. When I hang up, I'm initially much calmer. Talking to Nav always cheers me up. I'll even admit that Gia is cool, and I know when I get back, we'll become better friends. But that gets me into my jealousy spiral again. If Gia were terrible, it would be so easy to hate her. But she isn't! She's kind and funny and helps me with my stupid problems. And I see how much Nav loves her. I see it in her relaxed body language, hear it in her lovesick voice. I should be so happy for her, and I'm not. And that's on me. I'm just worried this is a characteristic of Real Hallie and not something I can discard.

I get back to Cabin 11, and it's so empty and silent and lonely that for a second, I just want to burst into tears. I think I'm depressed. I think it's getting close to my period time. I think I need to shove that entire chocolate bar into my mouth.

But no, that would be the ultimate failure. What I need is an emergency pick-me-up. My gaze slides to my laptop, and I know what I have to do. Horror movies are supposed to be off-limits, but I think it's time to break out *Halloween*.

CHAPTER 16

I grab Reginald and hug him to my chest. It doesn't help as much as I thought it would, but I'll take it. I sit at the desk (it almost feels like blasphemy to be in Julia's space, but she packed away all her study materials this time) and set up my laptop. I feel guilty for doing this, but it's an emergency. It's either a slasher or devouring my entire chocolate bar like a rabid dog.

The internet isn't the best here, but luckily for me, I downloaded all my favorite movies onto my laptop a few months ago. I debated deleting them and starting over as New Hallie, but I'm glad I didn't. I grab my comforter off my bunk, my water bottle, and boot up the first *Halloween* and settle in to watch Michael Myers wreak havoc on Haddonfield.

I know it's weird that horror movies relax me. But it's not just the scares that get me! Horror movies, more than any other genre, are almost always passion projects. A small group of people come together to create something they really care about, and it shows in the editing, the acting, the practical effects (for the older ones, anyway). I've always found that idea sort of romantic. To come together as a team and present something to the world, not always just to make money. To care about something endlessly, doggedly, until you look up one day and it may not be perfect but it's undoubtedly loved.

I drag my comforter over my head to block out the little light from the window as the opening sequence I've seen at least a dozen times plays. Reginald sits in my lap, and I hug him as I admire the perfect pacing and simple, terrifying idea of a man in a mask with a knife (and superhuman abilities, but we ignore that).

As Michael Myers stalks his next victim, the hair on the back of my neck raises. Did I hear something outside? I pause the movie and take out my earbuds, arms tense around Reginald. Complete silence. But the goose bumps on my arms keep going, and I turn, heart hammering in my chest.

A shape is standing at the door.

I scream and rocket to my feet. And a second later, my eyes adjust to the darkness of the cabin, and Julia's startled expression focuses. Relief smooths the goose bumps down, and I laugh.

"Sorry, you scared me!"

"My bad." Julia's smiling now, almost a full one instead of her normal half smile. She nods to my computer. "What're you doing with all the lights out?"

"Watching a horror movie."

I want to die as Julia's gaze immediately lifts to my vision board. I groan and sink down into the chair before she can speak.

"Don't say it. I know."

"I didn't say anything." Julia doesn't seem judgmental, at least. In fact, she seems curious. She steps closer, peeking at the screen. "If you like them, why'd you cross them out up there?"

I sigh before I can help it. A few months ago, this answer would have been simple. But now . . . "It's complicated."

Julia tilts her head to one side, which is so damn adorable I almost have a heart attack. Her attention is fully on me, looking right into my eyes. My ears burn fiercely in the dark, and that makes me feel even worse. It's going to be hard to pretend this crush doesn't exist. "Try me."

I sigh again. I want to close up, shut down, make a joke like I do with my other friends. But I'm just tired. Nav's the only one who knows what's going on, and she's a hundred miles away, enjoying her new relationship. Well, I have Walter and Reginald, but they can't give advice, so it doesn't count.

"I love horror movies now, but I didn't used to. I dated a girl last year who was obsessed, and she got me into them." I lean back against the desk, mood already lower. "Which would be fine! We broke up and I kept watching them, but I just . . . you ever think about how pieces of your personality come from other people?"

Julia seems thoughtful. "I guess I've never thought about it before, but that makes sense. I'm assuming this ex was shitty if you don't want to even touch something associated with her."

"Oh God, one of the worst. She did this thing where she'd make me feel like I was crazy. We'd argue, and she'd say 'I never said that.'"

Julia shakes her head. "Been there."

"And she threatened to stab my best friend because I was apparently hanging out with her too much." I rub my temples. I should stop, but I'm spilling my guts, and they all have to come out. "And you know, I'm ashamed that's what it took for me to end it. I was tolerating so much, and I probably would still be doing it if she hadn't threatened someone important to me. How sad is that?"

"It happens," Julia says wisely. Yeah, but probably not to her! She's way too smart to get caught up because a girl is hot and willing to look your way.

"I just feel gross when I think about it. So much of me is . . . them, you know? I like horror because of Ashley, I joined the basketball team for a crush that never went anywhere. It's pathetic, you know? This summer, I decided to change. No more horror movies, no more K-pop, no more basketball. I'm just going to be me." I look hopelessly at Michael on my frozen laptop screen. It's just before one of my favorite parts. "But I have a bad day and I go right back. I'm not changing anything."

Julia breathes out. "Heavy."

"Sorry, I—"

Julia holds up a hand to stop me. "Don't apologize. I get what you're saying. When my last relationship ended, I burned all her stuff. It was cathartic."

Oh, Julia gets it. And I'm making a mental note that she has dated a girl before and might be single now, just for science.

Julia continues, oblivious to my evil thoughts. "But I think you're being too hard on yourself."

I frown. "What do you mean?"

"Do you like horror movies? Just now, without Ashley, were you enjoying yourself?"

I waffle between lying to preserve my dignity and the truth. I cave on the truth. "Yeah. I was."

"Okay. Then it's not the same as burning stupid stuff that

gives you bad memories. If horror movies make you happy, even without her, then it's no longer her thing. It's yours now."

Something about Julia's gentle, simple certainty bothers me. I want to believe her, but . . . if it's not the horror movies, or basketball, or the music I like that's holding me back, then it has to be me. The real me.

Julia must sense my unease and depression because she says, "Okay, listen to this. I met Ms. Flores in the library the other day."

I'm paying extra attention now. I avoid the library (because it's right next to the music room, which gives me bad vibes). Is that where Julia goes to study?

"She said studying is important, but breaks are just as important. I didn't believe her, so she encouraged me to try it." Julia shrugs. "I played a game on my phone for thirty minutes and then went back. It helped."

I nod slowly, picking up what she means. "Horror movies are my break."

"Yeah."

"But I promised myself I wouldn't watch them. . . ."

"Then it's like a cheat day on a diet. Fuck diet culture, but even I know that if you quit something cold turkey, you have a bigger chance of relapsing."

Oh. Oh! That makes way more sense. This is like when I had to replace basketball workouts with running. I can't just quit everything at once. I have to microdose New Hallie.

"Thanks, Julia. I feel better now."

Julia gives me a half smile. "You're welcome."

I just watch her for a second, feeling rosy and warm. She didn't have to talk to me this much, and about something not related to Life Skills or music! But she did. I like Julia, but maybe we can be actual, real friends. Maybe I'm not doomed. "Do you want to study now? I can—"

"No, finish your movie. I'm gonna take a break too."

And without another word, Julia kicks off her shoes, climbs into her bottom bunk, and pulls the comforter over her head. I look at her back, slightly in disbelief, and in minutes, her breathing is soft and even. Asleep.

I turn back to *Halloween*, a goofy grin on my face. I watch the rest of the movie with lightness in my chest and a sort of peace. When it's over, Julia's still napping, so I sit in the dark and meditate on my lack of progress, my lack of chocolate, and slipping into bad habits. But I also think about Julia's words, her cool assurance that everything will be all right. And for once, Julia's voice is a little louder than the one in my head.

CHAPTER 17

I head to SAT prep after waking Julia, but today, there's a note on the door.

Go to the main hall for Pop-Up #2.

"Oh boy, here we go again."

Two approaching campers look at me, eyebrows raised. My ears burn, but I just point at the sign and hustle back to Cabin 11.

I ease open the screen. Julia's bed is a mess but empty; the door to the bathroom is closed. The faint sound of running water reaches my ears. I wait until it stops before I call, "Julia?"

Julia doesn't answer. She opens the door instead and pops her head out of the bathroom. She's still in her pajamas (black tank top again) and there's a glob of toothpaste in the corner of her mouth. She rubs one eye sleepily, and it's so cute I want to melt. "I'm assuming this is an emergency."

"Pop-up day again! We have to go to the main hall instead of SAT prep."

Julia heaves a sigh. "Another day on madman island." She retreats back into the bathroom but leaves the door open. "You go ahead, I'll be there in a minute."

I turn to go, but Julia speaks again.

"Hey."

I look back in surprise, but Julia's still hidden in the bathroom. "Yeah?"

"Thanks for telling me."

I smile at her, even though she can't see me. "No problem. See you there!"

I practically skip to the main hall. This time, there's no Amira to greet us; the doors are wide open, and a bunch of kids are already milling around in the massive room. I step inside, unsure. There are no card tables with games on them, or sectioned-off cabins. There's just one long table with a bunch of paper on it near the stage, and about thirty kids standing around. Even Ms. Flores isn't here yet.

Cam and Teddy wave me over, and I join their group. Cam bounces on their heels, like they're ready to run a marathon.

"Love pop-up day!"

"That's because you won the last one," Teddy says, sighing.

"I like them too!" I chime in.

"Once again, that's because you almost won." Teddy shakes his head, his shaggy curls bouncing. "I'm terrified of what she'll make us do next. We might have to eat live eels or something."

I shudder, and Cam laughs. Caroline enters the room, and I wave her over. When she joins us, Cam asks her, "Would you eat live eels for a hundred points?"

"Hell no." Caroline makes a horrible face. "Nothing's worth that."

A medal might be. Maybe eels wouldn't be so bad? With

the right seasoning, I'm willing to try anything once. I don't know if I could do it if they were alive, though.

Cam and Caroline argue over doing anything for points, but I check my phone—8:49. I glance at the door, but everyone who wanders into the main hall isn't who I'm looking for. I waffle between looking at my phone and the door, half listening to the conversation.

"What're you doing, Hallie?" Teddy asks.

I turn to face him, but Caroline speaks before I can.

"Looking for Julia."

I frown at her, hoping she can't see how red my ears are. "How do you know?"

Caroline grins at me. "You do this every day in SAT prep."

Well, shit. Even Caroline can see how in love I am! I hate this. I grimace while the queer cabin laughs without me.

"Do you like her?" Cam asks. I hate the way their eyes shine with interest. Reminds me unpleasantly of my gremlin best friend.

"I like everyone," I say diplomatically. I'm pleased that my voice is strong and clear and not at all as wobbly as my knees are. "And we're cabinmates. Cabin Eleven camaraderie, you know."

Cam shakes their head and so does Teddy. "I'm not friends with my cabin. We're polite, but that's all," Cam says.

"Mine are straight-up dickheads," Teddy adds.

Well, I guess it could be worse. I'm once again glad I have Julia, prickly exterior and all. And, speaking of! Julia enters the room, stifling a yawn. I wave at her and catch her attention.

She glances at the queer cabin and then looks longingly to an empty corner. I lower my hand, uncertain. Maybe she wants to be left alone so early in the morning—

Julia meets my eyes again and walks over, and my heart sings with happiness. She chose me over solitude!

I'm grinning as I gesture to Cam, Caroline, and Teddy. "Julia! This is the queer cabin."

Julia gives them a curt nod . . . and that's all. I can't hide my smile. As friendly as ever.

"Hi," Teddy says. "We never see you! Are you a hardcore studier like Cam?"

Julia looks like she wishes she were anywhere else, but she says, "I try to take camp seriously."

"Same," Cam says, grinning. "Good game last time, by the way."

Julia says nothing, but there's a weird tension now. Cam's smiling, but they look intrigued by Julia, maybe even appraising. And Julia regards Cam coolly, her expression much icier than I've seen in a week. They look like two opponents squaring off in a boxing ring. Or two bears getting ready to scrap.

"Anyway!" I say to rescue the mood. "We were taking bets on what today's pop-up will be. Would you eat a live eel for a hundred points?"

Julia considers her answer for a second. Then she says, not taking her eyes off Cam, "I would if that's what it took to win."

Ms. Flores picks that opportunity to enter the main hall, and everyone's attention is on her. Thank God. I don't think Julia likes Cam, but why? Maybe it's just their competitive spirits clashing. Cam is currently number one, where Julia and I are aiming to be, so there's bound to be some friction.

Ms. Flores (wearing a stunning red dress today, wow!) steps up to the mic and grins at us. "Welcome to pop-up number two, campers! Are we having fun so far?"

I'm surprised when I'm not the only one cheering this time. A few other kids yell their approval. Caroline claps, and even Teddy gives a small whoop. Julia and Cam are dead silent, though.

"Today, we will be testing your ability to solve puzzles and work under pressure. It's a scavenger hunt!"

Oh, fun! I'm not great at puzzles when I'm alone, though. I have to talk them over with others. But if it's split by cabins again, then I have nothing to worry about—

"The rules are a bit different this time. You can join a team, or you can do it alone. The winner gets a massive fifty points, but that's split between your team. The more members you add, the more you dilute that grand prize. Think carefully."

I deflate instantly. Oh, great. I guess I'll have to do it by myself . . . but maybe I can find just one teammate? Twenty-five points is still huge.

"Second place gets twenty points, third through fifth gets ten. And then nothing after that. No participation trophies!" Ms. Flores grins at the collective groan. "But participating is its own reward, if you choose to do so. Remember, these are optional. Campers who want to join, come up and get your riddles from the table here. Campers who want to sit out, enjoy your day off! Oh, and this is a timed challenge.

You have exactly one hour, starting when everyone gets their papers. Okay, go!"

Amira pops up from somewhere and waves at us from the long table in front of the stage. But I'm surprised when about ten kids turn to leave. They're not going to try? Even if they get fifth place, ten extra points is huge. Julia watches them go too, eyebrows raised.

"I can't believe they're leaving," Teddy says as we move to the table at the front. We're at the back, so it'll take a while.

"I'm not doing it either," Caroline pipes up.

We stare at her in disbelief as she shrugs.

"I'm not good at riddles. And I'm not getting the top spot, so I don't see why I can't relax."

"Makes sense," I tell her. I almost wish I was with her. Aiming for number one is so stressful. "What'll you do while we do this?"

Caroline gets a funny look on her face. It's not disappointment or apathy, or even general happiness. She almost seems excited. "We'll see!"

I note that as strange, but Cam has already started talking to Teddy, and the line is moving. I hurry to catch up.

"Look, my cabinmates are teaming up! That's so stupid," Cam says.

My stomach drops to my toes. I wanted to team up with one of them. . . . "But if you work together, it's easier surely?"

Cam snorts. "I don't want to share my points with anyone. It's dumb to do so now. We're almost halfway through the competition."

"Oh, umm, yeah." I know it's not Cam's fault, but they've unintentionally stabbed me in a sore spot. I don't think it's stupid to share the work, especially on a challenge like this . . . but according to my ex, I'm just a "dumb jock." What do I know?

I let Cam and Teddy go ahead of me to pick up their forms, dejected. I guess I'm going it alone—

Julia clears her throat behind me. I turn, and Julia says, "Do you want to be a team?"

I can't speak for a second, profoundly shocked. "I—I thought you'd want to do it by yourself! For maximum points."

Julia gives me a wry smile. "It's not stupid to think you'd need more than one person for a scavenger hunt."

I want to cry. I want to hug Julia. Your Honor, I am in love with her. I shake the cursed thoughts out of my head and pretend I'm not a lovesick puppy enough to answer Julia. "Let's do it! We'll crush it."

Amira gives us our form. I write my name at the top, and Julia puts hers next to mine in elegant handwriting.

Amira beams at us. "Good luck, girls!"

We stand to the side and wait for the last three people to pick up their forms. It's folded in half with a bold *DO NOT OPEN UNTIL TOLD TO DO SO* written across the front. Some people are already peeking, but I wait patiently, Julia at my side. Even if we get dead last, I already feel like I won.

"Okay, campers, open your clue sheet!" Ms. Flores calls. "Time starts now. Be back here at ten fifteen! Good luck!"

I open the form, and Julia crowds close to me. I'm momentarily too distracted by her touching my arm to read, but the whispers of confusion around us pull me out of the happy fog. I scan the instructions:

You will have to find a combination of people and places. When you find them, stamp your form with the corresponding clue.

Then there are twelve questions, and under that, twelve small boxes where the stamps go. I read the first clue, dread in my gut.

1. A tough duo who work tirelessly to protect Carnegie Camp and all its scholars.

Oh. That's Maxine and Walter! Easy. I read the next one.

2. A helpful guide to all your camping needs.
Hint: Fashionable!

Amira! It has to be, right? She's wearing a pretty handmade skirt today, and all her clothes are gorgeous. Wait, are they all this easy? I scan the other questions, and there are a few I don't recognize, but the rest are all people I've met and places I've been.

"Isn't this too easy?" I whisper to Julia. But Julia blinks owlishly at me.

"You understand this? I only know one of these."

I blink back. Wait, really? I look around; hardly anyone has moved, and the few teams whisper to each other anxiously. Teddy looks defeated, and even Cam's frowning fiercely at their paper.

I look back at Julia and grin. "I have a good feeling about this."

I lead Julia out of the main hall and around to my suspected answers. Maxine (sans Walter—maybe he's not good with crowds?) enthusiastically stamps our paper outside of the guard cabin. We find Mr. Green in the Communication classroom, Barbara at the nurse's station, and Sharon in the mess hall. There's a stamp beside one of the hydration stations, the campfire where the s'mores are, and the lake. Julia shakes her head in disbelief the entire time.

"How are you so good at this?"

"I'm not perfect," I say, happily embarrassed. I guess my hidden talent is scavenger hunts! Who knew? "I don't know this one about the eagle. Or the treats one."

"I know these," Julia says. She seems a little relieved. "There's an eagle statue in the library, and the treats is about the canteen."

"I've never been to the canteen," I say as we head in that direction. It seems like a bad idea to get tempted by all the fun things I can't buy because I'm saving my points.

"I go to stare at what I can't have," Julia says, and I can't hold in a laugh. She smiles as we enter the air-conditioned room and spy three campers already at the stamp. They gawk at our almost-full worksheet.

We go to the library, and then there are just three more. Amira is one, but I'm sure we're supposed to get her last, since she's at the main hall. We puzzle over the final two.

8. A budding creative with enormous potential.
Hint: You should be more sociable!

11. A friend to hard workers and underdogs.
Hint: Loves animals!

"I'm lost," Julia says. "Maybe the forest for eleven? But what is eight about?"

I consider the page for a second. "Is it okay if I think out loud?"

"Go for it."

"There weren't that many places without someone manning the stamp, probably because someone could steal it and screw over everyone else. So these two are probably people."

Julia nods, and I continue, the thoughts coming rapid-fire into my brain and straight out of my mouth.

"We've visited most of the instructors, so I don't think it's them. That would be too easy."

"So who's left?" Julia asks. "Do you know any more guards? I didn't even know that woman existed."

I laugh and start to explain about my morning runs, but then it hits me. "No, but I bet I know who eight is!" I backtrack to the main hall, where there are a few campers hanging around the edges of the room, Amira waiting patiently at the table, and . . . Caroline.

I skip to her side, grinning. "Stamp, please!"

Caroline matches my grin while Julia looks on in blank confusion. "You're the first one to figure it out! How'd you know?"

"First, you acted weird when I asked what you'd do while we were playing. And then you're writing that awesome book, and you said you'd talked to Ms. Flores about it. So I thought maybe she'd feel close enough to ask you to do this. And the hint is shaming people like Michelle for being dickheads and making you have a separate cabin."

Caroline's grin widens. "That's awesome, Hallie. I bet no one else will get it."

"Cam and Teddy will! And the rest of them can choke."

Julia laughs and tries to cover it up with a cough. She nods at Caroline. "Hope the boss is paying you for your service."

"She offered points, but I asked for unlimited ice cream instead." Caroline winks at me while I try not to combust with jealousy. "I'm not the only one who fits the prompt, but so far you're the first people to guess it can be a camper at all. Go ahead, you only have two left!"

We separate from Caroline so we won't give her away to everyone else, but there's still the last clue to figure out. Julia collects Amira's stamp while I hang back and turn over the last clue in my head. Underdog . . . hard workers . . . friend . . . and the hint about animals . . .

Julia rejoins my side. The blank eleventh square haunts me. "Any luck?"

I shake my head, starting to feel down. "I'm sorry, Julia. I can't figure it out. . . ."

"We can do it." Julia's eyes burn with determination. "Talk it out."

"I'm getting tripped up about the animal hint. A friend to

hard workers could mean anyone at the camp, and I'm not sure what underdogs means, but it's not specific enough either. The animal one is the key." I glance up and Ms. Flores is still onstage, sitting down now with her legs dangling off the edge. She meets my gaze and smiles, then turns back to Amira to chat.

But I don't look away. Because who else, besides Julia, can say they've been a friend to me? Not just me; to Samantha asking about business school, to Caroline who needed advice on her book, to Julia who needed driving practice and encouragement in the library. And Ms. Flores rewards hard work—no participation trophies. She's an underdog as well, clawing her way up to millionaire status from humble beginnings and being a minority in a majority white field.

And, if that wasn't enough—because she's sitting down, I can see her socks. They have bright blue dolphins on them.

I grab Julia's hand. She starts, but I can't look at her as we walk to Ms. Flores. She smiles down at me, and I shyly lift up our form.

"Can you stamp number eleven, please?"

Ms. Flores gives me the biggest, warmest smile. "It would be my pleasure."

Ms. Flores stamps the last empty square, and Julia grins at me, and I must be floating because I hardly hear Ms. Flores announce, "We have a winner!"

Julia gives me a high five, and my hand tingles where she touched me. Victory has never felt so sweet.

We sit down to wait for the others, and Julia is happier than I've ever seen her. "I can't believe you knew all these. I feel like I didn't do anything."

"Not true," I argue. "I didn't know the library or the canteen."

"Still!" I've never seen Julia smile this much. And it's because of me! What I did! "You should be a detective."

"Eww! ACAB all day."

Julia laughs. "I meant a private detective. Like Sherlock."

No one's ever said that to me before. It's all "You should be a doctor, Hallie," when I'm not sure if I can handle open wounds. Or "You should be a lawyer," when arguing makes me cry. I get lost in a brief fantasy of trench coats and chasing down crafty criminals, but it's more like a 1940s noir in my head. I'd have to develop a smoking addiction, and that's a no thanks.

"Wait, what about Watson?"

"I can be Watson. I did a good job of it today," Julia says.

We look at each other for a stunned second, and then away at the same time. My ears are on fire. If I was any more delusional than I already am, I would take that as a love confession. Because hello? Sherlock and Watson were so gay for each other. It's practically canon.

Any awkwardness and Sherlock-noir fantasies disappear when Samantha, the girl who we beat in the first round of the games, approaches Caroline shyly and asks for the stamp. Caroline is clearly pleased, and they chat even after she's done stamping the page. They part ways after several minutes, both their faces a little redder than before, and Ms. Flores declares her the second-place winner. Julia grins beside me.

"I bet Cam is shitting themself right now."

"Not so stupid after all," I mutter, but Julia hears me. She doesn't say anything, though; she just smiles like a satisfied cat.

We watch the top five drift in. A team of three gets third

place, Teddy and a blond-haired boy get fourth, and a co-ed group gets fifth. Cam frantically bursts into the room right after, but it's too late—they're sixth. They look mad as hell as Caroline stamps their page, but they shrug when they make eye contact with me. Julia doesn't look too impressed at my side, but I'm sure they'll eventually be friends.

Ms. Flores parades the top five teams on stage at ten fifteen, and she surprises us all with a cute goody bag. I peek inside and smile. It's a mini chicken Snuggable designed to sit on a desk. Hope Cabin 11's desk is ready for two new decorations.

"Congratulations, campers!" Ms. Flores says, beaming. "Of course to our winners, but also to everyone who participated. Wasn't it fun to get to know people you haven't met? See a part of camp you haven't seen? Keep that in mind for next time. Remember, you're not here just to study. You're here to grow. Blossom. Become a better you. And that starts with waking up and looking around you."

I can't stop beaming. This is a huge step in the right direction for my goals—even Ms. Flores thinks so! I'm finally getting settled into camp, and maybe even a new me. This chicken is proof. Stuffed chicken today, medal of achievement tomorrow.

Ms. Flores claps her hands. "Dismissed! Enjoy your day, campers!"

Julia and I smile at each other. I have a feeling we'll be riding this high for a long time.

CHAPTER 18

I think life is on an upswing.

Julia and I have been studying Life Skills and Fine Arts a lot, and I've managed to disguise my pining as regular friendship. She's more relaxed now, and she even laughs at some of my jokes. Not often, and she disguises it as a cough, but I heard her! She won't play her violin yet, or go to dinner with me, but I feel like it's less of a lost cause and an eventuality now.

My relationship with Walter is also growing. He now follows me to my cabin after my run and waits for me to shower. Then he escorts me to the mess hall before trotting home. Some people have started looking at me strangely, but it's whatever. I'm so proud of my grumpy boy.

And biggest win of all—thanks to the boost from pop-up number two, Julia and I are crushing Carnegie Camp. We moved up the ranks from mid-twenties to ranks eleven and twelve, with Julia just above me. Cam is still number one, but Michelle is in the thirties, so I feel on top of the world. Everything is going fantastic.

Well. Almost everything. I still haven't gotten much chocolate. I keep longing to watch *Halloween* again, and I catch myself listening to BTS far too often. But slowly, I'm sure I'm getting it. I haven't stalked Sarah's Instagram in days. We take the wins where we can.

Julia enters the cabin while I shuffle note cards. I'm sitting on the floor, Reginald beside me. The desk feels like Julia's space for some reason, though she always cleans her books and notes off by the time I get up to run. I wave her over.

"Julia! Come study with me."

I expect a gruff no as usual, but Julia tosses her bag onto her bunk and sits across from me. "Okay."

I'm too stunned to speak. I did not think that would work. Julia smiles at my shocked expression.

"What? I can do group work sometimes." She nods to Reginald. "Helps when one party member can't talk."

That jump-starts my brain again. I have got to stop being so weird around her! "He can't speak, but he's the smartest one here."

"That's offensive to George, and you know it." Julia grabs the Snuggable she won, a black chicken, off the desk. And after a brief consideration, she grabs the brown chicken I won too. She puts them beside their full-sized cousin. "Henrietta doesn't have anything going on behind those glass eyes, I'm afraid."

"You're not supposed to say it out loud," I whisper, and my heart flutters pitifully when Julia lets out a genuine laugh. I can't believe we're close enough to talk like this now. Three weeks ago, she would have bitten my head off. And now we have inside jokes, and she's willing to sit on the floor to study with me. Unreal.

Julia smiles down at my scattered note cards. "SAT?"

"Yeah. I already know most of it, but it's a warm-up."

Julia holds up a card, hiding the back from me. "Define *acumen*."

I get it right, and the next five. We swap, and Julia gets hers right too. We get excited as we rack up the right answers until we have no more cards left.

"We're getting a sixteen hundred, easy," I say as I pack up my cards.

Julia chuckles. "You might. The math portion always kills me."

"I can help! I'm good at math."

"I don't think I've ever heard a gay person say that."

I snort out a laugh, and Julia smiles again. I fake bow, my heart fluttering meekly in my chest. Surely it's not too much to enjoy this? It can't be against the rules to simply enjoy Julia's company. "I contain multitudes."

Julia rocks back on her hands. She looks at me for a few seconds, and I get nervous. Did I ruin our moment somehow?

"Can I ask you something?"

I nod, a little afraid of what she'll say.

"You mentioned you learned to cook when your mom traveled for work. Did you teach yourself?"

I nod, relieved. This is a question I'm not afraid of answering. "Yeah. My best friend helped—she's way better at it than me. I don't really enjoy cooking, but I can do it in a pinch. And it's useful at weird Life Skills camps, I guess."

Julia smiles. "But you're good at all the life skills. Everyone's struggling except for you."

"And Cam."

Julia's eyes narrow. "Yes, and Cam. But this isn't about them. How'd you get so good at it?"

I reflect on the question for a moment before answering. "I guess it's just experience? My ex, Gabriel, had a panic attack when he blew a tire, so I had to figure out how to change it by myself. And Ashley got me into parties, but I'm usually the drunk mom, so I know how to do first aid." I laugh at the memories. "Honestly, a lot of them taught me shit I don't care about, but my brain holds on to them for some reason. I can tell you all about bonsai tree cutting, if you want."

Julia shakes her head. "No, thank you." She's quiet for a second, dark eyes studying my face. "Seems like you date interesting people."

I don't know about that. Peter was in a band, which was kind of cool, but he wasn't what I would call interesting. Same with Ashley, Gabriel, Natalie. They were just . . . normal. But they were all passionate, which I liked. I wanted to be passionate about something too, I guess.

"Maybe it's more that everyone has something to love about them."

Julia seems incredulous. "I don't think that's true."

"It is! Like when you think about it, everyone you meet has unique experiences and a life you've never lived. And they all have good things about them." Sometimes so good, it's hard to see the bad.

"Even psychopath Ashley?"

"She had the prettiest, waviest hair," I answer immediately.

Ashley, as I crushed on her from the beginning, pops into my mind as easily as the first day I met her.

"And she adored her cat, almost an unbelievable amount. She loved oranges, but only the kiddie kind that were easy to peel, and sketches before they turned into their final product, and horror movies, of course."

I hug my knees, the memory fading and turning sad. She loved a lot of things, but I wasn't one of them. I'm depressed now, but I smile at Julia anyway.

"We won't talk about the stabby part."

Julia studies my face again. She has an unreadable expression.

"You're good at that."

"At what?"

"You pay attention to people. And you remember things about them."

My ears burn with a sick combination of pleasure and embarrassment. No one's ever said that to me before! I hardly know what to say.

"It's not a big deal."

"It is," Julia insists. "You know that's why we won the pop-up, right? You noticed all the little things about people, people I'd never even seen before. I never would have looked at Amira's clothes or Ms. Flores's socks. But you did."

Now I'm so flattered, I'm sure I'll combust. I want to say something cool and intelligent, but all I can squeak out is a quick "Thanks."

Julia looks away, toward her hidden violin case under her bed. "I'm not like that. I don't pay attention at all. Half the time I feel like I'm drowning, so I don't have the patience."

I frown. What does she mean by drowning? I thought she was unfriendly at first, but she's not. Maybe she just has a lot going on. I don't want to push her, but I am curious.

"Is that why you won't go to dinner with me?"

Julia laughs, her gaze still on her violin. "I came here all business, you know? Before I knew about the top prize and the laptop, I had it in my mind that I wasn't here to make friends. I came here to work." Julia looks at me now, and her expression is sad. "This camp means a lot to me. I don't have a college fund. I don't even have a laptop that works, and I'm too broke to get a new one. I have this, my grades, and the SAT to get me a full ride. Anything less is . . ." Julia trails off, and I can practically see her shutting down.

Before I can lose my nerve, I inch closer so our tennis shoes are touching.

"Same here. I mean, changing my life is important too, but I don't have much scholarship money either. My parents try to hide it, but when I was in middle school, Dad lost his job and was out of work for a year. I know there's no savings left for me."

Julia looks up, and for a second, I feel like we're closer than we've ever been. I understand what she's saying, because it's my reality too. I try not to worry about it, because that won't change anything, but I get why it would affect her. And I get why she was so standoffish now. If Carnegie Camp is a job to her, then she can't afford to goof off with her roommate when she's on the clock.

"I'm glad I broke my rule, though." Julia's looking right at me. "Turns out, I study better in a group."

I beam back at her. "I told you! It's way more productive!"

Julia scoffs, but she's a lot more relaxed. Friendly. Somehow, I broke through the top layer of her armor. There are layers and layers to go, but I don't mind waiting until she's ready. I don't mind learning all of Julia's good parts, day by day.

"Do you want to go to dinner?" I ask after a moment.

"No," Julia answers immediately. But there's no annoyance, no bite.

"You're telling me you don't want to hang out with the queer cabin?"

"Fuck no." This time Julia laughs, and taps the top of my foot with hers.

Shivers snake up my entire body from the touch.

"You and the Snuggables are the only study group I need."

I'm tingly all over. I should be embarrassed at my failure, but I can't even focus on that right now. "You know I'll keep asking."

"I know." Julia picks up a note card and raises one eyebrow. "But for now, let's go over math. Then you can go eat."

"Aye, aye, captain."

Julia rolls her eyes, and I laugh, and we study together until nightfall.

CHAPTER 19

"Walter, you can't just follow me around everywhere. You have a camp to protect."

Walter yawns at my scolding, then curls up in a ball by my feet. I guess that's dog for *I don't care.*

I'm studying outside for a change; I discovered a pavilion that has a fan at the top! It's late evening, so most kids are doing fun camp stuff, but I have Finance flash cards. I can't neglect the other subjects just because I'm focusing hard on music and the SAT. After Julia and I changed a tire successfully (which Julia aced, I'm proud to say), we both moved up to ranks ten and eleven. We have to keep the momentum going, so studying instead of making s'mores it is.

Walter spotted me from a mile away and trotted over to visit. But now he won't leave, even though it's been over an hour. I hope Maxine doesn't get mad at me for accidentally kidnapping her dog. He's not doing a good job guarding the camp from robbers or whatever, but maybe it's fine.

I cycle through my cards, memorizing my own handwriting. *Bear market* has a tiny loop in the *t. Elasticity* has a gap between the *l* and *a* where my pencil slipped. I remember that first, then the word itself, then the definition. I don't know if that's how everyone studies, but it works for me. I pause, thinking of what Julia said. I guess I do this with people too. I see the small things, then the medium, and only at the end can I see the whole. Sometimes—most times, it feels like—the whole picture isn't a good one. But by that time, I'm in too deep and don't know how to let go. I frown at my cards. Maybe that's something else I need to work on before the end of the summer.

Walter gets to his feet. I look down, and he's staring to my right, posture stiff. I look up and into the bewildered face of Julia.

"Where the hell did you get a dog?"

I laugh and put down my note cards. "This is Walter. He's my best friend at the moment."

"I see." Julia steps closer, and Walter slinks beneath the table and behind my legs, then settles with his back to Julia. I meet my roommate's eyes, smiling sheepishly.

"He doesn't mean it. You can sit down, he won't bite."

"He's got teeth, doesn't he?" Still, Julia sits at the picnic table, as far away from Walter as possible. She eyes him uneasily, but he's still sulking under my feet. "When did you get him?"

"He's not mine, I swear. He's Maxine's security dog, and he runs with me every morning. He doesn't like that I'm out of bed." I push a bag of Cheetos I snagged from the mess hall toward her. "Here, feed him some of these. You'll be friends in no time!"

Julia looks doubtful, but she bends and offers Walter a puff. He ignores her at first, but when I point to Julia, he follows my finger and sees the cheesy snack. He takes it from Julia's fingers gently, then army crawls closer to her, cute triangle ears pricked.

"See? Told you."

Julia shakes her head and gives Walter another Cheeto. "I swear, every day it's something new with you. Who did you learn dog whispering from?"

"No one. I've never had a dog."

For some reason, this makes Julia laugh. It's a short one, and Julia even seems surprised she let it out. She quiets almost immediately and looks down at her lap. I wait for her to say something, but she doesn't. She just feeds Walter another Cheeto, moving slowly and carefully.

This is strange. Julia normally studies by herself at an unknown location, and then if I'm studying in the cabin when she gets back, she'll sometimes join me. But I'm not in the cabin. She had to deliberately look for me. I want to ask her about it, but she's tense and avoiding eye contact, so maybe now isn't the time.

I waffle for a minute but finally settle on: "I'm studying Finance. Do you want the cards I've already done?"

Julia shakes her head. "No, thanks. You go ahead, don't let me distract you."

"Okay. Just let me know." I keep studying, but really I'm pretending. I'm watching Julia out of the corner of my eye. She dutifully feeds Walter the entire bag of Cheetos, one by one. When it's empty, Walter licks the cheese dust from her fingers and puts his head in her lap. She strokes his head slowly, over and over, for at least ten minutes. Walter stays still, sighing in contentment occasionally, but not moving. I'm dying to ask Julia what's wrong, but I don't. I just cycle through my cards silently, waiting for her to reach out to me first.

After ten more minutes, Julia says, "Do you want to hear me play my violin?"

I jump to my feet. "Yes! Finally!"

Julia rolls her eyes, a ghost of a smile on her lips. "I changed my mind."

"Noooo," I whine. Julia pretends to be offended, but she's smiling her characteristic half smile.

"Fine, fine," she agrees after a minute of me begging. "Come on, let's go to the music room. The dog can come too, I guess."

I gather up my books and notes with lightning speed. Julia heads to the music building, and I follow, but Walter decides he's had enough of us at that point and trots toward home. I wave at him, but I can't focus on the dog. I'm so curious what's going on with Julia. I've done nothing but beg her to play for me, and now she's ready? Why now? I don't say anything as we get to the room and Julia unlocks her case. She withdraws a beautiful, polished wood violin and a . . . stick? Whatever the thing is called to play it.

"It's so pretty," I say, kind of dazzled. It's clear she takes good care of it; the rich mahogany wood is polished, and there's not a single scratch on it anywhere.

Julia waves me off. "Go sit over there."

I follow her instruction and sit in a chair a few feet away. Julia messes with the instrument for a bit, tugging at the strings and examining the stick. Then she lifts the violin and tucks it under her chin. She closes her eyes and touches the stick to the delicate strings.

And she plays.

I can't move for an entire three minutes. I'm enraptured by the haunting sound, the swell and ebb and flow of the music. It's fast and furious in places, slow and haunting in others. But as beautiful as the music is, Julia is even more so. She's completely lost in the sound, her face smooth and worry-free, only a slight wrinkle between her brows as she concentrates. Her movements are fluid, even though her fingers dance over the strings with speed and complicated rhythm. I can't name the song or the key, but the sheer emotion from Julia and her instrument brings tears to my eyes. I've been to band practices and concerts, but this concert, personal and just for me, is one of the best experiences I've ever had.

Julia draws the stick across the violin's strings one more time, and a long note fills the room. She lowers the stick and violin, then opens her eyes. I stand up and cheer like I'm at a football game. I don't even care how stupid I look—Julia is so fucking cool and amazing and talented, and she deserves to know it.

"Stop, stop." Julia looks embarrassed, but pleased too.

"That was incredible!" I run to her side and start to give her a huge hug, but I stop myself just in time. She'd probably murder me.

"I messed up in a few places," Julia says.

"Luckily for you, I'm a musical idiot. It sounded perfect to me."

That gets Julia to finally grin at me. "You're great for my ego, you know that?"

"I try, I try."

Julia chuckles and puts her violin away. She hesitates before adding the stick to the case. "I play best when I'm sad. I didn't want to miss an opportunity to show off."

My euphoria dampens immediately. I know I shouldn't ask, but I think now's the time. She wouldn't have played for me if she wasn't ready to talk, at least a little. "Did something happen?"

Julia closes the violin case and snaps the locks closed. She traces one of the stickers on it, one I recognize as some sort of Pokémon. "Remember when I said I didn't have a college fund?"

"Yes."

"Well, it's not because my parents can't pay. They don't want to pay." Julia closes her eyes. "They don't believe in college, and they want me to work at their businesses when I graduate. My brother did, and he makes good money, but I don't want that. I want to be an architect."

Julia takes a shuddering breath, still not looking at me. "They're throwing an absolute fit because I'm here. I guess they thought I was bluffing? Which is stupid because when have I ever, but anyway. I'm here, and not working at their car wash for free, and they're mad as hell because they didn't hire anyone to cover me for the summer. They called to scream at me an hour ago." Julia rubs her eyes wearily and finally looks at me. Her expression breaks my heart—confused, vulnerable, deeply sad. "I'm just so tired. I know this is what I have to do to get where I want to be, but it's like . . . why does everyone have to make it so hard for me?"

I desperately want to give Julia a hug. I don't know much about her exact situation, but I've seen the damage parents can do. Nav's mom left her family, and I watched my best friend fall apart. Sarah's parents are kind, but they're forgetful and never around. They forgot her birthday last year and have been groveling ever since. And as much as I love my parents, they're not perfect. Mom's fierce judgment and inability to ever be satisfied hurt me more than I'd like to admit.

But Julia won't want a hug. She opened up to me for the first time, and maybe that means she can trust me. At least with this. I can at least be someone who doesn't make things harder.

"Okay, first of all, your parents are unbelievably shitty."

Julia's sadness seems to lift a little. "Agreed there."

"Second, why didn't I know you wanted to be an architect? That's cool as hell."

Julia's smile gets a little wider. It's working! Last one . . .

"Third, you are crushing this camp, and you've won so many prizes already. You're smart, and you deserve all the good things. Plus, there are so many other scholarships out there! And I mean, I'm sure you'll still get an excellent scholarship here for second place."

Julia quirks a brow. Her expression is almost back to normal, but not nearly as detached and cold. She almost looks like she's having fun. "Second?"

"I'll be in first place, of course. To get my medal."

Julia rolls her eyes, but she's smiling, a real, genuine one that lights up her face. I smile too, taken in by her strength and beauty and all things Julia. Julia, who was holding in something so heavy for so long and allowed me to share the weight for just a little while. I'm so happy, so honored, I want to cry.

"Yeah, right," Julia says. "What's the make and model of my violin?"

"How should I know?" I complain. "I don't even know what the stick is called."

Julia bursts into shocked laughter, and I join her. When she catches her breath, she says, "It's a *bow*. Good Lord, forget second place, you're not staying in the top ten with that knowledge. Let's practice."

I complain some more, but as Julia grills me on music terms, plays notes on the piano for me to name, points out the notes on sheet music, I can't help but look at her the whole time. Because the entire lesson, she's smiling.

CHAPTER 20

I hold the cool chocolate bar in my hand before bed. I'm manifesting progress. I'm borrowing power from the universe. *I will eat you, chocolate. I will earn the right soon.*

Julia is studying at the desk, valiantly ignoring my meditation, but I still feel awkward about it. I sit the bar on top of the fridge while I go change into my pajamas. I read about speaking with intention, but so far, I don't think it's working.

When I get out of the bathroom, Julia leans back in her chair to face me. "Don't forget to start studying art tomorrow."

"Please, you'll give me bad dreams." We're moving on from music, which is a relief, but I'm still scared of what's ahead. I can't even draw a decent circle! Meanwhile Julia isn't only good at music but also art too. She has so many talents. "Weird question, but are you going for music or art in addition to being an architect?"

"I'm going to be Watson, like I said," she says easily. We both laugh, and I'm rosy all over. Julia sits up straight in her chair after the moment passes. "But no, neither. Architecture is no joke. I won't have time."

That makes me sad. She's so good at playing her violin! And if she drew the stickers on her violin case, she's an excellent artist too. "You could minor in it. You're just so talented, I'd hate for you not to get to do what you love."

"Art doesn't make that much money." Julia seems sad when she says it. "I have to focus on what will make a living."

"Maybe, but surely there's time for art too? You should do what makes you happy." I glance at my anti–Jung Kook poster and turn away. "Or whatever. What do I know?"

Julia seems pensive for a second, but her expression quickly turns serious again. "That's Future Me's problem. I have to live through this first."

"We'll do it! I'll study art tomorrow, and you start on swimming safety, okay?"

Julia sighs but gives me a thumbs-up. I climb onto my bunk, grinning to myself. I hug Reginald, and it takes no time at all for me to fall asleep, dreaming about architect detectives who can somehow play the violin.

* * *

I wake up with a start. I freeze, confused. I'm in my bunk, facing the wall. The tail end of the vision board is in front of my eyes. I was asleep, I think? Something woke me up.

I jump again when my phone rings. My phone . . . someone's calling me. I roll over, and I'm wide awake when I see two things: It's 11:30 p.m., and Nav's picture is lit up on my home screen.

I sit up in bed and answer in one motion. "Nav? You okay?"

"Did I wake you up?" Nav's voice is uncharacteristically soft. It also sounds strained and not at all like her usual cheerful self.

"No, I'm good. But hang on a second."

I glance down and meet Julia's eyes. She's sitting at the desk, frowning, headphones around her neck. I wave at her and scramble down my bunk. I shove my feet into my tennis shoes without socks and hurry outside. I'm met with unbearable heat right away. I barely notice it.

"Okay, back. What's going on?"

Nav is quiet for a second. Then she says, "I just needed to talk to someone. You're sure it's okay?"

"Yeah, of course!" I've only been asleep for thirty minutes, so I'm not tired. I adjust my feet in my shoes (ugh, blisters here we come) and head to the track. "What do you want to talk about? How's work? I won a chicken in a tournament."

"What?" Nav laughs, and she sounds a little more like herself. "A real chicken?"

"Thankfully, no. Though I wouldn't put it past Ms. Flores to add animal handling to the curriculum."

"God, don't I know it. She made me sign up for swimming lessons. Can you believe that?"

I grin at the star-studded sky. "Yeah, I definitely can."

"And she never lets me keep the door closed when I'm at her house."

"Cruel," I say, barely containing my laugh. I pass the s'more station, and I'm stunned to see a few kids there! Amira's by the fire, gesturing at three boys to hurry up. They're all laughing and having a good time. Ms. Flores would be proud. I hurry by before Amira can see me and scold me for being out of bed so late. "At least she isn't like Gabriel's mom."

"Eww, don't remind me." Nav groans.

Gabriel's mom was a self-proclaimed "cool mom" and offered to give us beer as long as we stayed at his house. Once, she cornered me and gave me a box of condoms and a disturbingly in-depth lecture on her son's sex life. Gabriel and I broke up shortly after that.

"Speaking of—how's it going with Julia?"

I'd love to talk about Julia and how cute she is when she smiles and how good it felt to win the pop-up together instead of individually, but if we get started on that, Nav will never talk about her thing. And she wouldn't have called if it wasn't important.

"Let's talk about you instead."

Nav takes a deep breath, and I know the preamble is over. Luckily, I've reached the track, so we won't be interrupted. I start my trek around the worn oval.

"So you know the family reunion we used to go to?"

I do. It used to be a big deal; all of Nav's extended family would cram into her grandma's shoebox house for three days of food and games and fun. I used to look forward to it every year, because they were loose with the guest list and my family was considered hers . . . at the time. When her mom left, the reunions stopped. Nav hasn't been in three years, and neither have I.

"Yeah."

"It's next week." Nav takes a weak breath. "And I think I should go."

I pause in my walk, surprise rooting me to the spot. That's a big deal for Nav. It's technically her dad's side of the family, but she always said it didn't feel the same without her mom there. "That's a big step."

"I know. I'm sick about it." Nav sighs heavily in my ear. "I really wish you were here so you could go with me."

I start walking again to distract myself from the pain in my chest.

"I wish I was there too. I would kill for your grandma's banana pudding."

"So you were just friends with me for the pudding? I knew it." Nav laughs, but it still has a tinge of sadness.

"Of course! But listen, don't go alone. Maybe you can take Gia." As bad as I hate the idea of potentially being replaced, Nav needs this. She needs some support, and I'm not there to give it to her. I may be a jealous, horrible person, but I love Nav more than anything. I can't bring myself to be upset about this.

"I asked her already. And she said yes."

"Then . . . ?"

I hear Nav fidgeting on her end. I pass the guard station, and an alarmed Walter lifts his head and hustles to my side to huff disapprovingly. I pet him adoringly while I wait.

Finally, Nav speaks. Her voice is so soft I can barely hear her. "What if she's there?"

"Oh, Nav." We never talk about what happened with her mom. It was so sudden, and we were all blindsided. I used to call that woman Aunt Nicole. I never saw her unhappy. And one day, she just decided she was tired of being a wife and a mother, and she just packed her stuff and disappeared. I'll never understand it. And I'll never forgive her for what she's done to my best friend. Nav changed after her mom left. She became more closed off to everyone except for me. She started filling her life with flings and drinking too much. She stopped studying and just gave up. I supported her through it all and would do it all over again if I had to. But hot anger curls around my ribs at the thought. Just when Nav's finally a tiny bit happier, the mere thought of her mom is enough to bring her to tears.

"She won't be there," I assure Nav. I know because she's too selfish. Too much of a coward. "And if she does have the nerve to show her face, you have my permission to fistfight her."

Nav laughs. It's a lighter one, thankfully. "I wish I could."

"You should! But seriously, if she's there, you just grab Gia and Uncle David and get out of there. She doesn't get to upend your life twice."

"Yeah," Nav says tentatively, like she's struggling to believe it. "You're right. I haven't seen my family in years because of her, and that sucks."

"Hell yeah it sucks! You deserve to eat your banana pudding in peace."

"It always comes back to the pudding, huh?" Nav laughs again, and this time it's genuine. Almost back to normal. "Thanks for talking me down. I felt like I was having a heart attack or something. My chest was really hurting, and I wanted to cry."

I start walking again. Walter follows me, grunting his displeasure. He'll start herding me toward Cabin 11 soon, I feel it. "Sounds like a panic attack. Have you talked to your therapist about her yet?"

"No. It feels like . . . too much. Does that make sense?"

"Yeah, I get it." I think over her words before I speak. "Is that why you called me instead of Gia?"

"Yeah," Nav says. "Is that bad? I like Gia a lot. Like a *lot*, Hallie."

I smile to the ground. "I know."

"But this feels like a lot to spring on her. What if she decides I'm too damaged to date?"

"Nav, stop saying stupid shit. Gia would never think that, and you know it."

"Fine," Nav grumbles. "I'm insecure, okay? And I guess I knew that you'd make me feel better."

Walter licks my bare calf and nudges me toward the cabins. I scratch behind his ears, trying to pick apart how happy and cripplingly sad that makes me. How I'm fiercely proud of her for facing this horrible hard thing. How I'm devastated I'm not there to help her do it. How, soon, she may turn to Gia instead of me, and I'll be well and truly alone.

I don't say any of that to Nav. I can't. Instead, I say, "I'm here for you, Nav. Any time, whatever you need. Always." And I mean every word.

"I'm sorry for all this. I feel like such a baby." Nav doesn't sound sorry or guilty at all, so I know she's feeling better. "How's the camp? Tell me about the free chicken."

I tell Nav about the scavenger hunt, and she's practically cheering when I'm through.

"Yes! I knew you'd kill it. Also fuck Cam, though, for real."

"No, they didn't mean anything by it. Everyone is just so weird and paranoid about the points."

"And they didn't get any for not believing in you! Serves them right." Nav pauses, and I just know whatever she says next is gonna piss me off. "Sounds like Julia was real protective of you then."

"No! Don't start." I knew it! "Julia doesn't like me." She did say that she would be my Watson, not once but twice . . . "We're not even friends. Julia said so."

"Uh huh." Nav sounds like she definitely doesn't believe me. "I still don't really get your rules thing. You don't need changing, Hallie."

"I do," I insist. "And I'm doing it. Don't try to convince me."

"All right," Nav says, still laughing. "Help me out for a second: Do you think we should ditch the ice cream and only sell baked goods at Sweet Teeth?"

We talk about Nav's new job until we're both laughing and delirious and I can tell Nav is all right. I let Walter herd me toward home as I say goodbye.

"Thanks again, Hal," Nav says.

"You're welcome. You can call me if the reunion gets to be too much, okay?"

"Okay." Nav yawns in my ear. "God, work is gonna suck tomorrow."

As will SAT prep . . . I grimace at my phone proudly declaring that it's 2:02 a.m. But that's a problem for In-a-Few-Hours Hallie. Cabin 11 comes into view. "Night, Nav."

"Night. Love ya, babe."

I smile into my phone. "Love you too."

I hang up and rub Walter's ears. "And I love you, you excellent boy. Go guard the camp in peace."

Walter huffs at me and then stalks toward home. I enter my cabin, drained but feeling oddly calm.

I'm surprised when Julia turns her head when I walk in.

She's still awake? Did she wait up for me? My heart pounds pathetically against my ribs.

"Everything okay?" Julia asks.

"Yeah, sorry, my best friend was having a tough time. I feel bad I made you wait for me!"

"You didn't make me wait," Julia says, her characteristic half smile curling her lips. "I'm up at this time every night."

"Well, no wonder I have to wake you up for SAT prep!"

Julia's grin widens while I laugh. I'm more than a little delirious. I need sleep, bad. I climb into my bunk and collapse face down on the bed. I should have washed my face at least, but I'm exhausted. Five o'clock comes early.

"Is your friend okay?" Julia's voice floats to my ears.

I replay the conversation in my head. How Nav was brave and talked through her panic attack. How she admitted she needed support and got it. How we're finally able to talk about her mom for the first time in over three years. "She will be."

Julia is quiet for so long that I start to doze off. But then she says, her voice soft and sincere, "You're a good friend."

My brain helpfully reminds me that I was just viciously jealous of my friend going to face her fears without me and I sigh. "I'm trying to be. I'd like to be better. Like everything else."

"Shut up," Julia says, but there's an affectionate edge to it. "Go to sleep."

I mumble out a reply, but in seconds, I'm in dreamland where I belong.

CHAPTER 21

I'm eating an entire chocolate cake. I don't have a fork; I'm just shoveling the rich sweetness into my mouth with both hands. It's fucking delicious. Jung Kook has an affectionate hand on my shoulder, but I shake him off so I can eat more cake. For some reason, the entire basketball team is cheering me on. *Hallie, Hallie . . .*

"Hallie?"

My eyes pop open. I blink in confusion. Julia's standing under my bunk, expression anxious. Her braids are flat on one side, and she's in her pajamas. Oh—a beach-themed tank top and shorts with pastel Easter eggs on them. Cute!

"Hallie, wake up."

"I'm awake," I mumble, though I'm not. I'm halfway back to my cake buffet. God, I'm exhausted.

Julia stands on her bunk and pats my cheek. My body immediately shivers in confused, embarrassed delight. I'm wide awake now.

"I'm serious. You overslept—it's after eight thirty."

I sit bolt upright. "Please tell me you're joking."

Julia's face is grim. "Wish I was."

Shit, shit, shit—I stayed up too late! I know when I go to sleep past eleven I'm in trouble! Why the hell didn't I set an alarm?! I scramble off my bunk, and Julia shoves clothes into my hands.

"These are yesterday's—"

"No time," Julia urges. She has her own wad of clothes under one arm. "We can make it if we hurry, but sacrifices have to be made."

I follow Julia's instructions, in a blind panic. I *hate* being late for anything, especially school. I have a strict sleeping schedule for a reason! I groan and tear off my pajamas and tug on yesterday's stale, grimy clothes at top speed. I tie my tennis shoes, and Julia's already dressed and shoving books into her bag. I try to go to the bathroom, but Julia snags the tail of my shirt.

"No time. You can pee after class."

"But my teeth—"

"I have gum." Julia grimaces. "Sorry, emergency measures."

I want to cry. I'm in yesterday's clothes *and* I'll have bad breath? But it's better than being late. I jam my notebook into my backpack and meet Julia at the door. We don't speak—just run at top speed to the SAT building. Everyone's already seated when we get there, but Mr. Lin isn't here yet. I take my seat beside Caroline, wheezing, and I'm surprised when Julia follows me to the back and sits beside me. Caroline looks at us like we're nuts.

"Overslept," I manage.

Julia passes me a piece of gum, and I shove it into my mouth. A lot worse than dream cake, I'll tell you that much.

"Not bad," Julia says as Mr. Lin walks in. "Eight fifty-nine."

My laugh has a hysterical edge to it as the adrenaline fades and other emotions creep in. Shame, from not waking up on time. A tender sort of happiness that Julia not only woke me but also helped me get ready and not be late. And she woke up by herself! I'm so happy and proud, the shame doesn't bother me as much as it should.

Caroline leans forward, clearly curious. "This is the first time you're sitting with us! Is this a permanent thing?"

Julia's expression changes alarmingly fast. From smug victory to disinterested and mildly hostile in seconds. "We'll see." Then she opens her book and starts taking notes, even though Mr. Lin hasn't said anything yet.

I smile at Caroline, but I'm still feeling proud. At least Julia didn't ignore her. "She is, and today she saved my life."

Julia doesn't say anything, but I see the ghost of a smile on her lips. Mr. Lin starts class, and we take notes, Julia's arm brushing against mine every so often.

* * *

A new Life Skills counselor, Mrs. Yarrow, claps her hands. She's a short Asian lady with salt-and-pepper hair, and she's wearing the cutest beige vest against a dark green shirt. She looks like she's ready to wrangle some unruly wildlife. "Okay, campers! Let's do some wilderness training."

Julia grimaces at me. "I'm about to be shit at this too."

I don't answer because I'm feeling deep dread in the bottom of my stomach. I've finally found something in Life Skills I can't do.

I thought the day would get better after SAT prep, but I

didn't have time to go back to the cabin and change clothes, or brush my teeth before Life Skills. I had to choose between a shower and class, and class (obviously) won. I rub my tongue over my fuzzy teeth. But at what cost?

I was so embarrassed on the walk over when our conversation was drowned out by my grumbling stomach. Julia passed me a granola bar out of pity, but I'm still starving. And my whole body feels off—itchy from the old clothes, tingly from Julia being nice to me, achy from my legs wanting to run. I miss Walter too. I'm having a bad day.

And it's about to get worse, because I can confidently say I've never been into wilderness anything. I've gone on a total of two hikes, both of which ended in disaster, so I can't help Julia here. I like taking walks in my neighborhood when the weather's nice, but that's the extent of it. I don't think I could start a fire if someone put a gun to my head.

Mrs. Yarrow passes out maps to everyone. I glance over mine and feel sick. I have no clue how to read this.

"You'll read this map and try to reach the marked area! It's a beautiful waterfall; you'll love it."

Okay, sure, makes sense. If I could read a map, this would be easy. Everyone around me is muttering, but they look as equally confused. Even Cam is frowning fiercely at their map.

"Try to get there in one hour. Please pair up in groups of two or three. I know you lone wolves love your points, but it's a safety issue."

Julia leans close to me. "Do you know how to read this?"

"Umm . . . sort of?" I'm lying, but I don't want to let Julia down. I'm irrationally scared she'll leave me to pair up with Cam or someone else. Just what I need, now that Nav is going to the reunion with Gia . . . God, I hate living in my brain.

Julia doesn't say anything, but she seems determined. Maybe I'm reading too much into it. We're smart! We won a whole pop-up together! We can figure this out.

Mrs. Yarrow checks everyone's groups, then allows the first pair to go into the woods. We wait for five minutes before she allows the next pair. A way to prevent us from cheating, I guess. Julia and I are the fifth to go in. I feel an immediate dread as Mrs. Yarrow's grinning face disappears into the gloom of the dense trees.

"Okay, now what?" Julia says.

I study the map. It's a mess of red and yellow and tan lines, with some markings like *big tree!* and *small pond!* I hate it here. Ms. Flores is getting an earful after I'm done with camp.

"I think we look for this, uh . . . goldfish rock?" Allegedly it's straight ahead, but I'm not sure. There's no path, but there are three different sets of footprints leading in three wildly differ-ent directions. Everyone is just as confused as we are.

Julia nods. "I think we go straight, then curve to the right."

Who am I to argue? We head the way Julia points, passing lots of trees, dead logs, a lizard, but no rock that looks like a goldfish.

"Did you go camping with your family?" Julia asks.

"No. Never. We're city people."

"Same." Julia frowns fiercely at the map. "I wasn't even a Girl Scout."

"I was, but it was only for the cookies."

Julia looks up at me, an amused smile on her lips. "They're not even that good."

"Blasphemy! Samoas are God's gift to mankind."

"Eww, coconut?" Julia shakes her head. "You think you know a person."

"Same to you! I can't believe you don't like—"

I cut myself off as I notice a smooth gray surface below me. We somehow hiked uphill, on an embankment, but I think we found it. I point to it excitedly. "The rock! We did it!"

Julia peers over the hill and grins. "Fuck yeah, we're so good at this."

"Okay, now we go forward to the 'big tree.' Real helpful, Yarrow."

I wait for Julia to reply, but she's staring at something behind me. I follow her line of sight, and there's a rustling in the bushes, headed toward us. And it's not a squirrel—it's something big.

"Did one of your exes teach you how to fight off a bear?" Julia's tone is joking, but her tense posture is not.

"It's not a bear. There are no bears in Alabama." I'm fairly sure that's true. . . . But whatever it is, it's coming fast. "Probably a wild hog or something."

"A pig?!" Now Julia's voice is high-pitched with fear. "Do you know how to fight a pig?!"

I don't get a chance to answer. Something big, with a short snout, and black glistening fur pokes its head out of the underbrush.

It's a fucking bear.

"Run!" I scream at Julia.

She bolts without a second's hesitation, and I take off after her. But my left foot slips, and suddenly I'm sliding down, down off the embankment. Julia screams, and I tumble over the hill to the rock below.

I blink up at the blue sky, in shock. Am I dead? No, I think I'm okay . . . I'm not hurt, but I'm definitely muddy. Julia's face appears above me, her expression anxious.

"Are you alive?"

"I'm fine—the bear! Get out of here!"

"Heroic, but it's fine." Julia looks over her shoulder, and then another familiar face pops into view.

Walter, with all his shiny black fur and short snout, whines when he sees me. I almost start laughing. He probably came to find me because I missed my morning run. God, I feel like such an idiot.

"Are you sure you're okay?" Julia calls. "Nothing broken?"

I take a mental assessment. My butt's starting to hurt, but everything else is fine. There's water on my neck, though, so I must have landed on my water bottle. Ugh, I loved that one! I touch my neck, sighing. "I think I broke my water bottle. It was so cute too . . ."

Julia doesn't say anything. She just looks at me, eyes wide in shock. What? I bring my hand away from my neck, puzzled, and my palm is bright red.

I love horror movies. I love watching supernatural killers pounce on their unsuspecting prey. I even like medical shows like *Grey's Anatomy*. But the real thing? Seeing *my* blood that should definitely be inside my body and not on my hand? No way.

My head tips back as my brain protests being conscious to

see this anymore. But someone catches me, and Julia's suddenly right by my side, holding the back of my head.

"I'm dying," I whimper.

"You're not dying." Julia's tone is simple and certain. "It's just a scratch."

"Scratches don't bleed this much!" I know I'm hyperventilating, but I can't stop. I don't want to die, I haven't changed, I didn't get any chocolate, I don't even have a will yet—

"Breathe," Julia says. "Head wounds bleed a lot, that's all. I promise, it's just a scratch."

Walter licks my hand, which leaves a horrible mix of blood and saliva on me. I start panicking more, and Walter lets out a mournful howl.

"Even the dog thinks I'm dying!"

"He's upset because you're upset." Julia presses her hand more firmly to the back of my head. What I now know is blood creeps down my neck, mixing with sweat and mud.

"I'm gonna throw up." As soon as I say it, I feel bile rising to the top of my throat. My mouth waters ominously. "I'm gonna throw up and then pass out and then die."

"You're doing none of those things." Julia's voice is so sure it beats back the intense nausea. "I'm gonna tie something on your head, okay? And then I'll get Yarrow."

"Okay." I'm in tears, but I manage to hold the granola bar in my stomach as Julia searches in her bag to find a bandanna and ties it around my forehead. The blood isn't cascading down my back anymore, so maybe it's working? Or maybe I'm losing sensation in my body as it prepares to shut down.

Walter keeps howling, a lone requiem to the sky.

"Please take care of Reginald," I tell Julia. "And Walter. Maxine won't give him Cheetos."

"You're so dramatic." Somehow, Julia is laughing. Even as she moves forward and both her hands are stained with my blood. She casually wipes it on her shorts, leaving horrible rusty stains in large streaks.

"I'm so sorry about your clothes."

Julia grins at me. "Nothing a visit to the laundry basement can't fix."

I consider confessing my love to her right now.

"I'm going to get Yarrow. Stay with the dog, stay awake, keep breathing. You're gonna be fine."

"But what if you get lost?" My breath hitches in my chest. The panic attack is over, but now I'm feeling the steady throb in my head as my blood leaks out of my body.

"We didn't go that far. I can—"

But Julia doesn't get to finish her sentence. Because Mrs. Yarrow, Maxine, and another counselor appear on the embankment. Maxine gasps, Walter stops howling, and Julia sighs in relief. I wave meekly to the adults above, trying to ignore my hand stained with blood.

"I think I need to go to the nurse."

CHAPTER 22

I don't think I've done anything more embarrassing than this in my whole life. The time I misspelled *amicable* in the seventh-grade spelling bee and everyone laughed? Nope. The time I was up for the game-winning shot and tripped over my untied shoelaces, whiffing the ball completely and dooming us to over-time? Not even close. Being paraded in front of dozens of other gawking kids while looking like I'm the final girl in a slasher is the worst. *And* they make Julia go back to the cabin and Walter with Maxine, so I'm alone in the nurse's office while Barbara the nurse picks gravel out of the back of my head.

"How is it?" Ms. Flores asks. She's here too, holding my hand, which is extra mortifying. A millionaire reduced to babysitting a girl who thought a dog was a bear. I want to curl up and die.

The nurse pauses. "She needs stitches. She'll have to go to the hospital."

Ms. Flores gasps louder than I do. "The hospital! Please say you're joking."

Barbara glares at Ms. Flores. "Why would I joke about that? I don't mind patching her up, but I ain't a miracle worker. Take her to a doctor."

Ms. Flores paces in a tight circle, muttering in Spanish under her breath. She looks so scared and panicked, and it's all my fault. Now I want to burst into tears!

"I'm so sorry, Ms. Flores, I—"

Ms. Flores blinks at me, then closes her eyes and takes a breath. When she opens them again, her expression is calm and kind. "Nonsense! Everything will be okay, Hallie." Ms. Flores looks at the nurse, her eyebrows scrunched together. "You patch her up best you can, Barbara, I'll get the car ready. I've already called her parents, so I'll update them on where we're going."

Ms. Flores hurries away like a woman on a mission. I sit silently while Barbara ties a fresh bandage around my head to keep my brain matter inside my skull, I don't know. I have a vicious headache now, which also sucks. Mom is going to have a fit. Dad too, but for different reasons. Mom will be disappointed in me, and Dad will think I'm dying. They'll probably make a scene, and I'll have to be embarrassed by *that*. I sink lower in my chair, and Barbara scolds me for obstructing her view.

Ms. Flores comes back and waves me toward the door. "Come on, Hallie, we'll go to urgent care so we won't have to wait."

"Thank you," I tell Barbara.

She smiles and pats my back but doesn't reply. I shuffle out of the office and into the bright, punishing heat. Ms. Flores leads me to her Mercedes and buckles me into the front seat like I'm two years old, and then we're off to urgent care.

"I'm sorry," I tell her again. I don't know if I can ever apologize enough. I can't keep doing this. I keep fucking up in everything, even Life Skills, which I'm supposed to be good at. I'm so ashamed. I want to disappear.

"Don't be! Accidents happen." So she says, but she's biting her pinky nail anxiously. Ms. Flores glances at me. "Any pain? Do you feel faint? I have some water."

"I'm fine," I assure her, though I do feel faint. And my head is killing me. "Is Julia okay? And Walter?"

"They're fine. I should promote the dog to a rescue animal, though."

I smile at the idea. "He's not friendly enough."

"Touché." Ms. Flores drives in silence for a few minutes. The radio plays a pop hit I barely recognize. My head throbs in time with the bass. I pick out the high part, the soprano, which surprises me. Before camp, I didn't even know what that meant. And it makes me think of Julia and how lame I must look to her now. I said I'd help her in Life Skills, and all I did was ruin her clothes and rob her of her points.

"You still okay?" Ms. Flores asks.

"Yes, ma'am." It's the biggest lie I've ever told.

"You got quiet on me! You have to stay conscious in case you have a concussion. Let's chat."

"Okay." I wish I could just go to sleep, but that's probably the opposite of what someone with a concussion should do. It would be my luck to actually have one, and since my luck so far has been shit, I better stay awake.

"Gia told me Nav invited her to go to a family reunion." Ms. Flores seems happy, if a little confused. "I'm so happy Gia is being more social, but don't you think they're moving fast?"

"U-Hauling isn't a lesbian stereotype for nothing," I say, and then immediately regret it. Why did I say that?! I have *got* to have brain damage.

"What's U-Hauling?" Ms. Flores asks, and then I have to explain a part of lesbian culture to my best friend's girlfriend's millionaire mom. Someone kill me.

But Ms. Flores seems amused by the idea. "I don't think marriage is in the cards just yet, but I do think Gia's happy. She's been so down about moving around, and now it seems she's found someone who gets her. As a mom, that's all you want for your children at the end of the day. To be happy."

I nod, which makes the world swim a bit, but I'm not in a good mood. Thanks for reminding me that my terrible love life probably makes my mom sad too!

"We're here!" Ms. Flores says suddenly. I look up from my pit of despair to see a squat, square medical building surrounded by a shopping mall. At least I can get Panera afterward. If I'm not dead.

Ms. Flores gets out, and I clumsily unbuckle my seat belt. She opens my door for me and smiles. "Your parents are on their way, so we'll just get you in and get paperwork started. Okay?"

"Okay. Thanks, and sorry again."

"No problem at all. This is part of my job! Can't leave campers bleeding from the head. They'll never let me come back." Ms. Flores winks, and that makes me feel a little better. At least she doesn't seem too upset about my colossal mistake.

Ms. Flores escorts me to the door, one arm protectively on my back. She makes me sit down next to a sniffly kid and her mom, who is looking at me with abject horror. Oh yeah, my shirt . . . the collar of it has dried into a disgusting patch of reddish brown. I don't want to know what the back looks like. I give her a weak smile.

"It's okay. Head wounds bleed a lot."

She grabs her kid and sits on the other end of the lobby.

Soon, I'm in a tiny exam room, Ms. Flores beside me. We

have to wait for what feels like forever, but I'm comforted by Ms. Flores's steady hand on my shoulder. I can tell she's nervous, but her hand doesn't waver. I take deep breaths to calm myself. If Ms. Flores can be calm, I can too.

A white, balding doctor with friendly-looking bushy eyebrows enters the room. He glances at the chart, then at me. "What happened?"

Before I can say anything, Ms. Flores explains my injury. When she's done, she looks at me guiltily. "Sorry, I should have let Hallie explain."

"No, it's okay." I'm too tired to talk. I just want to go back to my bunk and check on Julia and then pass out.

The doctor examines my wound. His gloved hands feel strange against my hair and tender scalp. "Bumped yourself good, huh?"

"Yeah," I mumble. Ms. Flores squeezes my hand encouragingly.

He pokes around in my wound a little more, and when I flinch, he backs away. "Definitely need stitches, but it's a shallow gash. You'll be fine soon, I promise."

That's when Mom and Dad burst into the room. Both look panicked and are breathing hard. Mom takes one look at me, rounds on Ms. Flores, and says, "I'm suing you for all you're worth."

Okay, not a great start.

"Mom, please," I beg. "It's my fault. I slipped and fell, that's all."

"Hallie, look at you." Dad is close to tears. He comes to my side and wraps me in a huge hug. I lean against his chest, and I'm a little kid again, huddled in Dad's arms after I skinned my knee playing outside. Now I'm close to tears too.

"All this blood, it can't be good. We should be at a hospital!"

"She just needs a few stitches," the doctor says. "It looks much worse than it is."

"Says who?!" Mom is so outraged she's shaking.

"Says the doctor," I point out, my voice muffled by Dad's embrace. I reluctantly push away from him so Mom will take me seriously. "Please, you guys are embarrassing me."

That gets Mom to shut up. She always used that line on me when I was little, so it feels a little good to use it now. Dad is still weepy, patting my shoulder and holding my hand. Ms. Flores doesn't say anything, just watching the scene serenely from the corner of the room.

The doctor calls in a nurse, and she puts a pair of electric clippers in his hand.

I eye them warily. "What's that for?"

He seems apologetic. "I have to shave the affected area so I can see it better. Sorry, but it'll grow back in no time."

A part of me dies right then and there.

The next hour is a haze of pain and exhaustion and crippling sadness. They numb the back of my head, which is a bizarre feeling, and shave my hair. I can't feel it, but I hear the clippers whirring, and it takes everything in me not to cry. Dad holds me like I'm about to disappear, and Mom keeps handing me stuff—a cup of water, a stress ball, a Tylenol. The doctor threads a needle and goes to work on my head. By the time he's done, the headache is worse, but my actual wound feels like nothing.

"Okay, all done!" The doctor pats my shoulder. "It wasn't that bad, truly. Keep the cut clean and dry for at least twenty-four hours, and if you feel sick, come back. Make sure you eat a good meal tonight, and drink plenty of water. Try not to sleep for another hour, and no physical activity for a few days. Okay?"

"Yes, sir."

The doctor glances at Ms. Flores. "Do you have medical staff on-site?"

"Yes! Barbara is excellent."

"Okay, good. She can take the stitches out in about ten days." The doctor pats my arm again. "You're gonna be fine."

Dad gives me a hug. "Let's go home, okay, Hal? We'll order your favorite tonight."

As much as I'd love China Wok's delicious shrimp lo mein, I pull away. "I have to go back to camp."

"No!" Mom is still fighting mad. "You're coming home, where we can be sure you're safe."

For some reason, this makes me think of Julia and how her parents also don't want her at camp. Very different reasons, but I think I understand her more now. I want to agree with them and just leave that cursed camp behind, but I can't. If I give up now, that means I'm giving up on New Hallie. I'm not ready to do that. And, admittedly, the thought of leaving Julia alone in Cabin 11 makes me sicker than I already am.

"I'm going back. I started something, and I'm going to fin-ish it."

"This is different. You're hurt, and—"

"You're the one who always says I have to be the best in everything. I can't do that at home. I'm going back."

Mom and Dad are shocked into silence. I'm shocked too. I've never once talked back to my parents, but all the frustration and pain and sadness bubbled up and out of my mouth. I cringe, waiting for them to get mad at me, but they just stare instead.

"I think it's important for kids to not only face adversity but also overcome it with grace and determination," Ms. Flores chimes in. She smiles at my parents. "Hallie has incredible courage, and if she were my daughter, I'd be very proud."

Mom and Dad are uncertain. I reach for their hands tentatively, and they take mine. "I'll be okay. I promise. I just want to get back and take a shower."

"What can you do to make sure this won't happen again?" Mom asks Ms. Flores.

"Well, Hallie's banned from the woods from now on."

Ms. Flores and I smile, but Mom doesn't. She clears her throat and her expression turns serious.

"I know you're worried, Mrs. Griffin, but Hallie is in good hands. She'll have regular checkups with Barbara, our nurse, and I'll personally keep an eye on her while she recovers."

That seems to convince them. "All right," Mom says reluctantly. She looks at me, a complicated expression on her face. "But you call me if you feel sick or something goes wrong, Hallie, and I'll be right there."

"Okay." I hug them both, a softness creeping into my messy tangle of emotions. "I love you, Mom and Dad."

"Love you, Bean." Dad kisses the top of my head, and Mom squeezes me tight.

And soon, I'm out of urgent care and back in Ms. Flores's front seat. I wave at my parents as Ms. Flores pulls out of the parking lot. I watch Panera pass forlornly. I forgot to ask if we could go. Horrible camp food it is.

"Well, that was a nerve-racking adventure!" Ms. Flores says when urgent care disappears in her rearview mirror.

I laugh, wincing when the action irritates my headache. "Sorry about my mom. She can be intense."

"No kidding!" Ms. Flores laughs. She slowly relaxes as we get onto the highway. "Though I can't blame her. I'd be livid if anything happened to Gia. Next year, we'll have to adopt some new safety measures. I really shouldn't have just sent the kids into the woods cold turkey, but I thought it would build character. . . ."

Ms. Flores mumbles absently to herself for a while. I don't say anything, because I'm intrigued. With the crisis now over, I'm realizing Ms. Flores may have been as scared as I was. Which is surprising! I thought she was a perfect camp sponsor, millionaire, kind, and generous. But she gets nervous too sometimes. That thought comforts me, just a little.

"I'm proud of you for staying," Ms. Flores surprises me by saying.

"I have to," I reply, attempting a smile. "I can't win first place if I'm at home."

Ms. Flores laughs. "That's absolutely right."

CHAPTER 23

By the time I get back to Cabin 11, I feel like I'm made of glass.

It's nearly four o'clock, and I'm stinky and dirty and my fucking *hair*. I have no idea what the doctor did to me. I spent a whole year growing it out, and now I may have to chop it all off. But most important, I need a shower. Immediately.

I open the screen and Julia jumps to her feet. She changed her shirt and shorts, thank goodness. "You're still alive, I see."

I try to smile, but I'm on the verge of tears. "Apparently."

Julia takes a hesitant step toward me, then stops. "Was everything okay? No brain damage?"

"None that wasn't already there." My joke doesn't land. Neither of us laugh. I want to sink into the floor. "I'm gonna take a shower."

Julia nods. "Good idea. We can study tomorrow, don't even worry about it."

I nod and grab clean clothes and go to the bathroom. It takes me forever to peel out of my ruined clothes, and I stuff them in a garbage bag to go to the dumpster. RIP, pineapple shirt. You will be missed. I shower, but only for a few minutes; the steam makes me dizzy, and I can't get my hair/wound wet. I give up and towel off, and put on clean clothes. That'll have to do.

When I emerge from the bathroom, Julia's sitting at the desk.

I want to talk with her, to make sure she's okay after literally being bathed in my blood, but I feel like crying again. I choked down some of Sharon's horrible cooking under Ms. Flores's watchful eye, but now I need some emergency sweets. My gaze slides to the mini fridge. The chocolate bar. I haven't changed, but dammit I need something positive to happen to me today. This is an emergency break, like *Halloween*. I go to the mini fridge to open it, but freeze.

The chocolate bar is on top of the fridge.

No. No, please . . . I touch it, and my suspicions are confirmed. It's a liquid, gooey mess. The punishing heat melted it. When did I even leave it out? When did I last— Wait. I took it out to do my meditations. I went to change, and then Julia talked to me . . . and I forgot to put it back in the fridge. I left it out last night because I was happy a girl talked to me, and now it's melted. Ruined. My entire plan to change, reduced to a liquid disaster leaking from the tiny tear at the top where I'd only eaten two bits of chocolate.

"Hallie?" Julia's voice is uncertain. "Are you okay?"

I turn to her, but I can't see her through the water in my eyes. I try to blink the tears away, but they just keep coming. The dam keeping my emotions back all day shrivels to nothing, and I'm sobbing into my hands. I know it's not cute or attractive to be leaking snot, but I just can't take it anymore. My head hurts, I failed Life Skills, I'm a terrible friend who is a jealous monster, and I am never changing into who I want to be, and even the chocolate knows it.

Julia says something and touches my arm, but I just shake

my head. I crawl to my bunk and lie down, facing the wall. I can't even say my "It'll be better tomorrow" mantra because I can't even think about tomorrow—the shittiness of today is all-consuming. I hold Reginald to my chest and sob until I have no tears left, and then mercifully, my probably concussed brain allows me to sleep.

* * *

I wake up with a sore face. Like my entire face feels like it's hot and swollen, and both eyes are crusty with gunk. I'm not sure how long it's been, but from the light filtering in from the window, it must have only been an hour or two.

"Real attractive," I mutter to myself, but I'm feeling so pathetic I can't care. At least my headache is better; the feeling is back from my wound, but the skin around it just feels unnaturally tight. No real pain.

I hug Reginald, who is valiantly tolerant of me dripping tears and snot on him. I should get up, bounce back from this, and keep going, but I just can't. I failed in every possible way. I shouldn't have come back to camp. I should've let Mom and Dad take me home like the failure I am.

The bed creaks below me. Julia. I can't believe she didn't run away screaming after my embarrassing meltdown. I hear her stand up, then shuffle her feet. I want to turn over, but I can't face her.

"Are you awake?" Julia asks after a full minute of silence.

I sniffle, but there's no point in hiding it. "Yeah."

"Okay, good."

195

More silence. I would normally break it, reach a hand out to her, but I'm broken inside. I just want to sleep for days. I want to disappear.

Julia takes a breath. "Do you want to eat dinner with me?"

Fresh tears fill my eyes. All those times I asked, she turned me down. She hates people, so much she avoids them in class and all meals. But she's willing to face the dinner crowd just to cheer me up. Julia is so perfect. I don't deserve to be in her presence.

"Thanks," I choke out. "But I'm n-not hungry. M-maybe tomorrow."

"All right." Julia's voice is hard to pin down. It sounds neutral, but I hear the undercurrent of concern. Footsteps pad away from the bed, and I hear the screen door creak open. She must have been waiting for me for a long time. I close my eyes against the fresh tears and try not to think about anything at all.

I'm dozing in a hazy, self-pitying loop when the screen opens again. Back already? It can't have been more than ten minutes. Or it's an ax murderer come to pounce on me while I'm vulnerable. Today, I'd welcome it. God, I'm the worst right now.

"Hallie," Julia's voice calls. Not a murderer, then. "Stop avoiding me and roll over."

I grimace at the wall, but I do what I'm told. I wipe my eyes to try to preserve some dignity before looking at her. Julia's standing directly below my head, hands on her hips. She looks unamused, and that makes me feel worse.

"Get up," she says. Her tone has no room for argument, but I whine anyway.

"I'm fine up here."

Julia points to the ground. "Now."

I know I'm feeling bad because I don't even get a secret thrill over being bossed around. I just sigh and crawl out of my bunk. I hit the ground a little too hard and wince at the slight twinge in my head.

Julia points to her bed, which is neatly made for once. "Sit down."

I do, and Julia reaches above me. She comes back with Reginald, and I take him, grateful to have some sort of anchor to hold on to. Julia sits beside me, and I'm a little stunned when our knees touch. I'm looking at them when she speaks.

"Okay, first, do I need to take you back to the nurse?"

I shake my head, which irritates it again. "No, I'm fine. I mean, they just told me to rest."

Julia lifts an eyebrow. "You're crying because you're not in pain?"

I sniffle again and hug Reginald. I don't have the strength to lie. "No. I'm just really sad."

Julia nudges my knee with hers. It's warm and soft, and my mind wanders to the scar on the right one. "So talk about it. I'm right here."

I don't even know where to start. But I'm emotionally wrung out, empty, and Julia is reaching a hand out to me for the first time. I take it.

"I just feel really bad that I failed today. Like, who thinks a dog is a bear?"

"Me," Julia says. "And to be fair, Walter's a big dog."

"But I should have known," I insist. "I'm so embarrassed. I

don't know how to read a map, and I'm supposed to be good at Life Skills. And I dragged you down and messed up your points—"

Julia holds up a hand to stop me. "No one can be good at everything. The others couldn't read a map either. Plus, I got full points today."

I blink, confused. "But how? Did you find the waterfall by yourself?"

Julia gives me a small smile. "Turns out, preventing your roommate from dying is worth five points."

I sniffle, and my mouth smiles on its own. I'm not happy but relieved. At least Julia isn't caught up in my mess.

"What else?" Julia asks.

"My hair." My voice is small and heartbroken. "I worked so h-hard to grow it out, and the doctor shaved it like it was nothing. I'm so scared of what it looks like."

Julia makes a circular motion with her pointer finger. "Turn around. I'll see."

I do, dread in my heart. I hold my breath as I feel Julia's fingers gently lift my hair.

"Okay," Julia says, her breath pleasantly warm on my neck. "It's not bad. There's a bald patch, but it's small, and your pony-tail will cover it. I couldn't even see it at first. You're good."

Julia touches my shoulder, and I turn back around. I'm overwhelmed; my emotions are back in full force, and they're threatening to burst out of me again. Julia doesn't have to sit with me and soothe me about my hair. But she is, and I'm so grateful she's here that I want to resume sobbing.

"Thanks, Julia." I wipe my eyes, willing the tears to stay back.

"It's no problem." Julia puts a hand on my arm and looks into my eyes. "Now, tell me about the chocolate bar."

I can't help it—I burst into tears again. That's the worst of it, the raw reminder that I'm a failure in every aspect of my life. My hair will grow back, and I'll earn more points, but the chocolate hurts.

I'm surprised when Julia hugs me. I'm so surprised, I almost stop crying. Julia pats my back anyway, saying "Shh" in my ear. I focus on the feeling of her hands on my skin, her fingertips unusually rough, her touch unusually gentle. Her hug is soft and intimate, my head under her chin, and her thumb traces a soothing pattern on my back. I can hardly convince my brain to form a thought. In all my gay panic, I've never dreamed of a moment like this. I didn't know Julia, prickly on the best days, could be this gentle. I didn't know she *would* be, especially for me. But as she holds me, I allow myself a second to believe it. That she cares, and has for a while, and now she feels comfortable enough to show it. And those thoughts make me so warm, the tears dry and I'm okay again.

Julia eases back when I stop crying. She fussily wipes my tears with a tissue, then gives me another.

"Blow your nose."

I do, still sniffling. I attempt a smile. "Is your brother younger or older than you?"

Julia frowns. "Older. Why?"

"You have major big-sister energy."

Julia rolls her eyes, but she's smiling. "Don't try to change the subject. Tell me about the chocolate bar."

I take a deep breath. "It's hard to explain."

"Luckily for you, I'm one of the forty-eight smartest teenagers in Alabama. I'm confident I can keep up."

I laugh, and that gives me the push I need. "So, when I came to camp, I wanted to change. That's what the rules are for. I decided that every time I made progress toward my goals, I'd eat a piece of chocolate." Despite myself, my eyes well up again. "But I haven't been getting much chocolate. I feel like I haven't changed at all. And when I saw it was melted, I just . . ." I trail off, my throat burning. It's harder than I thought to talk about. "I feel like I'm a failure."

Julia's annoyed now. "You're not a failure. Getting bludgeoned by a rock isn't in your control."

"I guess," I admit, "but it's other things too. Like how I really miss watching horror movies. I said I wasn't going to do that anymore! Why can't I stick to something?"

"I still think it's fine for you to like them," Julia says. "But what's so special about the chocolate? I ate all mine on the first day."

"That's the problem, though. I always eat the chocolate on the first day. With basketball, I train until I throw up. And I watch horror movies over and over until I can quote them. I throw myself into my relationships, and they fail every time. Being impulsive and obsessive is the problem, you know? So I'm practicing some restraint."

Julia's frown deepens. "And this is because of your exes?"

"Right. I try so hard with my partners, and I always make the wrong decision. My best friend, before she fell in love anyway, was adamant that hookups were the way to go. She never got attached. But I . . . I do. And I can't do it anymore. I'm tired of being hurt."

The admission shocks me. That's it, isn't it? I told myself I wanted to change because Peter called me a dumb jock, or because I missed all of Ashley's red flags while sporting my rose-colored glasses. But that's the crux of it, isn't it? I don't want to be hurt again. I keep putting myself out there, but it's just not worth it.

Julia nods slowly. "Okay, I get that. But honestly, I don't think liking horror movies or basketball a lot is a bad thing. Or even having a bunch of crushes. I like it when you're happy."

I stare at her, speechless. My brain is short-circuiting because it just keeps repeating *"I like it when you . . ."* which can even be shortened to "I like you" if I'm delusional enough.

Julia gets up from her bunk and goes to the mini fridge. She comes back and holds out a chocolate bar to me. She smiles warmly as I gasp.

"Now, will this get you to stop wailing? Some of us have to be up at eight thirty in the morning."

I take the chocolate bar, the cold packaging soothing my too-warm skin. "Thank you, Julia. I mean it. You've been so nice to me."

"Well," Julia says, looking away. "I guess you're not the only one trying to change."

I can't help myself—I hug Julia. She complains but doesn't pull away. I feel electric. Understood. Deliriously happy. I just said I can't do relationships anymore, but with Julia, I think I want to. I want to eat dinner with her, study with her, listen to whatever she has to say. I want her to be able to talk to me about anything. I don't want to be hurt again, but with Julia, I'm starting to think maybe she would be worth the risk.

I stop hugging Julia, and she looks at me. She suddenly seems nervous. "Listen, I have to tell you something."

I'm nervous too. Is she . . . maybe . . . ? No, no it can't be. But my heart lifts with traitorous hope.

Julia fidgets for a second. "I'm sorry for what I said earlier, when we first made our deal. That I only wanted to learn Life Skills, and that we couldn't be friends. I don't have a lot of friends, but . . ." Julia smiles at me. "I don't think I can pretend you're not one."

I almost want to laugh. Julia sees me as a friend. A FRIEND. Of course she does! What else could go wrong on this horrible day?!

But honestly—maybe it's for the better. I said no romance, literally it's rule number one, and she's holding me to it. Plus, I like Julia as a friend too. If that's what she can give, I'll be happy to accept.

"I'm glad you think so," I say, smiling back. "But you've been my friend for like two weeks. Sorry."

Julia laughs, and my frustrations and pain and insecurity melt away. Because if I can make Julia laugh, then I've done something right.

I open the chocolate bar and break off two pieces. I give one to Julia, who accepts it.

"For changing," I say, "from acquaintances to friends."

Julia taps her chocolate against mine. "Cheers to that."

We both pop the pieces into our mouths. Sweetness melts on my tongue, and for the first time today, life isn't so bad.

CHAPTER 24

I bat my eyelashes at Julia, hoping to appeal to her better nature. "Can I go running tomorrow?"

Julia doesn't even look up from her notebook. "Not a chance."

I groan and lie on my side. It's been two days since my brush with death, and Julia has been militant about making sure I don't die of residual head trauma. I've been banned from running, and she makes me drink an ungodly amount of water. I would be lying if I said I didn't enjoy every minute of the attention. "You're so cruel! I won't die!"

"Tell that to Barbara." Julia pauses as scratching sounds from the screen. "And your dog. He's driving me nuts."

I get up and sheepishly open the screen. Walter trots inside and immediately settles where I was sitting, rolling to his back. This is also a problem. Walter hates that he can't run with me anymore, so he's been following me around and howls when we won't let him in. Maxine keeps collecting him, but he's back two hours later, without fail.

Julia looks at Walter through narrowed eyes. "I don't know how you convinced a guard dog to become a pet."

"He's still a guard dog! He's just guarding me." I rub Walter's belly, and he wriggles with delight, tongue lolling out of his mouth. "Aren't you, boy? Aren't you a good boy?"

"Sickening," Julia says, but she's smiling. She goes back to her notes, but her pencil isn't moving with the normal note-taking cadence. I watch for a few seconds, and then I see it—she's drawing.

"What are you drawing?"

Julia pauses and looks at me with the same expression she had for Walter. "Don't ask if you can see it."

"I would never!" I know artist etiquette; Nav protects her work-in-progress paintings like a rabid dog. "I just want to know what it is. Just what a friend would ask, you know."

Julia rolls her eyes and lifts her notes so I can see. It's a dog! A black-and-white herding dog in a cutesy style, way cuter than I would think Julia's drawings would be. And it's really good!

"Holy shit, that's amazing!"

"It's just a doodle." Julia puts her notes back on the desk. She gives me a small smile over her shoulder. "Friend perks that you can see it."

I'm beaming, but I can't help it. Since we publicly declared ourselves friends, we've really been acting like it. Julia isn't nearly as prickly as before. She's been in charge of my medical care, but she's also been hanging out with me more, studying like normal but with a playful edge, teasing me in her own severe way. And now she's showing me her drawings! I've wondered about them for weeks. Now I know she likes to draw cute dogs over her SAT practice problems. I'm overwhelmed by simple happiness. I still like Julia in a fuzzy, romantic way, but I really like being friends with her.

We study for another hour, separate but cozy in the same

room together. Body doubling, like Gia said. Walter snoozes in my lap as I read about art history, because we've officially swapped to art in Fine Arts. I know even less about art, despite my hobby of looking at it on Instagram. But I don't feel scared. I feel determined, and like I have a safety net; Julia won't let me fail at learning the difference between acrylic paint and watercolors. And I won't let her fail swimming lessons in the lake. For the first time since camp started, I feel like I'm part of a team.

Julia stretches her arms to the sky. "I'm tired."

"Same," I say, though I'm kind of interested in van Gogh's life. Dude had it hard for real. "I'm getting hungry."

Julia looks at me, her expression serious. "If we go to dinner, will the dog bite everyone in the mess hall?"

"God, I hope Michelle's there."

Julia cracks a grin and stands. "Let's go."

I gasp. "You're really wanting to go?"

"I asked you when you were sobbing your eyes out and you turned me down."

"I thought that was a pity ask!"

Julia rolls her eyes. "Get up, Hallie. Let's go eat."

I happily follow Julia to the mess hall. It's six, so the building is nearly full of hungry kids. I sense Julia becoming uncomfortable; she lets me pass her in the line for food and sticks close to my side while casting a dark look around her at the other chatting campers. Her shoulders are up by her ears again.

"What time do you normally eat dinner?" I ask her as I get

a tray. Looks like it's spaghetti night . . . but the noodles are dry, and the accompanying vegetables look weirdly wet and wilted. Ugh. Just let me take over the cafeteria, Ms. Flores. You can pay me in points!

Julia gets her tray before she answers. "Nine, if I don't forget."

"What do you mean? You forget to eat?"

Julia shrugs and unceremoniously dumps a lump of congealed pasta on her tray. "I'm usually not hungry. Too stressed."

"Oh my God." I skip the wilted lettuce and opt for corn. Hard to mess that up. "We have to eat together every night. This cannot be healthy. And we need to look into stress relief."

Julia grumbles behind me, but I can't quite make it out. I cheerfully ignore her protests as we grab dessert (a single, non-chocolate cookie for me and a giant piece of strawberry cake for Julia) and head to queer cabin's table.

"Hi!" I say as I take my normal seat beside Cam. "Julia's here today!"

"Welcome!"

"Hey, Julia!"

Julia grunts as she sits on my other side. She reminds me of Walter, sulking under the table when other campers approach him.

Cam leans forward, grinning. "Are you part of the queer cabin now?"

Julia sighs so heavy, her napkin flutters. I laugh and rescue her.

"She's still deciding, but we're eating dinner together now."

"You're welcome at any time," Caroline says warmly. She turns to me. "We were just talking about what we think the next pop-up will be."

"Lord, who knows," Teddy groans. "I'm about ready to give up. I'm never breaking top twenty."

"You can!" I say. "Maybe the next one will be something with hand-eye coordination. You were good at cornhole."

"You mean video games," Cam says, elbowing him teasingly.

Teddy shrugs, but he's smiling. "They're right. If this was a fighting-game competition, I'd be in first place."

That's so cool. I didn't know Teddy was good at games! I'm not great at them, but Peter got me into *God of War*. The story was really good. I feel like I understand Norse mythology better now (despite Kratos being Greek? Was that ever explained?). I want to ask Teddy about it, but Cam speaks up before I have a chance to.

"I still think the second one was rigged," Cam grumbles. "Who's even met the camp guards?"

"Hallie did," Julia speaks for the first time. She picks at her spaghetti pile without eating. Her cake is already gone.

"Yeah, I met Maxine while I was running."

"You run?" Caroline seems stunned. "On purpose?"

"Well, I was trying to replace basketball workouts, and—"

"You were on a basketball team?" Teddy asks. "Makes sense, you're so tall."

That bugs me. Yes, I'm tall, but I'm actually good at basketball? I practiced for years? Well, I mean, I *was* good, until I quit . . . "Umm, anyway, I was just running at five thirty, and—"

"Five thirty a.m.?!" Caroline's eyes bug out of her head. "Girl."

"That's more dedication than even me," Cam says. "I can't get up before seven on a good day."

"But you're here at seven thirty every morning."

"I have to hurry!"

I don't say anything as their conversation drifts in a new direction, Maxine and Walter's story forgotten. I pick at my spaghetti, trying to ignore the prickle of hurt.

Julia nudges my knee. I start, and she meets my eyes.

"I'm listening," she says.

"What?"

"Your story. You went running at five thirty and then what?"

Your Honor, I am in love with Julia Brown.

I tell Julia the rest of the story, and she listens closely, smiling when I tell her Gia said rottweilers are needy. She tells me she's always wanted a dog, but Walter is pretty intimidating, and then we get into a friendly argument about whether Walter is still a good guard dog or if I've ruined him. I'm so happy that I barely notice a lull in the conversation with the rest of the queer cabin. When I look up, all three are grinning at me.

"Do you two want to go get s'mores?"

"Yes," I say immediately. I will never turn down free marshmallows, but this is exciting! It's a queer cabin outing!

Julia sighs, but says, "Yeah. Lead the way."

We happily dump our half-eaten dinners into the trash and head to the firepit.

"I'm going to study, but you kids have fun," Cam says as we leave the mess hall.

"I need to work on my book, too," Caroline echoes.

They both head toward the cabins, Caroline taking a left when she gets far enough away. So much for a queer cabin activity. . . .

I look at Teddy. He smiles. "I'm still in. It might be fun."

"It is! Ms. Flores went all out."

"Of course you've already been," Julia says, smiling too now.

"I went the first day it was announced. Free food, hello? But no one showed up except for me. I felt so bad for her."

"Yeah, I feel kind of bad too," Teddy says as the fire comes into view. "Ms. Flores is so nice. She talked to me about the pros and cons of going to an art college the other day. She didn't have to do that."

"She's great," I say, beaming. I'm glad Ms. Flores has been chatting with everyone and not just the tiny Cabin 11. She really cares about all of us. It's nice.

We reach the fire, and Teddy gets distracted by talking to his cabinmates. Julia and I get two marshmallows each and sit on the log I was at last time. But it's not like last time; today, the s'more station is a lot more crowded: Teddy's cabinmates, someone from Michelle's group reading a cozy mystery book, a few more kids I don't remember the names of but I recognize. Ms. Flores is in the thick of it all, chatting happily to Samantha, the girl who won second place in the second pop-up. I know Ms. Flores is happy to have more participants. She catches my eye and waves, and I wave back as I carefully rotate my marshmallows.

Julia sits close to me, observing the other campers. She doesn't seem as tense as she did at dinner, but she's not fully relaxed either.

"Can I ask you something and you won't get mad at me?"

"You can ask, I can get mad." Julia aims her half smile at me. "Two-way street."

I waffle but decide to go for it. "Do you have social anxiety?"

Julia laughs, a loud one that shakes her whole body. She's full-on grinning when she can speak again. "Oh, no. I just don't like people."

Now I'm laughing too. I'm relieved she wasn't mad at me, but surely she can't hate *everyone*. "That can't be true!"

"It's true. I had friends in middle school, but when I stopped hanging out in favor of studying, they dropped me. Doesn't seem worth it to make more."

I frown at the fire. That sucks. I can't imagine my life without Nav in it. But in a way, I sort of understand. If something happened and Nav and I weren't speaking, I wouldn't have anyone to talk to. Not on a deep level, anyway. I have a lot of friends, but maybe it's just that I know a lot of people. Sarah is the only one from the team who's bothered to text me this whole time. I'm always texting people first. And if I don't . . . I stare at my rapidly browning marshmallows. I guess that's something else I need to work on.

"Well," I say to dispel my disturbing thoughts. "Now you have the queer cabin!"

"I don't like them either."

I shake my head, but I can't hold in a laugh. "They'll grow on you."

"Yeah, yeah." Julia smiles at the fire. She's not roasting marshmallows, I'm just now noticing. They're sitting untouched on a napkin at her side. "It's infuriating, but I think you're right. I kind of like Caroline now. I can tolerate Teddy."

"And Cam?"

Julia snorts. "I'll like Cam as soon as I rub my medal in their face."

God, everyone is so competitive! I like winning as much as the next person, but Cam and Julia are like two pit bulls wrestling over the only toy. "You shouldn't let competition ruin your friendships."

Julia rolls her eyes. "I'm only invested in one friendship at the moment."

I'm struck silent, too in love with the fact that she means me.

When my marshmallows are ready, perfectly golden brown and not at all burnt, I carefully stick them between two graham crackers. Julia frowns at my creation.

"Where's the chocolate?"

"I can't have chocolate until I change, remember? That means s'mores too."

Julia huffs out a disbelieving laugh. "Your self-control needs to be studied. If the detective stuff doesn't work out, you could be a Buddhist monk."

"If I was religious, I'd consider it."

"You are religious. You pray to your chocolate bar and vision board every night."

"I'm manifesting!"

"Yeah, which is prayer for atheists."

Julia and I laugh, and the fire is warm and smoky, and Teddy is talking in earnest to Ms. Flores now. When I take a bite of my modified s'more, it's full of gummy sweetness, and graham cracker crumbs fall down my shirt and into my bra. It's messy. It's a bit too smoky. It's perfect.

"This is nice," Julia says as she turns to me.

"Yeah," I say, staring right into Julia's gorgeous dark eyes. "It really is."

We sit in cozy silence for a long time, laughter and cicadas and the sound of Julia's soft breathing promising everything will be all right.

CHAPTER 25

I sit in the gazebo I found, Walter's head in my lap, and cycle through SAT cards.

I'm starting to get a little more worried about the test. The early days were a breeze, but now Mr. Lin's talking about specific strategies for the test like pattern recognition, skimming versus reading each passage fully the first time, and even what to eat that morning and how much sleep to get the night before. I didn't realize I needed to consider so many things! I was feeling pretty confident, but now the looming date seems closer than ever.

And it's not just the SAT. Taking the test means camp ending, and the deadline on achieving my goals. I feel sweaty all over when I think about it. Hallie 2.0 still seems so far away, but I have to achieve my goals. Failure isn't an option.

I start when my phone rings beside me. Nav's name flashes across my screen, and for a second, I consider letting it go to voicemail. But before I can even think about it, I'm answering. I always have time for Nav, horrific test breathing down my neck or not.

"Hello?"

"What're you doing?" Nav sounds muffled, like she's eating something. I glance at the time. She must be on her lunch break.

"Studying for the SAT. I'm so anxious, Nav, I'm gonna puke."

"Don't do it on the test! They'll kick you out, and you'll have to start over."

I groan, ready to launch into a playful scenario where I vomit all over my test, but Nav cuts me off.

"Hey, so, quick question—when were you gonna tell me you almost died?"

I tense up, immediately defensive. How did she find out? I didn't tell her because I didn't want to rehash the whole thing . . . and have someone else know about my failures.

"It wasn't a big deal. I just hit my head on a rock."

"Aunt Cathy said you had a concussion and were gushing blood from your head."

I groan. Mom is so dramatic. And of course she's telling everyone! Ugh.

"Mom's exaggerating. I'm fine." I tentatively touch the back of my head, where I self-consciously cover the stitches with my ponytail. "I didn't even go to the hospital."

Nav is unusually quiet. The silence isn't a good one—it's tense. Tension sneaks into my shoulders too.

"Is something going on with you?" she finally asks.

I frown at my lap, where Walter's woken up and is blinking sleepily at me. "Like what?"

"Like you not calling much. And I have to hear about your near-death experience from your mom! What's going on?"

My stomach roils with a sick feeling, just like I get before a fight. "I didn't want to tell anyone about it. I only told Mom because Ms. Flores called her. I wouldn't have said anything."

"And why not?" Nav sounds so strange. She's clearly mad, her voice creeping up in volume, but there's an undercurrent of something I can't quite place.

"I don't know! I just—it's complicated."

"I can handle complicated. Is there a reason you haven't called me specifically?" Nav takes a breath. "Did I do something wrong?"

I stare at my phone, speechless. I'm stunned, but guilt creeps in too. I didn't want Nav to know, not because of anything she did; it's just my own insecurity. I really didn't want anyone to know because I was embarrassed.

"Oh God, I'm sorry, Nav. No, nothing's wrong! I just didn't tell you because I'm bald in the back of my head now."

"What?" Nav sounds noticeably cheerier. "Are you serious?"

"Yeah, the doctor had to shave my head to give me stitches. It was humiliating. I felt like a skinned rat."

"Send me a picture right now."

"No! I just told you I was embarrassed!"

"Send it to me now! I leave for the reunion tomorrow and I wanna show Ben."

I stare at my phone for the second time. I . . . I forgot. I forgot about Nav's reunion. Something she's been so worried about, and I was so wrapped up in my own shit, I didn't even realize. Now I understand the emotion underneath her anger—she's hurt. I'm being a horrible friend. Tears prick my eyes, and Walter licks my hand sympathetically.

"Nav, I'm so sorry. I meant to call you before you left, but the SAT stuff, and queer cabin, and—"

"It's all right." Nav's voice is a little softer. "I know you have a lot going on."

"I do, but it's no excuse! Tell me all about it now. How are you feeling?"

I can practically hear Nav tensing up. "I don't know. Nervous."

"Well, it's going to be great. I know it."

"I hope so. I'm glad Gia's going with me, because she's almost as nervous as I am. She's asked me a hundred times if ten pairs of underwear is enough. We're gonna be gone three days!"

"Tell her to pack twelve," I say, my mind on my laundry debacle. "Did you know you have to separate white clothes from dark clothes?"

"I thought that was a myth."

I tell her what happened (and that I now own five pairs of pink socks) and we end up chatting for a full twenty minutes. I pet Walter's soft fur. It's like normal, like I never left. Nav doesn't have the undercurrent of hurt in her voice as she complains about her new manager duties and the fact that Uncle David burned bacon so badly it set the smoke alarms off. But I'm not back to normal. I'm upset. It's not like me to forget something so important. Unfortunately, it is like me to ignore a problem until it gets out of control. That's why I'm having to make so many changes at once, instead of gradually. Tackle the big picture problems, like Ms. Flores said.

But maybe I shouldn't do that. Maybe I should take a tiny step forward instead.

In a lull in our conversation, I say, "I'm sorry for forgetting about your reunion."

"Don't be," Nav says lazily. She yawns in my ear. "Not a big deal. And now that we talked it through, I feel better."

"I'm sorry about not telling you about my head too. I didn't tell you because . . ." I struggle for words. Instinctively, I want to hide my shame and embarrassment. But I've never looked past the surface of why I felt embarrassed. I still want to shield myself, to turn away from Nav and make a joke or talk about nothing. But I shouldn't. Nav and I fought a little, raised our voices. I got sick and sweaty like I always do before a fight. But now we're both calm, and for once, I don't want to bury my feelings.

"Because?" Nav prompts.

I swallow and decide to just go for it. "Every time something like this happens, when I'm not paying attention or I can't do something that I should, I feel like a failure. I hit my head because I thought Walter was a bear and slipped. I should have just calmed down, but I panicked, and then I made my head injury everyone's problem. I felt so stupid and small, you know?"

"Hmm." I imagine Nav nodding to herself. "Heard that before."

"What? When?"

"When Ashley was making fun of you for not knowing the theme of some stupid movie. Remember? I watched it too, and it was so boring I fell asleep. She said we were both small-minded idiots."

I blink at Nav's name on my phone. I didn't remember that until just this second. It was *The Menu*, a movie I thought was pretentious and Ashley argued me down about how it's supposed to be pretentious and I missed the point. She was so frustrated with me and Nav, she was almost in tears. I had no idea I internalized that. "Oh."

"Yeah. But don't listen to that psycho, listen to me. You didn't hit your head because you're stupid. You hit your head because Ms. Flores is a maniac who sends a bunch of city kids into the woods with no training."

That gets a small laugh out of me. "I guess. I just . . . I feel like I'm taking so many steps back from becoming New Hallie."

"I know, but don't feel bad over this. You're doing great at that weird camp, okay? And don't feel like you have to hide anything from me. I do dumb shit all the time. Did I tell you I mixed up salt and sugar for Mrs. Everdeen's cake?"

I gasp. Mrs. Everdeen works in our school's cafeteria, and she's also the meanest old lady in the world. "How are you still alive?"

"I have no idea, honestly." Nav laughs. "But actually, yeah, I do. She might hate me for the rest of her miserable life, but it's whatever. I made her a new one for free. I labeled every jar in the kitchen and told the new girl to stop moving my shit around. It's all good."

It's all good, huh? I touch the back of my head again. There's a bald patch, but I already feel peach fuzz against my fingers. Julia wasn't upset about her ruined shorts, and Ms. Flores wasn't mad at me either. It was all fine. "Yeah. I think so. I'm sorry again for not calling. I just . . ."

"Hold on to things until they blow up, yes," Nav says wisely. "But don't worry—we're cool. Just don't be afraid to call me next time you get maimed." Nav pauses, and I can sense her gremlin side coming out. "Or did you not call me because now you can talk to Julia about it?"

"I'm hanging up. Goodbye."

Nav cackles in my ear, and I hang up to spite her. I send her a text right after.

I hate you

But also I love you and I hope the reunion is amazing

i think it will be. now go study!
love ya babe

I put my phone in my lap and stare pensively at the trees swaying in the summer wind. I usually feel so awful after arguments. Sweaty, heart racing, about to vomit. But today, I barely feel a needle of guilt. Actually, I feel good. Better. I didn't know the head injury was still weighing that heavily on me. I'm glad we squabbled and made up, because now I feel like I understand why I was so upset. That couldn't have happened if Nav didn't care enough to check in, and if I didn't open up to her.

Disturbingly, my thoughts shift to my arguments with my exes. Ashley's vicious words after we couldn't agree on a movie.

Peter shouting at me over a missed practice and upsetting me so much I ruined my SAT score. There's a stark difference between those fights and the one I had just now.

I start out of my deep reflections when Julia pops into my field of vision. She's wearing a cute red tank top with the Carnegie Camp logo and black shorts. She's also out of breath.

"It's rough finding you. You study everywhere."

I try not to squeal with glee from the fact that she was searching for me. "What's going on?"

"Pop-up number three," Julia says. She sits on the bench beside me, still breathing hard. "At the main hall. But it's in twenty minutes. Hold on, give me a second to breathe."

Oh fun! I'm glad I don't have to go to Communication now. Although, based on my talk with Nav, I think I've already done well with that today. "You should come running with me in the mornings to build your stamina."

Julia doesn't say anything, but she does flip me off. I laugh so hard I snort.

We sit in silence as Julia's breathing evens. Walter swaps to lounging in her lap and she strokes his cute little eyebrows with her thumbs. I watch her, but I'm thinking about a few months ago again, Peter in my face, screaming at me. I don't like to admit it, but I think that fight and the subsequent failed test traumatized me. It's a huge reason I even wanted to change in the first place. I've been holding that secret fight close to my heart, humiliation and shame keeping my mouth shut, but maybe that's not the way. I opened up to Nav, and the world didn't end (though she'll probably tease me about my bald spot for weeks). I glance at Julia.

"Question," I say, before I can chicken out. "What would you think if your partner argued with you the night before the SAT and you failed it because you were upset?"

"Trick question," Julia says. "Because I wouldn't think. I'd kill them."

I want to laugh, but it sticks in my throat. That's such a Julia response. But I can't be Julia. I just cried for days, endured my parents' disappointment, and tried to shove it to the back of my mind so I wouldn't have to think about it. I didn't even break up with Peter. We were together for another month after that, until he cheated on me.

"But honestly," Julia continues, "I'd think they did it on purpose. The *night* before the SAT and they pick a fight? They had to know the SAT was important. And it's not like you can take it for free! I'd be so fucking mad."

I hold Julia's words in my head, carefully turning them over and over. I've always focused on my response to the argument, but Julia's seen something I missed—Peter absolutely knew about the test. He knew I'd been studying for months. He was mad that I'd missed a practice, not even a show. Through Julia's eyes, and Nav's calm expression of her feelings, I see the situation a whole new way. He could have spoken to me respectfully. He could have waited to argue with me until after the test. He didn't. That wasn't love. It was retaliation.

"Is this a hypothetical question?" Julia asks. I meet her eyes, her expression calm and curious. Earlier, I would have just let it go and said nothing. But now . . .

"No. It happened last time I took the test."

"God, they sound like the fucking worst." Julia sits up

straight and stares right at me. The eye contact is intense, and makes me a little uncomfortable, but I don't look away. "That will not happen again. The night before this one, we're both going to sleep early and eating pancakes or whatever the hell Mr. Lin told us today. No one is gonna ruin our shot."

A slow smile spreads on my face, and I get a bit misty-eyed. Some invisible worry dissipates, and tension I didn't know I was carrying eases. I was hurt before, but Nav and Julia are promising, as long as I let them know what's going on, that it won't happen again. I'm so moved and happy, I can barely contain myself.

Julia stands, startling me out of my mushy thoughts. Her eyes are full of flinty determination. "Anyway, that's in the future. Right now, we gotta go crush a pop-up."

I smile and stand too. "Let's do it."

CHAPTER 26

Ms. Flores (wearing a summery green dress with sunflowers at the bottom—amazing fashion sense, right along with Amira) greets us as we walk in. "Welcome to the third pop-up!"

"I swear this camp is just baby *Squid Game*," Julia says beside me.

"Except they can't kill us," Cam adds.

"Yet," Julia and I say at the same time. We look at each other and grin.

We're all gathered in the big building, our instructors flanking the sides and Ms. Flores on the stage. I'm excited! There are several tables set up in the middle of the room, like in the first pop-up. But instead of games, each table has a mysterious plastic box on it. The box has two big green buttons on top.

Ms. Flores gestures at the tables. "In today's pop-up, we'll be testing you on all five subjects you've learned. A pop quiz!"

There's a collective groan, me included. I work best when I know a test is coming. . . .

Ms. Flores holds up one hand. "Don't worry, I have incentives for you. You will be paired up, and the winning team will get a massive one hundred points."

Now I'm paying attention. A hundred points! Fifty points each! That's huge. That may just be enough to overtake Cam.

I look at Julia, and she's already staring at me, fire burning in her eyes.

"As a fun twist, you aren't limited to working with your cabinmates! You can pair up with whoever you'd like. It might be fun to work with someone new, hmm?"

I glance at Julia worriedly, but she smiles at me. "Don't even ask. I don't like anyone else here."

I grin back. "We're gonna crush this."

"As usual," Julia says breezily, and I've never loved her more.

Ms. Flores gives us time to pair up. I expect people to mostly stick to their cabins, but it's a free-for-all. Lots of new couples form, including Caroline and Samantha. I watch Teddy approach Cam, but I'm surprised when they shake their head and grab a girl with fascinating blue hair. I recognize her as someone in the top ten, but I can't remember her name. Teddy pairs up with one of his roommates instead. I want to say something, but Teddy doesn't seem too put out. Maybe he's okay. . . .

There are only eight tables, so we draw straws to determine what group goes first. Teddy and Caroline are in group one, Cam in group two, and then me and Julia in three. Amira ushers us into a side room so we can't hear the questions and cheat. I strain to listen, but the walls are solid concrete—can't hear a thing.

"This is fun!" Cam says, sitting by Julia.

Julia looks disgruntled, and I hold in a laugh.

"It does seem fun," I agree. I'm honestly pretty nervous, but it sounds like a game show. I've always wanted to try *Jeopardy!*

"Extroverts," Julia mutters. I grin and elbow her.

"It'll be fun! And we're definitely winning."

Cam shakes their head, a wicked gleam in their eye. "I'm afraid not. Everyone's fighting for second place."

"Says who?" Julia's getting prickly again. "You don't think Hallie and I can do it?"

"I didn't say that," Cam says. "But I know Hallie struggles with music, so—"

Julia stands abruptly, before I can even think about what Cam said. She glares down at Cam, who is just as shocked as I am. "Hallie is perfect in music now, thanks. You say we're fighting for second place? Watch us."

Julia stomps off to grab some free water. I watch her for a stunned second, then my heart lifts with secret joy. Cam's not wrong that I'm bad at music, but Julia was so offended, she couldn't even be in the same space as Cam after what they said. I'm so lucky to be friends with Julia. Cam chuckles beside me. "She's so cool."

"Honestly, she is." I grin at Cam, my confidence boosted by how much Julia believes in me. "But she's right. Good luck with the silver trophy."

Cam's group is called next, so Julia and I have to wait. Then it's group three's turn, and we file into the cavernous auditorium. Julia's arm brushes against mine, and I get the urge to hold her hand. But I'm only a little nervous—with Julia on my team, I can't lose.

Ms. Flores stands in the middle of the eight tables. Each pair of campers stands behind one, our group only using seven of the tables because of our missing members. Ms. Flores waves at us enthusiastically. "Welcome! Let me explain the rules. For this round, you can choose what category you want, and I'll ask you a question. The catch is, if your team gets the question wrong, you're out. We'll continue until there are four teams left. Make sense?"

We all nod, but I'm starting to get nervous now. Will we be okay? Have I studied enough?

The game starts. The first team gets out immediately with a music question, and the second and third pass their questions. Ms. Flores turns to me and Julia. "Hallie, Julia, what category?"

I look at Julia, but before we can deliberate, she confidently says, "Life Skills."

Jesus, okay. It's on me, then.

Ms. Flores nods, then asks, "True or false: when someone is drowning, you should jump into the water to save them."

Oh, I know this! But like Julia trusted me, I trust her too. I nudge her hand. She seems startled, but answers, "False."

Ms. Flores grins. "That's correct! Next team."

Julia is practically vibrating with excitement. She leans close as the fifth team gets their question wrong. "You didn't know I knew that."

"I did," I whisper back. "Because I trust you."

Julia's eyes seem to sparkle beneath the fluorescent lights, and I wish I could sweep her into my arms and kiss her. But I don't, because that would definitely be breaking rule number one. And I sternly remind myself—she doesn't like me! We're friends! I need to scrub my brain with a Brillo pad. I take a deep breath and focus on Ms. Flores's questions. More important than my lovesick freakout, we have a competition to crush.

And we do. I answer an SAT question right, and then round one is over. Round two is the same, but with a mix of other groups, and we dominate that one too. Soon, there are only eight teams left. Me and Julia, Cam and Diana (the blue-haired girl), Teddy and his roommate, and, to our dismay, Michelle and another girl I don't recognize.

"Last round!" Ms. Flores calls.

Now all the eliminated teams are in the auditorium, watching us and cheering us on, so there's extra pressure. But Julia looks as calm and focused as a cat about to pounce on her prey.

"This one will be harder. The questions will be random, and you will use your buzzers. Also, it will be timed. If you can't think of an answer in time, you'll be out, as well as if you answer wrong."

"Let's fucking go," Julia whispers. I turn a laugh into a cough as Ms. Flores asks the first question.

"We'll focus on Life Skills first. Hallie and Julia. What is the first thing you should do when getting into a car?"

Julia buzzes in without me having a second to think. She practically yells, "Put your seat belt on!"

Ms. Flores grins. "Correct! Now, Michelle and Fran. What should you use to get a stubborn stain out of clothing?"

I'm disappointed when Michelle answers baking soda, but happy when Teddy gets his right about first aid. Ms. Flores turns to Cam's team.

"Cam and Diana. About how long does it take to hard-boil an egg?"

Oh, this is easy. Sharon overcooks hers, but the idea is about the same. Egg in cold water, bring to a boil, let it ride for at least ten minutes. Mom makes me add vinegar so the shells are easier to peel, but it's not hard.

But . . . Cam doesn't say anything. And neither does Diana. They stare at each other, wide-eyed, and Julia straightens up beside me. No way Cam doesn't know this. But a little piece of conversation, way back at the beginning of camp, snags in my brain. A comment Cam made about barely paying attention in cooking class because it wasn't important.

"Hurry," Ms. Flores urges.

Cam buzzes in and says, hesitantly, "Five minutes?"

Ms. Flores shakes her head, and Cam's face falls. "I'm sorry, but that's incorrect. Please stand to the side."

I watch Cam and Diana leave in disbelief, but I don't have time to dwell on it. Ms. Flores is already asking the next set of questions. We fight through round after round, nearly missing a Finance question before Julia saves us at the last second. I barely hold in a cheer when Michelle and her partner get out on a Life Skills question about daily cleaning. Soon, it's just me and Julia versus Teddy and his roommate I now know as Harvard-bound Kent.

"Last two!" Ms. Flores is practically dancing with glee. "The questions will get harder from now on, but you're not necessarily out if you miss one. If you get it wrong and the other team does too, we'll keep playing. But if your team gets it wrong and the other one gets it right, then the other team wins. Make sense?"

We all nod. Teddy grins at me and mouths, "Good luck."

I return his smile and give him a thumbs-up. Kent and Julia, however, look like they're ready to break out into a fight.

Ms. Flores asks us increasingly difficult questions. My heart stutters when we get a Finance question about the different types of IRAs wrong, but the boys do too, so we keep going. Ms. Flores turns to the boys.

"This one has a visual aid! I'll show it to you first, then the other team will have a chance." Ms. Flores gives Teddy and Kent a piece of cardboard. They frown at it fiercely.

"Name this."

I can't see what they're looking at, so I'm a little worried when they can't agree and time runs out.

"Sorry, Teddy and Kent. We'll give Julia and Hallie a chance. If they get this right, they've won."

Ms. Flores passes the carboard to me. My blood runs cold when I see a familiar graph, little beans, and trouble—treble—clef on the lefthand side. Ms. Flores taps one bean and smiles. "Tell me what this is."

I look at Julia for help, but she beams back at me. "Hallie's got this," she says.

No! I'm a musical idiot! This is the game-winning point! I'm panicked, but Teddy gives me an encouraging nod, and Ms. Flores is watching serenely. Julia bumps my hand with hers. I shake off the anxious sweats and take a closer look.

I'm too scared to remember anything our instructor taught

us, but I can see Julia's notes in my mind. I hear her voice repeating "*Every Good Boy Does Fine*" like a mantra. Her little doodles and sticky notes of encouragement dance in my memory as I count the beans. I notice the little hashtag beside a fat, open bean.

"Almost time," Ms. Flores says.

"It's a . . ." I take a deep breath, then squeak out, "It's a whole note. G sharp."

Ms. Flores stares into my eyes. The auditorium is silent, brimming with anticipation.

"Hallie . . ." Ms. Flores grins. "That is correct."

The auditorium erupts in cheers. I'm too shocked to move as Julia screams and hugs me. I hug her back, and then the shock wears off because I'm laughing and screaming too. For some reason, we link arms and skip in a circle while Teddy and Kent clap along.

"Great job, Hallie and Julia! You both receive fifty points each, which means"—Ms. Flores pauses and does some mental math—"you two are in the fourth and fifth ranks, respectively!"

"Yes!" Julia is shouting, which I've never heard before.

I'm laughing, tears in my eyes, because goddammit, my hard work actually paid off.

"Do you two want to say anything?" Ms. Flores offers her microphone to us.

I shake my head, but Julia takes it.

"To Cam, I just want to say I told you so."

Cam sighs but shrugs good-naturedly.

"And also, to Michelle: eat shit."

Michelle turns beet red, and Teddy and I dissolve into hysterical laughter. Ms. Flores is smiling too but pretends to put on a stern face.

"I have to take a point away for unsportsmanlike conduct," she tells Julia.

"Take it off my tab," Julia says. She glares right at Michelle. "I can afford it."

I love Julia so much it hurts.

With that, the tournament is over. Ms. Flores brings us two Burger King crowns and puts them on our heads like we're princesses. Amira gives me a box of Sour Patch Kids and Julia snags a box of peanut butter M&M'S. And as I look into Julia's sparkling, triumphant eyes, I don't think I've ever been as happy as I am now.

CHAPTER 27

I show Mom my hard-won Sour Patch Kids. "Julia and I won a tournament!"

Mom beams at me. "That's amazing! I'm so proud!"

It's been a few hours since the win, and I'm still buzzing with excitement. Julia promptly went to the cabin to pass out, so I've been wandering around the camp, cradling my box of candy like it's a baby. I haven't talked to Mom and Dad in a while, so it felt like a good time to FaceTime them. Dad's in the background, drying dishes.

"What did she win?" he hollers.

"A tournament!" Mom yells back.

I roll my eyes, laughing. They're in the same room. Why are they screaming?

"Is that why you're wearing a Burger King crown?"

"You bet it is." I straighten my crown proudly. It's stupid, but I love it. I'm never taking it off.

"How's your head, Bean?" Dad asks, crowding Mom so he can see me on her giant phone.

"It's good. Barbara took the stitches out the other day and said I was good as new!"

Mom gasps and Dad looks horrified. "Why didn't you tell us?"

I didn't want to bother them . . . I'm having unwelcome

flashbacks to my conversation with Nav. "It was fine, I swear. Took like five seconds and didn't even hurt."

My parents look doubtful, so I try to placate them.

"I'm getting plenty of sleep and eating a ton, don't worry."

"Okay . . ." Mom still sounds worried but thankfully moves on. "How is camp, other than the tournament win? You never tell us anything!"

Well, there's a reason for that. Mom doesn't want to hear about near misses and almost points. I only called her today because I won. If I got second place, I wouldn't have bothered.

"There's not much to tell. I mean, I just study a lot—"

"What about your roommate?" Dad asks. "She seems nice whenever you talk about her."

I feel my ears burning, so I hide them under my hair. "She's good."

"Am I?" A voice says in my ear, and I jump. Julia is standing behind me, grinning.

"You scared me," I hiss. I angle my phone down, but my parents are as quick on the uptake as they are overbearing.

"Is that Julia? Are you talking to Julia?" Dad yells.

"Hi, Julia!" Mom says, leaning close to the phone. "Don't be rude, Hallie, let us meet her."

I want to die. Julia looks pleased with herself, though, so I reluctantly lift the phone's screen. She waves at my phone, smiling. "Hi, Mr. and Mrs. Griffin. I'm Julia."

"Nice to meet you!" Mom says. To Dad, she whispers, "Wow, what a pretty girl."

"Goodbye," I say loudly as Julia silently cracks up behind me.

"No, wait, Hallie! I wanted to talk to you about something."

I rub my temples, my face burning. "Please hurry."

Mom fidgets, which is unlike her. She's normally poised and serious. I can't remember the last time I've seen her uncomfortable. "I'd love it if you called more."

I frown and glance at Dad, but he nods enthusiastically. "We never hear about camp! We'd love to hear more."

"It's boring," I say. "Just studying."

"Did she tell you we won a chicken in a tournament?" Julia asks, shooting a mischievous glance at me.

I glare at her, and she grins.

"No! See, that's what I'm talking about," Dad complains. "Julia, tell my daughter to call home more."

"Will do, Mr. Griffin," Julia says sweetly, and I've had enough.

"Goodbye! I have to study."

"Okay, but we love you, Hallie," Mom says. It's unnerving how intense she's being.

"Love you too. We'll talk later." I hang up, and I've suddenly sprouted a headache.

They're going to be the death of me, I swear. Julia sits next to me at the pavilion I camped out at for the call. She leans her head down to rest on her fist, grinning like a smug cat.

"I'm glad your mom thinks I'm 'such a pretty girl.'"

"Please never speak of them again."

"They seem fun." Julia's smile turns a little sad, but just for a moment. She sits up, seemingly all business now. "Are you busy?"

"No, just celebrating my win." I adjust my crown, and Julia laughs.

"Eat the candy, Hallie."

"I'm saving it! New Hallie has restraint!"

Julia shakes her head. "Here we go with the monk training."

"You just want to eat my Sour Patch Kids."

"That too." Julia chuckles and sits up straighter. "Do you want to go over Finance tonight? I'm worried that we missed that question about the stock market."

"Bold of Ms. Flores to assume I'll have any money to invest in the first place," I say, but I'm already packing up my candy. I'm less worried about Finance, but I'd never turn down an opportunity to study with Julia.

"The dangers of being at rich people camp." Julia starts to get up but pauses.

I follow her line of sight and find Teddy waving at us enthusiastically. Cam and Caroline trail behind. Caroline is looking at her phone, and Cam has a moody expression.

"Hey! Look who it is, pop-up champions!"

I straighten my crown playfully, and even Julia manages a smile. "Teddy, you're in the presence of royalty. Please address us by our titles."

Teddy mock bows, and we laugh. Caroline joins in, but Cam still has a sour look on their face. My laughter fades into worry. Is everything all right?

"We're going to eat s'mores," Caroline says. "Wanna come?"

Julia glances at me questioningly, but there's no need. "Sorry, we're going to review Finance. But maybe tomorrow!"

"I should go too," Cam says. "I wasn't prepared today."

"There were hard questions," I say sympathetically.

Cam snorts before I can say anything else. "Yeah, but I can't ease up. I don't have luck on my side like you two."

Luck? Is Cam saying we got lucky in our win? I feel myself shrinking, cringing around an old wound that I'm not that smart after all and I just got lucky.

"What do you mean by that?"

Every eye turns to Julia, but she's staring at Cam with cold, laser focus.

Cam startles. "Nothing, just that—"

"That what? That Hallie and I aren't smart enough to win the tournament?" Julia's voice is quiet but lethal. "Or are you saying that you can't believe we're smarter than you?"

Uh oh. Julia's body is tense like she's ready for a fight, and Cam is sputtering, pure panic on their face. Caroline and Teddy stare at us, wide-eyed, but no one's saying anything.

"It's okay, Julia," I say, trying to rescue the conversation. "I'm sure Cam didn't mean that."

"Well, that's what they said," Julia says, not looking at me. She's staring down Cam with an expression so murderous, I'm sure I'd crumble to dust if it were directed at me. "So come on. Explain."

"I—I just thought that the questions were hard, that's all," Cam rushes to say. "I didn't mean anything by it."

Julia looks like she doesn't believe them, and honestly, I don't believe them either. Cam is fiercely competitive, so they have to be smarting from the loss. But they don't have to take it out on us. Teddy got second place after he had to team up with someone he doesn't like because Cam wouldn't join him, and he actively encouraged us in the middle of the face-off. Cam isn't being a good friend.

The thought shocks me. I don't know if I've ever thought that. I always just put up with everyone's bad behavior, until I can't anymore and I explode, like Nav said. That reminds me of our argument, how Nav was able to calmly explain her feelings and the world didn't end. And how Peter walked all over me until he ruined my SAT, and I let him.

I'm scared, but I think I have to be brave here. I think this is another small moment of change. "I don't like it when you do that, Cam."

Julia turns to me, surprise on her face. The rest of the queer cabin also looks stunned, but I keep going. "Julia and I weren't lucky. We studied really hard together, and it paid off today. And I'm not stupid for caring about Life Skills as much as the other subjects, and for liking to study in a group. I . . . it makes me feel bad when you don't respect me."

I feel like I'm going to throw up at the end of my speech. No one speaks for a full three seconds, and then Cam runs to my side. I'm startled when they give me a hug.

"Oh my God, I'm so sorry. I'm being such an asshole! I didn't mean to make you feel like that."

I hug them back, stunned. It's okay? Cam isn't mad at me? They pull away, and I'm surprised to see their eyes are wet with tears.

"I won't do that again, I promise."

"Okay," I say, still so shocked that I didn't get blowback I can barely think. "Thank you."

"Don't worry about them, Hallie," Caroline says. She smiles. "They're a sore loser."

"I'm not," Cam grumbles.

"You are," Julia says curtly. "But it doesn't matter. We still won fifty points each."

"Forty-nine for you," Teddy reminds her. "But God that extra point was worth it. I thought Michelle was gonna shit herself."

The conversation moves on, and I soak in what just happened. I think, somehow, I actually managed to change something for the better. For the first time since coming here, I feel closer to New Hallie.

"Anyway, s'more time," Teddy says after a minute. "Cam, you coming?"

"No, I'm going to study." They look at me sheepishly. "I really am sorry, Hallie."

"It's okay," I say, and honestly, it is.

Cam puts a hand over their heart. "I've learned my lesson. I'll never underestimate the power couple again."

I'm dazzled for a second. A power . . . couple? Me and Julia? I turn to Julia to see what she thinks, but she's just scowling triumphantly.

"Hell yeah we are. And don't you forget it."

Julia links her arm with mine, and I don't think I've ever been as happy as I am now.

We wave at the queer cabin as they go off to study and eat s'mores. Julia watches them go, but I'm looking at her.

"Thanks for sticking up for me."

Julia turns her radiant half smile to me. "You did a good job of it yourself."

I take a shuddering breath. "It was so hard. I don't . . . I don't like confrontation."

"Well, lucky for you, I do." Julia punches her fist into her palm. "Cam gets mouthy again, you call me."

I laugh and get up. "Noted. Let's go study."

I shoulder my backpack, and Julia does too. We head back to Cabin 11 to study, but I feel a little different. A bit stronger. And when Julia offers me some of her peanut butter M&M'S (after devouring almost all of my Sour Patch Kids), I take two. The chocolate is sweet on my tongue, and I finally feel like I've earned it.

CHAPTER 28

I wake up in the middle of the night.

For an entire ten seconds, I'm deeply confused. I'm not the type to wake up for anything, not even to pee. I don't really have to pee right now either; I'm cozy and warm under my comforter, Reginald snuggled in my arms. Something had to wake me up. This happened before, with Nav. But my phone isn't ringing.

I hear it then. A small sound, like a mouse squeaking. Wait, no—someone crying.

I'm wide awake now. The cabin is pitch dark; the lamp isn't on, and Julia's not at her desk. I sit up in bed, listening. The sound is right below me. "Julia?"

The sound stops. There's a heavy silence.

"Don't pretend to be asleep."

"I'm fine." Julia's voice is soft and strained. Definitely crying. "Go back to bed."

"You know I'm not." I grab my phone and squint at the light. It's just past midnight. I've only been asleep for an hour. "Hang on, I'm coming down."

I ignore her protests as I clamber out of the bunk bed by the weak light of my phone. My eyes adjust to the darkness, and Julia comes into view. She's bundled up in her comforter, eyebrows pulled together in distress. "Can I sit down?"

Julia nods, and I sit on her bunk, far away from her. She's giving off major *Get away from me* vibes, like she was when we first met.

"What happened?"

Julia doesn't say anything for a while. Then, she gives me her phone, which is open to a text. I scan the message—it's a picture, seemingly taken in late afternoon, of a bunch of stuff on tarps on a front lawn. A yard sale? But nothing looks that old . . . there are several books, DVDs, and clothes. A Cornell flag and art supplies. A sweatshirt with a Novia high school logo. Wait.

These are Julia's things.

There's a single line of text. It says: If you don't come back today, you won't have a home to come back to.

"Fuck," I whisper.

"Yeah." Julia's voice breaks. "I knew they were upset, but this sucks, even for them." Julia's voice breaks again, but she presses on. "It's fine, I'm fine. I just—I'll get over it. Sorry I woke you up."

I can hardly contain the sorrow in my chest. This is incredibly shitty of them. "Julia . . ."

"It's fine, really." She takes her phone back and stares forlornly at the screen. "I bet they'll keep it outside all night. And it's supposed to rain. Fuck, I'm so tired of this."

If I were Julia, I'd be a blubbering mess. I'd want her to hold me and stroke my hair and tell me everything will be okay. But she's not me. Julia is already shutting down, hiding behind her tough shell, closing the door and bolting it shut. Even then, I can see this is important to her. This is her life, strewn on her front lawn for strangers to steal and rain to ruin.

I would want comfort. But Julia will want a plan.

"Get dressed," I tell Julia, already on my feet and searching for my discarded clothes in the dark.

Julia looks at me, frozen in shock. "What?"

"Get dressed," I repeat. I find the shirt I wore today and tug it on. "Come on, hurry!"

Julia seems bewildered but doesn't argue as she changes out of her pajamas and into the clothes she wore today. While she's changing, I scroll through my phone and touch the Uber app. Thank goodness Mom set up this account when the team went to nationals in Florida and she was paranoid I'd be stranded. I just have to hope she won't get an alert I'm using the family credit card to briefly escape camp.

I tug on my shoes and grab my backpack, and I'm ready. Julia is ready a second after me. She follows me to the door, uncertain.

"Where are we going?"

"To get your stuff. You live twenty minutes away, right? Novia?"

Julia gapes at me. "We can't leave—"

"No, we can leave. We just can't get caught." I smile at Julia. "Put your address in here and we'll be back before anyone knows it."

Julia stares at me for a long moment but takes my phone when I put it in her hands. She types her address in slowly and gives it back. I quickly finish typing in the details and pick a car with a woman driver. I brace myself for a furious call from Mom, but nothing happens. My phone just declares that Jan the Uber driver will be here in twenty minutes.

"Done! Let's go." I shoulder my backpack and ease open the screen door.

Julia doesn't say anything else. She just follows me out of Cabin 11 and into the hot, muggy night.

I guess Ms. Flores takes it for granted that this is a camp for nerds, because it's horribly easy to sneak out. Maxine is doing rounds, but she's yawning and almost asleep on her feet. We wait until she's passed us and is walking toward the main building before moving. Walter is snoozing on the porch of the guard cabin and doesn't even flinch as we sneak by. The gate isn't closed, because Maxine leaves to get snacks sometimes. Thank God this isn't the setting of a horror movie because we'd all be extremely fucked.

Julia and I sneak past the gate, and I lead the way down the gravel driveway to the main road. We stand together in silence as my phone tracks the Uber's arrival.

"This is insane," Julia says into the darkness.

"Maybe a little."

Julia doesn't say anything, but she grabs my hand. I hold hers tight in mine as the car arrives.

We get into the back seat of the car, and Julia confirms her address with Jan. She falls into silence, and I reach for her hand again. She takes it and squeezes it tight, like she can hold on to hope. I want to tell her it'll be okay, and her parents are huge assholes, that I'm here for her, but I don't say anything. I just hold her hand for the entire silent twenty-minute ride to her house.

When we pull up, my stomach sinks. The yard is clear and the grass shining with dew—no tarps. No stuff at all. Julia makes a small whimpering sound, and I squeeze her hand.

"Let's check inside, okay? Maybe they put it in the garage."

We leave the car, thank Jan, and walk to the front door. I'm so nervous I barely take in the cute blue house with white shutters and pretty white flowers flanking the sides. There's a basketball hoop outside the closed garage. It's far too cute to house such assholes.

We reach the porch and then stop. Julia can't move. She just stares at the door with blank fear. The lights are on in the living room—apparently Julia's family are night owls, like her.

"Do you want me to knock?" I ask.

Julia meets my eyes. She nods, so I lift my fist and knock on the door.

It's quiet, but not for long. There's a clambering of footsteps, and the front door swings open. A man with an impressive beer gut and equally impressive mustache gawks at us.

"Jules! Honey, Julia's home!"

Another pair of footsteps, and a woman dressed in a pink nightgown, purple bonnet, and pink slippers appears from upstairs. She glances at me, but just for a second; soon, she's out the door and hugging Julia. Julia is like a stone statue. I wince. Not the family reunion I think they're hoping for.

"Come in!" Julia's dad, I guess, opens the door wide.

She stalks inside, and her dad notices me for the first time.

"Oh, hello! Are you Julia's friend . . . ?"

"Yep." I smile, though I feel like I've eaten rocks. "Just here for moral support."

"Well, come on in, support team." Julia's dad laughs at his own joke, and I go inside Julia's house.

It's cozy, but weirdly grandma-ish on the inside. The living room is decked out in fake flowers, and there's even a white doily on the polished wood coffee table. It's cramped with antique furniture displaying silver cups and fine china, and someone's laptop is open on the kitchen table. Someone has displayed a baseball trophy on a high shelf, and there are several family pictures of a young guy in a graduation cap. No art resembling Julia's, though, or even pictures of Julia on the cramped walls. It doesn't feel like she lives here at all.

Julia takes a shuddering breath. "I responded to your threat. What happened to everything?"

Julia's mom winces. "Jules, don't say that. We just want you to—"

"Where is everything?" Julia's eyes fill with frustrated tears, but her voice is remarkably calm. "I can replace everything but the photo albums from Grandma, so I hope you at least saw who took that."

Julia's parents are deeply uncomfortable. They're both fidgeting and glancing at each other. Her mom twists her sleeve in one hand. Her dad speaks first.

"Baby, we couldn't think of anything else to get you to come back. You know we need help, and summer is the busiest time—"

"Where is it?" Julia says. Her voice has no life in it. Just neutral, bland defeat. "Did you sell it?"

Julia's mom glances anxiously at her dad.

He nods, seemingly embarrassed. "We, uh . . . we didn't give your things away. We just took them out of your room to show you we were serious."

"So . . . ?"

"Everything's back upstairs where we found it," Julia's dad says. "No harm, no foul."

It's dead silent in the living room. The tension is unbearable; this must be what it feels like before a bomb goes off. Julia's face melts from her mask of neutrality into pure, terrifying rage.

"No harm, no foul?" Her voice hasn't raised in volume, but her words are dripping with venom. "You drag me out of bed with a threat, you make me leave camp, and that's no harm, no foul?"

Julia's dad shuffles his feet nervously. "Like I said, it was a last resort—"

"You know what, Dad, I'm glad this happened." Julia's physically shaking with rage. "This is the last time I'm playing your stupid games. You're damn right I don't have a home to come back to, because I'm never stepping foot in this house again."

"Julia Marie!" Julia's mom says, shocked. "Don't speak to your father that way."

"You don't speak to me at all." Julia's spitting mad. "I'm getting my stuff and getting out of here. Have a great life."

Julia stomps upstairs. Julia's parents looked shell-shocked, and honestly, I am too. I would be dead if I talked to my parents like that. But maybe Julia doesn't care what happens now.

I start to say something to her parents, but Julia's voice, distant but no less angry, yells, "Hallie, get up here and help me pack."

She doesn't have to tell me twice. I motor up the steps before Julia directs her wrath at me.

I don't really get a chance to do anything. Julia is clearly in a blind rage, tossing her already-torn-apart room into various bags. I just hold open a duffel and two canvas bags while she shoves clothes, art supplies, sheet music, and two heavy-looking photo albums into them. Then she zips everything up and storms downstairs and out of the house. I pause, meeting her parents' dumbfounded expressions.

"It was nice to meet you both," I say weakly before shouldering my bags and following Julia into the night.

CHAPTER 29

I follow Julia down the sidewalk. I have no idea where we're going, but I don't think now is the time to ask.

Julia power walks for five minutes, and then we arrive at a park. She storms past a rickety gate and collapses on the nearest swing, throwing her duffel bag to the ground.

Then she tips her head back and screams.

It's a rage-filled, mournful sound, like an injured wolf howling at the moon. When she's out of breath, she puts her head in her hands and starts to cry. I don't move, conflicted. I want to wrap her in a hug so bad, but I know that's not what she needs. A hug would probably make things worse. So I wait, and after only a minute, she's done crying. She stares at the sand beneath her untied tennis shoes, expression painfully blank.

I sit in the swing next to her. My legs are too long, so I'm still while Julia's swaying slightly. I pick through a ton of *I'm sorry*s and *I hate that this happened*s before I land on "Parents can be real assholes."

Julia huffs out a tiny laugh. There's no humor in it, but her eyes have more life in them now at least. "You can say that again."

We sit in silence for a few more minutes. I set Julia's bags down next to me, careful not to get any sand on them.

"This was a long time coming," Julia says, still staring at her feet. "You know the movie *Matilda*?"

"Yeah. Great movie."

"Except when it's your real life." Julia laughs a humorless laugh. "I'm not saying my parents are abusive, but I've always felt like the black sheep. We butt heads over the stupidest things. Violin lessons. Soccer practice. Not getting a job because I have to work at the car wash for free. And the fucking camp. What other parents would say, 'No, Julia, you can't go to smart camp! Who will do free labor for us?' My fucking pair of idiots, that's who."

I can't say anything useful, so I say nothing. I don't think Julia's finished.

"They're the reason I'm so bad at Life Skills. Every time we're in the same room, we're fighting. I didn't have time to watch my mom cook or ask my dad how to change a tire. I was always trying to get them to leave me alone so I could do my schoolwork. 'No, Julia, I'm not going to teach you how to drive a car. Your brother can drive you!' The reason they wouldn't teach me is because they knew as soon as I learned, I'd use it to get the fuck out of here."

I'm still quiet, but the raw pain in Julia's voice is almost tangible in the hot night air. I didn't know her situation was this bad. What kind of parents are not only unsupportive but actively praying for her downfall? They sabotaged her on purpose. Like clipping a bird's wings so it'll stay caged for the rest of its life. I think back to the beginning of camp, the first day we met. I remember her quiet fury, her extreme frost and wariness. But I understand it now. Julia had to literally fight tooth and nail to be there, and everyone, including me, must have seemed like a threat to getting away from this. And just when she finds a small amount of relief, Michelle immediately attacks her with homophobia. I can't believe she didn't tear the cabin down with rage. She's so much stronger than I am. I couldn't have shouldered all of this without it crushing me.

"And you know, it really hurts." Julia's voice breaks and so does my heart. "How they're never satisfied. They're never proud of me."

I nod, my heart sinking. "I know that feeling."

Julia looks at me then, eyes full of tears, and I wish I could take all the pain she's endured away. "It's different for you, though. Your parents want the best for you. Mine want the best for themselves."

"Yeah, true. But mine are delusional in the opposite way. They think I'm going to be a doctor."

Julia blinks, then the tiniest smile I've ever seen blooms on her face. "Miss 'I faint at the sight of my own blood'?"

"There was a lot of it," I groan. "Point being, I get it. Some of it, at least. And I'm here for you."

Julia nods and closes her eyes. "Fuck. I guess I'm homeless after camp, huh?"

"No way. What about Sarah?"

"What about her?"

"Umm, you're really close, and you have nicknames for her parents, and they live in a giant house. She'd help you, no questions asked."

Julia shakes her head. "I can't burden her with this."

"First of all, you are not a burden. You're her family, and we both know she would love for you to stay with her," I say.

In fact, Sarah would be ecstatic; she gets lonely a lot, and is always inviting the team over for sleepovers and parties. Having company would be a godsend.

"I know it's probably a bad time to say this, but you can trust some people. Not everyone will let you down."

Julia meets my eyes. Hers are tired and soft. "Yeah. Not a lot of people would do what you did."

I blink, a little shocked by her words. I guess . . . I guess she's right? I didn't even think about going on this rescue mission. I just acted. Julia needed me, and I was there. If I was abiding by my rules, I shouldn't have done this. I'll be dead tomorrow, and possibly oversleep and ruin my points. I won't get that medal acting like this. But I look at Julia, who's meeting my eyes with soft gratitude, and I decide that tonight, I don't care about my rules. The old, impulsive, lovesick Hallie has her good points. Tonight, New Hallie can wait.

I smile at Julia. "And I'll do it again, whenever you need. But we should probably get back before Ms. Flores suplexes us."

Julia laughs, a tiny one, but genuine. "Okay. Let's go."

I type in my details to Uber, but it's going to be forty-five minutes before Jan can get back to us. I groan and show my phone to Julia, who sighs heavily.

"What a horrible night. I'm homeless, and I somehow brought a cowboy hat."

"You're not homeless—you now live with your cousin." I

open the canvas bag near me, curious. I grin and pull out a stuffed bear with honey-colored fur. "Cowboy hats and bears? Impeccable packing skills."

Julia rolls her eyes. "Don't laugh. I need him. He helps me sleep."

"Oh, really? After all you said about my precious Reginald?"

"Butterbeary isn't ugly," Julia says, a smirk curling her lips. "Big difference."

We poke through the rest of her belongings, laughing at the odd assortment. She withdraws a mini basketball, and I make a show of shooting it through the hoop in the park. Julia laughs and claps, and I bow like I've done something actually impressive. When Jan pulls up in the same car, I'm wearing Julia's cowboy hat and she has a Hawaiian lei around her neck. She has Butterbeary (cutest name in the fucking world) tucked under her arm.

"You kids have fun?" Jan asks as we pile into the car.

I look at Julia.

She smiles. "It started out terrible, but the latter half wasn't so bad."

Jan drives us back to the camp in cozy silence, me grinning to myself in the dark.

We sneak in the way we came. Maxine is still doing rounds, and we wait for her flashlight to disappear before we slip through the gate. A low growl makes me freeze. Walter stalks toward us, body stiff, poised to bark. Julia lets out a tiny squeak of fear.

"Walter, it's me," I whisper. "You wouldn't bark at your best friend, would you?"

The answer is no, because Walter immediately relaxes and sprints toward me to lick my hands. Julia shakes her head in wonder.

"Remind me to call you if I ever need to rob a bank."

We sneak back to Cabin 11 without a hitch. Walter graciously escorts us but turns to rejoin Maxine when we enter the cabin. Julia dumps her stuff on the floor and crawls into bed fully clothed.

"Do *not* wake me up tomorrow."

I change into my pajamas, smiling. "I'll see you bright and early."

Julia sighs, then falls silent. I change and go to her bedside, but she's fast asleep, bear tucked under her arm. I get into bed as quiet as I can and check my phone—3:11 a.m. I know I'll be dead tomorrow, so I set an alarm for eight fifteen. Won't make that mistake again. And . . .

I open a text to Sarah.

When you wake up, can you call Julia?

I lock my phone. And in seconds, I'm fast asleep.

CHAPTER 30

My alarm screams at eight fifteen. I peel my face from my pillow, my head throbbing distantly, my eyes full of grit.

I'm dead. I'm human garbage. I died in my sleep, and I'm a zombie now.

Julia shifts under my bunk, and that's the only thing that convinces me to move. My entire body is sore, as if I did an intense workout for basketball. I cannot exist on just five hours of sleep! I don't know how Julia does it.

"Julia," I call, my voice unattractively husky, "it's eight fifteen."

"No, it isn't," Julia groans.

"I'm so sorry, but it is." I climb down from my bunk, but I'm so tired I just lean my head against the hard wood and wish for death. I hear the bed creak and Julia's footsteps, but I can't move. Last time, adrenaline and panic woke me up enough to sprint to SAT prep. The alarm somehow made it worse. I know I'll be late if I don't move, but my itchy eyes are begging me to risk it all and go back to bed.

"You're just like an herbivore. Asleep standing up."

Julia pats my back, her touch gentle, but that's not what wakes me up. It's the open affection, almost adoration in her voice. I look at her in disbelief and for a split second I see it reflected in her expression too; her lips curled in an amused grin, her eyes soft and gentle and locked on me. I can't move, but this time it's for a very different reason than being sleepy after our midnight shenanigans.

Walter saves me by woofing huffily at the door. Julia rolls her eyes and lifts her hand off my back. I use that opportunity to scramble to the bathroom before I suffer cardiac arrest. When I examine myself in the mirror, I predictably look like death warmed over. But there's also a faint blush on my cheeks, and my ears are bright red.

I cover my ears, paranoid Julia will somehow develop laser vision and see just how down bad I am after she touched me just one time. But no one's ever looked at me like that! Like I wasn't an insufferable disaster. Like I wasn't annoying, a failure, too much. She looked at me like I look at my multitude of crushes.

She looked at me like I was someone to be loved.

"Get it together," I growl to my hopeless reflection. But Mirror Hallie is so in love; my face is turning red before my eyes, and I'm already thinking about how amazing it would be to just tell Julia that I like her, that maybe we could work something out. . . .

No. No! I have rules! I can't change if I fall in love with my bunkmate! Even if she opened up to me for the first time, and held my hand when she needed support—

"It's all right, Walter, don't cry," Julia's voice says beyond the bathroom door. "Your mom'll be right back."

Even if she's kind to my dog best friend, despite saying he's scary—

"Hurry, Hallie! We don't want to be late."

Even if she knows how much being on time means to me, despite me never saying so—

"I'm coming!" I yell, just to stop thinking for a second. I glare at Mirror Hallie. Look at the problems in front of you, not problems down the road. I have to be on time for SAT prep or my points will suffer. My cursed crush will have to wait.

I brush my teeth at lightning speed and think of the least romantic things I can imagine—taxes, gum stuck to my clothes, cracking my head open on a rock—and that convinces my face to stop blushing. When I open the door, Julia breezes past me and grabs her toothbrush, completely comfortable sharing the space. Unfortunately, I'm not half as cool as she is, so I flee to the main room to change out of my pajamas.

Walter's waiting for me by the bunk, so I pet him and try to calm down. Now that I'm out of the danger zone, details from last night creep into my head and with it, unease. Julia seems fine, but maybe reality hasn't set in yet. She has to be stressed about that massive fight with her parents and what it means for her now.

I reach for my phone, and I have texts from Sarah.

I heard what happened.

I'm working on it

also thank you for being there for her.

I smile at my phone. Julia said once that I was a good friend, but I don't think I did anything amazing. Julia needed help, and I was there. Same with Nav. It's not unlike anything I would have done for my exes. But, as I watch Julia emerge from the bathroom, yawning and wearing mismatched shirt and shorts as usual, maybe it's different this time. Julia smiles when she meets my eyes, and I automatically smile back. I can't say why, but this feels different from Peter or Gabriel or Ashley. For the first time in my life, I feel like someone sees me.

"You ready?" Julia yawns again. "Fuck, I'm tired. You take notes; I'm taking a nap."

I breathe in slowly. Because even when I'm a puddle of gay sludge, being around Julia's calm confidence grounds me. She just had a monumental shift in her life, and she's babying me into being on time to SAT prep.

"I'm ready." I grab my backpack and pocket my phone. "But we'll have to sleep in shifts because I'm dying."

"Hope Caroline takes good notes."

"She doesn't. She's always writing her novel about man-eating bears."

Julia sighs as we leave Cabin 11, Walter panting happily at our heels. "Can't trust anyone but ourselves."

I smile at the ground, basking in the glory of inclusion. Julia used to depend on only herself, but now there's me.

Julia's phone buzzes. She glances at it, and I glimpse her screen—several texts and missed calls fill her phone. Julia's face darkens as she scans the crowded screen.

"Are you okay?" I ask tentatively.

Julia glances at me and her expression softens. She pockets her phone without answering it. "I will be."

There's nothing left to say. We head to SAT prep, but I can't help but notice that Julia's walking close to my side.

* * *

After SAT prep ends, Ms. Flores appears at the door. She crooks her finger at me and Julia. She's not wearing her characteristic, slightly manic grin. Today, she seems serious. "You two, come here."

My stomach drops to my toes. Oh fuck, we're dead! Walter somehow snitched on us! I glance at Julia, panicked, but she just looks grim.

"Hallie didn't have anything to do with it," Julia says.

Her voice is calm and even. I want to tear up. I can't believe she's protecting me—

Ms. Flores shakes her head, cutting my weird mix of panic and gratitude short. "Follow me. Both of you."

I take a deep breath to calm myself. I should have known we wouldn't get away unscathed. But honestly, as we follow Ms. Flores to a small, air-conditioned office, the anxiety fades. I did what I had to do. I'd happily do it again.

Ms. Flores sits at the desk, and Julia and I sit across from her. The chair is uncomfortable and cold, but I try to block it out. I glance at Julia, but she has the most incredible poker face. She's looking at Ms. Flores with an emotionless expression. But I can see her hands shaking, gripped tight around her notebook.

Ms. Flores sighs. She meets both of our eyes. "Why did I get a call at six a.m. from Mr. Brown saying his daughter and her friend showed up at his house?"

"He gets confused," Julia lies easily. Even I almost believe her. "Don't worry about it. I'm sure Mom has calmed him down by now."

"I applaud the instinct to lie to authority, but unfortunately for you two, we have security cameras at the gate."

Ah, damn. I should have known it wouldn't be that easy. Julia grips her notebook harder, so I jump in. "We're really sorry, Ms. Flores. We won't do it again, but it was an emergency."

"You certainly won't do it again." I've never seen Ms. Flores look so stern. "You could have gotten hurt, or worse. You realize you jeopardized not only your own safety but also the safety of the other campers?"

Julia and I mumble apologies. Ms. Flores massages her temples.

"But I also know you two wouldn't have done this without a good reason. So, I'm listening. What was so important that you had to sneak out of camp after midnight?"

Julia glances at me. She seems conflicted, her eyebrows pulled tight with distress. I know this has to be excruciating; she just told me what's going on, and now Ms. Flores is breathing down her neck like an extremely pissed-off dragon. But I think back to Ms. Flores's gentle—if unusual—methods and advice. And how much she loves every camper and is invested in their success. She'll understand.

I put a hand on Julia's arm. "You should tell her."

Julia sighs but gives me a tiny nod. I take my hand away while she finds the text and hands her phone over to Ms. Flores.

Ms. Flores scans Julia's phone. Her eyes narrow the more she reads. Suddenly, I know she wasn't mad at us before, because she's livid now.

Julia and I wait in uncomfortable silence as Ms. Flores scrolls up to read more of the conversation. Then, she gives Julia's phone back. Her expression is openly furious but not directed at us.

"Hallie, you can go."

I stiffen, shocked by the pace of this conversation. "I'm not in trouble?"

"No. Well, we'll talk about you ruining my security hound later." She gives me a small smile that's almost her normal one.

I glance at Julia, who's struggling to keep her poker face. "If it's okay, I want to stay—"

"I need to talk to Julia alone." Ms. Flores's tone is calm and gentle. "It's all right, she's not in trouble either. Go on to Finance."

I look at Julia one more time, and she nods. "I'll be okay."

"Okay . . ." Reluctantly, I get up and go to the door. Julia and I don't look away until the door closes behind me.

I can't focus at all during Finance, and I flub my points on an easy question about economics. But I can't bring myself to care. What are they talking about? Ms. Flores said Julia wasn't in trouble, but she was so mad when she saw the texts. I type out a quick text to Nav under the desk.

Nav types for a long time. Then—

I breathe a sigh of relief. I quickly tell Nav I'm in class and can't talk yet, but I promise I will later. I count the minutes until Finance is over, and then I sprint back to Cabin 11 at full speed.

I open the screen, and Julia's sitting at the desk, headphones on, completely normal. She turns around and lowers her headphones, a small smile on her face.

"Are you okay? Ms. Flores didn't kill you, did she?"

"No, but I was about to throw up," Julia says, laughing a little.

I sit on the floor beside our beds, my anxiety still ramping up. "What happened?"

Julia blows out a breath. "I think Ms. Flores is gonna adopt me."

I blink. That wasn't what I was anticipating at all. "Umm . . . congratulations?"

Julia's grin widens. "She was so mad when I showed her the texts. She made me talk about what Dad and Mom have been doing this whole summer, and before. It was like a really aggressive therapy session." Julia seems pensive, a little in awe. "She asked if I had anywhere to go after camp, and I said maybe Sarah's, but I don't think she was satisfied with that. She said she would personally make sure I didn't go home to an unsafe environment. Then she called Dad and chewed him out right in front of me."

"Oh my God."

"Yeah. It felt so good. I don't think anyone's ever stood up to him like that." Julia shakes her head in wonder. "After that, she gave me a hug and some homemade cookies and said I could skip the rest of classes today. And that if push comes to shove, I could stay with her. Apparently she has a daughter our age?"

"Oh, Gia! You'll love her, she's great."

Julia rolls her eyes, a soft grin replacing the wonder. "Why am I surprised you know her? Of course you do."

"Just because my best friend is dating her—"

"Stop, stop." Julia laughs, and it's so clear and happy that I just soak it in. For the first time since we've met, she doesn't look exhausted. It's like a weight has been lifted from her shoulders. Julia meets my eyes, and hers are softer than I've ever seen them. "Thank you so much for everything, Hallie."

"No, it's not a big deal."

"It is to me," Julia insists. "You dropped everything to help me, even though you know you're dead without getting nine hours of sleep."

"It's good for you," I argue, but I'm smiling.

Julia is too. "I know. But you sacrificed so much for me, and I didn't have the courage to tell Ms. Flores what was going on until you helped me. I'm so . . . I don't know. No one's ever done that for me before."

"Well . . ." I have to hold in my love confession with all the strength I have. "You deserve it, you know? And I'd do it all again."

Julia looks into my eyes for a long moment, and neither one of us breathes. Then, so quickly I almost miss it, Julia glances at my top bunk. Before I can figure it out, she gets up from the desk and stretches.

"Anyway," she says, her words a little quicker than normal. "Let's go to lunch. I'm starving."

I get up from the floor. I glance at my bunk too, but I just see a messy bed and Reginald. Oh well—maybe I'm imagining things. I grin and grab my backpack. "To some awful food! Wish you'd saved me some cookies."

"When you've had the night I've had, you can have some cookies." Still, Julia passes me half of a massive cookie, the top shining with cinnamon-sugar. "I ate the chocolate one, don't worry."

I shove the cookie into my mouth so I don't admit I love her right now. And then we head to the mess hall as usual, even though nothing can ever be the same again.

CHAPTER 31

I feel like something has shifted between me and Julia.

I can't prove it, but I'm putting my apparent-detective skills to good use. Julia walks closer to me now, and goes to dinner with me a lot more often. She's still studying hard, but takes more breaks, sketches more things in her notebook. Yesterday, she asked me to hold a dandelion between my thumb and middle finger, and after twenty minutes, she showed me the most perfect sketched hand I've ever seen. I know hands are hard because Nav complains about them all the time. And when I practically yelled how impressed I was, she tore it out of her notebook and gave it to me! I've dated an artist or two, and I know they don't do this for anyone.

If I didn't know any better, I'd say Julia liked me as more than a friend.

But I do know better. Julia is just my friend—she said so herself! And she has to be feeling better from not having her parents' threat hanging over her head. We FaceTimed Sarah the other day together, and Sarah was so excited about converting the guest room into Julia's room. Julia will have to change schools for her senior year, but she doesn't seem to mind. She looks ten times happier than the first day we met, when she was ready to bite my head off.

I'm also noting that if—*if*—we dated, we wouldn't have to worry about long distance anymore . . .

"Someone kill me," I mutter as I study flash cards for SAT. The final test is creeping closer, and I'm a bit panicked now. I'm ignoring the gay panic part and focusing on the test panic. If I ace it here, I won't have to stress at all my senior year. I have the grades, I have extracurriculars—the SAT is the last piece. I could get into any college I wanted if this test goes well. It would be pure, indisputable proof that I'm not the dumb jock Peter said I was. Also getting a 1550+ would be the ultimate symbol, besides the medal, of course, that I've changed. The mounting pressure is almost enough to distract me from Julia. Almost.

"SAT?" Julia asks. She just got out of the shower, freshly changed in Easter-themed pajama shorts. I try my hardest not to stare at her slightly flushed face and how she wipes leftover sweat from her forehead with the towel around her neck.

"Yep," I manage to choke out.

Julia studies my face for a second. "Does the cocoon help?"

"The what?"

She gestures at my suitcase. I have it squished against my right side, my left pressed against the bed frame. I guess it is a cocoon. I just thought of it as an anti-stress chamber.

"Yeah! But it could be better. Sometimes at home, I study in my closet."

Julia smiles, her characteristic half one that makes my heart stutter in my chest. She glances upward, toward my bunk. Then she reaches up and returns with my duffel bag. "Let's see what we can do."

I watch while Julia piles my duffel bag on top of my suitcase, then hers, and then the extra one she brought from our journey to her house. She balances a final bag longways in between the bunk and the piled suitcases. I'm enclosed in a dark, cozy cave, the harsh overhead light blocked out. Julia leans down, so all I can see is her face bathed in light.

"Better?"

I am in love with Julia Brown.

"Yeah," I manage to whisper, my eyes locked on Julia's. Not for the first time, I want to throw my rules in the garbage and grab her face and kiss her. But I can't. I can't do that to myself when I'm so close to becoming the best version of myself. I can't do it to Julia either; she deserves me at my best. Hallie 2.0, when she's gotten everything figured out, can ask Julia on a date. But this current disaster can't do anything.

Julia nods and goes to her desk to study. I try to focus on the flash cards in front of me, but after each flip I just think of Julia. Her smile. Her nose ring. The cute purple streak in her hair. How all her pajamas are holiday themed for some reason. How talented she is in art and music. How she is already decided on what she wants to major in. How strong and resilient she is, and how happy I am that she finally has some peace.

I throw down my cards. I'm not studying tonight.

"Mood," Julia says from the desk. She stretches her arms to the sky as I peek out of my cubby hole. She glances at me. "You want to take a break?"

"Yes, please."

"I have something to show you, but it's too early." Julia stares out the window, so she thankfully doesn't see me perk up like Walter does when I open a bag of Cheetos.

"What is it? A surprise?"

Julia returns her attention to me, grinning. "If it's a surprise, I'd ruin it if I told you."

I groan and Julia's grin widens. "For now, let's watch a movie."

Oh, that'll be nice. I'm combusting with anticipation for this mysterious surprise, but I hold it in. New Hallie is calm and can wait for her crush to surprise her. I crawl out of my cocoon and grab my laptop from my bed. "I have some saved. What genre?"

Julia tilts her head. She glances at my vision board before smiling. "Horror."

"You're just saying that because you don't believe in my manifestations."

"I didn't say that. I want you to take real breaks. And you like horror movies, so why not?"

Julia sits on the bottom bunk on the other side. I follow her with my laptop, sighing. She doesn't know it, but I'd do whatever she wanted. I shudder at the thought of breaking my rules, but it's fine. The horror movie one is just a guideline. "What do you want to watch?"

"What's your favorite?"

"*Halloween*," I say immediately. I pause, smiling. "Do you like horror movies?"

Julia gives me a serious look. "I have never once been defeated by a movie, and I won't start now."

"Okay! But let's try *Scream* instead." I like that one almost as much, and it's less scary, more funny. "Have you seen it?"

"No, but I know the memes."

I laugh and boot up the movie. "Prepare to experience some culture."

Julia, as I suspected, does not like horror movies. She watches almost the entire film through her fingers, flinching and squeaking with terror at each kill. I grin all throughout, even managing to hold back my pitiful excitement when Julia grabs my hand when the killers are revealed. When the credits roll, Julia turns to me.

"I may have been overconfident."

I laugh and close my laptop. "I picked a not-too-scary one on purpose."

Julia mutters darkly under her breath. She glances out the window and stands. "I'm regretting telling you about the surprise, but I have to do it now."

"What is it?"

Julia just smiles. I brighten when she grabs her backpack and violin case. "You'll see. Follow me."

Julia sets off without another word. I gather my own backpack and hurry to follow her. We walk toward the lake, and slowly, the sounds of the other campers talking fades into cicadas screaming and frogs singing to the sky. She takes the normal path, until she suddenly swerves into a smaller, barely visible path. I don't say anything, but I'm getting more and more curious by the second. How did she find this? Where are we going?

We walk for a few minutes, until the underbrush clears and

we're beside the lake. But it's not just the normal, still blue water; it's completely covered in fireflies. I gasp.

"Oh, wow." I watch the bugs light up the area, entranced. "It's so beautiful."

"Isn't it?" Julia smiles toward the water. "I found it on accident, when I stayed too late one day. And saw this."

I'm overwhelmed with the green-yellow lights all around me, the hush of the water, the alive, electric sounds of the wildlife surrounding us. This place is gorgeous. And Julia . . . wanted to show me. It's deeply romantic to take me to a firefly-lit lake, right?

I turn to Julia, and she walks a few steps ahead. She sits by the lake and pats the space next to her. I follow, a little nervous as I settle down beside her. Is something about to happen? Is this how she tells me that she doesn't want to be just friends anymore?

Am I ready to hear that?

Julia points to the fireflies. "You know how rare it is to see these now? They used to be everywhere. Global warming is taking them out in droves. But for some reason, they're thriving here. Why?"

I blink at her for a second. Global warming is decidedly not romantic. "Maybe because there's less pollution and stuff here?"

Julia nods seriously. "Less human interference. I think Ms. Flores would body-slam us if she saw us littering."

I laugh at the image of the petite woman WWE-slamming kids into the ground. "It's Ms. Flores, with the steel chair!"

"My God, she's doing a tombstone!" Julia says in a mock

announcer voice. Then she laughs and says, "I'm sorry, I don't know anything else about wrestling."

"Unfortunately, Michael was a big fan. I can name quite a few names and moves."

"Someone needs to study your brain. It's like a steel trap." Julia smiles at her lap and opens her catch-all notebook. She doesn't study her notes but instead flips to a new page. She carefully begins to sketch the outline of the lake, adding tiny graphite dots for the fireflies. She tapers the dots to a point, then carefully erases them, making them perfectly round.

I watch her draw, and the nervous tension melts away. This isn't a confession. This place is Julia, in a way—gorgeous, mysterious, secluded. And somehow, I'm the only one who gets to see both.

I stay quiet until her sketch is finished. She shows it to me, and I applaud.

She rolls her eyes, grinning. "It's not that great."

"It is and you know it!"

"Fine, fine." Julia looks pensively out on the lake. "Ms. Flores checked on me today."

"Yeah?"

"Yeah. She just wanted to see how I was doing. We talked about college and stuff." Julia meets my eyes, hers dark and soft. "She said the same thing you did. About minoring in music."

"See? I told you it's a good idea!"

Julia pretends to sigh. "I'd honestly never considered it. I picked up violin because the concert band teacher asked me to. It was just something to do so I wouldn't have to be at home."

Julia's expression turns pensive again. "I told Ms. Flores about how hard architecture school is and she said, 'So? You think you can't do it?' And I guess I'm thinking . . . I can. This camp showed me I can. I can have it all."

"You absolutely can."

Julia nudges my shoe. "So can you, you know."

I frown at her. "What do you mean?"

Julia chuckles. "Never mind." She stands and opens her violin case. My heart races pleasantly.

"Are you going to play for me?"

"I'm going to play, and you're free to listen." Still, Julia grins at me. "If I'm going to minor in music, I'll have to learn how to play when I'm happy too."

Julia touches her bow to the delicate strings, and the clearing fills with music. I watch her play, a happier, upbeat tune now, fireflies darting around her instrument and illuminating her face. Not for the first time, but definitely for the strongest, I fall head over heels in love with her. These last two weeks are going to be torture.

Julia finishes her performance, and I cheer. She seems vaguely embarrassed but also radiant and so, so happy. We pack our things to go back to the cabin, though I never want to leave.

"I know the bugs are cute at night, but I really regret coming here after that movie."

I'd forgotten all about *Scream*. I grin, ready to tease her. "If Ghostface came into the cabin, he'd get you first." I nudge her playfully with my hip. "Should have let me have the bottom bunk."

"Why would you say that?" Julia's voice is tinged with genuine despair. I can't hold in a laugh as we troop back home. "I can't believe this. I'm such a wimp."

"Why'd you ask to watch a horror movie if you were so scared?"

"Is it a crime to want to look cool?"

I grin into the dark. I've had this conversation many times with my exes, my parents, even Nav. No one loves horror movies like I do. The initial viewing is pretty scary, but afterward, you just have to focus on the filmmaking. And obviously, it's not real. No one gets scared of fantasy movies coming to life. Though admittedly the stakes are lower if they did.

"We'll pick a rom-com next time."

"No," Julia says immediately. "We can watch your favorite one next."

I blink, shocked. "Are you sure?"

"Yeah." Julia's voice is confident. "I want to see the movies you love."

I'm stunned into silence. No one has ever said that to me. Ashley and I of course bonded over horror, but after that, no one wanted to watch with me. Peter even went so far as to say it was "unnatural" for a girl to like horror movies. Nav will watch with me, but she complains and is on her phone the whole time. For an entire year, I've been watching my favorite movies alone in my room with enough popcorn for one, my lights out so I don't ruin the ambiance. And now Julia's saying she'll join me? Even though she's clearly frightened, though she watched through her fingers, she wants to try again? Just because they're my favorite?

I piece together all the puzzle pieces from today, growing more and more alarmed as they click into place. Julia building my study cocoon. Showing me her sketches though she once guarded them like Walter does the camp. Bringing me to her secret, secluded clearing, though she was feeling jumpy from the movie, and giving me a performance for me and only me. And most of all, reaching out her hand to me, showing me that what I like matters and she's willing to experience it with me.

My hunch from before rears its head, but this time it's harder to refute. Julia Brown might just have a crush on me.

CHAPTER 32

I head to the track after Life Skills, on a mission. Walter jogs behind me, tongue lolling, as I FaceTime Nav. She picks up on the first ring, because we scheduled this call.

"War council is in," Nav says, angling her phone to Gia, who's sitting on her bed with a notebook and pen, a serious expression on her face. "Let's figure out if Julia has a crush on you."

My heart skips a beat, even though I told Nav the reason for the call via text. Hearing her say it out loud . . . "We don't know for sure."

"Exactly," Nav says. "We're gonna figure it out right now."

"Defense, please present your evidence." Gia pushes up her glasses with one finger, and I can't hold in a laugh. Nav and Gia are total goofs, perfect for each other. I don't know why any of us ever thought it would end up any other way.

"Okay. So this is all just a hunch—"

"Are hunches admissible in court?" Nav asks Gia.

Gia seems to seriously consider it before nodding. "We'll allow it."

I roll my eyes, their elaborate play taking some of the nerves away. I tell them about what happened with the scary movie, and the firefly field, but also all the little changes I've noticed. When

I get to Julia building my cubby hole for me, I nearly swoon. It could be the oppressive heat, though.

When I'm through, Nav nods gravely. "Sounds like a grade A crush to me. Like she took you to a secluded lake with fireflies and played her violin for you? Hallie, come on."

I hate how happy and light those words make me feel.

"Agreed," Gia says. She's holding her dog, a corgi named Jordan, while she thinks. "And the fort! That's so cute."

"I mean, it wasn't a big deal—"

"It is!" Nav says. "She paid attention to you and actively tried to make you more comfortable. I didn't even know you studied in your closet. Which is so weird—why do you do that?"

"I can laser focus without distractions when I'm in there. But that's not important, what's important is what do I do about it?"

"What do you mean?" Gia asks. "You ask her out now, right? It doesn't have to be as dramatic as Nav's."

"I will never live that down," Nav groans. "But yeah, you gotta go for it. You've been here before, you know what to do."

The comment stings. Here we are again: Hallie Griffin, who has dated endlessly and has nothing to show for it. Yes, I've been here before. I asked Peter anxiously to homecoming, Ashley to get after-party Waffle House with me before that, Diya to the arcade before that. I also remember how god-awful I felt before each of them, like I was going to vomit up my intestines. And those were the successful ones! The no's were a hundred times worse.

But what's really hanging me up this time is that somehow, despite my best efforts, I like Julia more than I have anyone else. I've never been friends with someone before dating them. I never shared s'mores and studied with someone. I never held their hand in the face of something hard. I never won tournaments with someone and shared custody of hard-won candy. I've never had someone draw a picture for me and only me.

A sick feeling replaces my earlier butterflies. Julia means a lot more to me than my exes ever did, and that's why we can't be together. If I did something wrong because I haven't changed enough and hurt her, I think it would kill me.

"I can't do it."

"I know you're scared," Gia says, her tone kind and soothing. For a second, she reminds me of Ms. Flores. "But it'll be worth it! She clearly likes you back."

"You don't understand." I can't get all my tangled thoughts in order. "My number one rule for the summer is no romance."

"Not this again," Nav complains.

"You're the one who told me not to fall in love!" I'm snapping at Nav and she can tell. Her teasing expression falls into a frown.

"I meant don't fall in love with douchebags. I didn't mean people who love your horror movies and built you cute forts."

I look away from the phone. "Still. That's what I said and I'm sticking to it. I said no romance, and I meant it. I'm clearly not good enough yet, and I'm not hurting Julia while I figure myself out."

There's a loaded silence. Walter nudges my knee. Even his big brown eyes are concerned. I'm starting to hate myself. Why am I whining about this to Nav and Gia, who are happily coupled up? This is a single girl's issue.

I start to apologize and change the subject, but Nav beats me to it.

"Okay. You can wait until you're ready." Nav's voice is unusually subdued. I look back at my phone in surprise, but the moment's already passed. She already looks mischievous again. "Now give me details on how you escaped from camp and almost got away with it."

I exhale, relieved. "I can't really tell you the details, but Julia had an emergency, and I went with her."

"No wonder she likes you," Nav mutters under her breath.

"Mami said she might come live with us?" Gia seems anxious. Jordan licks her chin and forces her to pet her. "I've been an only child for so long! What if I mess up?"

"Don't I know it, Gia. I got so worried that she'd hear me pee in the bathroom." We chat about only-child problems until the sun is low over the horizon.

"Are we keeping you?" Nav asks. "I know you gotta study for the test."

I hesitate. I should go, but I need to address the other elephant in the room. I pick my words carefully. "Do you want to talk about the reunion?"

Nav blinks, then breaks into a grin. "It was great! Did you know Ben cut all his hair off? He's bald!"

I gasp. Nav's cousin had such beautiful locs! "That's a travesty."

"I know. I called him Shrek all weekend." Nav laughs, and Gia smiles at her, all the love in the world in her expression. I try my best to ignore it. "But no, it was great. She, uh . . . Mom wasn't there."

"Good." I keep my tone firm. "Gia, did she tell you I gave permission to whoop her mom's ass if you saw her?"

Gia flexes her skinny bicep. "I was ready and willing."

"Stop." Nav holds Gia's hand, and a lump rises in my throat. She is so incredibly happy, it's like staring into a bright light. It's beautiful, but it still hurts. "I will probably have to have years of therapy, but I'm glad I went. And we got to eat the banana pudding!"

"Oh my God, it was so good." Gia's eyes are as wide as saucers. "I loved it so much that I shook Nav's grandma's hand. It was really embarrassing."

"You mean adorable." Nav affectionately pushes Gia's hair behind her ear, and Gia turns a happy shade of pink.

I've seen enough. "I gotta go before you two start making out."

"I would never be that rude!" Nav says. "Plus I never know when Ms. Flores is coming home, and she would probably kill me."

I smile, despite feeling waves of jealous revulsion. "Still, I have to study. Bye Nav, bye Gia."

"Bye! Good luck, Hallie."

"Love you! Go tell Julia that too!"

Nav hangs up, and I crouch in the dirty track. Walter leans his weight on me, and I hug his neck, overwhelmed with emotion. Tears prick my eyes, but I refuse to let them fall. New Hallie isn't jealous. New Hallie doesn't cry frustrated tears over her best friend's relationship. New Hallie isn't horribly, terribly lonely.

Walter licks my face and I hug him tighter. "It'll be better tomorrow, Walter," I whisper. He nuzzles under my chin, as if he's agreeing. I will be better tomorrow. I cling to that as I stand, take a breath of soggy summer air, and head home to Cabin 11.

Julia's not at her desk when I get back. She's lying on the unused bottom bunk, staring at the bed above, headphones firmly around her ears. She glances at me when I come in, but doesn't move except to take her headphones off.

We look at each other for a second. It's unlike her to not be studying. And she seems kind of distressed, her eyebrows pulled together with worry. I've never seen her in the stare-at-the-ceiling stage.

"Tough day?" I venture.

"You too," she counters.

I shrug, but my heart is singing. She noticed! She noticed something's wrong! I shouldn't be happy, but by God, I am.

Julia sits up and sighs. "I don't want to talk about it. Wanna get s'mores?"

My mood instantly lifts. Hell yeah I do! And maybe she knows how happy the invitation makes me, because she smiles at me as she gets up and gathers her backpack.

CHAPTER 33

When we get to the s'more station, we stand at the edge, stunned. Almost every camper is here! The s'mores table is crowded, surrounded by all cabins. Someone has broken out the hot dogs, and there are people roasting them around the double-sized fire.

"Whoa," Julia says, her eyebrows raised. "I thought we were all too cool for s'mores."

"Maybe everyone isn't so competitive now?" There's only a little over a week left of camp. If you're not in the top ten, you're probably out of luck getting number one. Julia and I are still four and five, but I spy two and three chatting with Amira by the hot dog station. And, though I can't believe it, Cam is here! They're sitting next to Teddy, cramming an entire s'more into their mouth and dancing with glee.

Julia shakes her head with wonder. "I'm gonna get in line. Find us a seat?"

I salute, and Julia rolls her eyes, smiling. I pick my way through the crowd toward Cam. They catch my eye and wave me over, cramming close to Teddy while he complains.

"Hallie! You've got to try these, oh my God."

"Are you saying you've never had a s'more before?" I sit down next to Cam and put my backpack on the log next to me for Julia.

Cam seems a little embarrassed and I gasp.

"You haven't!"

"I've never gone camping!" Cam says, already defensive.

I laugh and shake my head. "Finally, something you're not good at."

"I assure you, now that I've had them, I'll be a s'more-eating champion." Cam puffs out their chest. "Wait, where's Julia?"

"In line. She's getting ours."

Cam smiles, but it's a sly one. I lean away, wary.

"What?"

"Nothing!" Cam's expression turns thoughtful. "Actually, that's not true. I've been thinking, and I wanted to apologize again."

I blink at them. "For what? You already apologized. No big deal."

Cam rubs the back of their neck. They're staring sheepishly at their shoes. "No, I know, but I wanted to say I really am sorry. I guess I came here expecting to be the best, you know? Even before Ms. Flores announced the points system, I thought my way of doing things was the only way . . ." Cam trails off, looking across the fire at something. I follow their line of sight, but all I can make out is the dancing flames.

"But I was wrong. I told you that you shouldn't work with anyone because that's how I work best. But you and Julia are killing it! I'm a little worried y'all are gonna win."

"We are," I say automatically.

Cam and I smile at each other.

"But it's okay. You can only know what you know, right? Studying alone works for you, so you were just trying to help."

"Yeah, but I didn't even stop to consider how others felt. Not just you, but Caroline, Teddy, my cabinmates . . ." Cam returns to staring into the fire as Teddy shoots me a knowing glance over their head. "I feel like I've learned a lot in five weeks."

"Yeah?"

"Yeah. Not just how to change a tire, though that is huge for me. But like . . . I can't just stomp into the room with a chip on my shoulder. I can't hurt my friends because I'm too stubborn. And I'm not gonna be the best all the time."

"Still taking those pop-up losses hard, huh?" Teddy chimes in.

Cam elbows him, but they're grinning. "Shut up! But honestly, yeah. I'm not the best at everything, and I think that's okay?"

"It is," I urge. "Ms. Flores would be so proud of you, Cam."

Cam puts their hand over their heart. "That's my life goal from now on. Live a life that will make Ms. Flores proud."

We laugh, but Cam has the right idea. I want her to be proud of me too. And I think Ms. Flores's dream is coming true—the camp is full of laughter and sweets, people sword fighting with their skewers, some reading leisure books or playing games on their Switches. I think this is what Ms. Flores meant when she said she wanted us to be well-rounded. I find myself speaking aloud.

"I thought I was pretty smart too, but music humbled me real quick. But you know, I'm not mad about it. I'll never be amazing at it, but I learned so much about Fine Arts. Everyone, my parents included, told me they weren't important, and I believed them. But that's not true. I actually know what a soprano part of a song is. And I read a biography about van

Gogh, and I loved it! I never would have done that without coming here."

"*And* you got to study with Julia," Cam says, batting their eyelashes innocently.

I kick their shoe while they cackle. My ears are on fire. "Julia is my precious cabinmate and that's all."

"Sure," Teddy says, grinning.

I start a heated denial when Julia appears at my side, arms full of marshmallows and graham crackers and chocolate. She sits next to me and dumps half of her prize in my lap.

"Had to fistfight Michelle to get these," she says.

"Why didn't you call me? I would have backed you up!"

Julia turns her half smile to me. "Can't share all my fun."

"Teddy, let's get some hot dogs," Cam says, hooking their arm through Teddy's.

He agrees, and we wave as they skip in tandem to the table. I narrow my eyes at their backs. I know what they're doing. They're leaving me and Julia alone on purpose! But I'd be lying if I said I minded. In fact, I need to remember to get their addresses so I can mail them Christmas gifts.

Julia passes me a stick with two marshmallows on it. We stand closer to the fire, me roasting mine patiently, Julia plunging hers deep into the fire immediately. I watch, amused, as she withdraws a burnt clump of marshmallow.

"Do you like them burnt?"

"I like them fast," Julia says, smiling. I watch her assemble hers without any finesse whatsoever, and she's done eating hers by the time mine is perfectly browned. She's already loading up another when I reach for the graham cracker.

"Wait," Julia says. She sifts through the assembled ingredients and withdraws a cube of chocolate.

"I can't have chocolate—"

"I know, I know. But it's not chocolate."

She drops it into my hand, and by the firelight I read the wrapping—it's caramel. I meet her eyes, and she smiles.

"Your dry marshmallow-graham cracker combo made me depressed. You can have caramel, yeah?"

"Yeah," I whisper, but for some reason I think I'm gonna cry? I blink rapidly against the smoke and wipe my eyes. This is so thoughtful. Where did she even get this? I didn't see any caramel squares last time. For a second, I imagine that I throw away my rules and grab Julia and kiss her right in front of everyone. But that would be Old Hallie, not the new, cool, self-actualized Hallie. That's the Hallie she deserves. Not impulsive, not petty and jealous, not "too much." So I take a deep breath and smile at Julia, despite wanting to kiss her.

"Thank you."

Julia shrugs, but I can tell she's pleased. I feel like I know the subtle movements of her face as well as my own. The tiny downturn of her left side when she's disappointed, the way her eyes light up when she's excited. The slight divot she gets in the middle of her brows when she's worried. And now, her half smile in full bloom, her eyes soft and content—she's happy. Simply because of me.

I assemble the modified s'more as I try not to burst into complicated tears. The sweetness of the s'more almost gets me, though. Knowing mine is special because Julia made sure

I could still enjoy it is about to take me out.

"Campers," Ms. Flores calls from the s'more table. Everyone looks up and quiets down immediately. "We have a final pop-up!"

"Now?" Julia mumbles, her mouth full of her third burnt marshmallow.

"This one will be unique. There will be no points awarded."

Oh. I expect everyone to deflate, maybe even go back to what they were doing, but no one does. Every eye is still on Ms. Flores.

"We will have stargazing near the lake. There are telescopes for everyone to share, but also finger food and sandwiches if you'd just like a nice night under the stars. Remember, you won't get a view like this in the city!" Ms. Flores smiles at everyone warmly. "There will be no points, and it's optional, as always. But I hope to see you there in ten minutes."

I glance at Julia. She swallows and wipes her mouth with one thumb. "You don't even have to ask."

I smile and stand. And try not to think about how romantic stargazing really is, or get paranoid that somehow even Ms. Flores sees my crush and is trying to be my wingman. I just hold out a hand to Julia and stifle a shiver of delight when she takes it.

"Let's go get a good seat."

CHAPTER 34

Almost everyone troops to the lake, led by Ms. Flores. There is indeed a snack table, so I gather a bunch for us while Julia finds a place to sit. I grab as many sweets as I can find for her, plus fruit and sandwiches for me. I turn, arms full, but Julia surprises me by standing by my side. She's holding two beach towels.

"Since there are no points this time . . ." Julia hesitates but smiles. "Do you want to go to the secret spot?"

I barely hold in a gasp. Do I want to go back to that romantic-as-hell firefly lake? Does she even have to ask? "Absolutely!"

Julia's grin widens, but she doesn't say anything as we sneak away from the crowd. I can barely see two feet ahead of me, but Julia expertly picks her way through the underbrush until we get to the clearing. Fireflies float around our heads, their soft glow and the full moon casting enough light for us to see each other. Julia lays down the blankets for us, and I carefully spread out all the sweets I grabbed.

Julia's eyes light up when she sees the cake slices I brought. She pops one into her mouth immediately, then sheepishly takes a grape from the pile.

"You can have all these," I say, laughing. "The caramel was enough."

"I'm sorry, I have a terrible sweet tooth," Julia admits.

"I know." I say it without thinking. We both look away, my ears burning hotly under the starry sky.

Julia recovers before I do. She takes a handful of M&M'S and pops a few into her mouth. "I'll eat all the chocolate so you won't be tempted."

"Appreciate it," I say, the burn fading from my ears and settling into a strange type of warm comfort in my chest. I take a piece of white cake from the pile and try it. I kind of get Julia's sweet obsession; these were clearly not made by Sharon. Has Ms. Flores been secretly supplying us with homemade sweets this whole time? I've been missing out.

We sit in comfortable silence. For once, I'm not thinking about anything really. Not changing, or worrying about the upcoming SAT, or my past failures. I'm just listening to the cicadas humming and the lake lapping at the rocky shore. And feeling Julia's presence beside me.

"The stars are so pretty here," Julia says after a while.

I look at her, and she smiles.

"Any of your exes know about space?"

"Diya. She went to space camp one time and never got over it."

"That'll do it." Julia sits up straight and looks right at me. "Go ahead. Tell me what you know."

If anyone else said this, I'd be embarrassed and play it off. But Julia's attention is only on me, her expression open and curious. She's not teasing me. She doesn't even care that I learn a lot from my exes. She just wants to know what I'm thinking.

"I don't actually know that much," I admit. "Diya wanted to

work at NASA, but she didn't want to do the go-to-the-moon part. Just the math."

"Disgusting," Julia says, a smile in her voice. "But you like math."

"I do, but not like . . . rocket science." I look up at the sky. "I wish I'd learned more. Back then, I wasn't that good at listening. I was just happy a girl was talking to me."

"Mood." Julia looks up at the sky too. "Do you know anything about constellations?"

I sit up straighter. "No, I don't."

"Calm down, I don't either." Julia laughs. "I barely know my star sign."

"What is it?"

"Aries. And don't ask about my rising or whatever because I don't know."

"But it would be fun to find out!"

Julia rolls her eyes. "I guess so. We could learn it together."

I nod enthusiastically. I get lost in the idea of learning something new, but not to impress someone or desperately try to form a connection. Just learning something for the sake of it, because I'm curious. Learning something new *with* someone and not alone. We talk a little about our star signs and what we know (I'm a Taurus, which is boring, but Aries sounds really interesting).

"You're doing it," Julia says.

"Doing what?"

"Your steel-trap thing." Julia nudges me playfully, which sends pleasant shivers throughout my body. "I can practically see your mind storing info away forever."

"That's not true!" It is. I will never forget this moment for as long as I live.

"Yeah, yeah." Julia looks back at the sky. "My grandma loved stars. I wish I'd paid more attention."

Julia's tone turns sad, and some of the playfulness disappears. I think back to her a few hours ago, staring at the top bunk with a cloudy expression. I inch closer, so our hands are almost touching.

"Do you want to talk about earlier?"

"Only if you do," Julia says immediately.

I sigh. Julia is direct and authoritative. I'll never get away with not talking through my feelings ever again. Somehow, that doesn't seem so bad. "Deal. But I asked first."

"*Who's* not competitive?" Julia teases, then looks at her tennis shoes. "I think the good part has worn off. About not living with my parents, I mean."

"That means . . . ?"

"I was just thinking about how I don't want to be a burden on Sarah and her family."

"We already discussed that you are not a burden."

Julia sighs. "I know. But I still *feel* like I will be."

"I'm telling you, Sarah will love having you there. She gets so lonely sometimes. I worry about her."

Julia glances at me. "Yeah, me too. I'm not great company, though. I just eat and sleep and study."

"And make s'mores and stargaze," I say. "And win smart-people tournaments."

Julia laughs. "You know what, that's true. I'm exponentially more interesting after this summer. Can't say Ms. Flores never gave me nothing." Julia sits up and hugs her knees. "I was also thinking about how insane it is to change schools in my senior year."

"Mapleton has a weirdly good college-ready program," I say. My brain pops out a risky line, but I can't stop myself from saying it. "And I'll be there."

Julia considers this for a few seconds. She finally meets my eyes, hers soft. "Yeah. That's worth it."

Tingles run from my scalp down my back. I don't know if anyone has ever said that to me. That I'm worth a hard and scary change. That I'm a positive in the midst of a lake of misery. I'm so pleased that I can't speak, and the moment passes. Julia nudges me with her shoe.

"Your turn. Why were you crying?"

"I wasn't," I say. "There was dust in my eyes."

Julia rolls her eyes. "Sure, okay. Why was there dust in your eyes and you also looked upset?"

The tingles fade, and I'm left with the ugly truth. I haven't spoken it out loud. When I do, I can't take it back. A part of me is terrified to air this ugly part of me, something I've been working hard to scrub away all summer. But Julia might not judge me. I hope.

"I'm jealous of my best friend's relationship."

Julia raises her eyebrows. "Elaborate."

"My best friend, until this summer, always said she just wanted hookups. And then she just falls in love in a whirlwind four weeks. I'm so happy for her, but I . . ." I hesitate but decide to go for it. I have to let it all out. "I also wish it had been me."

"Do you like your best friend's partner?" Julia asks.

I shake my head. "No, not romantically. But that's another bad thing! Gia is so sweet and kind, and she treats Nav so well. I should be happy for them, shouldn't I? But I see them happy together and I just want to puke. I spent so long searching for that kind of love, and she found it when she wasn't even looking." I rest my head on my knees. I can't look at Julia. "I'm a terrible person."

"No, you're not." Julia's voice is gentle. "You're just a person. Jealousy is normal."

"With your best friend?"

"Sure," Julia says. "For instance, I am extremely jealous of your bear-trap brain. I want to take it out and dissect it so I can get mine to work that way."

I peek at Julia through a curtain of my hair. She's smiling, and that helps me relax.

"Listen, it's normal to want what others have. Do you know how much I wished for normal parents?"

I sit up. That makes a lot of sense, but it makes me feel worse. Julia has actual problems and I'm just a jealous goblin pining after what my friend has. "That's different."

"It isn't," Julia insists. "I would sit in my room and seethe at how easy everyone else has it. I was so bitter that I pushed everyone away. I kind of lied to you earlier. My friends in middle school dropped me because of studying, but also because I was rude and irritable because they had what I thought were perfect lives."

"But you had so much going on. You can't blame yourself for that."

Julia puts a gentle hand on my arm. "Is being hurt and

disrespected for so long not a good enough reason to be jealous of your friend? Is it crazy to want that for yourself?"

I don't have an answer to that. I've been focusing on the facts: I am bitter and jealous of Nav. But Julia's asking me to consider the why behind it. My brain balks at the idea. Does it matter why I'm doing bad things? I don't think so.

Julia eases closer. My breath catches in my throat. "The fact that you're so torn up about it means you're not a bad person. It's okay not to be perfect."

I take a steadying breath before I reply. "I will take your words into consideration."

Julia rolls her eyes, grinning. "You really should go into politics."

"No, I'm gonna be a detective! I've already decided."

"Don't go the doctor route, I'm begging."

And just like that, we're back to normal, the conversation ship steered safely away from the rocky edge of Deep Thoughts. But it's a bit different. Julia doesn't move away, despite the heat. I don't either. We talk about everything and nothing, eating grapes and cake under the moonlight, looking up at the stars. And when it's over, when we make our way back to help Ms. Flores pack up the blankets and break down the table, when Julia gasps with glee when Ms. Flores gives us the leftover sweets, I allow myself to think about Julia's words, just a little bit. Maybe I'm not a bad person. Maybe I don't need to change. I reject the idea immediately, but one fact does stick with me: this was the best non-date I've ever had.

CHAPTER 35

The next three days are the best of my life.

By all accounts, they shouldn't be. Julia and I are now in third and fourth place, with us just a fraction of a point away from second and third. The SAT looms in the background, and the top ten have renewed interest in clawing their way to first place. Every class is like heading to the Colosseum to fight to the death.

But they're the best days because of Julia. We've somehow become even closer. We study like mad for hours, bouncing SAT words and problems off each other at incredible speed, but then we take a break to do something fun. And, God, has it been fun. Julia tried to teach me how to play her violin, and when I made the most horrible sound known to man, she just laughed and showed me how to position the instrument under my chin. I convinced her to run with me and Walter yesterday, and she almost collapsed after only one lap, and Walter woke Maxine with his panicked howling. We used the music room to paint something, and we both ended up painting Reginald (mine very badly). I lectured her on how to appropriately care for bonsai trees, and she somehow didn't fall asleep. If I squint and turn my head a little, it's almost as if we're already dating.

Which is a problem! I hate myself after every almost-kinda-date, because of the number one rule I'm breaking every time. I want to believe our hangouts are simple friendship, but they aren't. I don't think about kissing Nav, or imagine holding hands with Cam, or plan a nonexistent future with Sarah. Julia is not just my friend, and that's a problem.

I'm brooding in my study hole when Julia enters the cabin. She peeks inside and smiles, and despite my best efforts, I smile back. I can't even pretend I don't like her! Someone strike me down right now.

"SAT?" she asks, nodding to the note cards at my feet.

"Yeah. I'm so nervous."

"Me too." Julia sits at the entrance of my suitcase cave. "I know we can take it over, but honestly I never want to look at this shit again."

"The math section is interesting . . . ! Though, honestly, I didn't use to love it. I practiced a ton of math to impress Diya."

"Oh boy, here we go." Julia leans back on her hands and looks at me with barely disguised adoration. I'm ashamed that I get a shiver of pleasure at the expression meant only for me. "I was thinking. Do you think you're attracted to interesting people just so you can hoard their knowledge like a dragon?"

"That's exactly it." I'm grinning too, and I know I have the goofiest expression on my face. I'm not strong enough to resist Julia and her offbeat charm I've grown to love. I almost tell her I'll absorb her artist skills too before I remember that she specifically said "attracted to." I cough and adjust my study cards. "It hasn't been too helpful so far, though."

"No way. I'm kind of interested in bonsai trees now."

"And running?"

"Fuck no," Julia snorts, and we laugh.

Walter uses that moment to scratch at the screen, and Julia lets him in. He beelines toward me and immediately knocks down my study cave. I groan and lecture him while Julia stifles a laugh.

"Walter, no! You are being so bad today, oh my God."

"That's what you get for spoiling him." Julia helps put away our bags while I continue to scold Walter and he ignores me. I end up hugging his fluffy neck, so maybe she's onto something.

"He just needs more playtime. Maxine is always too busy."

Julia sits on the floor again, and Walter trots up to her. He rests his heavy head in her lap, and she strokes his head gently. "You're doing your thing again. Where you notice things about people. And dogs, in this case."

"I swear, it's not a big deal."

Julia gets a mischievous gleam in her eye. "Then use your superpower on me."

I blink and my heart decides that we're running now. "What?"

"Tell me something you've noticed about me. And then I'll say yours."

"Is this a bet?"

"A friendly one! Whoever wins gets extra s'mores tonight."

Julia waits, her eyes sparking with a challenge. She doesn't think I can do it! Unluckily for her, I'm practically in love with her, so . . .

"You love studying at the desk. With music, always."

Julia nods, still smiling. "True. Continue."

"You love sweets."

"Doesn't count, I told you that."

"But you didn't tell me that it's because you often forget to eat due to stress, so the quick calories and sugar boost help."

Julia blinks in astonishment, then holds her hands up in surrender. A wry smile graces her lips. "My bad for doubting Hallie Holmes."

I could stop there. I should stop there. But something is tugging at my heart, telling me to keep going. To show in this subtle way how much Julia means to me. To show her that I see her and I care, but I just can't do anything about it yet. Not until I'm better. Hallie 2.0 in every way.

"You carry your stress in your shoulders. They must get tight, because you rub them a lot."

Julia's impish smile fades, but I keep going.

"When you don't know something, you feel embarrassed and don't like to ask for help. Your shoulders go up like this." I mime the hissing-cat motion I've seen time and time again. "But you trust a few people to help you, and you're a lot more relaxed now."

Julia meets my eyes. Her expression is complicated: intrigue, wonder, something I can't quite name. "Who?"

"Who you trust?"

When Julia nods, I swallow the lump in my throat.

"Ms. Flores."

"And?"

We're playing a very dangerous game of chicken, and I'm losing. Because how do I back out of the situation I created? Willingly created, at that. My brain is screaming to stop and play this off, but my heart convinces my mouth to say, "Me."

Julia's eyes soften. She smiles, a full one, and my breath is momentarily stolen. "That's right," she says. She lets out a low chuckle. "I don't usually play games I don't think I can win, but shit, you've got me. That was amazing."

"Thanks," I manage, dizzy at the speed of our conversation. I feel like I somehow survived this round, but just barely. Every word is like we're on a tightrope, so it's hard to keep up.

"But," Julia says, sitting taller. "You're not the only one who can do that."

"Oh yeah?" I smile, trying to disguise my rapidly thudding heart. "You can do better than Holmes?"

"I can try." Julia clears her throat. "You're great at giving advice but spectacularly bad at taking it for yourself."

"That's not true," I argue. "I listen to all advice."

"But do you hear it?" Julia raises her eyebrows. "Are you still sulking over being jealous of your best friend?"

My shoulders slump automatically, and I'm caught. Here I am sulking right in front of her! She got me.

"Okay, okay, fine. What else?"

"You twirl your hair when you study."

I blink. I've never noticed. "Really?"

"Yep. Just your pointer finger on your left hand."

I don't know what to say. Julia told me earlier that she doesn't notice anything except what's right in front of her, but that's not true. I didn't even know I did that when I'm studying. . . .

Before I can be overwhelmed with the fact that Julia knows me slightly better than I know myself, she continues.

"You're effortlessly thoughtful. Not just big things like helping Teddy study when Cam isn't looking or brainstorming with Caroline for her book. You noticed I was embarrassed about laundry and helped me."

"Well, that was partially because I can't stand a messy room," I say, trying to dispel the building tension.

Julia grins. "Fair, but you also didn't have to give me allergy meds when I was too proud to go to the nurse. Or in the mornings when you go for a run, you don't slam the screen. Even on the first day, when we were strangers, you put my chocolate bar in the fridge so it wouldn't melt."

I did do all those things, but I . . . I never gave them a second thought. I can't believe Julia noticed all that and remembered. She doesn't give me a chance to catch up as she continues.

"You're genuinely interested in what people say. When we talk, you always look right into my eyes. And it doesn't matter the subject. If I'm explaining music notes or art or just bitching about Finance, it doesn't matter. You always pay attention."

Julia eases closer to me. I'm frozen. I think I'm in shock. I expect her to stop, but she doesn't.

"You think you're a bad person, but you're not. You're such a good person, in fact, that people take advantage of you. But that's their problem, not yours. It's their fault for seeing someone as smart and wonderful as you are and not appreciating you." Julia is right beside me now. I don't think either of us are breathing. She carefully, deliberately, places her hand on top of mine. She looks up, her eyes soft and so close to mine. "If I told you that you were enough without that medal, would you believe me?"

"I would want to." My voice is barely a whisper. My whole body is tense, but the good, anticipatory tense. As bad as I hate to admit it, as much as it hurts when Nav said it, I have indeed been here before. I know the tension, the lean, the intense gaze that flits briefly to my lips.

She's going to kiss me.

My brain is screaming that I can't let this happen, that it's against the rules. My heart is screaming for me to lean in and meet her halfway. I'm in a tug-of-war, so I don't move, but I'm willing it to happen. I want Julia to kiss me so bad it hurts.

Julia stares into my eyes for a heartbeat, but then she glances up, over at my bunk. Then she closes her eyes and lets out the tiniest sigh before opening them again, smiling, and saying, "I want you to believe it, because I'm obviously getting the medal when I get first place."

I'm dumbfounded as she grins and leans away. I . . . did I get that wrong? I thought for sure—she was saying all these great things—

Julia gets up from the floor and stretches. "Let's call it a draw. We both get extra s'mores."

I take a deep breath to steady myself. The shock has worn off and now I'm just disappointed. I wanted it to happen, but she pulled away at the last second. I won our game of chicken, but at what cost?

"Okay," I manage. I clear my throat and gather my note cards. My brain is fried now—there's no way in hell I can study. "Let's get early dinner."

"Hopefully they have hot dogs at the campfire tonight. I can't take much more of Sharon's cooking."

I stand and get my backpack, and Julia gets hers too. Walter trots to the door, tail wagging. But I pause to look at the top of my bunk, where Julia's gaze has been drifting for the past week. And the first thing I see, in my own handwriting, is: *1. Absolutely no romance!*

* * *

I stare into the campfire, trying to divine answers from its dancing flames. I have somehow screwed everything up, so much that I don't know what to do. I want Julia to kiss me, but I'm scared. Julia might want to kiss me too, but she respects the stupid rules I made for myself too much to make a move. So I have to do it. I have to decide. But I can't! I always make the wrong decision. Every single thing in my life has been wrong. I don't want to ruin what I have with Julia, but every scenario I run tells me that's exactly what I'm doing.

"Help me, fire gods," I say to no one.

The camp is deserted, because it's getting late. I should be back at Cabin 11 myself, but I can't focus. All I can think about is Julia telling me, in her own way, that she cares about me.

That she notices. That she thinks my thinking is wrong, but she still respects it enough to not kiss me.

It's nowhere near Sad Girl Hours, but I'm already depressed.

"That bad, huh?"

I look away from the fire and into the friendly face of Ms. Flores. She sits beside me, and I attempt to smile at her, but I don't feel so good. I look back into the fire.

"I'm thinking about mistakes again."

"Hmm." Ms. Flores sits in silence for a full minute, just waiting for me to speak. It takes me a while to pick out a thread of coherency from the hurricane that is my thoughts.

"I wanted to use this summer to change. Everyone is being brave around me—Nav is in therapy and dating Gia, Cam is having important realizations, Julia is facing a huge change with such grace—and I'm just me. I tried to cut out the bad parts of myself, but I haven't done anything except give myself a headache. And . . ." I trail off. I want to explain how much I like Julia, but I can't put it into words.

Ms. Flores nods slowly. "It's true that change can be scary."

"I know, but I'm not scared! I want to do it."

"Maybe what scares you isn't change." Ms. Flores meets my eyes, hers warm and kind. "Maybe it's that you don't like the person you are now, and you're afraid if you don't change, no one will like you either."

I wince. Ms. Flores somehow stabbed a dagger right into my heart.

Ms. Flores continues in my wounded silence. "But, consider this: we don't have to be perfect to be loved."

"I know," I say automatically. I mean, I know that on paper, but when I think about all the bad parts of me, the jealousy, the inability to stick to my rules, my tug-of-war in my brain and heart over Julia . . .

Ms. Flores isn't buying it either. She raises her eyebrows at me. "No one's perfect, Hallie. Everyone's made mistakes."

"I know, like you said with you and Gia's dad." I hesitate but go further than I did last time. I'm working on that tiny change toward honesty. If Julia can trust me, I can trust Ms. Flores. "But you had a net positive. I don't get anything good out of mistakes."

Ms. Flores shakes her head. "You kids love your overthinking, don't you? And math! Never seen so many children who love numbers." Ms. Flores laughs to herself while I sit in confusion. When she collects herself, she continues. "Listen, life isn't about numbers or keeping score. Do you think I got a net positive out of forgetting to get the air-conditioning fixed in the main hall and fielding complaints from twenty sets of parents? Or realizing I made the points system too competitive and some campers were crying from stress? Or the million other little things that went wrong during camp? I had no idea how stressful being a hands-on sponsor would be."

I blink at Ms. Flores. The admission is shocking, but it all makes sense when I think about it. While I was stressing over the SAT and if Julia looked at me, Ms. Flores was dealing with stress of her own. "Don't you feel . . . bad, about the mistakes?"

"I did, for a little while. But you live and you learn, right?

Now I know what to do for next year. I'm definitely tweaking the points system." Ms. Flores winks at me. "And beefing up security so my campers can't sneak out in the middle of the night."

My ears burn with embarrassment while Ms. Flores laughs. I think about her words, and that she's made a lot of mistakes too. Maybe it's normal. Maybe she's just a person, like Julia said about me. I feel like I'm understanding, that I want to, but there's a mental block. I can easily forgive Ms. Flores for her mistakes, but I can't say the same for me.

"I know what you mean, but it's hard. I'm trying to look at all of my mistakes at once so I can change them all, like you said. Looking at the big picture."

Ms. Flores frowns. "That's definitely not what I meant."

"Oh . . ."

"Here, let me give you a hint. You need to change your thinking." Ms. Flores gestures to the empty campground. "Imagine yourself as a s'more night."

I frown, trying to picture it. The image of a s'more pops into my head. "You mean that I'm like a s'more? With different layers?"

"No. I mean the entire night." Ms. Flores looks into my eyes. "You're not just a s'more. You're the whole experience."

I stare back, completely lost. "I don't get it."

Ms. Flores grins. "It's okay. You will."

"You're really serious about the no participation trophy stance."

Ms. Flores laughs, and I smile along with her. I'm still confused, but just being heard makes me feel better. Just being honest instead of bottling these feelings up is a step forward, I think.

Ms. Flores gently tucks a strand of hair behind my ear. "For now, study hard, ace your test, and enjoy the last few days of camp. And just think about it." Ms. Flores stands, but just before she leaves, she pauses. "Hallie?"

"Yes, ma'am?"

"For what it's worth, I don't think you should be so hard on yourself." Ms. Flores smiles at me. "I like the Hallie you are right now very much."

CHAPTER 36

Julia and I stand in the bathroom, shoulder to shoulder, game faces on.

"Do you have your pencils?" Julia asks.

I lift my backpack full of freshly sharpened black-and-yellow pencils. "Yes. Water bottle?"

Julia holds her plain blue one up. "Yes. Backup plans for what happens if we fail?"

I meet Julia's eyes in the mirror. "None, because we won't need any."

Julia grins at me in the mirror, and I know we're ready.

Today, we take the SAT. We took our last Fine Arts and Life Skills classes yesterday. Camp is over in just a few days. Julia and I inched up to second and third place, her in second, so the test will make or break us. One test between me and New Hallie. This is do or die.

And I only have a few days to decide what I'm going to do about our tense non-relationship, but I'm ignoring that for now.

"I feel so sick," Julia says as we leave the cabin. The test is at nine o'clock sharp, and it's eight fifteen. Julia asked to wake up early for once, but when I went to kick the bed, she was already awake and staring at the bottom of my bunk with open dread. "If I fail this, I will lose my mind."

"You won't!" I grab Julia's hand without thinking. I start to pull away, embarrassed, but she just tightens her grip on my hand.

She doesn't look at me, but she doesn't have to. I feel the strength radiating between us. All the late nights, all the flash cards, all the math problems and practice essays. She's nervous, but somehow, I'm not. I think back to everything we've done, and I know we'll be okay.

My phone ruins our moment. I fish it out of my pocket and groan—my mother. All the confidence I had is out the window. If she lectures me before this test, I might actually bomb it.

"Hello?" I answer, dread boiling in my gut. It's just a call, not FaceTime, so at least she can't see how sick I feel.

"Hallie! I hope I'm not bothering you."

"You're not, but I can't talk—I have the SAT in like ten minutes."

"I know! But I wanted to talk to you before the test." Mom takes a deep breath. "Good luck. I know you can do it. And I wanted to, umm . . ." Mom trails off, like she can't find the words.

"What's wrong?"

"I'm really proud of you," Mom says, her voice hushed. "I haven't been the best about saying it, so I want to say it now."

I'm so surprised I stop walking. Julia slows, one eyebrow raised. Mom isn't like this. She's such a drill sergeant. I don't think I've ever heard those words from her.

"Oh, umm . . . thank you."

"It's been bothering me since you hit your head," Mom

rambles. "I thought you'd want to come back to recuperate, but you acted as if you couldn't come home."

"I mean, I still wanted to finish camp."

"I know, but I don't want you to feel pressured. And then you don't really call, or talk about camp, and I think— I'm beating around the bush. What I mean to say is, I'm sorry."

Now I really don't know what to say. I don't think Mom has ever apologized to me in her life.

"I know I'm hard on you, and I was extra hard because of the SAT debacle. But I never said I was disappointed in you. I just hated that Peter boy, and I was trying not to kill him for hurting you."

I grin at nothing. "Good thing he's gone, huh?"

"Yeah, thank God. But I— Hallie, I'm sorry if I made you feel bad about the test. I know you'll do great this time. But even if you don't, I'll still be cheering for you."

My face heats up. I don't know what to do with my hands. I wish Mom was here so I could hug her.

"Thanks, Mom" is what I say. And because I'm feeling a little extra brave, I add, "I don't think I want to be a doctor. Almost passing out from the blood leaking from my head kinda sealed the deal for me."

Mom sighs, but it's not disappointed. It's a little resigned but also amused. "That's all right. I know you'll be great at whatever you choose to do."

I blink back tears. I can't believe it. I've been avoiding this conversation for so long, convinced that telling Mom the truth would somehow disappoint her, or make her stop loving me . . . and I was dead wrong. It was just that easy. I always think of Julia as having layers of armor, but I guess I had layers and layers of hurt. And slowly, Mom, Nav, Ms. Flores, and always Julia, are pulling them back one by one.

I can't say all that to Mom, so I opt for "I love you."

"I love you too, Hallie." I hear the smile in Mom's voice. "Knock 'em dead."

We end the call, and I just stand still for a second, soaking in Mom's words. Julia joins my side.

"Everything okay?" she asks, her tone tentative.

"My mom said she's proud of me."

Julia smiles. "She'd be an idiot not to be."

I look at Julia, my eyes stinging in a way that has nothing to do with dust. "I think I'm gonna cry."

"You can, but you gotta wrap it up in thirty minutes."

I laugh, and the burning in my throat lessens. She's right—test first, then I can dissolve into an emotional puddle. Julia and I head to our final SAT class—the real thing—and I've never felt stronger.

The feeling persists even as we're separated by last name and all our belongings are confiscated at the door except for our pencils, calculators, and water bottles. When I'm seated with the test in front of me, I just stare at it for a moment, shocked by how different things are this time around. In March, I was exhausted, hurt, and thinking how nothing I ever did was good enough for someone I loved. But today, it's the opposite. I repeat Mom's affirmations in my head, imagine Julia's hand in mine, replay Ms. Flores's words that she likes *this* Hallie. I can do this. I'm ready.

When time officially starts, I open my packet to the first question. I flip through the rest of the packet quickly, and a slow smile spreads on my face. I feel exactly the way I did at the second pop-up, when I saw the clue for Maxine and Walter. Every practice question, every morning spent in SAT prep and study night in the cabin with Julia paid off, because there isn't a single question I don't know.

I pick up my pencil and get to work.

I finish my test right after Cam, well before most of the others. I try to send mental good vibes to Julia, Teddy, and Caroline as I recheck my answers for the last section. When the time is called, I hand in my test and just sit still for a second. I did it. It's over.

I leave the testing room in a fog. Caroline meets me outside, smiling. "I'm so glad that's over!"

"Me too," Teddy says. He runs a hand through his hair and sighs. "I hope I got everything. Testing is brutal."

They talk, but I look for Julia, who hasn't come out of the room yet. Cam joins us and immediately launches into what answers they weren't sure about, but I don't relax until Julia emerges from the building. She scans the crowd, and when she sees me, breaks into a beautiful grin.

Somehow, over the course of six weeks, Julia started looking for me too.

She rushes to my side. "How'd you do?"

"Good." My voice is quiet, because I'm almost afraid to speak it out loud. "Really good."

"Thank God, because I'm sure I killed it!" Julia is almost

yelling. She looks startled, then we both give in to hysterical, relieved giggles.

We did it. We did it! It's all over!

I hug Julia and she hugs me back, and I'm so delirious from happiness that I don't even have time to be embarrassed. I look at her, and her eyes are alight with victory and happiness, and for a long second we just hold each other, gazing into each other's eyes. If I leaned down to kiss her, this would be the perfect moment.

Someone clears their throat, and we spring apart. The queer cabin is watching us with open amusement, maybe even some mischievous glee from Caroline. My ears burn hot. I forgot they were even there.

"We're heading out," Cam says. "Apparently, there's some kind of celebration tonight? We'll see you lovebirds there!"

I'm speechless and so is Julia as Cam and the rest of the queer cabin walk away.

"We should go back to our cabin," Julia says after a moment. She's staring firmly at her shoes. "Honestly, I want to go back to sleep."

I smile. I should have added "perpetually sleepy" to our game. "Let's go."

We don't talk as we troop back to Cabin 11, but every step gets less awkward. And now that the test is over, I don't have an excuse to avoid thinking about my feelings. What am I going to do? I like Julia so much. Liking her, despite setting clear and firm rules for myself, is fundamentally what's wrong with me. I'm so confused about what I want and what I need, whether New Hallie can exist in a world where Old Hallie has struggled against rule number one all summer. I'm starting to think it's impossible to accomplish all my goals, and that makes me want to cry.

I frown when we get closer to our cabin. Two people are sitting on our porch. Two people . . . and a dog? What the—

"Who is that?" Julia squints as we pass Cabin 8. "Don't tell me I have to deal with something else right now."

When we get to Cabin 9, the two people jump up. And I gasp as one I recognize waves, a familiar corgi jumping at her feet.

"Hallie!" Nav bellows. "Get over here, you smart bitch!"

CHAPTER 37

I run to Nav, screaming. She hugs me, and we twirl around, laughing and jumping up and down.

"You're here! I can't believe it!"

"Surprise!" Nav puffs out her chest arrogantly, and just that small, familiar moment makes me tear up again. It almost feels like being home.

We separate, and I realize we're being so rude; Gia is standing awkwardly to the side, and Julia's probably wondering who these strangers are camping out at our cabin. I backtrack and stand next to Julia.

"Julia, these are my friends! Gia is Ms. Flores's daughter, and that idiot is Nav."

"I'm hurt," Nav says while grinning.

"Hi," Gia says. She's clearly uncomfortable but sticks out her hand to Julia. Julia seems surprised but completes the handshake. "I heard you might live with us."

Julia's eyes widen, and then she laughs. "I didn't think Ms. Flores was serious! No, no, I'm good. But that's amusing she really was thinking about it. Your mom is so cool."

Gia finally smiles. "Please don't tell her that. It goes right to her head."

Julia turns to Nav, but they both frown at each other.

"You look familiar," Nav says, studying Julia's face.

"You do too . . ." Julia gasps. "It's you! The Head Bitch."

Gia and I look at each other while Nav cracks up. Uh . . . what's going on? Where on earth could they have met before? Julia lives two and a half hours away from Mapleton.

"Sarah's party!" Nav says between wheezes. And as she says it, I remember. I was fuzzy-headed from the vodka Sarah gave us. I was chatting with Milly from the team. I saw Nav talking to a very pretty girl, and I wanted to check on her, but she gave me the *Don't bother me right now* stare.

And that girl was Julia.

Julia laughs too. She playfully punches Nav in the arm. "That's for ditching me under the stairs. I was about to have some fun, and then Sarah tells me you're in party jail and I have to clean up puke all night. Terrible party."

"Sorry," Nav says breezily. "I was in love with Gia at the time, which made making out with you pretty difficult."

Gia blushes happily, and Julia shakes Nav's hand, finally getting an introduction, but I don't feel so good. Nav literally got everything I want—even Julia! I would kill to kiss Julia even once and my best friend not only made out with her, but left her alone at a party! My good mood from the test is gone. I grit my teeth so hard, I'm scared they'll break.

"Are you okay?" Nav asks me.

I swallow my hot jealousy and deep burning rage and a tiny bit of despair and force a smile. "I'm good. Wanna see the camp?"

"Hell yeah we do!" Nav whoops. "Show me the rock that almost took you out. I just wanna talk."

My smile turns genuine, just for a second. But that reminds

me of how rotten of a person I am. Nav didn't know I liked Julia at Sarah's party. We hadn't even met. And Julia doesn't seem awkward or weirded out. She just looks vaguely amused by the whole thing. Even Gia, who should be the closest to feeling the way I do, doesn't seem to mind. I'm awful. I'm the worst person. This is why I'm having so much trouble changing. There's a horrible part of me that just won't let go.

I put the conversation out of my mind as Julia and I play tour guide. We meet the queer cabin briefly by the mess hall but quickly move on due to Gia's shyness. Nav loves the main hall and track, and Gia is enamored with the music room. We're headed back to Cabin 11 when Walter joins us from his guard station, triangle ears pricked with interest.

"Walter, this is Nav and Gia," I say.

He sniffs Nav's shoes suspiciously, then turns away. Nav makes a choking sound in her throat.

"I can't believe this! Dogs love me!"

"He only has eyes for Hallie," Julia says, smiling at him. "Took him ages and a whole bag of Cheetos to tolerate me."

I stroke Walter's back as he touches noses with Jordan, whose nubby tail is wagging furiously. Savagely, I'm glad Walter doesn't like Nav. At least I have one goddamn thing to myself. "Good boy."

We all head back to the cabin. I take a few breaths to calm myself. "How'd you convince Ms. Flores to let you come visit?"

"It was brutal." Gia grimaces at the ground. "But she said it would be okay right after the test, since everything is basically over. Oh, how'd it go?"

"Great!" I beam at Julia, and she returns my smile. "I think we crushed it."

"I knew you would," Nav says affectionately, and that makes me feel even worse for our one-sided feud. "But honestly I'm ready to party."

Julia and I exchange a confused look. "What party? Ms. Flores said those days were over."

"Nav, it's supposed to be a secret." Gia frowns at her girlfriend, who at least has the decency to seem sheepish. Gia returns her attention to me. "Tonight, there's going to be a big party to celebrate the end of camp. Mami said she'll go to bed early and won't ask anyone what happened."

"I changed my mind. I do want Ms. Flores to adopt me," Julia says.

Gia looks anxious again, so I lean closer and whisper, "She's just kidding."

Julia hears me, and she clarifies. "I just think your mom is the best. Possibly some sort of angel?"

"A god for sure," I chime in. "We're basically the Ms. Flores cult here."

Gia groans. "This is terrible. She's gonna be talking about this all year."

We talk a little about building a shrine for Ms. Flores, and then the queer cabin comes over to celebrate the end-of-test win. Nav is a social butterfly, and outwardly cool until you get to know her better, so the queer cabin is instantly enamored with her. Julia and Gia separate from the group to chat about Gia's favorite game, and Julia enthusiastically talks about some recent art she's done. I sit back and listen. In a way, this is incredible—all my friend groups (and crush) mingling, getting along. But I'm too upset about Nav, and my own jealousy, and the crucial decision I have to make to enjoy it. How pathetic is that?

Gia's corgi waddles to my side. She hops into my lap without any preamble and starts licking my face. I hug the dog like she's a lifeline. At least I have dogs. They won't judge me for my spineless indecision.

"Aww, all dogs love you," Julia calls from her bunk bed.

I smirk and hold up Jordan, who pants happily. "It's a gift."

"Jordan's a therapy dog," Gia says. "She might respond if you're feeling anxious. Are you feeling okay?"

I meet Jordan's eyes, who licks my nose. If a dog I've never met can clock that I'm not doing well, something has to change. And quickly.

"I'm fine," I say. "Promise."

CHAPTER 38

Like everything at Carnegie Camp for Young Scholars, the party is over the top.

Someone has decorated the main hall with all silver and gold decorations, and there's an honest-to-God disco ball hanging from the ceiling. It looks like a heinous eighties prom. I love it so much.

"This is so corny," Cam snorts.

"I know! Isn't it amazing?" Caroline gushes.

Teddy nods approvingly. "Now, someone point me to the booze table so I can forget I'm looking at a disco ball."

I look back for Nav, Gia, and Julia, but they're stalled at the door. Nav looks worried as the massive room fills with forty-eight campers and a few more guests.

"Are you sure you want to do this?" Nav asks Gia.

Gia nods, her eyebrows scrunched together in determination. "I do. I'll be okay."

"If you get overwhelmed, just tell me, okay? We can leave any time."

I smile at the scene, trying my best to ignore my jealousy. Nav used to be incredibly selfish, but now look! She's taking such good care of Gia, who has so much social anxiety that when we met, she couldn't speak to me. It's so sweet I could cry. I've been wanting to cry a lot lately.

Julia joins my side, also watching the couple curiously. "Just for clarification, this is the relationship you're jealous of?"

"Please don't," I groan.

Julia flashes me a grin and pats my arm. "It's okay, I get it. They're so cute, it's disgusting."

Julia is a perfect person. She's even willing to be a hater with me! I rub my temples to refocus. I'm at a party. I probably just got a fantastic score on my SAT. I have one night to just relax. I can get it together for one night.

"Let's go! I see some snacks with our name on them."

Julia and I raid the snack table, and Nav and Gia join us after the pep talk. Gia does seem anxious, so I make a mental note to make sure someone she knows is around her at all times. Nav and I like to separate at parties to cover more ground (better stories that way), but Nav's changed. She sips her plain water happily, her free hand brushing against Gia's every so often. I sigh and eat more Cheez-Its.

"Campers!" Amira calls from the stage.

We all focus on her automatically. True to form, she's wearing a lovely midnight-blue dress tonight that matches the decor perfectly.

"I expect you all to be responsible tonight. If anyone feels sick, Barbara is in the infirmary until midnight. At one a.m., you all better be back in your cabins and asleep or I'll lose my mind."

We cheer. I'm laughing, but I'm struck with a sense of sadness. Though I hated it at first, I think I'll miss this chaotic study camp.

"It has come to my attention that a bottle of Barbara's alcohol has come up missing. If any of the food or punch tastes funny, please report it right away. On an unrelated note, if any of you start fighting or getting sloppy, I'm canceling the party and you're all going to bed." Amira glares at the front row.

I love Amira so much. I glance at Julia and she meets my eyes, her half grin already on her face. We all put on our best innocent, *We'll be careful* faces for Amira.

"If we're all clear, then have fun tonight. And congratulations, young scholars, for completing Carnegie Camp!"

A much louder cheer resonates through the building as Amira leaves the stage and pop music blares from speakers around the room. Already, people are dancing, infamous red SOLO cups in their hands. I glance at the ruby-red punch, then at Julia. Julia pops the rest of her chips into her mouth and tugs playfully on my shirt.

"Let's see how good the punch is."

I smile back, and Nav meets my eyes. I think it'll be a fun party.

And it is. I have half a cup of mixed punch (tastes nothing like alcohol, which is the most dangerous of them all), but I don't drink much of it. Because I'm focused on dancing, and laughing at Julia's jokes, and making sure Gia is having a good time. And then someone starts up a trivia night, which Julia and I completely dominate.

Cam starts a chant: "Power couple! Power couple!"

And Julia flexes her bicep while I try not to pass out from glee.

I'm taking a break at the snack table again after we win at trivia. I consider another cup of punch, but I'm not feeling it.

Normally I like getting shit-faced at parties, but my stomach kind of hurts, and the buzz I have now isn't very fun. Maybe it's because I'm always trying to escape outside pressure, from school and Mom and usually one of my exes treating me like shit. But today, I don't have any pressure—not externally, anyway. The test is over. Mom apologized to me. No one's treating me poorly and hasn't since I implemented my no-romance rule. All my misery comes from me.

I throw my SOLO cup away and grab a bottle of water instead.

Gia approaches me, and I wave. She waves back and stands next to me. "I think I'm gonna go."

"Yeah?" When she nods, I do too. "Was it fun?"

"Kind of." Gia looks at Nav dancing wildly while Cam looks on in alarm and her eyes soften. "I'm glad I tried it for Nav."

I don't say anything, just let that soak in. I look for Julia, as I have since I started camp six weeks ago, and I find her chatting with Teddy. Her posture is loose and relaxed. Not a worry in the world. She looks my way and waves. I wave back.

Gia nudges my arm, calling my attention back to her. She grins. "I think you should go for it. Tell her how you feel."

"I can't." I'm whining, which is pathetic, but Gia just nods sympathetically.

"It's hard. I get it. But a certain someone told me I have to be brave."

I did say that to Gia, when we were brainstorming on how to get Nav to stop sulking and actually admit her feelings for Gia. Julia's words come back to me. I'm good at giving advice but really bad at taking it.

"Maybe," I say, doubtful, and Gia just smiles. She leaves and joins Nav, and they both step outside. I watch them go, a heavy pit in my stomach. The party isn't nearly as fun as it was before.

"Who ate all the salt-and-vinegar chips?" Julia grumbles at my side, startling me. She glares at the picked-over snacks. "I bet it was Michelle."

"What a bitch," I say automatically, and we both laugh.

"Did Nav and Gia leave?"

"Yeah." I sigh again. I've also been doing a lot of that lately. "Probably going to go cuddle or something. I want to spit blood."

"In our cabin too! Heinous work." Julia looks at me, her eyes shining in the well-lit auditorium.

We stare at each other for a while, and it's so nice to just be by Julia's side. To complain about snacks and have inside jokes and be haters together. I always thought I was looking for a sweeping romantic love story, but I think this is what I was really waiting for. A study partner. Someone who hugs me after I gave myself a concussion. Someone who listens to my long-winded stories even when the rest of the group moved on. Everything I wanted is standing right in front of me.

Why can't I accept it?

"Hallie," Julia says. Her voice is soft, and my heart rate kicks up faster. "There's something I have to tell you."

"Okay," I whisper.

"I shouldn't be saying anything, but I'm losing against this mystery punch. Amira should probably throw it out."

We both smile. Even though I'm scared, Julia's humor manages to make me happy. Julia shifts from one foot to the other and clears her throat. She looks just as nervous as I feel. She takes a deep breath and says what I've been longing to hear for what seems like all my life.

"I like you."

My heart is going triple time. She just said it. Out loud. I wasn't imagining things—Julia likes me! I want to grab her face and kiss her. I want to cry. I haven't changed. I'm not ready.

"I know you have your no-romance rule," Julia continues. "But maybe . . . maybe it's okay if you break that one?"

Julia's eyes shine with hope and affection, and I find mine tearing up. I want so badly to say yes, but I'm so mixed up and afraid and I don't want to be hurt again—

I don't have to say anything. Julia, who is smart and quick on the uptake, who knows me better than I know myself, reads my answer in my face. Her face falls, and she steps back.

"No," I say, trying to pick the right words to make her stay. Trying to take it all back. "Julia, I—"

"No, it's okay." Julia's tone is still so gentle, and it breaks my heart. "I knew you had the rules, and they're important to you. I shouldn't have said anything. I'm sorry."

Julia turns away, and I can't speak over the lump in my throat. I want to call her back, tell her she shouldn't be sorry, that *I* should be sorry, that I want nothing more than to be with her. But then I think of all the times I made a mistake, all the times I made the wrong decision, all the times Ashley and Peter and Gabriel hurt me, and I say nothing. I just watch the girl I love leave the auditorium and disappear into the night.

CHAPTER 39

I sit outside the main hall, listening to the faint thump of bass from inside. I'm numb. I am such an idiot. I'm afraid. I should have drank that entire bowl of mystery punch.

I hear footsteps approaching, but I don't even recognize the familiar shoes until I hear my best friend's voice.

"All right. What did you do?"

I look up into Nav's face. She has her hands on her hips, one eyebrow raised. I blink tears out of my eyes. I love Nav, but I really don't want to discuss this with her right now.

"I don't know what you're talking about."

"Really? Because Julia just came back to the cabin and looked like she'd been crying."

I feel as if someone is squeezing my heart in a tight fist. "Is she okay?"

"I don't think you get to ask that question." Nav frowns fiercely. "What is going on with you? You've been acting weird this whole summer."

I'm so upset, so mad and bitter and hurt. I feel like I've let a bunch of tiny cuts build up my entire life, and I'm just now feeling the pain from them all. But what really sets me off is Nav's nonchalant assumption, made even worse because I know she's *right*.

"I'm jealous of you, okay? Are you happy?" I hate how vicious my tone is. Nav doesn't deserve me being so nasty, but now that I've started, I can't stop. "You have everything I want, even Julia! You kissed her and laughed about it like it was nothing."

Nav blows out a slow breath. Normally she'd be hot by now, rising to my anger. But she isn't. She just looks disappointed. "Is that what this is about? That I kissed Julia before you even met her? I call bullshit, because you've been acting off all summer. You don't want to talk about your crush at all, even though we always scheme together. You're being so weird about these arbitrary rules you made up. What is going on? And don't lie to me because I'll kill you."

I hug my knees to my chest. I don't have it in me to pretend to be angry with Nav anymore. Underneath the anger, and the jealousy, and the bitterness is just hurt. Years and years of it, so vast I can't hope to heal it all. I rest my head on my knees.

"I like Julia, but I don't like me," I mumble. Hot tears prick my eyes, but I keep going. "I hate how gullible I am. I hate that I can't ever make it work with anyone. I hate that I can't even stick to a few stupid rules for six fucking weeks." I look up at Nav, but I can barely see her because of the tears in my eyes. "I wanted to change, so I wouldn't feel like this anymore. But I couldn't do it. And now I'm stuck. I want to tell Julia how I feel, but I'm scared I'll make the wrong decision again. But this time, if it's wrong, I'll hurt me and Julia, and I just can't do that. I can't take it."

"Oh, Hal." Nav sits next to me and gives me a hug.

I still don't cry, but I hug her back, sniffling so the dam doesn't break.

"Okay, listen. I feel like this is partly my fault." Nav wipes my eyes with her thumbs, where a few tears fell. "I always tease you about your exes because they truly are god-awful, and I told you not to date anyone here. But I didn't mean Julia."

"What's the difference?"

"You know the difference, shut the fuck up." Nav glares at me. "Julia isn't a Peter or an Ashley. She actually cares about you. You two are so sickening to watch—you're always looking for each other wherever you are."

I manage a miserable smile. "We were just saying how gross you and Gia are."

"Don't change the subject." Nav shakes her head. "I didn't want to see you get hurt a hundred miles away where I couldn't help you. But don't you see? You *are* hurt now. I hate to see you like this! I hate to hear you say that shit about yourself. It's breaking my heart. I don't want you to change, and Julia doesn't either. She doesn't like a mythical new version of you. She likes *this* version."

I don't know what to say. Nav makes sense, but something is still holding me back. I'm still missing a crucial piece for me to understand. I still don't know how to reconcile how others feel about me and how I feel about the old Hallie, the dumb Hallie who let her exes walk all over her, the Hallie who is bitter and jealous and might not be the smartest person at Carnegie camp.

Nav stands. She wipes my face one more time. "Don't go

after Julia just yet. I'll tell you like you told me—don't talk to anyone until you get your shit together." Nav gives me a small smile. "And wash your face before you talk to her. You look like shit."

"Fuck you," I say with all the love in my heart.

Nav gives me an affectionate middle finger, and then I watch her as she walks away, toward Cabin 11 and Julia. Just where I want to be.

* * *

I end up at the campfire.

It's still going, and someone has left out a few s'mores for people who didn't want to party. *Thoughtful as always, Ms. Flores.* I sit on my normal log, wincing at the hardness. I try to conjure up Ms. Flores so she can tell me what to do, but she doesn't appear. I'm on my own here.

I stare into the fire, but my mind is far away. It's turning over every mistake I've ever made. Sad Girl Hours on steroids. Every failed pop quiz, every close call between a B and an A. My relationships, obviously. And how I made Julia, someone I care about very much, cry. I feel like the rottenest person alive.

A warm wind swirls through the camp, sending smoke into my eyes. I cough irritably. It's like the camp itself is compounding my pain. I take my eyes away from the light for a moment to see two campers meet at the s'more table. Oh, it's Samantha . . . and she's with Caroline. I watch them as they shyly get marshmallows to roast, and retreat to the log farthest away from the fire. They're sitting close, and Caroline seems nervous but happy. I smile at them sadly. At least they're getting a nice summer romance.

I watch them for a second, and I'm painfully reminded of me and Julia. Is this how everyone saw us? Studying together and quizzing each other on SAT terms? Winning pop-ups, never alone but together? Me rushing out of breakfast to wake her up, Julia staring down Cam and protecting me because my feelings were hurt? And I ruined everything. Like I always do. I hold my head in my hands, trying to squeeze the imminent tears back into my face. Because I'm hanging my head low, I catch sight of my socks. The baby-pink ones with cacti.

I stare at my socks, and that day resurfaces in my brain. I was trying to be helpful, and I ruined Julia's and my clothes. I felt the ever-present shame of not doing something right. But Julia wasn't devastated like I am. She didn't yell or scream or tell me I'm worthless.

She laughed.

I blink at the ground and my pink socks. I tried to apologize, and Julia waved me off. She wore her newly pink pajama shorts proudly. She wasn't upset at my failure. The only one upset at my mistake is me.

I sit up, my body buzzing with a strange form of adrenaline. I think I'm on the edge of a breakthrough. Ms. Flores told me, on this very log, that I need to think in a different way. And Julia said I was really bad at taking advice, so maybe I need to try fixing that.

I told Julia that I always see the small parts, and when I see the whole picture, I'm in trouble. I told her about Ashley's good points, and how I ignored her possessiveness and jealousy, and how she often put me down.

What if I'm doing the same thing to myself, but seeing only the bad parts?

I take the small pieces I know. I trust too easily. I have bad taste in partners. I'm quick to fall into a depression spiral and easily hurt. I hesitate, but then I reach for the good parts Julia told me. Thoughtful. Good at listening. Love collecting details.

And the medium parts. I'm afraid of being hurt again. I want to change, but I'm frustrated with my lack of progress. And then Julia's assessment. I'm a good friend. She feels safe with me. I take what Nav and Ms. Flores said. They like this Hallie, not a new version.

Maybe . . . maybe this is it. Maybe this is the piece I've been missing. I've been so focused on the negative parts of myself, but that's not the whole picture, is it? We all have negative things about us. Mom can be overbearing. Nav can be blunt and selfish. Julia can be lazy and hard to connect with at first. But I love them all with every fiber of my being.

My eyes widen as I remember what Ms. Flores said: I'm a *s'mores night*. I'm not just a s'more, with clearly defined pieces stacked in neat layers. I'm the whole experience. I'm the sweet treat, but I'm also the log that's too hard, the smoke that always seems to be blowing in your eyes. I'm the laughter, the shy flirting between friends who want something more. I'm the warmth of the campfire and the stars above and the slight stomachache after eating too many sweets. I'm all of it. Because without the hard log, we'd have nowhere to sit. Without the smoke, there would be no fire to roast the marshmallows. Without the bitterness, there is no sweet. Without all the things I think are negative about myself, I cannot be Hallie Griffin. Julia and Nav and Ms. Flores, my parents and my camp friends—they all love *this* Hallie. All of me. Even the bad parts, because they make the good parts even better.

I rocket to my feet, startling Samantha and Caroline. "I figured it out!" I shout to no one, but I smile when Caroline says a tentative, "Good for you?"

I don't have time to answer her. I'm running to Cabin 11 to save the relationship I almost ruined.

CHAPTER 40

I run full speed to Cabin 11 as if demons are chasing me. I rip open the door, startling Nav and Gia, who are playing a game on her Switch. I search for Julia, but she's not here.

"Where's Julia?" I huff, out of breath. "I figured it out."

"Wow," Nav says, already grinning. "That was fast."

"Much faster than you," Gia teases her. "But I'm sorry, I don't know where she is. She left with an instrument case, I think."

I turn to leave, but Nav snatches the tail of my shirt. "What did I tell you? Wash your face, you look like you've been to war."

I don't protest, because I get it now. This bluntness is how Nav loves me. She wants me to look my best when I have to grovel to Julia. I smile and splash water on my face, and I'm glad I pause because I have an idea. I grab the chocolate bar Julia got me from the fridge, wave at Nav and Gia, and run back into the night.

I know exactly where she'll be. Because as well as Julia knows me, I know her too. She'll be hurt, and sad, and she'll want to play her violin. But she won't want anyone to hear, because only I'm allowed to hear the vulnerable sound of her bow on the strings. So somewhere private, where she can play and not be heard, where no one has a chance of walking in on her . . .

I run to the private clearing Julia showed me, where we ate victory candy and stargazed and she sketched the lake. I hear the music long before I see her. I follow the mournful wail until fireflies flit around my face, and I see her illuminated by their soft light.

I pant, but I don't speak. She turns and glances at me but doesn't say anything either. She closes her eyes and finishes the song. Tears fill my eyes as I watch her, feel the notes in my bones. When she's done and lowers her violin, I clap just like I did the first time I heard her play.

Julia gives me a small half smile. "Thank God you showed up. Thought I was gonna give the best performance of my life to bugs."

I wince at what she's not saying. She's the saddest she's ever been, even sadder than when her parents were harassing her, and it's all my fault.

I inch closer, but I don't know how to start. "Julia . . . I'm sorry."

"Don't be. I'm half drunk—Amira is trying to kill us." I smile, and Julia does too, though her eyes are still sad. "I shouldn't have said anything. I know your rules are important to you."

"They're kind of stupid, though, aren't they?"

Julia blinks for a second. "This feels like a trap."

I laugh. Somehow, even though I'm the most nervous I've ever been in my life, Julia manages to calm me down. I close the distance between us, finally ready to see the whole picture.

"I set those rules because I thought there was something

wrong with me. Like to my core, I needed to fundamentally change."

"That's not true," Julia interrupts. "As I said before."

"I know. I find it really hard to believe good things people say about me. It's one of my faults," I admit. "Along with not taking my own advice. But I'm listening now. No, I hear you, not just listening. You were right. I don't need to change."

Julia listens, giving me a slight nod. I take a deep breath.

"I was too scared to be hurt again, so I focused on what I could change, which was myself. But this summer, you've been telling me that I don't need to. And if I'd paid attention, I'd have realized it too. Basketball helped us get second place in the first pop-up. Being good at details won the second one and helped me memorize SAT terms. Being friendly, even when others tell me not to, let us sneak out when we needed to. Even though we did get caught later." I take a shuddering breath. It's almost painful to say all this out loud. "So yes, I trust easy, and it hurts me sometimes. I get neurotic if I don't do some kind of exercise. I can be petty and jealous, and if I stay up between the hours of one and four a.m., I start spiraling about everything I've ever done, which is why I try my best to be asleep by eleven. I'm not perfect, but it was kind of stupid for me to even try to be, you know? I don't want to pretend to be perfect around you, if that's okay."

I shut up, breathing hard for some reason. Julia considers me for a few seconds, then she bends and puts her violin away. I watch, anxiety at an all-time high, until she returns to me. Then, she smiles.

"You have changed," Julia says. "Because you never could have said this earlier."

"Sorry it took me so long to figure it out," I breathe. Maybe . . . maybe she accepts my apology? "I'm also bad at seeing the big picture until it's far too late."

"Who said it was too late?" Julia says.

My heart skips a beat as Julia gets closer, her smile widening slowly. "I happen to like that you're not perfect. I'm glad you're petty and jealous, because so am I. I'll never forgive Michelle for as long as I live, and hearing you hate her as much as I do really soothed my soul."

I smile, euphoria gathering in my chest. It's happening, I think.

"And I like that you have hobbies like running and horror movies. It makes you interesting, you know that? Complicated and contradictory. It's not a bad thing." Julia steps closer, just an inch at a time. She suddenly seems shy. "That's good to know about you spiraling at one o'clock. But I don't want you to worry about it. I'm up at those hours anyway, so if you ever want to talk, I'll be up to listen."

We're so close, I could reach out and kiss her. And I want to, but I have one more thing to say.

"I like you too," I whisper. Julia looks into my eyes, and I hold her gaze. "I liked you from the moment I met you."

"That can't be true." Julia's whispering too. "I was such a bitch."

"Not a bitch, just not very friendly. But I could tell that you had your reasons. I liked you when you stood up to Michelle and threw her shit outside. I liked you when you asked me if the lamplight bothered me. I liked you when we teamed up for the pop-ups, when you asked about my vision board, when you were just studying at your desk and listening to music. I've liked you always, this whole summer, and I'm so sorry I was too much of an idiot to say it until now."

Julia's eyes shine with a gentle adoration that's just for me, twinkling in the glow of the fireflies surrounding us. "Not an idiot," she murmurs. "Neurotic, like you said. And I happen to find it pretty cute."

"Is it okay if I kiss you?" I ask.

Julia smiles, a full one meant just for me. "Thought you'd never ask."

I bend down, and Julia presses her lips to mine. It's warm and sweet, and my heart is exploding with happiness. It's also a little salty from our tears, and my hands are kind of sweaty around the chocolate bar I've been holding on to for dear life. It's not perfect. But it's ours, and real, and that's better than unattainable perfection any day.

We pull apart and Julia strokes my cheek with her thumb. "I can't tell you how long I've been wanting that to happen. I would decide to tell you, then I'd look at your board and chicken out. I think I'll hate Jung Kook's face for the rest of my life."

I laugh. That's why she kept looking at my bunk! She's always respected my boundaries, and encouraged my progress, even when it was stupid.

"Speaking of the vision board . . ." I hold out the chocolate bar to show her. She raises her eyebrows and I elaborate. "If you think about it, I did it. I accomplished my goal. I set all those rules to find a way to be happy, and now I finally am. So I can eat the chocolate now."

"All of it?"

"Half," I clarify. "I want you to have the other half."

Julia chuckles, then full on laughs. She pulls me into another quick kiss, then rips the wrapping off the chocolate. I break it in half, and we toast, like we did when I hit my head and she reassured me that everything would be all right. The difference is that this time, I believe her.

"To not changing," Julia says. "Because who needs perfect? We're not, but we're still amazing. Second and third smartest people at Carnegie Camp."

I laugh and touch my chocolate to hers. "Hell yeah we are!"

We cram each of our halves of the bar into our mouths at the same time. It's partially melted because of the heat of the Alabama summer and my sweaty hands. Chocolate gets all over my fingers, and when we kiss again, Julia gets chocolate on my face when she touches my cheek. We howl with laughter and groan about the mess, but all I can think about is that I'll never have to say my mantra, *It'll be better tomorrow*, again. Because I can't imagine anything better than this, so tomorrow is finally here.

CHAPTER 41

Amira gestures at her full table at the entrance to the main hall. "Welcome, Hallie, Julia! Please select a graduation cap."

I meet Julia's eyes, hers amused. There's an assortment of hats in front of us, all multicolored with different tassels. It would be professional and cool of New Hallie to pick plain black, to show how serious she is about an awards ceremony.

I take a hot pink one with a purple and blue tassel instead.

Julia gets a black one, but it's been decorated with yellow and orange flowers. We put our hats on and go to the auditorium, hand in hand.

It's the last day of camp, and I'm really sad about it! Julia caught me blubbering in the bathroom this morning and she had to hug me for ten minutes before I could get it together. But the last day is perfect. We had terrible scrambled eggs, courtesy of Sharon, as usual. I had my last meal with the queer cabin. My parents are here to pick me up, along with Nav and Gia, who never left. I'm sad it's ending, but Julia's hand in mine reminds me that when one thing is over, something else is always beginning.

Someone calls my name, and I spy my parents frantically waving. I glance at Julia. "Do you want to meet Mom and Dad?"

"It's only fair, since you've already met mine." Julia grins. "Plus, I haven't forgotten that they think I'm such a pretty girl."

"Stop! Don't remind me, please!"

Julia teases me right up until we meet my parents. I start to introduce her, but Mom hugs me and Dad starts crying for some reason. I want to be embarrassed, but now I'm feeling weepy too. I missed them more than I thought I would.

"Oh, Bean, you look so happy," Dad says after Mom lets me breathe.

"And your hat! I love it." Mom adjusts it, and smooths down the wrinkles in my shirt. She zeroes in on Julia standing behind me. "Hallie, don't be rude! Introduce us."

I shake my head, laughing a little. I step back and take Julia's hand. "This is my cabinmate, Julia. And also my girlfriend."

Mom and Dad seem speechless for a second. Dad is the first to recover. He sticks out his hand for a formal handshake.

"Nice to meet you, Julia! I'm Hallie's dad. I hope she's treating you well."

Julia grins and completes the handshake. "Of course she is. I've never been happier."

Mom smiles, finally, and shakes Julia's hand too. "Aren't you sweet! Much better than her previous ones, I'll tell you."

"So I've heard," Julia whispers conspiratorially. Mom looks delighted. I smile at the scene. Before, that comment from Mom would have bothered me, but now I take it in stride. I made mistakes. We all do. It's fine, as long as we keep moving forward. I'm a little concerned my parents might like Julia more than me, though.

Ms. Flores approaches our group. She's wearing a stunning white dress with blue and yellow jewelry. And her necklace is a peacock! "Hello! We meet again!"

"Hi," Mom says. She looks incredibly uncomfortable. "I may have said some things at urgent care that were out of character—"

"Water under the bridge," Ms. Flores says breezily. "But I do have something to discuss with Hallie before we start."

"Me?" Oh God, what have I done now?

"Yes, ma'am. We need to discuss how you've ruined my guard hound." Ms. Flores laughs at my stunned expression. "I'm kidding. Walter is seven, so his guarding days are coming to an end anyhow. But it is a bit troubling that he allowed you to bribe his silence."

"Hallie's a dog whisperer," Julia says. "Totally not his fault."

"Even so, we have to find him a new home now." Ms. Flores smiles at me. "Would you like to bring him with you?"

I gasp and turn to Mom. "Mom, please, we have to."

"What?" Mom looks distressed. "What is a Walter? What's going on?"

"He's a dog, but he's such a good boy! We have to take him!"

"Hold on now—"

"We've talked about getting a dog," Dad muses. "Why not? We need more exercise anyway. Could be fun!"

Mom struggles for words but sighs. "You two are taking care of it, I mean it. And there better not be dog hair all over the house."

I turn to Julia, elated. She grins at me. "You're having a real good summer, huh? You get a free dog and a girlfriend."

"And five thousand dollars," I remind her.

Julia laughs. "Even better."

We chat with Ms. Flores and my parents for a bit, until I spot Sarah and her parents heading inside. I pull Julia away from Mom and Dad so we can meet them.

Sarah squeals and hugs Julia as soon as we're close. Julia freezes, eyes wide, and Sarah does an awkward-hug sway as she squeezes her cousin in a tight grip. "I am so proud of you! Look at your cute hat! I'm so glad you finally started dating Hallie, you were so emo for weeks!"

I'm beaming as Julia stammers out a response and Sarah cackles. It's nice to know I wasn't the only one pining! Sarah's parents save Julia by hugging her too. They're holding some signs, and when they move, I catch sight of the words—*Julia, we're so proud of you.*

Julia stares at the signs, seemingly dumbfounded.

"You've done such a great job, Jules," Sarah's dad gushes. "We're so excited to have you live with us too. We spent all day clearing out your room."

"Are you sure it's okay . . . ?" Julia still doesn't look like she believes it.

"Of course," Sarah's mom says. "I always wanted twins, didn't I say that, Marv?"

"Yep, you sure did." Sarah's dad is practically beaming.

"Campers, the ceremony is about to start," Ms. Flores says from the stage. "Please get your graduation caps and assemble at the front."

"Go, go," Sarah says. "We'll be right here when you get back."

Julia and I wave at Sarah and her parents and join everyone else up front. Julia takes an unsteady breath beside me.

"You okay?"

"If I start crying, just ignore me."

"No! I'll start crying too!" I blink dramatically. "I'm already sad that my parents love you more than me."

Julia grins up at me. "Ms. Flores, Sarah's mom and dad, your parents. I'm collecting them like infinity stones." Her expression softens as she glances back at Sarah, who's now chatting happily with Nav and Gia. "I can't believe they came. And they made signs for me."

"Why not? Is it so hard to believe that people love you?"

Julia elbows my side. "I don't want to hear that from someone who only figured that out two days ago." But she grabs my hand and squeezes it, and I know she's working hard to believe it too.

Ms. Flores claps her hands to get everyone's attention. "Thank you, campers and parents, for attending the closing ceremony! I am so honored to have served as this year's sponsor for Carnegie Camp for Young Scholars. I know you're all so proud of your children, and I am too. They learned not only how to do math and science but also how to develop practical skills. They learned how to work well with their peers, and that there's more to life than just studying. Scholars, I hope you take this summer with you for the rest of your lives. I know I will." Ms. Flores blinks rapidly as she smiles at the crowd. "And now, awards! We'll call everyone by last name, and you will receive your five-thousand-dollar scholarship."

The crowd cheers. Amira calls us one by one, and campers walk onstage to get a small square piece of paper. We cheer for all the queer cabin, and when it's my turn, my parents, Nav and Gia, and Sarah's family go nuts. I smile for the picture as I shake Ms. Flores's hand, trying my best not to cry. I can't believe that just six weeks ago, I was depressed because I thought I was so fundamentally broken that no one could love me. And now, I have a room full of friends and family and my girlfriend who show me otherwise.

When we've all gotten our certificates, Ms. Flores returns to the stage. "And now for awards! I promised the campers that first place would receive a twenty-thousand-dollar scholarship. The winner of that prize is Cam Lowell!"

I cheer, but I'm still a little sad as Ms. Flores gives Cam a shiny, oversized check. I worked hard, and I was hopeful I'd break into first place after the SAT was graded . . . but I forgot it takes two weeks! Our rankings were solidified before we ever took the test. But as I watch Ms. Flores put the medal around Cam's neck, the pinprick of hurt fades. I don't know if I met my goal and got a 1550+ like I wanted. I don't even really care. I did my absolute best, along with helping my friends shine too, and I'm proud. Turns out, I'm not all that competitive. I just really, really enjoyed playing the game.

"But that's not all." Ms. Flores's eyes twinkle with mischief. "This camp isn't just about who is the best academically. There are scholars who excelled in single categories rather than just overall. For highest score in Finance, Cam Lowell again!"

Cam blinks in shock and glee as Ms. Flores gives them another check. I clap and cheer, but Julia sighs next to me. I don't think she ever did truly warm up to Cam.

Ms. Flores continues. "For Communication, Samantha Dencore!"

Samantha climbs the stage while we all cheer. Ms. Flores calls out Kent Roberts for Life Skills.

And then she says, "And for Fine Arts, Julia Brown!"

Julia freezes beside me as the room goes wild. "That's me," she says in disbelief.

"That's you!" I scream. "Go, go!"

Julia wanders to the stage and shakes Ms. Flores's hand, still in shock. I clap and cheer as loud as I possibly can. Julia was dogged about first place, all because she wanted a new laptop to replace hers that died. And now she can buy one, and a whole lot more.

"And, one final award. For the scholar who excels in skills that are hard to quantify. Adaptable, clever, a hard worker. All while being friendly and helpful to everyone around her. The undisputed champion of the pop-ups." Ms. Flores looks right into my eyes and says, "Hallie Griffin."

I barely hear the room erupting in applause. My ears are ringing in pure shock. Someone pushes me forward, and I end up onstage somehow, shaking Ms. Flores's hand for a second time. Mom and Dad are screaming my name, and Nav is right there with them. Gia is covering her ears from the noise but beaming at me. Caroline and Teddy are practically dancing, and Cam leans forward to mouth, "Good job!" I stand next to Julia, who has a radiant grin on her face.

Ms. Flores beams at the audience. "All winning campers will receive a twenty-thousand-dollar scholarship in addition to their five thousand."

I almost faint on the spot.

"I have medals for you too, but sorry they're not the fancy kind."

Ms. Flores gives us each a medal. I hold it in my hand and start laughing. It has a shiny gold foil wrapping, but it's not gold. It's chocolate.

I meet Julia's eyes, and we tear the wrapper off at the same time. And, no longer waiting for change, we both eat our victory chocolate whole.

ACKNOWLEDGMENTS

Writing these never gets easier. Not because they're inherently difficult but because I'm still in awe of how many people love me and my book and have supported me enough to get me this far.

First thanks always goes to my beloved Grandma. We spent so many nights chatting about Hallie's journey and the finer points of Carnegie Camp for Young Scholars (despite you swearing up and down you weren't interested lol). I love you dearly, and I don't think I could write books without you.

Thanks also to my agent, Holly Root! I appreciate that you're never frazzled by my chaotic writing and pitching process, including my many meltdowns in your inbox. Thank you (and I'm sorry!). And my editor, Clare Vaughn!! You've been with me from day one with Hallie, and I'm so grateful you saw the diamond in the very messy first draft it was. I love your enthusiasm and all your wonderful Hallie-related memes. 😊 I can't wait to work on more books together!

Thank you to the whole Harper team: Julia Feingold, Alison Donalty, Shona McCarthy, Mary Magrisso, Danielle McClelland, Meghan Pettit, Shannon Cox, Taylan Salvati, Heather Bosch, and everyone else who worked on Hallie's story.

To Emily Chapman—thank you for always cheering me on

(and helping me with marketing judgment calls). To Sonido Reyes for our chats about life and gaming sessions. And special thanks to A. Z. Louise for all the memes, snippet sharing, and brainstorming on what is the cutest possible dog for Hallie to have. 😊

Early readers: you were invaluable. I literally could not have done it without your feedback. Belinda, who read the messiest outline and was basically my second editor for draft one. Chad, who helped me realize the book wasn't in fact trash (and by extension me!). Jacki, whose love for Ms. Flores was only rivaled by our favorite ice queen and Walter. Melissa, who relentlessly encouraged me to keep going. And A. Z. Lousie again, because they're just that amazing!

Innumerable thanks to my writing chats who kept me sane: Scream Town, WiM Crew, slackers, Word Smith Buddies, and many more.

And thanks to me, for staying. We're doing it, younger Jessica! Life is tough, but I'm so glad we stuck it out. Onward to many more books!